If Only
Family by Choice
Book 1

Robin Nadler

This novel is dedicated to my parents who taught me what true love was. Watching the way they were together made me believe that with love, all things are possible.

Prologue:

It's amazing how one moment can change everything you ever thought to be true about human nature. You live each day and expect the same results, some people are nice and some aren't. Some people expect things from you and some don't. Some people are there for you and others walk away. Treat others as you wish to be treated. These are simple truths we have all come to rely on. It's important to have these simple truths, because it allows us to condition our response to certain events, to know what to expect. It is when these truths fail us that we learn just what we're made of.

Brittany's Story:

Just keep running, she told herself as she made her way down the street and urgently searched for cover. The asphalt was wet and slick as the rain had just subsided and the ground was covered with worms seeking food and soil. Bits of rock and tar slapped her shins as she tore through the darkness, searching for anyone to help her, anyone but him. Crouching behind a large tree, she tried to catch her breath, her heart pumping blood thickly through her body, the air visible from her panting in the cool mist. Her chest was burning from the air and she was afraid she might pass out. Her red hair hung limply down her back and clumps stuck to her wet skin. She looked at her surroundings, trying to search for a way to get help. Counting to ten, she tried to slow her breathing and calm down. The view from where she stopped was dark and gray and foggy, and she saw the moon pierce through the dense cloud cover, illuminating the nothingness she saw. She began to feel her tears fall again as the panic gripped her chest, but there wasn't time for this. There was only time for survival. She ran again, looking back to see if she was still being followed, when her foot slipped on a pile of mud and she fell onto the harsh pavement, placing a hand down on the rough terrain of the street, slicing her palm and her knees. She cursed herself for wearing short pajamas, but she never expected to be outside. She never expected this. There was no time for tears or pain. This was her life and she was running to live.

The blood ran down her fingers from her sliced palm and her knees were on fire, but she kept going. Although she couldn't see anyone, she felt his presence in the silence; he was still there, lurking in the shadows. Her heart was louder than the sound of the silence and she was sure he could hear it. Just get to safety; there was no time to worry about anything else, she told herself. Wiping the beads of sweat off her forehead with her bloody hand, she continued running. She was almost back to the road when again she tripped again and fell flat on the ground. Almost giving up, she lay there, willing the darkness to just end this for her, but then she thought of her fans and of all the people who would be upset with her and she sat up. Hearing a noise behind her, she turned around just in time to see a skunk run across the street, spraying its disgusting scent all over. Great, just fucking great, she swore. Her eyes began to sting from the spray and her tears and she ran to the little puddle she saw to flush them out. That was stupid, she thought. She was sitting out in the open and she knew she made a fatal mistake. She turned slowly just in time to see a hand raised above her face. Everything went black.

This isn't real; this is a dream, a horrible dream. If I just wake up, all will be as it was. I am safe and warm and okay. A quick opening of her eyes told Barbara just how wrong she was. Pain shot through her hands and arms as she tried to move, the rope evident as it sliced through her wrists, creating the sensation of fire, which wasn't hard, given the state of her hands. Her heart was going a mile a minute and her head screamed from pain. Camera flashes began to go off in her face and she closed her eyes, the light blinding. The smell of chemicals was pungent as she saw the shadow of the figure that was tormenting her and her tears came as he approached and his hands were on her. Her screams infused the silence of her mind, but not the air around them. She couldn't speak. There was something in her mouth, a gag or something. She tried to plead for him to stop, but he just kept going, his filthy hands touching her in places that were sacred. He untied her hands and she tried to bite, claw and scream, but he threw her on the ground and tore her clothes. She scratched at anything she could reach, but then the chemical smell was covering her face again, and thankfully, she passed out. This happened numerous times, the same routine over and over. When she awoke the final time, she was naked, beaten and bleeding. She was alone in the dark room, images of her body hanging all over. She tried to get up, but her legs were like jelly. She looked around and saw her torn clothes nearby. She moved and pulled her shirt and what was left of her shorts back to her body. She got up slowly and ran out of the room, stumbling into the woods outside the place she was held. She couldn't see anything; her eyes were stinging. She fell numerous times and finally she came to a road. She saw car lights coming and she waved at them before

6

finally passing out. That was the last time Barbara Rose would be seen.

****

Tommy's Story:

How did this happen? One day you're graduating high school and going off to college, and the next you're sitting here, hearing the doctors tell you they did everything they could, but your parents are gone. No, not gone, because that implies they might come back. Your parents are dead. You sit there and listen and nod like you have an understanding of what the doctor is telling you and that you are okay. You are okay with the fact that your entire existence has been shattered and everything in the world that you thought was safe and untouchable has been wiped out. You let them lead you to a chair and you sit down. You take the cup of water they give you and you sip it, to make them happy. You do everything you should. You don't react, you don't feel, you don't cry.

You're 18 years old and suddenly you're an orphan.

"Tommy, what do you want me to do?" Jack asked his best friend as they sat in the hospital. He knew Tommy was in shock, but he didn't know what to do or say. How can someone live through this? What would he do?

Tommy looked at the Chaplain who was sitting with them. "What do I need to do next? I have to go and get my sister. I need to tell her," Tommy said softly, his voice sounding like it was far away.

Jack felt like he was going to be sick. Julie was 12. She was staying with friends while their parents had gone on a romantic weekend. She was only 12.

"Why don't you let someone else do that, young man? I think you need to stay here." The elder man said.

Tommy stood up to his tall 6 foot frame and ran his hand through his chestnut hair. "I'll tell her, no one else," he turned to walk away. Jack thanked the Chaplain and followed his friend. He thought about how they had gotten there, to that moment. Just a few hours earlier they were at the bar, having fun and partying.

******

Tommy looked at his best friend Jack and smiled. Here he was, enjoying college after he and Jack had finally gotten everything they had worked so hard for. They were both freshman at the University of Michigan and both had finished their first semester of classes. The year before, while they were seniors in high school, Tommy had helped Jack with the loss of his mother from Lung Cancer, and he was so glad his friend finally seemed to be smiling again. The year that should have been the best had been so difficult and Jack's father had been out of the picture since his mom died, so he felt truly alone.

"What are you thinking about?" Jack asked Tommy as he walked over to him. "You're staring at me like you want something and it's creeping me out," Jack laughed.

"Sorry, man, I was just thinking. You know, not everything is about you," he grinned. "How is it going with that blonde over there?" Tommy asked;

referencing the girl Jack was talking to. Standing at 6 foot 1, Jack was tall and handsome and even though only an inch shorter, Tommy was always in his shadow. He never seemed to have the way with women that Jack did, but he didn't care. His life was going to be different now that he was in college. He was going to finally be out on his own and be the man he knew he was supposed to be.

"She is a psychology major and she is trying to analyze me," Jack said with a twinkle in his eye. "She seems to like me," he grinned. "Not that I blame her, I mean, what's not to like."

Tommy rolled his eyes. "I am sure she appreciates your humbleness as well."

"Of course," Jack laughed. Tommy looked down as his cell phone buzzed. He didn't recognize the number.

"Hello?" he asked, not knowing the call would change his life forever.

"Tommy, hey, we're here," Jack said as he pulled up to the house Julie was staying at. He looked at his friend who had not said a word the entire drive. Jack wished there was someone else to do this. He didn't know how Tommy would make it through telling her. He fought his own tears back again.

Tommy looked at him and nodded. He had called ahead and told the mother of Julie's friend what happened, so she could help them. He walked up to the house and the door opened. The woman hugged Tommy and motioned for them to come inside. He still didn't cry.

"Where is she?" he asked.

"Why don't you go in the living room and I will get her. Are you sure there isn't anyone else I can call for you?" the mother asked.

"There's no one else," he said and turned to walk into the room. Jack went with him but kept his distance. He thought once again he was going to be sick. Julie jumped down the stairs and froze when she saw her brother and Jack. She knew immediately something was wrong.

Tommy flinched when he saw his sister. She was so happy and so innocent. He knew that what he was about to tell her would forever change everything about her. He motioned for her to come over to him and when she sat down, before he was able to say anything, she began to cry. "What happened? Where are mommy and daddy?" she asked in the smallest voice he had ever heard.

Tommy looked at her. "There was an accident, Jules. They are both gone," he said simply.

She sat there, stunned and then she screamed in terror. He moved closer to her and held her while she screamed and cried. Jack let his own tears fall as he watched the scene in front of him. Julie was sobbing and Tommy was just holding her. Tommy realized in that moment that his life was also changed. He had a new purpose and it was her. He needed to provide for her and instill in her what his parents had given to him. He pulled back and wiped her tears. She was breathing heavily and he stayed strong.

"What's gonna happen to me? Where will I go?" she asked in a scared little girl voice. "Are you going to leave me, too?"

Tommy smoothed her hair. "Never. We will stay together. I will take care of you. You will be okay," he said.

Her face crumpled and she put her head in her hands. "I want my mommy," she sobbed again and for the first time, Tommy held her and cried. "Me too, Julie Bean, me too."

Chapter 1:

12 years later

Present Day:

The wind whipped through Brittany's long red hair as she stood at the edge of the stairs that led to the huge expanse, which was the University of Michigan Hospital. The brilliant building was massive and looked like a city within itself. Doctors and patients entered and exited the doors on their way to and from the hectic pace of hospital life. The brisk Michigan air was cleansing as she tried to settle her jumping nerves. The end of fall and the beginning of winter were illuminated in the crunching of the leaves, which sat tousled on the ground. The smell of coffee and hot chocolate filtered through the arctic air. Hugging her arms around her waist and smiling at the familiar scene, she told herself again that this was the change she needed. It had been a surprise when Stephanie called and told her about the prestigious new women's center which was opening with the newly expanded children's medical center. Stephanie had recommended her for a new position in high-risk obstetrics, a field in which Brittany had recently made a name for herself. Knowing that her friend also desired assistance in matters of fertility, Brittany saw it as a chance to maybe help her oldest and dearest friend become the mother she always wished to be. Stephanie and her husband Jack had been unable to conceive and Brittany's research might shed new light on their issues. The halcyon atmosphere in London had been soothing for her for the past 12 years, and to be honest, she wasn't really looking for a change; but once the call came, she decided it might be just what she needed. Maybe it was time to stop running.

"So are you going to wear a hole in the ground or are you going to walk inside?" a familiar voice invaded her thoughts. Brittany turned and saw Stephanie approach her, her braided brown hair barely moving in the wind.

"What are you doing here? I thought orthopedics was on the other side of the hospital," Brittany smiled brightly as she exclaimed, referring to Stephanie's specialty of orthopedic surgery. Her demeanor immediately eased as she saw her friend and realized it had been too long since they had seen each other. Stephanie had been married for a little over a year to Jack, a prominent Cardiologist. They seemed to be a perfect match and Brittany was thrilled for her friend. "How have you been feeling?"

A little of the light went out of Stephanie's eyes at the mention of her health. As a 6-year fighter of Multiple Sclerosis, she had struggled with her duties as a surgeon and her need to never allow her disease to interfere with her life. Some days she lost that fight, an analogy she often used to describe her health.

"I think today I am winning, but tomorrow, who knows?" she laughed and Brittany hugged her.

"You amaze me," the redhead said and her admiration was mirrored in her friends' eyes.

"Enough of the flattery. I didn't have anything scheduled this morning, and I thought I would show you around," Stephanie waved the conversation away, opting instead to open the small paper bag she was carrying, handing it to Brittany who looked inside. "I know how you get when you don't eat with your meds, so I wanted to make sure everything was okay today."

The fact that Stephanie was the only person who knew everything about Brittany was something that made this move easier. It was important to have that connection, that person who would be there through anything. "I missed you, Steph," Brittany said, swallowing a lump in her throat as they walked into the building.

Chapter Two:

"Come on, just meet her for dinner. What's the worst that can happen?" Jack asked Tommy while they ate lunch in the hospital cafeteria. They were crammed into a small corner table near hundreds of other doctors and nurses who decided to take a break at the same time. Jack was trying desperately to pull his friend out of his funk.

Tommy smirked as he rolled his eyes. "When are you going to let up? Face it; there is not another Stephanie out there, so I will just have to live vicariously through your 'amazing' love affair. Can we just drop this already?" Taking a final bite of his burger, he hoped to change the subject. Jack was always trying to fix him up and to be honest, Tommy was nervous enough about starting at a new position; he didn't have any time for romance.

Jack grinned at his friend, who was more like his brother. "Nope, not gonna happen," he laughed as Tommy gave him a dirty look. "Megan is cute and funny. I think you'll really like her. Besides, you are the boss now and you need to get out and mingle with people around here."

"I liked you better when you were alone and miserable, at least then you never played matchmaker," Tommy sighed as he stood up. "Are you coming?"

Jack finished his drink and stood up. "Yep, got to go show my brilliance in the O.R," Jack smiled and continued, "I will just have to make sure you get out and party later. It is my duty to see you happy and in love," he grinned. "Working with the clients you do has to leave you wanting a little more adult time," Jack referred to the fact that Tommy was heading the new Pediatric Oncology and Surgical wing at Mott Children's hospital.

Tommy snorted. "I am as happy as I care to be, so you keep telling yourself that I'm miserable. Whatever helps you sleep at night."

Jack grinned. "Actually, being with my wife helps me sleep at night, so back to Megan,"

Tommy walked faster and laughed as Jack yelled after him.

******

"Thanks so much for showing me around, but I have worked in the hospital for awhile, I'm just new in this wing," Tommy said to Megan, the nurse in his department that Jack had mentioned. She had been beside him since he walked onto the floor and she acted like she was personally responsible for him being there. He didn't want to be rude, but he just wanted to find some things out on his own. She was cute enough, but not his type. He wasn't sure if she was just being helpful or asking for something more. He was definitely not interested. "I think I am just going to go to my office and get ready for my next consult," Tommy said politely.

"Okay, but anything you need, just ask." Megan cooed and walked away.

Tommy made his way to his office, dodging the people in the hall. He smiled at the stares he got; those were usual for him. He knew he was handsome, but he was also really nervous. Having just been promoted, he had a lot to prove. He was thrilled, though, to be closer to Jack and Stephanie. He walked into his office and sat at his desk, looking at the computer, which seemed to have been around for a while. He fingered the picture of Julie on her wedding day and the next picture of Julie with her student's in her classroom. He still couldn't believe she was a teacher, but he knew it was the most natural job for her. She was nurturing and caring and although he hated to admit it, better with people than he was. He was so proud of her and he knew that besides Jack and Stephanie, he needed to be closer to the only family he had. Julie and her husband Bill lived a couple hours away and Bill was an active member of the Army. He had served a year in Iraq and was now working as a homicide detective. Looking out the window, Tommy took a deep breath. This was going to be good. This was the new start he needed.

****

"Could this job get any crazier?" Brittany asked Stephanie as they sat down in the cafeteria to eat lunch. "I mean the paperwork is ridiculous. I want to see patients, not write a book for the insurance companies," she took a bite of her salad.

"I hear you, that's why I teach med students. They do the work, it's over, and we move on," Steph said and chewed her sandwich. "I did have one almost light himself on fire, but that was my only excitement," she shrugged. Suddenly Steph nudged her. "There he is, Jack's friend Tommy I was telling you about. He was just promoted," she said pointing to Tommy who was walking into the room. "He is going to be heading up the surgery and oncology center at Mott Children's hospital which is connected to your clinic. I'll call him over, you should meet."

There it was, the familiar flop of the stomach, the knowledge of the dreaded introduction and the complete shutting down of any and all emotion. Brittany shook her head, making the same decision she always had. She looked at her pager and sighed. "I have to go, I will see you in an hour for your appointment?" Brittany smiled at her friend.

"Nice dodge, but yes, see you then," the friends smiled at each other and Brittany stood up to walk out. She saw Stephanie wave to Tommy and as she turned to walk the other way, she got a look at him and had to admit, he was quite the specimen. He must have been at least 6 feet tall, with brown hair and green eyes. He had the most amazing smile, which he flashed as he saw Stephanie. He didn't seem to notice her and she shook her head, maybe in another lifetime.

Chapter Three:

Stephanie made her way to Brittany's office, her legs throbbing from walking so much. Sometimes she wished she worked in a small clinic where there were no more than a few steps between rooms. She pinched her thighs to try and stop them from throbbing so much. She hated this damn disease. She noticed some women walking down the hallway near her and stared at her, probably thinking the scene was a bit odd. That was the problem with MS. Looking at Stephanie; there were no obvious signs of a disease. That was both the curse and the benefit of Multiple Sclerosis. She couldn't remember how many times she had heard people exclaim. "But you don't look sick." Smiling, she figured if they saw her slapping her own legs in an empty hallway, they might think differently. It didn't matter, she had things to do and her appointment with Brittany was going to give her the hope and opportunity she and Jack needed. She approached the door and knocked.

"I looked over all of your test results that you sent to my office in London," the beautiful redhead said as she led Stephanie to the chair in her office. She sat down and smiled. "Everything looks great for trying the new round of IVF. Is Jack coming to the appointment?"

Stephanie nodded, "Yes, he will be there, he is so excited and nervous."

"Did I tell you how happy I am for you?" Brittany asked.

"Only a thousand times," Stephanie laughed. "You know I wish the same for you."

Brittany laughed. "I don't think that's in the cards for me. But I can live vicariously through your romance."

Stephanie touched her friends arm. "You know I used to think that, too. Don't close yourself off to love."

The tall redhead smiled a tiny smile. "I won't, but you know first hand the baggage I carry," she turned to walk back to her desk.

"I do, but you would be surprised at how amazing the right man could be. Besides, you're worth it," Stephanie stood up and hugged her friend. "I have to go to a meeting, meet you later for a drink?"

Brittany nodded, "Yep, after my next consult I think I will need it," she smiled at Stephanie's expression. "I'll explain later."

Stephanie laughed and walked out

****

"I have the room booked for a consult. I don't understand why it is a problem," Tommy gripped the phone and his knuckles were white as he tried to clear up the issue with the conference area he needed. He went to set up the room for a little boy and his family who were coming in to go over surgical options for his newly diagnosed cancer. The family was extremely concerned with making the boy's visit to the hospital as non-threatening as possible so Tommy had made arrangements to ensure their comfort. He was an hour away from the meeting and someone else was using the conference room. He was livid and was trying to find out who was inside.

"It doesn't matter if the paperwork got screwed up. Never mind, I will go and talk to the people in there myself," Tommy hung up the phone and walked to the room. He didn't know why he was so worked up over this, but the family he was helping had a rough road ahead of them and he really felt for the young parents. He walked into the room and saw a doctor he didn't recognize talking to a very pregnant woman and her husband. The whole room was basically empty. "Excuse me, I need the room now," he stated bluntly.

"*Excuse me*, I am in the middle of a meeting," the doctor said. She stood up and looked at the family sitting there. "I'm so sorry, I will be right back," she walked to Tommy and led him out to the hall. "What is your problem? Are you an idiot? Can't you see I am in the middle of something?" she seethed at him, astonished at his arrogance. "How about knocking and waiting for an answer? I would think a friend of Jack and Stephanie would have better manners."

Tommy was taken aback that she seemed to know him, but he shook it off. "I'm sorry, but why do you need an entire conference room to talk to a pregnant woman and a guy? You could accomplish the same thing in your office, you know, the things each of us have here?" he said in a sarcastic tone, noting she almost matched his height, shorter by only a few inches. Her long red hair was tucked neatly into a clip and as she shook her head in anger a few tendrils came loose. She hastily tucked them behind her ears and he realized he almost reached up to do it himself, a thought that completely stunned him.

"Who the hell are you? It is none of your business why I am in here and you are completely out of line. I have half a mind to call the chief of staff and report you for harassment," she yelled at him, her brilliant blue eyes flaming at him. The door of the room opened and the woman and her husband walked out.

"Dr. Anthony, I think it's best if we go," the woman said, nearly in tears. Her husband had her arm in a tight grip.

"No, please, it's fine, let's go back inside," Brittany said frantically, glaring at Tommy and trying to convince the couple to stay.

"Actually, you can continue this in Dr. Anthony's office. It is Dr. Anthony, right?" Tommy said, realizing there was probably more going on here than he thought, but too stubborn to change his demeanor.

The woman looked fearfully at Brittany. "You know I can't do that," she murmured. She turned to her husband who appeared livid.

"We need to go, now," he grabbed her arm roughly and they rushed off, the woman turning with another look of fear at the doctors.

Tommy moved to them. "Hey, I'm sorry," he began, but they didn't turn back. He forgot for a moment the fury that was standing behind him.

"Unbelievable, just unbelievable. Are you happy? Do you have any idea what you just did?" Brittany flamed at Tommy, her blue eyes full of fire. "What is wrong with you?" she stared into his emerald eyes, searching for an answer, her arms crossed in front of her chest.

He shook his head, trying to clear the flush he felt in his face. "I'm sorry, but I don't care. I have a consult coming in and I need this room, so if you will excuse me," he looked at her and felt the need to look away, as if she was seeing something he wasn't ready to share. He walked into the room.

"Oh, I don't think so. We are hardly finished here. You are the most arrogant asshole I have ever met. You can't come in here and boot my patient out just so you can have the room and then act like everything is okay," Brittany stated, her astonishment apparent. "You don't know what you just did."

"Look Red, I don't have time for this. I have a young couple coming in with their 6-year-old son who has a rare form of Leukemia. They want their little boy to have a good experience here and not see the hospital for what it is, the place where he will probably spend most of the rest of his life. I don't have time for your hissy fits or your soap box because your clients will have a beautiful bouncing baby soon enough and they will go on with their blissful existence and be none the wiser. Now move aside so I can make the room kid friendly," Tommy walked past her and closed the door, separating her from him and the room.

Brittany stood there in silence, the heat ruminating from her face. This wasn't over, not by a long shot.

******

"I can't believe we are finally ready to do this. I think it's fate that Britt came here from London," Stephanie said to Jack as they waited in the room for their appointment.

"I am sure it had nothing to do with you contacting the chief every moment you could," Jack smiled at his wife as they waited. He was more than a little nervous for this appointment, and he wasn't sure why. He just didn't want anything to go wrong. He knew he had been distant and cranky with her and it was all because he was scared.

"Sometimes you have to give people the push they need to see what's right in front of them," she took his hand in hers and held it tightly. He brushed his hand through her hair and leaned in to kiss her. "Besides, I know she and Tommy are going to hit it off wonderfully."

The door opened and Brittany came in, looking more than a little flustered. "Hi," she smiled at them and reached out to shake Jack's hand. "It's so great to see you again, Jack."

Jack smiled at her. "I'm so glad you came and joined the staff. You are going to be such a great addition."

Stephanie looked at her friend with concern. "What's going on with you? You look upset."

Brittany smoothed her jacket and exhaled. "No, everything is fine, I just had a run in with Tom, another doctor, and it was really unpleasant, to say the least. It's not important," she knew he was their friend, but this wasn't the time to bring it up.

Stephanie looked puzzled. "I'm sorry."

Brittany shrugged her shoulders. "It's not important and it doesn't matter," she took Stephanie's hand in her own and smiled. "Let's talk about you two and when you want to schedule your IVF."

Stephanie smiled and looked at Jack. "I think we are ready now."

Jack smiled back. "Are you sure everything looks good with Stephanie's blood work?" he asked her. "Have you consulted with the neurologist? I don't want the meds to interfere with her health. I am already worried about her being off her interferon for so long," Jack was referring to the injections Stephanie had to give herself because of the disease.

Stephanie held Jack's hand and looked at Brittany. "Jack is worried about me," she squeezed his arm. "I am, too, but I am feeling great, and I know the window of opportunity may not last forever."

Jack felt a twinge in his heart at her words. "That's not true. Nobody knows how long we have and I am not about to do anything to put you at risk."

Brittany looked at Jack. "You know that there is always a risk to a woman when she goes through a pregnancy, and because of Stephanie's Multiple Sclerosis, it makes her ability to fight off infection of any kind a little more difficult. But there are also many advances in fertility and obstetrics, which enable us to monitor and protect both the mother and the fetus. Having MS is a risk to Stephanie long term, but it isn't a reason not to have a child, and there is no risk to the baby. Because you both have been having trouble conceiving, I think it's worth a try at IVF. It is ultimately your decision, and you both need to be on board," she smiled at them.

She pulled up a chair and sat opposite them. "On a personal level, I can't think of a better person who deserves to be a mom more than Stephanie, and if she chose you to be her partner in life, you must be a pretty good guy, too. I know how scary this is, but it is also an exciting and amazing process," she walked over to the desk and picked up the chart. "I know some of your main worries, and I have some literature which might help you. You know that most women who have MS find that their symptoms get much better while they are pregnant," she looked at Jack, who was obviously unsure of everything. "I think you should take a few days and make sure this is what you both want. I will schedule the procedure for Thursday, and if you have any questions or concerns, we can talk before then."

Stephanie and Jack thanked her and walked out into the hall. They walked in silence and Stephanie turned to look at him. "How about we talk tonight? I have something I need to do."

He looked at her. "Okay, sure. I'll see you in a little while," he went to hug her but she had walked away. He felt terrible. He knew he had seemed distant and not totally on board with the whole idea, but that wasn't it. He was a coward and he didn't know how to deal with this. He ran his hand through his hair and turned to follow her, He needed to make sure she knew what he was thinking.

****

Stephanie walked to the hospital roof and let the fresh air run through her hair and over her face. She felt her tears fall and for the millionth time, cursed her disease. She tried not to dwell on it or really think about it in a way that made her feel like a victim, but sometimes it just got to her. She sat down on the floor and closed her eyes, trying to block everything out. She concentrated on her breathing and just listened to the silence.

"I hope you don't mind, but I needed some air," Jack said as he sat down next to her.

Stephanie looked at him and smiled. She scooted closer to him and leaned her head on his shoulder. "I'm sorry," she wiped her tears.

Jack put his arm around her. "I thought we weren't saying those words anymore."

She looked at up at him. "Sometimes it's necessary. All of this, this fear and uncertainty, I'm sorry for it."

He felt like a jerk. "Stephanie, I must be the worst husband in the world. I am a coward and because of that, you doubt yourself. All of these feelings of worry and concern I am having are not your fault. I guess I just never realized how much I was keeping to myself," he turned and faced her. "Let me be clear. I love you and I want to have children with you. I want to be with you through all of it, the struggles and the triumphs, but you need to understand how terrifying this is for me. I can't do anything but watch all of this happen. You will be going through all of this and I can't take any of it away for you. In case you haven't noticed, I don't like to be on the sidelines," he smiled as she laughed. "You will just have to learn to live with my neurosis."

She leaned in and kissed him. "I wish I didn't have MS. I know it goes without saying, but sometimes I need to say it. I wish I could worry about the simple things that every expectant mother worries about without thinking everyday that I am selfish for even wanting to give birth to my own child, knowing I may not be able to do all of the things other mothers do. If I think about the enormity of the problems we may face, it gets overwhelming. I need you to be with me 100% on this or we don't do it. It is as simple as that," she touched his face.

"I am the one who should apologize. I have made you doubt my willingness to be with you on this. Of all my doubts and fears, none of them have ever been because of your MS. I look at what you have been through in the time I have known you, and I just worry about you. I don't worry about the kind of mother you will be or the life we will offer our child, because I know it will be the best of both of us. I worry about being without you. I know it's silly, but I can't help it. To be honest, I think about having a child all the time. When I walk by the nursery I look at the babies in their bassinets and picture the name "baby Stephens" on one of them. I see you holding our baby and it makes me happier than I ever hoped to be. I want to do this with you. I want to have a child with you because our love deserves to grow," he leaned in and kissed her, feeling like he wanted to do more. "I think we should go home and give it one more try, naturally," he grinned as he nibbled on her neck.

She wrapped her arms around him. "I think that's a great idea," she kissed him deeply and smiled as they made their way back inside.

"There's Tommy, I need to talk to him about a case before we go, do you mind?" Jack asked as he spotted his friend.

"Not at all, I am going to make a couple of notes in the computer at the nurse's station," Stephanie said and waved at Tommy before walking away.

"Hey, how did it go with the boy's parents?" Jack asked, knowing how torn up Tommy had been about his case.

Tommy sighed. "It went well, after my run in with a certain doctor who has no idea about what it means to be a team player."

Jack was confused. "Care to elaborate?"

"No, not now anyway. I explained the course of treatment and the probability of success, and they want to go ahead with it. I just wish I had a better option, the kid is only six," Tommy wiped his brow.

"I know, man, but you will do your best. You are giving them the best option there is," Jack said.

There was a loud commotion in the lobby and Jack turned around in time to see a man standing there with a gun pointed at Tommy. He heard a loud shot and then he felt a strange sensation through his body. He heard Stephanie scream and he turned to look at her before he slowly sank to the ground.

"Jack? Oh God Jack," Stephanie screamed and ran to her husband through the cacophony of sounds and chaos. She saw the police subdue the man with the gun and Tommy was already tending to Jack. Stephanie threw herself onto her husband. "Look at me, oh Jack, look at me," she cried as she touched his face. He remained motionless and she looked at Tommy, who was screaming orders to the staff and holding pressure on the wound.

"Don't say it," she screamed at him. "Don't you dare say it!"

Chapter Four:

The dark metal doors were different than she remembered the hundred times she had walked through them on her way to surgery. Now they seemed cold, like iron, keeping her away from her love. Stephanie looked at her hands and the blood stained flesh and was lost in the memory of their time together when she truly fell for Jack. He was her lifeline and she was able to live again because of him. Now, everything was falling apart. She put her head in her hands and sobbed again, trying to remember what had happened, but it was all a blur. She remembered the talk on the roof; so much love had passed between them. They headed home, but Jack stopped to talk to Tommy. Then the shot and her heart shattered. She felt sick to her stomach and looked for a garbage can to vomit. She ran to the bin and spit up nothing, because she had already done that. She had nothing left in her to purge. There was an emptiness, which had settled in and was making a home inside her. She sank to the ground, feeling shaky and weak.

"Stephanie?" a voice called out to her. She looked up and saw Brittany looking for her as she same out of the O.R. doors.

"Here, I'm here. Can I go in now?" Stephanie stood up on trembling legs and wiped her face as she stumbled to her friend.

"No, not yet, they are still working on him," Brittany said. She took Stephanie to the bench and they sat down. "I need to make sure you are okay," she began to take Stephanie's vitals.

"I am fine," she pulled away from her. "I just need to be with my husband," she wiped her angry tears away.

Brittany sighed. "Stephanie, you need to look at me," she spoke with purpose and Stephanie felt her heart race.

"What is it? Dammit Brittany, tell me the truth," she yelled.

"I am trying. Jack is holding his own in there. I was able to get an update and they are working to repair the damage. The bullet nicked the right lobe of his liver and they are working to finish the repair," Brittany said.

"Oh God, he could go into liver failure and then kidney failure and then there is nothing we can do," Stephanie said.

Brittany rubbed her friends arm. "Or he could make a full recovery and you both will start the family you planned. I think you should look at that possibility. When they are done, Dr. Williams will come out. He won't leave the O.R. until everything is finished."

Stephanie felt immediate relief at the mention of the name. "Tommy is like a brother to Jack. He won't let anything happen in there."

Brittany sighed. "I know this is probably not the right time to tell you this, but I need you to know something," she felt tears prick her eyes.

Stephanie looked at her friend. "What is it? What's wrong?"

"It's my fault that Jack was shot," she let her tears fall. "He was shot by an angry patient of mine.

"How on earth is that your fault?" Stephanie asked her. "You are not responsible for anyone else's actions."

Brittany sighed. "Do you remember when I told you and Jack about my run in with that rude doctor who threw my patient out of the conference room?"

Stephanie nodded. "Yes, I think so, but I still don't understand."

"The couple he threw out were new clients of mine from the free clinic I volunteer at on the weekends. Kathy is an abused woman who I had been trying to help for a long time. She tried to leave Mason but never did and then she became pregnant. I gave her the best care I could, but he wouldn't allow her to get treatment," Brittany stopped and exhaled.

"I finally convinced her to come here with Mason so I could try and explain some of the reasons as to why she needed to be under a doctor's care. He wouldn't come unless I guaranteed he wouldn't be in a hospital room, but in a conference room and everything would run smoothly. It was going well and I think he was starting to listen to me when Dr. Williams busted in and threw them out. Mason went crazy. He came back looking for Tom and Jack got in the way. I am so sorry, Stephanie, this is all my fault."

Stephanie hugged her friend. "No, it's not. If there is one thing I have learned from being with Jack, it is not to blame myself for the actions of others," she touched Brittany's hair and smoothed it down. "Britt, you of all people should know that," the two friends exchanged an understanding glance, silently speaking of the past.

"Stephanie," Tommy came out of the O.R. and pulled off his mask as he called to her. Stephanie jumped up and ran to him. "He is stable. He is going to make it," Tommy said and Stephanie hugged him.

"Thank you," she said. "I need to see him."

Tommy hugged her. "They are moving him to recovery and you can go in then. We will need to monitor his bilirubin and ALT for the next few days, but I expect the numbers will settle down. Don't worry if he looks yellow."

Stephanie smiled. "I know. Hepatic injury can cause a lot of issues, but I have faith he will be okay," Stephanie saw them wheel Jack out and turned to follow the gurney.

Tommy walked over to the bench and sat down. He didn't seem to notice Brittany was still there. He put his head in his hands and let his emotions come out.

Feeling like she was intruding on a private moment, Brittany turned to walk away when something made her stop and turn toward him. She walked over and sat down next to him. She hesitated, but gently touched his shoulder.

Tommy looked at her. He wiped his face and stood up. "Sorry, I should go see Jack."

Brittany stood up like she was stung and crossed her arms over her chest. "Of course," she watched him walk away and she sank back down on the bench, her sadness taking over.

Tommy walked away and heard her cry. He turned to see her sitting there, crying softly. He didn't know why he cared, but he turned back and walked over to her.

"Why don't you come with me, Red?"

She looked up at him, embarrassed he saw her rare show of emotion. "I don't think so," she said as she wiped her face.

"Fine," he said and walked away with a shrug.

Brittany watched him leave. He would never be so nice to her if he knew her history. She was better off alone, she reminded herself again.

Chapter Five:

Tommy walked into the room later that night to see Stephanie and Jack relaxing in his bed. He smiled as he made his way to the chair next to the bed. "How are you both doing?"

Jack smiled. "Fine; and you?"

Tommy sighed. "I am tired of saving you, man. Can you stop getting hurt?"

They all laughed. "First of all, you didn't and have never saved me. And second of all, thank you," Jack said with all sincerity.

"No problem. I think you will be able to go home in a few days," Tommy said.

"I am going home tomorrow," Jack said matter of factly.

"No you are not. You will stay here until you are well," Stephanie said.

"I can recuperate at home just as easily if not better than here, and besides, you two won't let anything happen to me," Jack rolled his eyes.

"I think the pain meds are getting to you," Tommy said and shook his head. "There is no use arguing with you, at least not tonight."

Jack smiled. "Good, then it's settled."

"You will stay as long as needed," Stephanie finished the sentence.

Jack sighed. He decided to change the subject. "So what happened exactly?"

Stephanie looked at Tommy and he shrugged. "I don't know; some guy tried to kill me and shot you instead. I don't know why, I never saw him before," Tommy said.

Stephanie looked at him. "Yes you did."

The men looked at her.

"Brittany told me what happened," Stephanie relayed the story to them as close as she could remember Brittany telling her. She came to the end of the story and looked at Tommy. "None of this is either of your faults. No one is responsible for another person resorting to violence."

Tommy put his head in his hands. "This is all my fault. I was so angry that she was in there with those people when I needed the room, it never occurred to me to ask why."

"I didn't make it any easier for you by putting up an argument," Brittany said from the doorway. She walked in slowly, keeping her distance from Tommy. "I'm sorry, I don't mean to intrude, I just wanted to see how you were doing," she said to Jack.

He grinned at her. "I am great, and will be fine, so you both can stop looking so forlorn. How about when I get out of here you two come over for a home cooked meal? I can make a mean lasagna," Jack held Stephanie's hand.

Tommy looked at Brittany and then at Jack. "I have rounds, I will see you soon," he nodded at them and left, brushing past her without stopping.

Brittany felt tears prick her eyes as he walked by. "I am so glad you are going to be okay. Stephanie, I will catch up with you later about rescheduling your appointment."

Jack looked at her. "Nope, we are going ahead with the IVF on Thursday. Nothing is going to stop this."

Brittany smiled. "Okay, see you then," she turned and walked out.

Stephanie ran her hand through her hair and sighed. "They are both a mess," she turned to Jack and saw he had a smile on his face. "What is it?"

"I think Tommy is smitten," he said.

"Smitten? Why do you think that?" Stephanie asked him. She touched his face as he lay back in the bed, clearly exhausted.

"I have never seen him react to a woman like that," he said through his closed eyes.

"How did he react? He just left," she said as she rubbed his hair.

"Exactly, Tommy has a problem when someone gets to him. He runs when he can't deal and he gets that look in his face like he wants to throw up. Brittany did something to him," he smiled at Stephanie.

"If that's the case, they both have their work cut out for them," she crawled closer to Jack and he held her to him. They would deal with their friends tomorrow; tonight they would just hold each other.

*****

Tommy walked onto the hospital roof and tried to clear his head. He couldn't believe what had happened. He had almost gotten Jack killed. He had thrown a couple out of a consult because of his arrogance. He didn't even remember the man's face. How could he be so oblivious?

And then there was Red. He shook his head. What the hell was going on? She must have been the friend of Stephanie's from Paris, or London, he couldn't remember. He didn't want to remember, because he didn't have the time for this, or the energy. He thought back to his life just a few years before. Everything seemed so much simpler then. He walked to the ledge to look out and he saw her again, sitting in the corner of the roof, her eyes closed and her head in her hands. He approached her gently, against his better judgment.

Clearing his throat he asked her softly, "Are you okay?"

Brittany looked up, startled. Her long red hair was disheveled and hung around her shoulders. Her blue eyes were red from crying and her expression was one of utter loneliness. Tommy recognized it from his own face.

"I will be thanks," she said and wiped her face with her sleeves.

Tommy went over and sat down next to her, being careful to keep a good distance. "It has been one hell of a day."

She nodded, "Yep."

He turned to look at her, noticing her features for the first time. She was very pretty, and looked a little familiar. He felt his heart beat a little faster at her proximity. "So, you've known Stephanie for awhile?"

She looked at her hands. "Yes, we go way back. You have known Jack for a long time?"

"Yes, since we were six," he answered. They sat in awkward silence for a minute.

"You know, you could have just asked me to move my appointment," she said softly. "I can be reasonable."

"So it's my fault your client was a lunatic who came back shooting?" Tommy stood up angrily.

Brittany stood up and looked at him. "No, I didn't say that, but you were a complete ass and I became defensive because of it. I could have diffused the situation and we all could have been happy. I just wish you had given me the chance," she said, her pulse racing, realizing his close proximity. She was uncomfortable for so many reasons.

"Well, I'm sorry. I guess I have an emotional investment in my patients and the news I was going to be giving needed to be told in that room. I don't know what else to tell you," Tommy paced the roof, needing to keep his distance.

Brittany shrugged. "I guess that's it. You said your piece and it is up to me to believe it or not. I prefer my doctors to be team players, but I can also relate to the idea that your surroundings make a difference in how you perceive important news. You had a patient who you promised something to, and you did it. As angry as I am, I admire that."

"Thanks," Tommy said as he watched her walk away.

Chapter Six:

"How have you been feeling?" Brittany asked Stephanie as she went over her vitals, preparing for the egg retrieval. "How are you tolerating the hormone injections?"

Stephanie shrugged. "I feel good. I love getting a break from my MS shots, but the hormone shots are worse."

Brittany sat down and smiled at her. "I know, but I hope it's worth it. Things look good from my end. We should be able to go ahead with the egg retrieval today and then implant in a few days. How does that sound?"

Stephanie grinned. "Awesome. I am so ready to get this process started. I think we all need something good to happen."

Brittany nodded, "I couldn't agree more. Do you want me to send for Jack?"

Stephanie shook her head. "No, Tommy is going to bring him as soon as he is done with his release papers. I wanted to let them have some time to talk. I think Tommy is really beating himself up about what happened. He blames himself for Jack getting shot."

Brittany tried to hide her distaste at the mention of Tommy, but Stephanie caught on. "You two didn't quite get off on the right foot, did you?"

Brittany shrugged, "It doesn't matter. You and Jack like him, so I will just have to make nice," she moved to get the materials ready for the egg extraction.

Stephanie didn't want to drop it. "Tommy was wrong in how he treated you, but it was really out of character for him. He is a great guy and he is worth getting to know."

Brittany turned to look at her and sighed

"Stephanie, this is pointless, you know I am not going to get involved with anyone, so there is no point in even discussing it. I am sure he is nice and I am sure he is worth getting to know, but it will have to be with someone else."

"You know, it doesn't have to be that way. You are such a beautiful, smart and giving person, Britt. Why won't you let anyone see that?" Stephanie asked her friend.

Britt looked at her. "You know why," she wiped at her eyes. "I just can't bring myself to deal with certain things, so it's easier this way. I know it isn't right, and I should be able to move on, but it's just the way it is."

There was a soft knock on the door. Brittany opened it and Jack walked in, so the conversation ended.

******

"So what's on tap for today?" Stephanie asked Chelsea, the head orthopedic nurse, as they stood at the hub the next morning.

"I think you have a consult with Dr. Williams. The boy he is treating with bone cancer is up for a possible trial and the parents want to talk to someone about it. I know he mentioned you and he told me to send you over to his office when you came in," Chelsea smiled at her. "I am so glad Dr. Stephens is doing better."

Stephanie grinned. "You and me both. I think we all need a few things to go well for a change," she picked up the chart and her tea and walked off toward Tommy's office.

About an hour later, Tommy walked Stephanie out of the office. "I can't thank you enough for talking to the Jackson's for me. I hate that we are so limited in our options for their little boy. It seems that you might be able to offer at least a little hope."

Stephanie sighed. "I don't know. The trials in pediatrics are limited at best, but if there is anything I can do, I will make sure it happens," Stephanie felt a little woozy all of a sudden and stopped walking. Tommy noticed and took her arm.

"Hey, are you okay?" he felt her pulse.

Stephanie nodded. "I just need to sit for a minute."

She let Tommy lead her to the set of chairs and concentrated on her breathing.

"I am going to call Jack," Tommy said and picked up his phone.

Stephanie touched his arm. "No, it's the hormone injections. Brittany, please call her, she can help."

Tommy picked up his phone and called OBGYN. He asked the nurse to get Brittany over to where they were. He got up and got Stephanie a cup of water. She held it and her hand shook, spilling the water. "I don't like this, Stephanie. I need to call Jack."

"No, please don't worry him. He isn't in any condition to deal with this. He has only been home for a day," Stephanie felt her tears come. She was feeling worse by the minute. "I think something is wrong."

"That's it, come on," he helped her up and walked back to his office. He paged Brittany to find them there and looked up as she walked into the room.

"What happened?" she ran to Stephanie who was prone on the couch.

"She just got dizzy and then she was shaking," Tommy began.

Brittany began an exam on Stephanie. She called on her hospital phone and ordered some blood work and a room. She smiled at Stephanie. "You are going to be fine. I am going to order some tests and get you on an IV. They are getting a room for you," she touched her friend's face, which was flushed and burning up. She stood up to go talk to Tommy.

"Can you get Jack? He should be here, if you think he will tolerate it," she asked him.

Tommy nodded. "What's wrong?"

"I can't discuss anything personal with you. If Jack wants to, he can fill you in. I think it would be helpful if he were here. I don't want to call him and stress him out and I don't think he should be driving yet. I just thought maybe you could help," Brittany said.

"I'm on my way. Tell her not to worry," Tommy took one last look at Stephanie and left.

****

Jack was working on something for Stephanie that he hoped to finish before she got home. He heard a car in the driveway and cursed to himself. He would have to finish later. He tried to gather everything together when he realized the garage never opened. Maybe it wasn't her. He walked to look and saw it was Tommy. He smiled until he realized his friend was still in his lab coat. They never left in their lab coats. He opened the door.

"What is it? What happened? Is it Stephanie?" he felt his panic rise.

Tommy walked into the house and closed the door. "You need to relax. Stephanie is just feeling a bit run down and I didn't want you to drive like a freak. I will take you to the hospital and you can be with her."

"What aren't you telling me? You are here with your lab coat on which means you left quickly. If it weren't a big deal, she would have called me," Jack grabbed his jacket. "Let's go."

Tommy followed his friend out to the car. "Brittany wouldn't tell me anything. What's going on?" he pulled the car onto the road.

"Did she say what she was feeling?" Jack asked him.

"We were talking after she did a consult for me. She got light headed and her hands were shaking. I took her to my office and she told me to call Brittany. That's all I know. They are running blood work and admitting her for fluids and observation," Tommy said.

Jack ran his hand through his hair. "We are trying to have a baby," he said softly.

Tommy looked over at him. "That's great, man. You and Stephanie will make the best parents," he was thrilled for his friends.

Jack smiled. "Not if it costs Stephanie her health," he wiped his face. "I am trying to be optimistic about this, but I am scared to death that something is going to happen to her."

Tommy nodded. "Stephanie is such a fantastic woman Jack; I forget she is living with MS. She handles everything with such class," he spoke with admiration.

Jack nodded. "She does, but she isn't wonder woman. She wants so much to be a mother, and I want that too, but there is only so much stress a person can take, and stress brings on exacerbations. We haven't been able to get pregnant on our own, so Brittany is doing IVF."

They pulled into the staff lot and got out, making their way to Stephanie.

Chapter Seven:

"I don't know why I am here. I just got dizzy and worn down, nothing unusual. The mix of meds I am on is a reasonable explanation as to why I feel this way. This is ridiculous," Stephanie told Brittany as she lay in a hospital bed. "I need to get home before Jack begins to worry."

Jack and Tommy got to the room at that very minute. "Hey, what about me worrying?" he smiled as he pulled her to him in a hug. He felt her forehead. "You're burning up," he said concerned.

"I don't believe you guys. I am fine; it's just my body adjusting. You shouldn't have come. You need to be resting," Stephanie said, although she knew it was futile to argue with any of them.

Jack looked at Brittany. "What's the plan?"

Tommy stepped out, allowing them privacy.

Brittany was looking over the latest blood work results. She looked at Stephanie and Jack. "It could be nothing, but the fact that you have been under so much stress lately, with Jack being shot, your immune system is already taking a beating. The hormone injections on top of everything else might be too much for your system. You are running a fever of 101 and your electrolytes are out of whack. I think we need to reconsider the procedure."

Stephanie felt tears in her eyes. "No, we can't. We already prepared the embryos. They need to be implanted. I don't want to wait," she let her tears fall.

Jack felt his own heart breaking for both of them. His worst fears seemed to be materializing; yet he knew what Stephanie needed him to do. "I think we should wait a day like we planned and then proceed. We can give Stephanie a high dose of IV fluids and antibiotics. She will respond," he squeezed his wife's hand.

Brittany nodded. "I will give you a day, but I won't compromise your health. Let me go order your meds."

"Thank you," Stephanie said and Brittany walked out. Jack ran his hand through his hair. "I will be fine," Stephanie leaned back and closed her eyes. "Our baby needs me."

"I need you," he said brokenly. "Dammit, Stephanie, I don't think I can do this," he felt the panic rise in his chest. "I know what I said, but we haven't even really begun and you are already here. I just don't think I can do this," he walked to the window. "I can only imagine what you think of me. You married a coward," he turned and looked at her.

Stephanie motioned for him to come over to her. "You are not a coward," she said softly. "I will never understand why men think showing any signs of weakness automatically makes them a coward. It takes a real man to feel things and to talk about those feelings. I didn't marry you because you always agreed with me or because you rescued me from myself. I married my partner in every way and when you need strength you can take it from me. I don't intend on going anywhere, and I need you to know I will do everything it takes to be with you for as long as you'll let me."

Jack touched her face, "How did I get so lucky?"

"Actually, you haven't gotten lucky in a while, as soon as we are both feeling a little better, we shall both get very lucky," she pulled him to her for a sweet kiss.

"Ahem, am I interrupting?" Tommy knocked on the open door.

Stephanie grinned and wiped her face. "Of course not, family is always welcome."

Tommy came in and hugged her.

"How are you feeling?" he asked.

"I'll be fine in a few days. How did the family react to the drug trial information?" Stephanie asked about the little boy.

Tommy smiled. "Don't you ever take a minute off?"

Jack shook his head. "Never," he looked at his wife. "But then again, neither do we."

They all smiled.

After a few minutes, they were all talking about nothing, each trying to get the other to relax and not worry about things. Stephanie yawned and Jack tucked her hair behind her ear. "I think you need your rest."

Tommy stood up. "That would be my cue to leave," he turned when Jade, the nurse who worked with Brittany was in the doorway.

"Excuse me, do any of you know where Dr. Anthony is? She isn't answering her page and we need her in the E.R," Jade said.

"She was going to check on my meds, but she should answer her page," Stephanie said.

Tommy shrugged. "Is there something I can help with? I am off and was about to leave."

Jade shook her head. "No, this is a specific case. There was a young woman brought in who was sexually assaulted. She is refusing treatment and we thought Dr. Anthony could help. She has been great with our assault victims"

Tommy was confused. "I am sure there are other Gynecologists on duty."

Jade looked at him and turned and left.

Tommy looked at Stephanie. "Am I missing something?"

Stephanie didn't know what to say. She didn't want to betray her friends' confidence.

"I think you should ask her about that."

Tommy shook his head. "If I cared, I would. You guys rest and I will see you later," he left.

Jack and Stephanie were both surprised by his response, but didn't say anything. Jack looked at

Stephanie. "Brittany went through something bad, didn't she?"

Stephanie closed her eyes. "Worse than you could imagine," she drifted off to sleep with her husband holding her hand. After he was sure she was asleep, he stepped out of the room to find Tommy.

Jack saw him in the hall a little while later. "Hey, is everything okay?"

Tommy looked at his friend. "Yes, why?"

Jack shrugged. "I don't know, you seem to be a little rude when it comes to Brittany. As far as I know, she is a really great person. Stephanie doesn't trust easily, and she really respects her. Maybe you should give her a chance."

Tommy wiped his hand over his face. "I don't know what it is, man, she just gets to me. I don't know why. I'm sorry if I upset Stephanie, I didn't mean to do that."

Jack shook his head. "Don't be ridiculous, Stephanie just wants you to be happy, we both do. It just seemed like you were struggling with something. You never have to apologize to us for that. Why don't you come by the room later and have dinner with us."

Tommy felt terrible, but he didn't know why. "Sure, I'll be there," he patted his friend on the back and walked away.

******

Tommy made his way down to the emergency room without even realizing he was walking that way. He saw the police there talking to a woman who looked to be hysterical. He listened a little to what was going on. The woman was talking about her daughter who had apparently been attacked and sexually assaulted. The girl was in the exam room now. The police were trying to get information to help. Tommy walked past the door of the room where the girl was being treated. He heard Brittany's voice and he stopped.

"You will get through this, I know how it feels right now; you think your life is over and you will never get through this pain. I am here to tell you that it will get better. You have a strength inside of you that is just waiting to come out. You need to believe that you are going to be okay," Tommy moved a little and through a small opening, saw the young girl sobbing in Brittany's arms. She was rubbing the girls back and holding her.

"He hurt me so badly," the girl cried. "I tried to get away but he was so strong," she began to get sick and Brittany held her hair back. She moved the bin away and handed the girl some water. Tommy felt his stomach twist.

"He can't hurt you anymore. Don't let him take one minute more from you. You will survive and you will get through this. Look at me. I became a doctor and I have made it my life's work to help people. My attack could have been the end for me but I made sure it wasn't. You are not alone. I will be with you as long as you need me. Now there are things we need to do to help you. We need to perform an exam and run some blood work. We will start you on some antiretroviral medications on the small chance you were infected with anything."

"I don't want anyone looking at me. I don't want anyone to see. Can you do the exam, please?" the girl cried.

"Of course I will. I need a nurse to come in and help, but she will be someone you can trust," Brittany called on her hospital cell to Jade, who came in. "This is Nurse Sorad, she will help us."

"Hi, my name is Jade and if you need anything, please let me know. How about if I just hold your hand?" Jade asked and the frightened girl grabbed it. Brittany nodded to Jade and began the exam, getting the samples needed and checking for injuries. She finished as quickly as she could.

"All done. You don't know how much courage that just took. You are going to help to make sure this guy never hurts another woman. I am going to get your mom to come in and sit with you and I will be back in a little while. Jade will stay with you until then, okay?" Brittany said.

"Okay," the girl nodded and Brittany gathered her things and walked out.

Tommy moved quickly to the side when she came out, and she didn't appear to see him. He was overwhelmed with emotion as he watched her walk away. He wasn't sure he had heard correctly. She was raped? She was attacked like that? How does someone do something like that? He wanted to know more about her, about what she had been through. He hated himself for being such an ass to her. He knew Jack had been right, he was a jerk and he had no excuse. He was standing there, lost in thought when Brittany walked back over to the room with the girl's mom. She looked at him, standing there and he looked at her. She felt her heart sink. She had seen that look many times before. She helped the mother into the room and made sure they were okay before turning to walk out, closing the door behind her. She looked at Tommy and then turned to walk the other way.

"Red, I mean, Brittany, wait," Tommy said.

She turned around and eyed him. "No, I don't think that's a good idea," she kept walking until she got to an empty room, walked inside and closed the door behind her. She sank to the floor and let her emotions come out. She remembered that moment as if it were yesterday. She could hear the sounds and feel the pain. Her heart broke at the days and weeks ahead for the girl. She prayed that the news would be better than it had been for her. She heard a soft knock on the door. "Occupied," she said.

"Red, it's me, Tommy. I need to talk to you; please let me in. I know I have been an ass and I'm sorry, but I need to see you," he felt an urgency to make this right, to take away her pain.

She sighed. What was his problem? She wasn't in the mood for another argument. She opened the door. "I can't handle a fight right now. When someone goes off on their own, it usually means they want to be alone. I'm a big girl and I can take care of myself," she turned away, but didn't close the door.

"You are probably used to doing that, right?" he said and she looked at him before she sat down on a chair in the room. "Taking care of yourself. I recognize the trait because I'm the same way," he walked in and sat down on the chair next to her and exhaled. "I want to apologize for how I have treated you. We got off on the wrong foot and I have done nothing but reinforce your idea that I am an ass."

"So now that you overheard my personal business you have decided to be nicer to me?" she looked at him and sighed, her eyes red and tired. "Don't bother, there is more to me that you won't want to know."

He didn't flinch.

"Go ahead, I'm listening."

She looked at him, her eyes blazing. "Who do you think you are? You can't just come in here after hearing stuff about me that you had no business hearing and then poke around for more. You have no reason to be here and to be honest, I am simply not interested."

He smiled softly at her. "I didn't ask you to marry me; I just thought you might want to talk about it," he stood up and walked in front of her, crossing his arms as he leaned against the bed. "You know, I apologized for my behavior, it wouldn't kill you to do the same."

She was beyond flabbergasted. Who was this guy? She stood up and faced him. "Look, I know that Jack and Stephanie like you, so I know there must be something there to like, but I am not in the mood to find out or to have this conversation. I just need to be alone for a while, please. Can't you respect that?" she couldn't help it, but her emotions were at the breaking point. She turned way from him, put her head in her hands and cried.

Tommy felt terrible. He closed the gap between them and touched her shoulder. "I'm so sorry, I didn't mean to," he stopped talking and she turned and collapsed in his arms. He held her and tried to comfort her as she cried. He had never felt so helpless.

"Shh, it's going to be okay," he spoke to her but felt the hollowness of his words. She began to quiet down and pulled away, wiping her face.

"I ruined your jacket," she said as she saw the spot her tears had made on his coat.

"I think it will dry," he looked at her and wanted to hold her some more. "Can I get you anything?"

She shook her head and grabbed a tissue to wiper her face, totally mortified. "I'm sorry; I don't know what came over me. I don't usually do things like that."

"Show emotion? I think you're allowed. Anyone who witnessed what that girl had been through would be affected, let alone someone who," he stopped, not knowing if he was crossing a boundary he shouldn't.

"Someone who has also been raped?" she said softly. "Sometimes I feel like it happened yesterday," she sighed. "I have separated myself so much from that moment. It's bad enough I have to live with the scars every day, but I want so much for it not to be my defining moment. There is more to me than that event, and I can't let it have that power over me," she couldn't believe she was being so open with a virtual stranger. But something had happened between them, a wall was cracked and a small sliver of ice had melted.

Tommy felt tears come to his eyes.

"I don't know what to say. I wish I had profound words of wisdom to make you feel better. I know when memories hit us in our lives; sometimes we just need to go through them. You can't run from them and you can't bury them or they will eat away at you."

"You sound like you are speaking from personal experience," Brittany said to him.

"I am, although I don't mean to imply that I know a fraction of what you are going through. My parents were killed in a car crash when I was a freshman in college. After that, it was just me and my sister Julie. She was only 12. Sometimes I miss them with a profound sadness that just comes over me," he looked at her, this woman who somehow brought out his most innermost fears. He couldn't help it; he wanted to talk to her.

"I am so sorry for your loss. I can't imagine what you must have gone through," she felt her heart ache for him.

Tommy wiped at his eyes and cleared his throat. "It is what it is, that's what I tell myself. My parents raised me to believe in family and faith, and that has been their legacy. I raised my sister with those ideals and I try to make them proud," he cleared his throat. "Anyway, I have a consult in a few minutes. Can I take you to dinner later?"

Brittany felt her heart sink. "Tommy, there is something else you should know about me."

He looked at her. "Okay."

"I am HIV positive," she said and waited for the response.

Tommy heard her and the gravity of what she went through sank in. He didn't know what to say.

"Okay, but you still have to eat."

She looked at him and smiled. "That's true."

"So, dinner?" he pushed.

"Maybe tomorrow. I have something I need to do tonight. Will that work?" she asked him.

"I'll tell you what, I am going to visit with Jack and Stephanie and then I will be at my house. If you change your mind, call me or stop over. I'll leave you my address," he wrote his information on a sheet of paper. He turned to leave and stopped at the door. "I am honored you shared all of this with me and I am profoundly sorry you are HIV positive, but it doesn't change any part of the woman I see. I am sorry I was such a jerk and I want to work to make it up to you," he met her gaze and turned and left.

Chapter Eight:

"How are you feeling? Did you sleep?" Jack asked his wife as she sat in her hospital bed.

She shook her head. "I tried, but I am still a little nauseous," she sighed. "You would think I would be used to this feeling, but it's like my body is always telling me how angry it is that I have this disease."

He took her hand in his. "I agree with your body. I would fight it every hour of every day," he smiled at her. "You just keep reinforcing the fact that you're my hero."

She looked at him, his eyes filled with sincerity. "Thank you," she said.

"For what?" he kissed her fingers.

"For taking a chance on me. I don't know why you did, or what you saw, but it made my life worth something. You made me want more, and I never really thought I deserved that," she was getting choked up when she looked up and saw Tommy coming into the room.

"Hey, come in," Stephanie said as she wiped her face and smiled.

"I don't want to interrupt," he said.

Jack stood up and moved over.

"Stop standing on ceremony and get in here," he patted the chair next to him. He noticed Tommy had a different look on his face, one he didn't recognize. "Is everything okay?"

Tommy nodded. "Yeah, it's just been a long afternoon."

Jack agreed. His phone rang and he answered it. He spoke for a minute and then hung up. "I am going to head over to cardiology and give input on a case. They need my feedback. I will be right back, if you don't mind," he said to Stephanie.

"But you are on medical leave. Can't you get a day off?" Tommy asked.

Stephanie smiled. "It's fine, go and give your brilliant opinion and then come back so we can eat. Tommy will keep me company while you're gone."

Jack leaned in and kissed her. "I love you."

"I love you more," she said and watched him walk out. She turned and looked at Tommy. "So, spill. What's going on?"

He looked at her with fake innocence. "What do you mean?"

She laughed. "I know I haven't known you as long as Jack, but I am a very observant person. You have a different air about you, like something is on your mind."

Tommy took a deep breath. "I just found out some things about someone and I am having a hard time processing everything."

Stephanie looked at her friend. "I am a good listener, why don't you let me help you process."

He met her gaze. "It's about Red, I mean Brittany. I overheard her talking to a rape victim and she revealed some things. I talked to her about it and she told me things that I am having a hard time dealing with."

"Because it changes your opinion of her?" Stephanie asked gently.

He looked at her, "Actually, just the opposite. I feel like I need to do something to make it better. I don't think I have done enough to be the man I should be. She has made something amazing out of her life after surviving a horrible ordeal, and I have nothing to feel proud of. I have done nothing to deserve a quarter of the admiration she deserves," he realized he was rambling and he blushed.

"I don't think you need to do anything to deserve her admiration or friendship. Brittany doesn't look at people like that. She demands respect and accountability and doesn't feel sorry for herself," Stephanie smiled at Tommy. "I think you both could learn a little bit from each other."

Tommy sighed. "I just wish I had been a little less of an ass when we met. I just feel badly about things, there is nothing more to it," he shook his head. "I am not interested in anything else."

Stephanie shrugged. "Okay, if that's what you need to tell yourself."

He glanced at her. "Nice."

They both laughed.

******

"So, do you feel okay about waiting a few days?" Jack asked Stephanie as they sat at home a few days later. Jack had brought Stephanie home under the strict agreement that she would come back if she felt worse at all.

"I am just happy to be home and as long as we can go ahead with the implants next week, I am good. I just want things to go well for both of us," she touched Jack's hand. "I hope you know that I will never risk my health if I can help it. I won't go ahead with this procedure if it isn't safe, no matter how much I want to."

Jack tucked her hair behind her ear. "I know that, but how about we look at it as if it's going to work. I prefer to think positively and for once in our lives, things will go as planned," he leaned in and kissed her.

She wiped his cheek with her thumb. "How do you feel? You know, you are still recovering from a gunshot wound."

He grinned. "I am doing really well, but I think my wound might need a little TLC from a certain orthopedist with hands like butter."

"Oh, should I call her?" Stephanie said with a straight face.

"Funny, shall we go tend to our ills?" he looked at her seductively.

"I thought you'd never ask," she said. They began to get up when Jack's phone rang. He looked at the number and saw it was Tommy. Stephanie motioned for him to answer it. She walked to the chair and sat down.

"Hey Tommy," Jack said. "Where are you? I'll come get you."

Stephanie sat up with alarm and looked at Jack. She hoped Tommy was okay.

"Dude, how much have you had to drink? Sit tight and I'll be right there. Fine, but let me talk to the bartender," Jack said. Stephanie could hear him relay instructions for a cab to bring Tommy to their house. Jack made sure the bartender understood and then hung up the phone. Stephanie walked over to him.

"What's wrong?" she touched his arm.

Jack ran his hand through his hair. "I don't know, he wasn't making a lot if sense. He said something about Brittany and her telling him something. He was trying to tell me about it but it sounded like he was talking about a disease or something. I don't know, but the cab will be here soon and I'll figure out what his problem is," he walked into the kitchen and started some coffee.

Stephanie sat down, knowing what it was that had happened. She looked at her husband when he walked back out. "Come here," she patted the couch next to her. "Tommy shared a little with me when we were talking earlier, and I think Brittany would be okay if I shared a little with you."

Jack was confused, but came and sat down. Stephanie smiled sadly at him. "Brittany and I have known each other since we were little, like you know, but we sort of lost touch when Nikki and I moved to Paris," she began. "I had just started a new interferon injection and I was participating in a trial for the clinic. I was going in regularly to give blood and report on my symptoms. Sometimes I would counsel people who were recently diagnosed, or struggling with their diagnosis. Everyone had some form of autoimmune disease, MS, Lupus, Rheumatoid Arthritis," she paused and looked at her husband. "And HIV," she paused. "That's where I reconnected with Brittany."

Jack's eyes grew wide. "Oh God, Brittany is HIV positive?" he shook his head. "That's what Tommy meant when he was mumbling."

Stephanie touched his thigh. "There is a little more," she looked at him. "Brittany came to Paris after she was attacked. She tested positive on her second test, a month after she was raped," Stephanie felt tears come to her eyes as she remembered that day. "As hard as I think it is living with a disease like MS, what she went through was so much worse. This man took so much from her, and what he left her with is a constant reminder of the worst moment in her life," she wiped her eyes and Jack pulled her to him in a hug.

He held her tightly, thanking his lucky stars for the billionth time that he had found her. He sat back and looked at her. "As horrible as what happened must have been, Brittany is lucky to have you. I can't think of a more positive role model than you on how to live with courage and honor. You show me that every day."

Stephanie smiled at him. "Having MS is not like HIV. I am not communicable, and she is. That's a huge barrier for Brittany and something she has never been able to reconcile. She told Tommy a small part of what she went through, but I am not sure the extent of what he knows."

Jack nodded. "I understand. I will keep her confidence and let Tommy tell me what he knows," he heard the cab pull up and Stephanie stood up.

"I am going to go into the bedroom and give you some privacy. Let me know if you need anything," Stephanie kissed him and left.

Jack opened the door and Tommy walked in. The men looked at each other and Tommy put up his hand. "Don't even start."

Jack didn't say a word. He went to the kitchen and poured a cup of black coffee. He walked in to where Tommy was sitting at the table. He put the cup down and sat down across from his friend.

"What am I supposed to do with this information? I don't even know this girl and here I am, going and getting drunk because I can't get her out of my mind," he took a drink of the coffee and looked at Jack. "Do you know what some jackass did to her?" he continued to talk, even though Jack hadn't said a word. "She was attacked and she," he didn't finish his sentence; he stood up and stumbled as he walked to the couch. Jack followed. "She is HIV positive," Tommy let his shoulders sag as he spoke the words.

Jack looked at his best friend. "So what does that mean for you?"

Tommy glanced at him. "What do you mean?"

"I mean, what does her having HIV mean for you? Does that turn you off? Is she less attractive to you?" Jack was blunt for a reason.

Tommy glared at his friend. "Of course not, why would you even say that? She is a beautiful and intelligent woman who has suffered a horrific ordeal. How could I look at her with anything but admiration?"

Jack smiled. "Does she know you think that? Did you tell her any of that?"

He shook his head. "No, I asked her to dinner and she said no and then I left."

Jack sighed. "I have so much to teach you about women," he grinned at his friends glare. "Look, the reality that Brittany is HIV positive is huge, I get that. But the fact is, there is so much more to her. You need to get to know who she is, what she thinks about, what she feels. You need to give her time to get to know you as well. That is, if you want to."

Tommy looked at his friend, "I don't know how to break down the walls that are there. They are so high and I feel like an ant trying to scale Mount Everest."

"You might want to leave that part out when you talk to her again," Jack laughed. "Look, I know what it's like to have walls and to have to break through them. All I can tell you is that if you think she is worth it, nothing should stop you from letting her know."

Tommy nodded. "I think she's worth it, but I don't know if she thinks I am."

Jack patted his friend on the back. How about we add some food to that coffee and get you sobered up so you can go and find out."

Chapter Nine:

Tommy finished his final surgery of the next day and was exhausted. He sat down in the locker room and closed his eyes. His head still hurt from all of the stress of the previous day and the drinking he had done. He really hadn't been that drunk, but this emotional garbage he was feeling left him drained. He shook his head.

"Get yourself together, Williams."

"Talk to yourself often?" Brittany asked him.

Tommy glanced up, surprised. "Maybe," he smiled.

"Okay then, I hope you like the conversation," she smiled back and went to leave.

"Hey, Red," he said and she turned to look at him. "How about that dinner you owe me?"

She had a strange look on her face, like she suddenly remembered a feeling and it bothered her. "I don't owe you anything," she smiled, but he saw the look cross her face.

"Never mind, it's not a big deal," he said and tossed his surgical garb in the bin.

She sighed. "I'm sorry, that's not what I meant. I was just trying to be funny, and I guess I am not really good at that," she said sheepishly. "Dinner would be nice."

Tommy felt his heart leap a little. "Do you still have my address?"

She nodded. "Yes."

"Okay, why don't you come over at 7?" he smiled and she nodded before walking off.

"Shit," he said to himself. He couldn't cook. What the hell was he getting himself into?

******

Brittany stepped out of the shower and wrapped a towel around her body. She felt nervous and excited, and she knew how big of a step this dinner was for her. She had never really been on a date, ever. She had made a vow to herself to never get involved with anyone. Many people had tried to change her mind about that, but she was nothing if not stubborn.

But Tommy was different. He made her, well; feel. She brushed her long red hair and began to blow it dry. She finished and placed a few large rollers in her thick locks and began to put on some makeup. She never wore much, just a touch of lip-gloss and some mascara. She finished her hair and put on her casual jeans, which hugged her curves nicely. She pulled out a turquoise short sleeve sweater and pulled it on. The blue looked amazing with her red hair and she smiled at her reflection. She felt she looked presentable.

She didn't know why she agreed to this dinner, but she was going and she was determined to have an open mind. She made her way to his house with a bottle of wine she picked up. She walked up the steps and knocked on the door, waited a minute and knocked again. She got that feeling in her gut like she was in a bad dream. She felt her walls begin to come up again and she turned to leave when the door opened and she

saw Tommy. He was on the phone and he was
obviously upset. His eyes were watery and he
motioned for her to come in. She followed him inside
and closed the door behind her, but stood in the foyer,
not wanting to intrude on his phone call. She felt utterly
out of place, but she also had the desire to help him.
She wanted to know what was wrong. She stood
awkwardly in the small space and waited.

"Red?" Tommy called out to her after a minute. She
walked to the room he was in and saw he was sitting
on the couch, his cell phone on the table and a pad of
paper in his lap. "I'm sorry, I didn't mean to be so rude.
I had to take that call and I lost track of time," he was
rambling and looked on the verge of tears.

"Maybe we should do this another time," Brittany said.
She saw his face fall a little, but she didn't know what
was the right thing to do. "Do you want to talk about it?"

Tommy ran his hand through his hair and sat back.
"That was my sister, Julie."

Brittany sat down on a chair. "Is she okay?" she hadn't
heard much about Julie.

"Not sure, they found a mass," Tommy said and his
face crumbled. He put his face in his hands and
Brittany moved closer to him.

"Hey, hey, it's okay. Tell me what she said," she felt so
sad and helpless.

He looked at her and she saw just how green his eyes
were. She saw no pretense in his face, no judgment,
only anguish. "She hadn't been feeling right for a few

weeks, and when she went to the doctor for a physical, they found a lump in her left breast. She had a mammogram and it is a definite mass."

Brittany nodded. "Tommy, look at me," she spoke firmly and with authority. "I deal with this all too often and you need to know that early detection is key. If they caught this early, there is a good chance that if it is malignant, it can be cured."

Tommy sighed. "I am an ass. I totally forgot that you deal with this every day," he looked at her. "I want you to look at her chart, examine her, tell me what we should do."

Brittany smiled. "I will do anything I can to help, but right now I am concerned about you. You need to know you aren't alone in this."

Tommy shook his head and stood up, his hands shoved in his pockets. "That's just it," he said. "Without Julie, I am alone."

Brittany tried to hold her tears back as she stood up to face him.

"That's simply not true, but if you want to look at the worst case scenario, I can't stop you. What I can tell you is that attitude and approach are the only things you can control. Julie will look to you for support and guidance, but mostly she will need her brother. You need to be there for her and help her make the best decisions for her."

"What if I can't do that? She is my baby sister and I can't watch her go through this," he knew he was losing it, but he couldn't help it. He felt like he was drowning.

"Then when you feel like you can't take it anymore, you come talk to me and I will help ground you. I'm good at that, you know, removing emotion. People have told me I am an icicle," she smiled. "I know it wasn't a compliment, but perhaps now it will serve a purpose. Maybe I can help you face this."

Tommy smiled for the first time since she had arrived. "You are not so hard hearted. I think I see a little vulnerability in there."

"Where? Let me put that away," she said and laughed. "It is good to see you smile. I know this is scary, but try to put it in perspective. Wait until you have all the results and then we'll go from there. Chances are it is benign. You work in oncology, you know it's too soon to panic."

Tommy felt better and he knew it was all thanks to her. "Thank you. I didn't mean to spend our dinner like this. I feel like a jerk."

Brittany smiled. "Actually, this was quite the icebreaker. I was nervous about making conversation, but you handled that."

He laughed. "I'm glad. Do you like pizza? I'm afraid I didn't have a chance to make anything."

"I think that would be awesome. I like pineapple on mine," she said and smiled.

"Pineapple it is, although that's gross," he said under his breath as he dialed.

"I heard that," she said and laughed, feeling for the first time in a long time like she was where she should be.

******

Tommy sat back as Brittany gathered the plates after they finished their pizza. He watched her move and felt his stomach do flip-flops. He shook his head as if he wanted to clear it and stood up. "You don't have to do that, I will take care of it."

She turned and smiled at him, her long red hair covering her face. She tucked it behind her ear and walked back over to him. "It's a habit, sorry."

He motioned for her to sit down next to him. She did and suddenly felt nervous. "Maybe it's time for me to go home, that is if you're okay to be alone."

He sighed. "I don't want you to stay unless you want to. I will be okay, but I don't want you to leave just yet," he reached out and took her hand.

She felt her heart in her throat. She couldn't do this, she couldn't feel this way, it wasn't real, and it couldn't last. "Tommy, I can't do this, I'm sorry."

He held onto her hand and with his other hand touched her cheek. "Please don't run from me. I don't want to be alone. I'm not asking for anything, just company," he felt exposed and desperate for her to stay, but he didn't care. He was laying it out there.

Doing her best to ignore the feel of his touch, she took his hand and pulled it away from her face. "Tommy," she said, "You don't know what you're getting yourself into. I'm not worth it."

He cocked his head to the side and smiled. "I beg to differ."

Chapter Ten:

"Why didn't you call me? I would have come over and you wouldn't have been alone," Jack said to Tommy as they ate lunch together in the hospital cafeteria. Tommy had just filled his friend in on his phone call from Julie.

Tommy blushed a little. "I wasn't alone," he said quietly. "Brittany was there."

Jack stopped chewing for a minute and a huge grin spread across his face. "Dude, you are so telling me everything. Why did she come over? How did it go? What did she say?" he was so happy for his friend.

"What are you, a teenage girl?" Tommy laughed at Jack's exuberance. "We were two colleagues having dinner, nothing more."

Jack nodded. "Right, because both of you are out dating so often," he became more serious and looked at his friend. "Thomas, tell me what's going on."

"Thomas, really?" he smiled. "Look, I had asked her to come to my house for dinner, and when she got there I was on the phone with Julie. She did what any decent person would do and stayed to make sure things were okay," he downplayed the impact her visit had on him.

Jack took a long drink of water. He was deciding the best course of action before proceeding. "So when are you going out again?"

Tommy glared at him. "Who said we were going out again? I am not interested in anything like a relationship and I know she is totally against it. We had a nice time; she helped me through a rough patch, now it's back to normal."

Jack shrugged and dropped it, knowing how sensitive Tommy could be about his feelings. He also knew that Brittany had gotten to him and he was in trouble. There was no 'normal' anymore, "I'll call Julie later and yell at her for not calling me. For now, let's get back to the floor," he said and stood up.

"Good idea," Tommy said and followed, trying to convince himself that all was indeed, normal.

They made their way to the floor when they both received a page. It was 911 to the ER. There was chaos upon entering the triage area. There had been a bus accident and there were a ton of walking wounded as well as critically injured. Tommy and Jack went to work to assess the patients. Stephanie and Brittany joined them in the E.R, along with all available doctors.

"Dr. Anthony, I need you," an Intern called out to Brittany. She ran over to a woman who was doubled over in pain, her head bleeding from an open wound. She looked to be about 8 months pregnant.

"Hi, I'm Dr. Anthony, an OBGYN. What is your name?" Brittany pulled on her gloves and motioned for a gurney to be brought over.

"Her name is Lindsay and she is hurt badly. Help her now!" a man yelled at Brittany. She suspected it was the woman's husband. The yelling caught Tommy and Jack's ear and they both exchanged glances. Tommy walked over to the man.

"Why don't you let the doctor examine your wife is it?" the man nodded. "Good, let your wife be looked over and then we will see what needs to be done," Brittany looked at Tommy and said a silent thank you.

"Now Lindsay, can you tell me what hurts you?" Brittany was having the nurse set up the fetal monitor and was waiting for the ultra sound machine

"Everything hurts, I'm so scared, I can't lose my baby. Please help me." The woman sobbed.

Brittany held the woman's hand. "Look at me. You need to believe that everything will be okay and you need to concentrate on relaxing. Your baby needs its mother right now and you will do whatever you need to do to protect it. Lindsay, you can do this," she lost sight of where Tommy had taken the father, but she was not happy with the EKG readings. She looked at the nurse. "Please get Dr. Stephens in here," she said. The nurse nodded and left.

"Okay, now just try to breathe in and out slowly. I am going to check to see if the placenta is still in tact. She nodded as Jack came in. "This is Dr. Stephens, one of the finest cardiac surgeons there is. He is going to look at your test results before I do anything else."

"Cardiac Surgeon? Oh God, I need surgery?" Lindsay cried as her husband came in with Tommy.

"Surgery? Oh, I think I'm going to be sick," the husband ran into the bathroom. Tommy rolled his eyes and followed the husband again.

"I am just going to take a look," Jack said. "I am a cardiac surgeon, but that doesn't mean I always do surgery. Most of the time it just sounds fancy, when really I read charts. Now let me ask you a few questions and run a few simple tests," Jack smiled as he tried to calm the woman. He proceeded with a few tests and the woman seemed to be calming down a little. Jack smiled at her. "Good job. I think you just have a nasty bump on the head and are having some anxiety at the effects of the crash. We will need to stitch up your cut, but you should be none the worse for wear. Now your husband on the other hand," he smiled as Tommy helped the man walk back in.

"Marlon, I just have a bump on my head, it's okay," she said and her husband ran to her. "I will be, OOH," she yelled. "I think I am having a contraction."

Brittany walked over and checked the monitor. She motioned for Jack and Tommy to move over. "I need to complete my exam now," she put on her gloves. She walked to the side of the bed. "I need to inform you both that I am HIV positive. I take all necessary precautions and there is a minimal chance of any risk to you or your baby," she said to the parents.

The man looked at her. "I want another doctor," he said in a calm voice. He looked at his wife who nodded in agreement.

Tommy was enraged and Jack felt his heart sink. "What the hell is wrong with you? She is the best OBGYN you will ever see."

Brittany was surprised at his outburst. She held up her hand. "It is completely understandable. I will see to it that you have another doctor come in. It will be a few minutes, but you need to try to relax. Good luck to you both," she turned and walked out past Jack and Tommy.

Tommy went to say something to the couple when Jack pulled him out into the hall by the arm. "What the hell, man? I have to say something to that asshole. He is discriminating against her and it isn't right."

Jack sighed. "You need to respect Brittany here. I have learned that it does nothing but draw more attention and she doesn't want that. She has been fighting this battle for a long time and you can't just step in and make it better."

Tommy looked at him. "I don't accept that," he said and walked away.

Jack sighed and felt a pair of arms wrap around his waist from behind. He smiled and turned around. Stephanie pulled him into a kiss.

"How do you feel? This is quite a first day back."

He tucked her hair behind her ear. "I could ask you the same thing."

"Tired, but good. I saw a lot of patients, mainly contusions and people who were scared. I saw you go in with Brittany to a pregnant woman, is everything okay?" Stephanie walked with him to his office.

Jack shook his head. "I have so much to tell you," he sighed. He opened his door and led her in. They both collapsed on his couch. The couple Brittany was trying to help asked for a new doctor when they learned about her HIV," he saw the instant pain in his wife's face and again cursed the ignorance of some people. "Tommy was there and I thought he was going to rip the man's head off."

Stephanie leaned into her husband. "Did you rein him in?"

"I tried, but he was really mad and wanted to fix it. I tried to tell him what you told me when people treat you differently because of your MS. He walked away mad, but maybe he heard me," Jack said. He played with her shirt collar as they spoke.

"Maybe I should talk to him," she said. "Tommy is dealing with a lot right now, and sometimes it takes a small trigger to set someone off," she looked at her husband. "How did Brittany react?"

Jack smiled. "Like a consummate professional. She wished them luck and left the room. I know how hurt she must have been. I wish the prejudice would stop. I wish she didn't have to announce her medical status to perfect strangers and have them make judgments about her when they know nothing, and understand even less."

Stephanie felt her anger dissipating. "You always know the right thing to say. How did I get so lucky?"

"You know, I don't know," he smiled at her expression. "I am quite a catch, but then again, you were so far out of my league. I don't know how you tolerate me."

She was quiet for a minute. "It's a challenge, but I try to muddle through it every day."

"Oh yeah? Then muddle through this," he devoured her with kisses, leaving her self control at about a negative five.

Chapter Eleven:

"Can I come in?" Tommy asked Brittany as he stood in the doorway to her office. She was completing some paperwork and looked swamped. She lifted her eyes to see him and smiled. "Hi, of course. Did you talk to Julie yet?" she had been thinking about him most of the day, but one thing had led to another and she was worn down about the whole day.

"Nothing new to report with Julie," he sighed. "Look, I want to apologize to you if you'll let me," Tommy began and she looked him in the eye.

"About what?" Brittany asked.

He came in and sat down across the desk from Brittany. "I need to ask you something and I would understand if you didn't want to answer."

"Okay, I'm intrigued, but a little nervous," Brittany smiled at him.

"Why did you decide to become a doctor?" he asked her.

She was a little taken aback. "What do you mean? Why does anyone become a doctor? They want to help people, make the world a better place, all of the clichéd answers," she narrowed her eyes at him and saw him look away a little. "That's not what you meant to ask me, is it. Go on; ask what you really want to know," she spoke with a challenging tone.

Tommy met her stare. "Why did you choose a profession where you would have to tell people about your condition every day? I get wanting to help people, but being an OBGYN, well it doesn't get more hands-on than that. Doesn't it bother you to have to explain yourself to everyone?"

Brittany sighed. "Sure it does," she stood up and walked around the desk to the couch. She sat down and looked at him. "We haven't known each other for very long, but you seem to strike me as someone with integrity and vision. You have been through something terrible with the loss of your parents and you took it upon yourself to raise your sister and go to medical school and create a life that has meaning and purpose. Why didn't you just give up?"

He moved to the other end of the couch. "My situation is different."

"Not really," she said. "When you meet people, do you have to tell them about your personal issues before treating them? No, but you bring that baggage with you. In every relationship you build, in every patient you treat, in every consult you take, your past is with you. Your experiences have made you the man you are today and you bring those experiences with you to the office just like I do."

She looked at her hands and then continued.

"I hate that I am HIV positive. I hate that I have to tell everyone. I hate that I met a man who I truly enjoy being around and I know in my heart that it can never be anything more. I hate that people are still scared of being infected by being in my presence. I hate that the woman in the ER has a good chance that her baby will have complications because she had to wait for another doctor," she felt a tear come to her eye. "But do you know what I hate even more?"

"No," he said, choked up.

"I hate that I have no control over any of that. I can't control people's fears, and I am not sure I would want to. It saddens me that when you look at me you see my HIV. It hurts me that when that couple looked at me, they saw a disease, and not a doctor. I can't control any of that. But do you know what I can do?" she smiled. "I can give Jack and Stephanie the option of a family. I can help the woman who is scared her life is over because of mistakes in her past. I can show the world that I am so much more than my disease and although I may have to shout it from the rooftops before every procedure, I am in a place where I can still *do* that procedure. I am so thankful that I have opportunities and abilities, and I will not waste another minute feeling sorry for myself. I have done that enough for one lifetime."

Tommy felt weird. He tried to process everything he had heard. He felt like he wanted to pull her to him and feel her lips on his. He wanted to make it better, but he didn't know how. He felt powerless to say or do anything. He just stared at her. He opened his mouth to speak, but felt like he had a frog in his throat.

"I have to go, sorry," he stood up and left her alone, staring after him.

Brittany leaned back into the couch. "And there it is. Brittany 0, disease 7015," she stood up and walked back to her desk. She couldn't care about this, about him. She just had to do what she always does, move forward.

****

Tommy had the weight of the world on his shoulders. He paced in his office as he went over his colossal failure in Brittany's office. Two things she had said kept running through his mind.

I hate that I met a man who I truly enjoy being around and I know in my heart that it can never be anything more. That's what she said, and more importantly, she said *it saddens me that when you look at me you see my HIV.*

He was a jumble of thoughts and nerves and he felt like he wanted to punch the wall. No one had ever had the power to make him feel like this. He was scared and excited and angry with himself. He ran his hand through his hair and turned to walk out of his office, he had to do something.

****

Brittany looked at her watch and realized she had a few more hours before Stephanie's procedure. She sat down and pulled her long hair up into a ponytail. She took out her lunch and put her iPod in the dock next to her desk. She found the song she liked and began to eat her sandwich and read her magazine. She looked up as her door opened.

Tommy walked in and closed the door. He stood before her, out of breath. Brittany was startled. "Just listen before you throw me out," he said. "You said your piece and now I need to tell you something," he spoke fast and with an intensity that surprised even him. "You have to cut me some slack. You can't be here, at this hospital, and dictate how I react to you. You are irritating and confusing and you make me crazy," he sat down on her couch and continued. "But you are also wrong. You think I look at you and see your HIV. You think you aren't able to have a relationship. But you have convinced yourself of this without giving me or anyone else a chance. I am infuriated that some jackass would question your ability to be a doctor. It infuriates me that you just let it happen. I get that this is your issue, but really, it isn't going to change if the only people who fight against prejudice are those directly affected by it. You didn't choose to be attacked, you didn't choose to contract HIV, yet you are alone with the consequences and it isn't fair. I also don't know why I care. I don't know why you get to me and I don't know how to get through to you. I'm sorry if I didn't react the way I should have, but I don't know the right thing to do," Tommy stopped and sighed. He realized the extent of his rant and turned to look at her.

Brittany sat in silence and wiped the tears that had fallen down her cheeks. She stood up from her desk and walked over to him. She knelt in front of him and took his hands in hers. "You have nothing to be sorry about. You are right to feel the way you do and I am sorry I gave you the wrong impression about how you need to react. In case you haven't noticed, I am not the best at expressing my feelings. I think it has been a long few days for you and I think you are on overload," she stood up and he felt her break their connection. "Look, I am not the one to get involved with. You have so much to offer, Tommy, you need to leave me and go live your life. I am not your problem to fix and I don't need to be rescued. I am happy with my life," she lied.

Tommy stood up and nodded. "Okay. I get it," he turned and walked to the door. "But I don't think you're happy, and neither am I," he said and left the office, leaving her alone again.

*****

"So, are you ready for the transfer?" Brittany asked Stephanie and Jack as she came into the exam room. Stephanie had been prepped and was ready for her. Brittany sat down on a chair.

"Yes," Stephanie said as Jack held her hand. They were both grinning like little kids.

"You're sure Stephanie is okay to go through this?" Jack asked.

Brittany smiled. "Absolutely. Actually, this is the least invasive of all of the procedures she has had to endure for the IVF. I will insert a small catheter into the uterus and using an ultrasound guide, I will deposit the embryos. We are implanting two and hopefully at least one will take. It shouldn't feel any different than a normal pap smear," she smiled at Stephanie.

"Okay, and tell me again when we will know if it worked?" Stephanie asked.

"After the procedure you need to lie flat for an hour and then you can go home but you need to stay off your feet for the rest of the evening. Tomorrow you can resume normal activity. It should take about 9 days and we can check if a pregnancy has occurred," she stood up to get her gloves. "You know that the odds are in your favor, but it is not uncommon to have to go through all of this again. I just don't want you both to get discouraged."

Jack looked at Stephanie and grinned. "We can take it. We were meant to be parents and it will work out the way it was supposed to," he leaned in and kissed her.

Chapter Twelve:

Brittany and Stephanie were enjoying a lunch break on a last warm afternoon outside the hospital cafeteria a week after the procedure. They hadn't had a chance to talk in a while, and Stephanie was curious about what was happening in the life of her friend.

"So tell me what happened with Tommy. Jack filled me in on Julie, but he didn't say much about the night you were there," Stephanie took a drink of her water.

Brittany played with her hair as she smiled. "He is a really nice guy, Stephanie, despite our first meeting. He is smart and funny and he seems to be very sensitive under the tough exterior."

"And," Stephanie smiled at her friend.

"And nothing, you know that. I am not open to anything else," the red haired doctor said emphatically. She turned and looked around, suddenly feeling like they were being watched. She saw nothing and shrugged it off.

"Britt, you don't have to be like that. You know that Tommy is a good man. He and Jack are like brothers. He has a good soul," Stephanie met her friend's gaze.

"That's not the issue. It's not Tommy; it's me. I just won't go there," Brittany gathered her bag. "I am glad I am here at U of M and I am so thrilled to be working with you, but the fact of the matter is that I can't escape my past. It's just lucky that Tommy hasn't figured out who I really am."

Stephanie touched her friend's shoulder. "There is nothing wrong with the truth. You have nothing to be ashamed of."

Brittany turned to her and smiled sadly. "I can't risk the life I have now, the focus of my work and my commitment to medicine is everything to me."

"But don't you miss it? Don't you wish," Stephanie began.

"No, I don't," Brittany interrupted. "That life led me to the worst thing imaginable and I can't think about it without reliving everything. I just can't."

Stephanie stood up and hugged her friend. "I'm sorry. I didn't mean to bring all of this up."

"Don't apologize. I never want you to walk on eggshells around me. You know all about me, the bad and the worse, and you still choose to be my friend," she grinned. "How about we go get that blood work taken and see if we can find one more miracle."

The two women smiled and headed back into the hospital.

******

I can't believe I found her, after all this time. The strange figure that had been following the women thought to himself. He had searched for years, across countries and continents. He had one objective and one purpose and it was finally coming to fruition. He pulled the worn picture from his pocket and smiled at the face of the woman who just walked back into the hospital. He kissed the picture and put it back into his pocket. "Soon, my love," he spoke sinisterly and slunk off into the woods.

******

Tommy walked out of the hospital and was on his way to his car to head to the hotel and pick up his sister. She was driving in with her husband from across the state to go through more tests and to have Tommy with her. He saw a man standing in the corner of the parking garage, staring into space. He immediately got a bad feeling and walked over to him.

"Is there something I can help you with? Are you lost?" Tommy asked the man who smelled worse than he looked, like chemicals and dirt.

"No, I'm fine," the man said in a low voice.

"Well this is the physicians lot, are you a physician?" Tommy pressed the man for information.

"No, but I didn't think it was a crime to stand here. What's your problem?" the man got angry.

"Relax man, I was just trying to help. You can stand wherever you want," Tommy turned and walked to his car, making a mental note of the man's appearance and mannerisms. He got a really bad vibe from the whole conversation.

******

"So tell me about this new girl you met." Julie said to Tommy as they had coffee in the lobby of the hotel.

"What are you talking about and who have you been talking to?" Tommy said, trying not to blush.

"I know people and they talk," she smiled.

"You know your sister, man, always getting the most current info." Julie's husband Bill smiled at his brother in law.

"You don't need to remind me. I will talk to Jack and Stephanie," he smiled.

"Come on, they love you like we do and want you to be happy," Julie said.

Tommy finished his drink. "How about we get things taken care of with you and then I will tell you everything you want to know," he smiled. "I'll pick you up later and we will head in to the office, okay?"

Julie hugged her brother. "I am so glad to be here with you. I know everything will be okay," she said to him.

Tommy wished he could guarantee that. "I am glad you're here, too," he watched them walk towards the elevator and he turned to go home.

****

Brittany was finishing up some paperwork when she heard a knock on her door. She looked up and smiled as Jack walked in.

"Hi Jack," she said.

"Hi, I don't mean to bother you, but do you know where Stephanie is?" he asked her, trying to keep the worry out of his voice.

"Not since her appointment earlier. We had lunch and then we took her labs. She was going to work on some paperwork she had and then meet you," Brittany noticed his concern. "What's going on?"

Jack sighed. "I don't know, I haven't been able to reach her on her cell and she isn't in her office. We were supposed to meet a half hour ago and she never showed up. I don't want to make something out of nothing, but given all we have been through, she wouldn't just not show up or call."

"Okay, then let's go figure out where she is," she stood up and walked out with Jack.

Chapter Thirteen:

It had been three hours and Jack was losing it. He paced around the lounge while Tommy tried to get him to relax. Brittany went to get them all some water.

"Something is very wrong. I know it. I need to find her," Jack ran his hand through his hair in frustration.

"We just need to figure out her steps and retrace them. She was with Brittany for lunch and then to have labs taken. She went to her office after that and as far as we know she never checked in. We searched the hall and offices around hers and there has been nothing," Tommy said. "The police are on their way?"

Jack walked over to the cabinet on the wall and punched it. He was so angry at the helplessness he felt. "Fuck," he swore.

"Dr. Stephens, I have some news," an officer said as he walked into the room. Jack turned around walked to him.

"What is it? Did you find her?" he was desperate.

Brittany walked in as the conversation began. She came over and handed Tommy some water. He looked at her and smiled his thanks. She gave one to Jack who didn't want it. She put it down and walked to the side of the room, out of the way.

"There has been a strange man spotted outside the hospital, first by the cafeteria, and then by the garage reserved for physicians. He is on the security cameras, but he keeps his face covered," the officer said.

"So what the hell does that mean? Some strange man took Stephanie? Are you telling me that she has been abducted?" Jack yelled.

"We don't know. We need to find this man," the officer said.

"I think I saw him earlier," Tommy filled them in on his encounter with the man in the garage.

"Can you remember anything else about him?" the officer asked.

"The smell," he said. "He had an odor to him that was unique. It was like a charcoal and chemical smell, like an old film store would smell."

Brittany dropped her water on the ground and smiled apologetically when they looked at her. She listened to the conversation going on around her and began to feel sick. This couldn't be happening, it just couldn't. She felt like the room was spinning.

Jack's phone rang and he looked at it. "Stephanie?" he asked into the phone.

"You can pick up your wife in room 3268. I have left her there with a message," the phone went dead and Jack ran out of the room, the officer and Tommy close behind. Brittany stood frozen in fear.

Jack went to the room and the officer held him back, needing to secure the area. He opened the door and they went in, Jack felt his heart in his chest. He looked and saw Stephanie on the bed, unconscious. Her hands were tied and her mouth was gagged. Jack raced to her and felt for a pulse.

"Stephanie? Baby? Can you look at me?" he removed the gag and looked for something to cut the ties with. Tommy came over and helped him cut her loose. He called for a gurney and stepped back, allowing Jack some privacy.

"Stephanie, please look at me," he gently massaged her cheeks and looked her over for injuries as she began to stir.

"Jack?" she muttered softly, finally opening her eyes.

"Yes, I'm here, you're safe," he said and pulled her into his arms. She hugged him back and finally woke up more.

She looked around the room and her eyes scanned the people. She felt her eyes fill with tears as she realized someone was missing. "Where's Brittany?"

Everyone turned to look and realized she wasn't there. "I don't know; she must have stayed downstairs. Why? What's wrong?"

"He wasn't after me, he is after Brittany. You have to protect her, you don't understand who he is," Stephanie sobbed and Jack held her. He turned and looked but Tommy had fled back downstairs as soon as Stephanie spoke.

"Let's get you checked out, we need to admit you," Jack said.

"No, he didn't hurt me, he just gave me something over my mouth, like chloroform or something. When I came to he had me tied up and he kept talking about the redhead I was with earlier. He knew all about her past and he talked about how he had been looking for her. He knew when you all came to get me she would be alone and he could get to her. He put the smell in my face again and then you were here," she sobbed. "Oh God Jack, I think he might be the guy who attacked her. We have to find her."

Jack held his wife and tried to reconcile the fact that his wife was safe, but this lunatic may have taken Brittany. "What can we do?" he asked her.

"We need to help Tommy find her," Stephanie said. "I need to fill him in on the rest of her story."

****

Tommy tore through the halls to get back to the lounge. He couldn't believe he had just left her there. It was obvious that something was bothering her, but he figured it was just the fact that Stephanie was missing. Why didn't he notice she didn't follow them? Who was this guy? How did he know her? He rushed into the lounge and his worst fears were confirmed. The room was a mess and there, in the middle of the room, was a note with scribbled writing. He picked it up.

"I have her and we are together now. She will only ever sing for me."

For the first time since his parent's died, Tommy felt his world crashing around him. He looked up as Jack came in wheeling Stephanie. "She's gone," he said with anguish. "What am I going to do?"

Jack looked at Stephanie and she had tears streaming down her face. "Tommy, I need to tell you everything. There is so much you don't know about Brittany, and if this guy is who I think he is, then we need to get to her quickly because he won't ever let her go."

Tommy looked at Stephanie and Jack, the two people who would never lie to him or lead him astray. He thought of Julie and Bill who were coming to the hospital later for a consult, but all that mattered to him was Red. He didn't understand why, but until she was safe, nothing else mattered. "Who is this guy?" he asked.

Stephanie sighed. "I think the more important question is, who is Brittany?"

"What is going on here? What is it you aren't telling me?" Tommy yelled at Stephanie in frustration.

"Take it easy, none of this is Stephanie's fault," Jack said protectively.

Tommy sighed. "I'm sorry, I'm just concerned for her."

Stephanie smiled. "You really care about her, don't you?"

Tommy shook his head. "I don't know what I feel. She irritates me like no one ever has, she challenges me when I think I'm right, she makes me question what I though was happiness."

Jack and Stephanie smiled at each other and looked at him. "You really care about her and she cares about you, too," Stephanie said. "We will find her."

"How? We don't even know who this guy is. What did the note mean? Where are the police?" Tommy knew he was rambling, but he was really scared.

"The officer is consulting with the FBI. Come sit down, Tommy," Stephanie said and motioned for him to sit down next to the chair. Jack sat on another chair. "Tommy, Brittany told you about her attack, right?"

Tommy nodded. "Yes, she told me and that she tested positive for HIV after that."

"Okay, but did she tell you anything about the attack itself or anything before it?" she asked him.

Tommy shook his head. "No, and I guess I never pushed it. Should I have pushed it? Shit, I handled all of this so wrong."

"No you didn't man, there is no right or wrong here. You have nothing to be sorry about," Jack said sincerely.

"Jack's right. Brittany has made a life out of hiding her pain and her past. She isn't an easy one to crack and to be honest, you are the first person I know of who she has felt comfortable enough with to share any of this," Stephanie stopped and took a drink of water. "Do you guys remember Barbara Rose?"

Jack and Tommy were silent for a minute and then Jack spoke up. "Was she that teen pop singer who disappeared or something?"

Stephanie nodded. "Yes. She had the most number 1 hits for someone her age and she was on her way to becoming the biggest thing since, I don't know, whoever was really big at the time. She was beautiful and smart and really giving."

Tommy began to remember. "Right, she was our age, I think I remember her coming to Detroit when we were there. She was working for charity or something like that."

Stephanie smiled. "She was from here. She was the most charitable performer, especially for someone her age. She was very aware of how fortunate she was and made it her mission to give back. But that led her to a lot of fans that had an unhealthy fascination with her. One in particular, was very dangerous," Stephanie felt her tears come as she remembered.

Tommy was trying to wrap his head around this story, and how it related to Brittany. "I don't understand, how is this relevant? That girl disappeared or was kidnapped or something and it was all tragic, but so what?"

Jack was processing the story his wife was telling and was trying to put two and two together. "Did they ever find out what happened to her?"

Stephanie nodded. "It turned out that she was attacked by a crazed fan. He wanted her to be his and to sing just for him. She tried to escape and he beat her badly, and he sexually assaulted her. The FBI was involved in searching for her and when they finally did, she was rescued, but the damage had been done. She never sang again. She changed her name and moved back to London to go to medical school. We had been friends since we were little and a few months after the attack, she came to Paris to see me at the clinic for her HIV test," she stopped while the realization sank in.

"Are you telling us that Barbara Rose is Brittany?" Tommy asked almost as if he was talking to himself.

Stephanie nodded. "Yes, Tommy. Brittany changed her name legally and made a new life for herself. She is one of the strongest people I know, but if this guy has her again, I don't know how she will survive," she began to cry.

Tommy felt sick. "Didn't they catch the pervert who did this? How could he find her and get to her? Didn't anyone protect her?"

"They never found him. They found where he kept her and who he was, but he disappeared. He was some sort of photographer and had a ton of pictures of her all over his place. He also made her pose and do all sorts of things while he had her. He always smelled of photo chemicals and that was something Brittany had a hard time dealing with," Stephanie said.

"Fuck. That asshole in the garage smelled of chemicals. I had him and I just walked away," Tommy was frantic. "We have to find her, now."

"We will. The FBI is here and they will work with the police and they will find her. You need to believe that," Jack said.

"Tommy, Brittany is not the same girl she was then. She is confident and strong and she will fight. We need to believe in her," Stephanie said.

"I need some air," Tommy said and left the room. He had so much going on in his head. She was a famous singer? How did he not recognize her? What was this sick freak doing to her as they were just sitting here? How could she not have told him? He knew why, because he was an ass and he never gave her a chance. He stopped walking and leaned against the wall. His legs gave way and he sank to the ground, his arms on his knees. "What am I going to do? How do I find her?" he asked the hollow hallway.

Chapter Fourteen:

Just relax and you will be okay, Brittany thought to
herself. This isn't like before. You will not be a victim
again. Think about all of the things you learned in your
self-defense classes. You can get away. She repeated
the words to herself as she sat in the damp darkness.
He had tied her up and had been rough with her, but
then he was called away and had left her alone. She
knew they were in some sort of cabin in a wooded area
because he forced her to walk a long way through the
forest. She had fallen a few times and he yanked her
up to keep going. She was wet from the ground and
her whole body ached, but she could handle it. She
was going to get out of here. She thought of Tommy
and smiled to herself. This time she had something to
live for. She heard a noise and her heart sank. He was
back. The door opened and the lights flicked on. She
squinted as the light hurt her eyes.

"Hi honey, I'm home," the man said to her. He moved a
chair closer to her and sat down facing her. "You were
really hard to find, you know that? But so worth it,
Barbie."

Brittany felt her stomach churn as he spoke and the
memories of such a terrifying and painful moment in
her life came flooding back. She fought back tears, not
wanting to show him anything. She looked away from
him but he grabbed her face roughly and jerked her
back toward him. Her neck strained and a shooting
pain went through her body. She sucked in her breath.

"You will look at me when I talk to you. That's what's
wrong with people these days; they don't maintain eye

contact," the man sneered at her. "Now, how about some dinner?"

Brittany stared at him, not saying anything. She couldn't imagine eating anything.

He opened the package he had brought in and pulled out something that smelled worse than he did. "How about some dinner music before we eat?" he said to her. He walked over to his small tape player and brought it over. "I have waited for a long time to hear this again. I know why you never sang again after our last meeting. It was because you missed your inspiration, you missed me."

Brittany couldn't help it as her tears fell down her cheeks. She was having a hard time holding it together. "I can't sing for you," she said softly. She was stunned as his hand crashed across her face. She almost blacked out.

"You will do as I ask you, or you won't like the consequences," he said.

She tried to keep her eyes fixed on him. "What are you going to do that would be worse than what you already did? You ruined me. You took everything from me: my career, my family and my life. I can't have a relationship because of you and I am unable to look at myself without seeing what you did to me. There is nothing else you can take from me that you haven't already," she was trying to keep her voice even.

"That hurts. You can blame everything on me, but I would much rather we just let bygones be bygones. I have a beautiful gown you need to put on and a ceremony to perform. I'll give you some privacy, but don't try anything because I am right outside the room," he walked over and moved to untie her, leaning in and kissing her cheek. She jerked away from him and once again he smacked her. "I'll break you, just you wait," he said as he put the dress in her lap and walked out.

Brittany got up and ran to the corner of the room and vomited. She sat back on the floor and tried to control the pounding of her head and her heart. She silently wished and prayed for Tommy to find her, but she knew it was unlikely. She had totally shut him out. She stood up and walked back over to the gown. She saw it was too big for her so she pulled it over her clothes. She knew he would be mad at that, but she wasn't giving him an inch of her. She scanned the room for something, anything to use as a weapon. She saw there wasn't really anything around so she pulled off her shoe and held it, hoping the high heel would do something. She heard him come back in.

"What the hell is that? You aren't supposed to be wearing anything under the dress," he came over to her and grabbed her roughly by the arms, twisting her flesh.

"I know, I wanted to put on a show for you. I wanted to take it off in front of you," Brittany said as calmly as she could, the pain in her arms severe.

"Well now, that's more like it. He slid his hands around her waist. "Tell me how much you missed me," he leaned in and kissed her neck.

Brittany froze and tried to hold back her tears. "So much," she said and with a quick move, smashed her heel into his head with all her might.

"Bitch! he yelled as he felt the blood pour down his face. He threw her with force and she crashed into the table, tearing a slice through her stomach as the table splintered into pieces. She scrambled to her feet as fast as she could and ran out the door, not waiting for anything. She ran through the trees and the branches, scraping her skin and tearing at the gown she was wearing. Her foot was cut up from not having a shoe on, but she kept running. She didn't know if he was behind her or not so she kept going until she felt her legs get tangled in a branch and she fell hard to the ground, hitting her head and rolling into a pond. The water was freezing and she tried to pull herself out but as soon as her face was free of the water, she blacked out.

****

"Did you talk to Tommy?" Stephanie asked Jack as he helped her into their house. "We need to help him find Brittany. You don't know what this man might do to her."

Jack was torn, but his first priority was his wife. "You need to be safe, Stephanie. Do you know how scared I was? I can't lose you and I can't stand to see you hurt. I just need you to be okay."

She looked at him and touched his face. "I'm sorry, baby, I love you. I'm just worried about Brittany. I'm okay, really. I wasn't hurt at all."

He leaned in and kissed her. "I know, and I feel terrible being happy that you're okay while Brittany is in such trouble. I know what Tommy is going through and I don't know how to help him. I know when you were gone before; I didn't care about anything other than getting to you. It didn't matter what anyone said or did, I just needed to get you back. I know Tommy and Brittany aren't at the same place as us in their relationship, but I don't think either one of them realized just how much they care for each other," he pulled Stephanie to him and they just held onto each other, both praying for their friends.

*****

Tommy couldn't sit at home and wait, so he decided to head back to the police department to see if he could do anything else. He had talked to Julie and Bill and told them to go over to see Jack and he would fill them in on what was going on with him. When he got to the station, he ran into an officer and asked him for an update.

"I can't tell you anything. I'm sorry," the officer said.

"Please, do you know if they have any leads at all? No one will tell me anything and I feel like I'm going crazy," Tommy pleaded with him.

"Look, I don't know if it's anything, but the FBI have an address they think they suspect may have rented," the officer said softly.

Tommy listened. "Where is it?"

The officer shot him a look to keep quiet. He reached down and wrote something on a sheet of paper. "I don't know, I told you, I can't help you," he walked away, leaving the note on the desk.

Tommy was so frustrated until he realized the officer had left the address on the paper for him. He picked it up and turned to leave. He sat in his car and plugged the address into his navigation system. It was a cabin in the woods near the outskirts of the city. He drove at breakneck speeds to get there. He arrived on scene where the Police and FBI were all over the place. He got out and ran to the scene.

"Hey, stay back, what's your authorization?" an officer asked him.

"I am a friend of the woman who might be in there. Please, can you tell me if she is okay?" Tommy asked him.

"Just a minute," the officer turned and walked away. He came back a minute later and shook his head. "Sorry, I have nothing to tell you."

Tommy turned and walked away, trying to figure out a plan. He heard some members of the FBI talking and he hid and listened.

"The suspect is injured badly and he is off to County. The room is a mess, but there is no sign of the girl," one of the men said.

Tommy felt his heart sink. He listened some more.

"She's probably dead. He didn't say much, but if she is out there, the chances of finding her alive are slim. The Captain said we are calling off the search until morning because of the storm that's coming. We meet here at 6:00 am," the officers continued discussing their jobs, but Tommy had already heard enough. If Brittany was out there, he would find her.

****

Tommy pulled his car into a remote part of the park and got out. He closed his coat around him at the chill of the air and the impending storm. He took his gym bag out of his trunk, which he always had with him and put his medical bag inside. He had a flashlight and his cell phone and he locked the doors. He began to walk, not knowing where to go or where to look, but he had to try. The rain began to fall at a slow pace, so he put his hood on and continued. He called out to her and listened, hearing nothing. He kept going.

****

"What do you mean you don't know where he is? I can't believe you just let him walk away," Jack was furious with the officer after hearing about his conversation with Tommy.

"Look, I only gave him the address to the cabin. We haven't found anything there and that's all I know. Some guys said he came by the scene and they wouldn't give him any info and he left. I tried to call him and fill him in, but I can't get an answer. I only called you because he left your number on his card as an alternative," the officer said.

"Okay," Jack tried to calm down. "Look, I will check on him and let you know if I find anything. I'm sorry, I know you are trying to help," Jack said his goodbyes and hung up. He took the cup of coffee he had and threw it against the wall. "Dammit Tommy, you should have waited," he spoke aloud to nobody.

"Would you have waited?" Stephanie's voice caught him off guard.

He turned and sighed. "I'm sorry; I didn't mean to scare you," he sat down and put his head in his hands.

"Jack, when I was missing, there was nothing that would keep you away. It isn't in our nature to sit back and wait. It isn't in Tommy's, either," she sat down and took his hands in hers. "He is doing what he needs to do and we need to support him. He will find her and in doing so, maybe he will find himself," she smiled.

Jack looked at her. "How can you be so sure? I can't lose him."

Stephanie walked over and sat in his lap. She smoothed his hair and touched his face. "Because I know these things; and because you found me. They are meant to be together just as we are. Their story is not meant to end this way," she leaned in and kissed him. "Come back to bed with me and we will wait together."

He kissed her again, too filled with emotion to respond. He simply nodded and followed her to their room.

Chapter Fifteen:

It was hard to breathe through the thick air and Tommy had been walking for over an hour. He was wet and tired and exhausted and lost. He had tried his cell phone a few times but received no signal. The winds were picking up and he felt the rain droplets smack against his face. The smell of rain permeated his nostrils and he wasn't sure if he was walking in circles or in a line. The cold air went to his bones and he looked for shelter, not knowing what else to do. He saw an area of the trees where it was open and he went and saw a cave. It wasn't really a cave, but more like a large piece of rock that had been hollowed out. He could walk easily into the area about 10 feet and at least be protected from the rain. He thought about starting a fire, but realized he needed some wood. He left his bag there and headed out to gather some materials.

"Nothing like remembering how to be a boy scout while you are out searching for your girlfriend who isn't really your girlfriend," he said out loud. He shook his head and pushed his aching legs forward. The rain pelted him harder and he was about to turn back when he saw an area of water that had some nice rotted branches on the ground. He knew that would make for a nice fire, assuming they weren't all soaked. He turned to go over to the area when he lost his footing. "Shit," he swore as he fell on his knees. His weight pressed his knees deep into the mud and almost thought about just sitting there for a minute, but something made him look up and he saw a sight that stopped his heart. There was a figure on the ground near the trees, half in the water. He grabbed his flashlight and aimed it on the figure, getting up; he sprinted through the mud.

Oh God, he thought as he saw it was Brittany. His heart was in his throat as he gently lifted her lifeless body and turned her over. There was mud on her face and his hands were shaking as he felt for a pulse. Her skin was like ice and the pelting rain that was now steady prevented him from getting a read. He gathered her clumsily in his arms and made his way back towards the cave and into the shelter, gently placing her down. He couldn't tell if his face was covered with rain or his own tears. He leaned down and listened for breathing, but he felt nothing. He grabbed his bag and pulled out his stethoscope. His heart leaped at the sound of a faint heartbeat. Holding her face in his hands he spoke to her. "Brittany, please look at me, can you hear me?" There was no reply. He needed to do something. He saw she was injured and had areas that needed attention, but worse was the cold. She was hypothermic and he needed to warm her. He needed to start a fire. He left her to run out and grab some wood.

Tommy could barely control himself. His hands seemed to stop working correctly and he dropped the wood all over the ground. "Fuck," he swore. He grabbed what he could and made his way back, placing the wood a safe distance from her and fumbling in his backpack for a lighter. He lit the wood and carefully arranged it to gather a good flame. Pulling off his coat, he moved back to her. His hands hung above her body, waiting for his mind to work, but he didn't know where to start. "You're okay now; I'm so sorry I let this happen," he spoke to her without thinking, as he evaluated what he could. He cursed his cell phone again as he looked at it and found no signal. He had to get her to a hospital, but he knew there would be no moving her tonight. He felt the warmth from the fire and took out his blanket from his bag, happy at least for his survival kit. He moved to her and brushed the wet clumps of her hair which covered her cheeks. He had to get her dry and warm.

Looking at the torn up gown she wore, he felt sick at the thought of why she had it on. He also saw the gash near her abdomen and the bloodstain. He pulled out his knife and cut the fabric away, removing the gown and leaving her scrubs underneath. Putting on his gloves, he carefully cut away at the fabric covering the wound. She had sustained a deep tear, but the bleeding seemed to have eased, probably because her body temperature had dipped so low. He took out some gauze and covered the wound, taping it as best as he could. He looked her over some more and saw her foot that was uncovered. She had numerous cuts to her foot and he could only imagine how she had run away like that. He didn't care that tears were running down his face as he covered her foot with more gauze. He saw her arms were scratched from the trees and although it would be painful, there were no open wounds on her arms. He moved to her face and saw the bruise on her cheek and eye where she had been struck. Again, nothing he could do for that at the moment. He sat back and put his head in his hands, unsure of what to do next.

"I need some help," he screamed into the air. "I don't know what to do," he sat there, breathing heavily. "Okay, you're a fucking doctor, you know what to do," he said to himself. She needed to get warm. He needed to bring her body temperature back up. He turned to her. "Okay, I know you won't like this, but you have to get warm and the only way I know to do that is to get rid of the wet clothes. I promise I won't hurt you. I am a doctor and I am always professional. I won't look at anything and I won't disrespect you. You can trust me," he spoke gently to her as he cut away her clothes. "You're a doctor, you will understand," he removed the scrub top and sat her up in his arms to pull off the back. He gently moved her to the blanket and cut off her pants. He was careful not to move the bandage he had placed on her abdomen. He fought the urge to vomit as he saw the bruises she had sustained on her back, probably from being tied to a chair. He moved her body close to the fire and covered her as best he could with the blanket. Suddenly she began to cry, although still unresponsive.

"Hey, it's all right, you're safe now," Tommy said to her. He figured it was involuntary on her part, but it made him feel worse, if that was possible. He touched her skin and realized she was still freezing. He was worried she wouldn't make it through the night. He took a deep breath. The best source of heat was from the fire and from him. He knew what he had to do. He pulled off his clothes and moved onto the blanket. He pulled her to him and wrapped his body around hers, trying to keep her warm. He held her there while the storm raged outside and his heart broke. He rubbed her arms and back and tried to keep her warm. He used his body to protect her and shield her as he had wished he could have before. He also spoke to her.

"You know when you met me, it was not at one of my finest moments, but then again, you were using my room. I guess technically it wasn't 'my' room, but still, I was mad, like really mad, but not at you. I hate dealing with brain tumors and children. I mean, I hate them at any age, but with kids, it's just extra horrible, you know? How do you explain to a parent that their child is not going to live to see adulthood? More imortantly, how do you explain to a child that there are some things that you can't make better? I hate that part of my job," he moved a little to cover more of her. He wrapped her arms around his torso and tried to maneuver her so she was getting enough heat. He felt her skin again with his fingertips, but there was no change yet, still ice cold. He wondered how long she had been in the water. His panic began to settle in again and he fought the urge to give in to his fears. "We will get out of here in the morning. I will get you out of here, okay?" he told her, hoping she could hear him. He tried to fight it, but eventually he fell asleep, keeping her close.

******

Everything seemed so far away. She was running, trying to get away, but he was so close, right on her heels. She tried to run faster but her arms and legs were so heavy, nothing worked the right way. She knew he was gaining ground on her but she couldn't move. Something was holding her down. She opened her eyes and whimpered. "Please don't hurt me again."

Tommy wasn't sure he heard her correctly, or if he was dreaming. He woke up fully and looked down at her. Her eyes were wide open and she was silently sobbing. He quickly moved off of her, covering her with the blanket. "Shh, it's okay, you're safe, it's me, Tommy," he said softly to her. He took her hand. "It's me, you're okay. You were suffering from hypothermia and I didn't know how else to help you. I didn't hurt you, I promise," he held her hand while she processed what he was saying. He didn't know what she would say or do or think next. He looked at his watch, it was 3am. He must have fallen asleep for an hour.

"I need to go home," she said. She went to move but cried out in pain. Tommy held her face between his hands.

"Red, you need to listen to me. You have been through a horrific ordeal and you are hurt. We are in the middle of a forest and it is 3 am. There is a storm outside and until it clears and is light out, we need to stay here. I know you're scared, but you have to trust me. I won't let anything happen to you," he felt his own tears fall again as he spoke to her. He needed her to believe him.

She was panting, most likely from the pain. She closed her eyes and tried to take a deep breath. "I'm so cold," she said through blue lips. "I am just so cold."

Tommy nodded. "I know. I can help you, but I need to hold you to me if that's okay. My body heat can help warm you. Is that okay? I won't hurt you, I promise," he said. He looked down at himself and realized she was probably a little taken back by the fact that he was in his underwear. He locked his eyes on her. "I won't hurt you, okay?" he said. She nodded through her tears and he lay down next to her again, but this time she wrapped her arms around him and seemed to hold on for dear life.

******

Tommy opened his eyes as the light flooded in the cave. He realized he was still entwined with Brittany. He moved off of her and she didn't stir. He felt for a pulse and was relieved to feel it, but it was weak. She felt much warmer to the touch now, but she was not responding to him. He tried to wake her, but she was out. He looked at his watch and saw it was 6 am. He stood up and covered her with the blanket. He pulled his clothes on and his shoes and he stepped outside with his cell phone. He still couldn't get a reading, so he walked a little, keeping his eye on the cave in case she woke up. He tried to call 911 but still nothing. He tried to text Jack and tell him to have his cell phone traced to find their location. He didn't know if it worked, but he went back to the cave.

He saw now, in the light, just how rough of a time Brittany must have had. She was bruised all over and the scratches on her arms looked worse than he thought. He moved the blanket to check her abdomen and was pleased to see the bandage had held. He covered her tightly and looked at her foot, which was swollen and purple. He knew she was in trouble because of her compromised immune system. He had to get her out of here and get her on antibiotics. He knew she probably also needed her HIV medication. He ran his hand through his hair and sighed.

"Tommy?" she muttered through her closed eyes.

"Yes, I'm here. Can you open your eyes?" Tommy moved closer to her and touched her face. She opened her eyes and the slate blue color pierced him. "Hey, you're going to be okay," he said softly.

She looked at him and her eyes finally seemed to register. "Liar," she said with a tiny almost imperceptible smile. "Not coming back from this one," she closed her eyes.

He held her face in his large hands and spoke firmly. "I have thought a lot of things about you since we met, but I have never thought of you as a quitter," he spoke with passion, but his voice quivered. "You are not giving up, I won't let you."

She looked at him through her water filled eyes. "I can't do this again," she said as the water spilled down the side of her face.

He took her hand in his own. "Yes you can. You are not alone this time. You have people who love you and will not let you fall. You have Stephanie and Jack and you have me. I won't leave you alone," he didn't care that he was revealing so much of himself. All that mattered was her not giving up.

She closed her eyes again and he got scared. "Hey, please don't go to sleep again. Can we keep talking?"

She opened her eyes as if something had suddenly occurred to her. "You didn't get my blood on you, did you? You have gloves?" she was panicked for a moment and he brushed her tears aside.

"I am fine. I took universal precautions. I brought my bag and I have plenty of gloves and gauze. Please don't worry about me," he reassured her as best he could. He hated that she had to worry about that on top of everything else. He really had no idea what she went through on a daily basis.

"I'm sorry I didn't tell you who I really am," she said.

"That doesn't matter. All that matters is getting you out of here and getting you medical attention. We will have plenty of time to talk about that," he said. He didn't like her labored breathing. "Can you tell me what hurts?"

She nodded. "I think I have a broken rib. It feels like I may have punctured something," she struggled to talk. She looked up at him with watery eyes the color of the ocean. "I don't know how much longer I can do this."

"You will do this as long as you need to. We will get out of here," he prayed that Jack received the text.

"I'm scared," she said softly and closed her eyes again.

"Me too," he said. "I am going to see if I can get a signal on my phone," he waited for a response, but there was none. He stood up and walked outside. He made his way to the middle of the trees and found a clearing. He tried his phone one more time and dialed 911. He was shocked when it rang and he got an answer. He relayed what he knew although he didn't know where they were. He lost the call midway through, but hoped they had received enough information to trace the call. He ran back to the cave to tell her.

"Hey, Red, we are going to get out of here," he stopped when he saw her. She was sitting up and hunched over to her side. She had blood trickling down her mouth. He ran to her. "What happened? What is it?" he asked as he grabbed gloves.

"Can't breathe. I think my lung is collapsed," she struggled to get the words out and tried to block out the pain and panic. "Oh God," she cried.

Tommy tore through his bag, looking for something to use. He looked at her. "I don't know what to do," he yelled, frantic.

She looked at him and spoke volumes with her eyes. "Traumatic pneumothorax. Scalpel and syringe," she began to cough and yelled at the pain. She held her hand over her mouth to cover any blood contamination.

"Fuck," he swore. He needed to act fast or he would lose her. "Where is the ambulance?" he cried.

"Tommy, you can do this. I believe in you," she said in a steady, but weak voice. She was turning bluer with each moment.

He nodded. He spread out the blanket and moved her gently to a reclining position. He cringed at every cry she let out but he had to act. He looked at her as he took some gauze and swabbed her chest near the side. He looked at her and apologized again.

"It's okay, no matter what happens, you are not to blame. Thank you," she said and nodded for him to do it. He took the scalpel and cut into her skin. She cried but held it together remarkably well. He angrily wiped his tears away as he grabbed the syringe and inserted it in her chest. He listened as the air filled her lungs and the collapsed lobe inflated. She immediately began breathing better. He sat back and let out a sigh of relief. He looked at her and smiled. "Okay?"

She nodded, unable to speak, but smiling her gratitude. She began to shiver and he realized she was lying there still in her bra and panties. He put his jacket over her and moved to secure the syringe in place. He knew it was a matter of time before she would suffer serious complications if they didn't get out of there. He looked at her and she nodded her understanding. "I know," she said.

Tommy watched her as she slipped into sleep again. He was grateful for her momentary peace from pain. He heard a noise and ran outside. He saw the police and for the first time in awhile, he felt a tiny piece of hope. He waved them in and led them to Brittany.

Chapter Sixteen:

Jack and Stephanie ran into the E.R. looking for Tommy. Jack moved to the nurse's station when Stephanie stopped him. She motioned toward the hallway and he saw Tommy standing there, staring into space. They made their way to him.

"Tommy, what the hell happened? Are you okay?" Jack asked his friend, pulling him into a hug.

Tommy wiped his face. "I'm fine."

Stephanie was afraid to ask. "How is Brittany?"

He fought back his emotions. "In surgery. They are fixing her punctured lung and everything else."

Jack exhaled. "Can you tell us what happened?"

Tommy looked at them and shook his head. "I can't talk about it. I just need her to be okay," he said brokenly.

Stephanie took his hand and held it. "Tommy, you are a man among men. Brittany is lucky you care so much about her. She will pull through this because you are here. She knows it and she needs you. I have known Brittany for a long time and I have never seen anyone get to her like you have. I don't mean to make more out of it than it is right now, but I truly believe you have the start of something special."

Jack smiled at his wife. "You know when Stephanie says something, it's best to agree with her. I have learned that she is always right."

Stephanie grinned and Tommy smiled at them. "I love you both, you know that, right."

They nodded. "You're our family, man," Jack said. They all looked up as the doctor walked out. He looked at them.

"Please, tell us," Stephanie said. She felt Jack's arm protectively around her. She grabbed Tommy's hand.

"We repaired the lung and set her ankle, which was broken in 2 places. She will likely need further ortho work after it heals, but I suspect we know someone who can help with that," he smiled at Stephanie who nodded. "She has 2 broken ribs, one of which punctured her lung, as we suspected," he looked at Tommy. "What you did saved her life. She would have suffocated if you didn't insert the syringe."

Jack and Stephanie looked at Tommy, understanding a little more about what happened. The doctor continued. "She has multiple contusions and abrasions, and a serious bump on her head. I want a neuro consult but I'm waiting on the doctor to arrive," the doctor sighed.

"What is it?" Tommy asked, sensing the apprehension.

"I am seriously concerned with infection. Her compromised system has taken a really serious blow and her last tests before this showed an elevated viral count. This trauma and the shock to her system may plunge her into serious immune system failure," the doctor looked at Tommy.

"You mean AIDS?" he choked out.

"Let's not go there right now. I just want to focus on keeping her spirits high and helping her recover. She needs to feel support and love from her friends and family. We will take the next step if and when we need to. She will be in a room soon and you can see her if you want," he said and walked away.

"Oh God, this is all my fault," Tommy said.

Jack felt his heart break for his friend. He knew how terrifying it was when someone you cared about was fighting something you could do nothing to help. "This is not your fault, and you did nothing but save her life. You are her hero, man and you will continue to be."

Stephanie touched Jack's arm and he turned to look at her. "I think you should go home and get some rest, Tommy. I will go sit with Brittany."

Tommy shook his head. "No, I need to sit with her. I need to see her," he wiped his face and shook off his fear.

Jack nodded. He understood what his friend needed and he looked at his wife. "Call us if you need anything, okay?"

He nodded and walked toward the bank of rooms Brittany would be taken to.

Jack turned to Stephanie and pulled her to him in a hug. He couldn't help but thank his lucky stars that she was safe and healthy.

******

Tommy stood at the door to the room, afraid to go in. He couldn't do this. He wasn't strong enough. He felt like he was 18 again and his dad was lying in that bed. He knew what happened when people were like this; they died. His mother had never even made it to the hospital. He laughed when he thought about the fact that he was a doctor. He was a hypocrite. He crossed his arms in front of his body and watched her, not crossing the threshold, not connecting. He had already gotten too close, too involved. It was better this way. He closed his eyes but he couldn't get the image of her lying in the water out of his mind. He knew something had happened to him out there and he couldn't process it. He was always in control, always one step ahead of the game, and now he felt like a duck on the water. He looked calm, but underneath his legs were flailing.

"So are you keeping the doorway warm?" Jack asked as he walked up next to him.

Tommy looked at him and smiled. "Maybe. I thought you guys left."

"Nah, nothing to do at home. Besides, I thought you might need a brother," he looked at his friend. "Why don't you go in?"

"Can't. I was just getting ready to leave," Tommy lied.

Jack nodded. "Sure you were. And why is it you can't go in?"

He felt a tear fall and he angrily flicked it away. "Just can't."

Jack sighed. "Having some flashbacks?" he knew what Tommy was reliving.

His friend looked at him. "Something like that."

Jack motioned for him to walk over and sit down on the bench near the room. Tommy followed and collapsed onto the seat. "This is different, Tommy. Brittany is not your parents. Don't bury her already."

Tommy shot him a look. "I'm not, I just don't want to deal with this anymore," he knew he sounded ridiculous. "I am not made like you, I can't be the hero."

Jack laughed. "I'm no hero. Hey, did I ever tell you what happened when Stephanie first got to me?"

Tommy shook his head. "No."

Jack smiled. I had a full-fledged panic attack. I didn't know how to deal with any of the feelings I was having and I was scared I was going to screw it up."

Tommy looked at his friend. "What if I screw it up?"

Jack smiled. "That's part of your charm. It took me awhile to realize it, but it didn't matter if I wasn't perfect. Stephanie loves me in spite of my arrogance and my ego. She checks me and makes me grateful to be in a world with someone as amazing as she is. It's not perfect, but it's perfect for us and I will cherish every moment I am given with her because it's a gift. Screw your pride and screw your fears. If you want to be with her than go be with her. If you are scared, then tell her. Deal with this stuff or it will eat you alive. I know you. I have seen you at your worst and you have seen me

the same way. You can be an ass and you can be
stubborn but you have never ever been someone to
walk away from a fight. She is not your dad and she is
going to make it. The question is, are you?" Jack
squeezed his shoulder and stood up. "Stephanie and I
are here if you need us."

Tommy stood up and hugged his friend. He nodded
and watched Jack leave. He walked back to the door of
her room and took a deep breath; looking down, he
slowly walked in. He pulled a chair up to the side of the
bed and sat down. His resolve quickly faded. She
looked so small and fragile. Her red hair stood out
against the paleness of her skin. She had a purple
bruise on her temple and what looked like a handprint
on her cheek. He could only imagine how hard that
psycho had smacked her to cause a mark like that. He
looked at her vitals and was encouraged at her oxygen
saturation. Hopefully the repair would hold. He looked
down at her hand and gently put it in his own. He
covered it with his other hand and sat silently and
prayed. "I would appreciate it if you woke up," he said
to her. "I don't like sitting in hospital rooms. I realize
that sounds funny coming from a doctor, but it's true.
It's best you know about that now. I have issues, lots of
them. I am hard to get along with and I don't put the
seat down," he shook his head. "I don't know why the
hell I just said that," he let go of her hand and rubbed
his face. He looked at her after a minute and smiled as
she looked back at him. "Hi. I didn't know you were
awake," he said. "Should I get a doctor?"

She moved her head slightly. "No," she said in an
almost inaudible voice.

"You made it," he said lamely. "I mean you came through the surgery. Well obviously you made it through the surgery," he stopped talking and sighed. He looked at her, taking her hand in his again. "I'm glad you're here."

She smiled a small smile and tried to speak. "Thank you for saving me," she said as her lip began to quiver. She grasped his hand as tightly as she could.

He touched her cheek and smoothed her hair. He went to speak but couldn't find the words. He just looked at her, trying to speak with his eyes.

She closed her eyes and began to cry as the weight of all that had happened took its toll. He felt his heart shatter at her anguish.

"It's okay. You're safe now. Please don't cry," he asked her gently.

"I was so scared. It was the worst night of my life all over again. He touched me again and I was back in that night," she looked at him. "I don't feel well. Can you leave?" she thought she was going to be sick.

Tommy went to stand up but stopped. "No. I am not going anywhere," he grabbed a basin and moved to the side of the bed. He helped her sit up gently while she dry heaved into the bin. She cried at the pain the movement caused her broken ribs. She had nothing in her system, but she tried. He held her long hair back and let his tears fall unabated. She leaned back into him after a minute, exhausted from the unproductive effort. He held her while she caught her breath and then he grabbed a cup of water from the bedside table for her but she shook her head softly.

"No," she panted. "I can't."

"Okay for now, but you need to drink," he wasn't too worried because of her IV. He put the bin on the table and went to move. She stopped him with her hand on his knee.

"What is it? Did I hurt you?"

"I know you probably don't want to and you have done more than I could ever ask," she stopped and tried to catch her breath.

"What is it?" he asked her.

"Can you just stay for a little while? I don't like to be in the hospital. I know it's silly, being a doctor, but I can't help it. I just feel like everything is happening all over again and I don't want to feel like that anymore. I don't think I can take it," she paused at his silence and seemed to pull herself together a little bit. "You know what, it's okay, I don't mean to impose, I'll be okay," she said as her tears fell. She looked away, moving slightly away from him.

"Are you through?" he asked her. "We are a sorry sight. I think it's time to get out of our own way," he moved from behind her and stood up next to the bed. He helped her lean back in the bed and covered her with the blanket. He sat down and held her hand while she closed her eyes. "There is no place else I would rather be," he said as he watched her fall asleep from sheer exhaustion. He thought to himself that for all of his protests and his fears, and for all of his worrying about what might happen, Jack was right, this was where he was supposed to be and he felt more alive than at any point in his life.

******

Stephanie made her way to Brittany's room the next morning. She walked in as Brittany was sitting up and looking much better than before. The women smiled at each other.

"Hi. I am so glad to see you up. How are you feeling?" Stephanie came in and sat down next to the bed.

"I'm okay. I just hate being in the hospital. I am trying to convince Dr. Schmidt that I can go home," Brittany said as she looked at her hands. "I will have to figure out how to get around with my foot in a cast, but I will feel better in my own place."

Stephanie was concerned. "Are you sure that's a good idea? You just escaped from a horrifying ordeal and you almost died. It wouldn't hurt to spend a few days here."

Brittany sighed. "I just can't, Stephanie. The man who hurt me is in custody, so I'm safe. I feel like if I stay here I will fall back into that place I was in before. I have come so far and I can't go back there."

Stephanie put her hand on her friend's arm. "Did you talk to Dr. Schmidt about your viral load?"

She looked at Stephanie. "I know what's ahead of me. I can take care of myself at home and monitor my levels."

Stephanie nodded. "Okay, but what about Tommy?"

Brittany looked at her. "What about him?"

"He won't like you going home alone. He really cares about you," Stephanie said.

Brittany looked down at her hands. "I know and I really care about him, too. He saved my life."

Stephanie pushed her on the topic. "Why don't you give him a chance to help you? Tommy is a compassionate soul who is just as confused as you are. I can't imagine what you have been through, but as someone who is dealing with a disease, I know that there can't be enough support. I love you and now that your past is out in the open, maybe you can stop running. You are such a strong and resilient woman, Brit. I want everyone to see that."

Brittany smiled at her friend. "Thank you for everything. I really do appreciate it," she watched as Stephanie left to go on rounds.

******

Tommy walked off the elevator on Brittany's floor on his way to see her. He had gone home after he was sure she was asleep. He took a long shower and slept like a rock. He was eager to see how she was this morning. He walked into the room and saw the bed empty. He felt a momentary pang of anxiety but when he turned around he saw a nurse who smiled at him. "She went to the roof to get some air," the nurse said.

"Thanks," Tommy said and headed up. He walked onto the roof and saw her sitting in her wheelchair near the corner of the wall next to the bench. Her red hair was blowing in the wind and he was immediately concerned about the chill in the air. He walked over to her. "Hey, how are you feeling?" he asked as he sat down on the bench next to her chair.

Brittany looked at him and smiled at the concern in his soft eyes. "Better. I am waiting to go home."

Tommy was surprised. "Schmidt is letting you leave? Does he think that's wise?"

She rubbed her forehead. "I am leaving against his advice," she saw him begin to protest but stopped him. "Look, I appreciate everything you have done for me, but I need to go home. I need to be alone."

Tommy was so frustrated. "Why? Why must you insist on doing everything alone? My God, Red, do you have any idea how close you came to dying? Do you know how precarious your health is now? Going home could lead to a worsening of your condition and then maybe something you can't come back from."

She looked at him, surprised by his reaction. "Tommy, I am not your responsibility. I have so much going on in my head and I am just so tired of running. I just want to stop *feeling* everything."

He took her face in his strong hands and looked at her, blue eyes against green. "We are past this. I saw the worst. When I pulled you from the water almost dead, something happened to me. I don't know what it is or where it will go, but I know that from now on, you are a part of me, and I care about what happens to you."

She touched his chest with her fingers. "Tommy, we can never have a relationship," her voice broke.

"Why not? We are both looking at the future with our eyes wide open. I am not asking for anything other than a chance to see what we have," he was laying it all out for her. "There is nothing you can say to change my mind about you."

She looked down and exhaled. "You will want more than I can give you. I am HIV positive, Tommy, and my viral load is higher than it has been in a long time. My body is struggling to fight off this latest attack and if it can't," she stopped.

"Then I will help you fight harder," Tommy said.

"It's not that simple, Tommy," she cried. "There is so much you don't know, and when you find out, you will change your mind. I can't handle that, I can't bear it if you look at me with pity," she looked away from him. "I can't even let anyone touch me without feeling dirty. I am carrying so much with me; sometimes I think it's just pointless. All I know is what he did to me and what it turned me into," she looked at him and sighed. "When I was 18 years old he raped me and beat me and left me with so many deep scars," she started to talk again, but stopped.

"What is it?" Tommy asked her.

She looked at him. "Before that, I had never been with a man before. I had never been intimate with anyone. I was this all-powerful teen sensation and everyone knew everything about me. The one thing I wanted to keep private and share with only my husband was my body and my love. He took that from me and now that I am left with this disease, there is nothing more I can offer you."

Tommy cradled her cheek in his hand. "You are so wrong. You have never lost that. He couldn't take that from you, Red, because rape is an act of power, of control and of violence and has nothing to do with love. He took a lot away from you, but that part is still intact. You, and only you can decide who and when you give yourself to someone. If you believe nothing else I tell you, please believe that," he pulled her to him for a hug, holding her gently, so he wouldn't hurt her. "Can I take you back inside and into the warmth?"

She touched his face and with her finger, traced a line over his lips. She felt her heart beat faster and he looked at her with a look she had never seen before. "I'm scared," she said.

"So am I," he added. "But if you let me help you, maybe we can figure things out together? I have a big house with two empty rooms. If you insist on leaving, will you stay with me for a few days? I promise it will be totally as a doctor patient relationship."

She thought a minute and sighed. "I would like that, if you're sure, but first I need to talk to Jack and Stephanie. Can you call them?"

Tommy nodded and picked up his phone, silently thanking God for her decision to let him help her.

****
Jack and Stephanie met in the hallway outside of Brittany's room. Jack kissed her and pulled her to him.

"I missed you," he crooned into her ear as he nibbled.

Stephanie giggled. "It's only been an hour since I saw you," she reached around and squeezed his behind.

He smiled. "What do you think Brittany wants with us?"

Stephanie sighed. "I don't know. We had a nice talk earlier, but she is probably the most stubborn person I know. She has been through so much and I don't think she has even begun to deal with it."

He nodded. "I know, but I think with Tommy's help, she has a fighting chance," he took her hand and they walked into the room.

"Hi," Stephanie smiled at Brittany. She was sitting in the chair dressed in scrubs. Her hair was pulled back and for the first time, Jack saw the bruising on her face. He felt his blood boil.

Brittany noticed him looking at her. "Looks worse than it is," she smiled.

Jack shook his head. "I'm sorry, I just hate that you are going through all of this."

Stephanie nodded her agreement and walked closer to Brittany. "So, what can we do for you? Do you need some advice on how to make Tommy stop wearing those t-shirts all over?" she smiled.

Brittany laughed but held the small pillow to her chest to absorb some of the pain from the broken ribs. She took a minute until the pain subsided. Jack moved to help her. "It's okay, just some cracked ribs. No, this is professional. Can you guys sit down?"

Jack and Stephanie looked at each other and sat down. "What is it?"

"Well, it is my duty as a doctor to inform all expectant parents what they can anticipate during the first trimester," Brittany said with a smile.

Stephanie sat and looked at her and then at Jack and then at Brittany again. "Wait, us? Parents? Do you mean," she stood up, unable to contain her excitement. She looked at Jack who was trying to grasp what was said.

"Are we pregnant?" Jack asked.

Brittany nodded and Jack's face broke out in a broad grin. "Really? For sure? Really really?" he said.

"Really really," Brittany said. She felt tears come to her eyes as Jack picked his wife up in a bear hug and they celebrated.

"But how do you know?" Stephanie asked her.

"Before I was, well, before everything happened, we had your labs done," she began and Stephanie nodded. She had forgotten about that in the mess of everything else. I had the results pulled today after we talked and I just wanted to be the one to tell you both the news before you meet your new doctor."

Jack looked at her. "What do you mean new doctor?"

Stephanie sat down and took Brittany's hand in her own. "You are our doctor, Brit."

Brittany smiled. "I am a little limited at the moment of what I am able to do for you. I love you guys and I don't want to do anything but help you. It will be better for you both if you have someone else help you for now. Maybe after a little while, I will be able to resume my duties, but for now you have to think about what's best for you."

Stephanie felt her tears come to her eyes. "What's best for me is to have you help me through this."

Jack put his arm around his wife. "I think we all need to wait a few days before we make any changes. Is there anything Stephanie needs to do in the next few weeks?"

Brittany shook her head. "Not really, you are already off of the interferon, and we will monitor your iron and your liver and kidney functions. It is just really important that you take it easy."

Stephanie grinned. "I'll do anything for my baby," she looked at Jack. "Our baby."

"See, we don't need another doctor, you are all we need," Jack smiled.

"Who needs what?" Tommy asked as he stood in the doorway. Jack turned around and couldn't wipe the smile off his face. He walked to Tommy. "I'm pregnant," he said.

Tommy looked at him. ""Um, I'm going to take a wild guess and say that Stephanie is pregnant?" he smiled at them.

"You know what I mean," Jack said and Tommy hugged him.

"That's the best news I've heard in a long time," he said. He walked to Stephanie and pulled her into a hug, too. "I can't think of two people who deserve to be parents more than you do."

The friends all laughed and smiled together for a bit, Brittany watched and tried to smile with them. She needed to give them this news. She needed something good before everything else began.

Chapter Seventeen:

"So, are you sure you want to do this? I mean, you can stay here for another night if you want to," Tommy told her as he sat down near the chair she was on.

"I am ready. I need a change of scenery, but you know I will be okay on my own if you've changed your mind," Brittany said.

"Nope, I just spent the last hour getting the house ready for you," he felt his cell phone buzz and he looked down and frowned.

"What is it?" Brittany asked.

"It's a text from Julie. She wants to know if I would be here for a few minutes because she and Bill were coming by," he said.

"Maybe they have some results to go over with you?" she said. "Don't worry until you know things for sure, okay?"

"Okay," he said and turned around when he heard them at the door. He smiled at his sister and brother in law.

"Hi Tommy." Julie said and hugged her brother. She looked over his shoulder at Brittany and smiled warmly. She walked over to her. "Hi, I'm Julie, Tommy's sister and this is my husband Bill."

Brittany smiled. "It's nice to meet you both."

"How about we go to the lounge and let Brittany have some privacy," Bill said.

Tommy looked at Brittany. "I'll be right back, okay?"

Brittany smiled, grateful for the moment alone. She shook her head. "Sure."

Tommy walked out. Brittany, finally alone and exhausted, let the tough exterior drop. She did what she had wanted. She was able to give Stephanie and Jack the best news of their lives and she was able to see their happiness and witness their love for each other. She moved to the wheelchair carefully and gently. It took all of her energy to lift herself up and her torso and abdomen were wracked with pain. She sat for a minute until the sharp jabs subsided. She took a few deep breaths and looked up as Tommy came back in alone. She looked at him, trying to mask her pain. "Well, what is it?"

Tommy smiled. "You're not going to believe it, but you were right. The mass they found was benign," he sat down and ran his hand through his hair.

Brittany was beyond happy. "Oh Tommy, that's wonderful news. I am so happy for you and for them. You deserve some good news for a change."

Tommy looked at her. "That's not all."

"Okay, what's up?" she asked him.

"Julie is pregnant and she and Bill are moving to Ann Arbor," he said.

Brittany looked at him, surprised. "That's all good, right?"

He smiled at her. "Yes, it's really good. I am truly happy for her and for Bill and for Jack and for Stephanie. It's just that I wish everyone was happy," he looked at her with sincerity.

"How about you just take this for now?" she said. "Every child is a miracle and for that, we can both be happy for your family."

"Sure, I suppose you're right," he said. "Are you ready to go?"

She nodded. "I really am," she said as he wheeled her out.

******

"I made up the guest room for you, so after I help you get in, I will bring your bag to you," Tommy said as they pulled up into his driveway.

"You don't need to go through any trouble for me," Brittany said as she looked out the window.

"I'm not," he said and turned off the car. He looked at her, noticing the paleness of her skin and the pain in her face. "Are you sure you are ready to be out of the hospital?"

She looked at him and nodded. "Yes. I'm just tired."

"Okay," he said. He got out and walked to the other side of the car and opened the door, handing her the cane. She had on a removable walking boot and although she was supposed to remain off of her foot, the boot would enable her to get around without crutches. She was unable to put anything under her arms because of the broken ribs and bruising. He held out his hand to help her stand up.

She hesitantly took his hand and let him help her. "I got it," she said and steadied herself for a moment. She limped very slowly toward the door, grimacing at each move but not making a sound. He walked behind her in case she faltered, but he kept his distance. She paused halfway to the door.

"What is it?" he asked her, concerned.

"I just need to catch my breath," she said.

"I don't mean to be pushy, but will you just let me carry you in? It will be much easier for you," he rubbed his face.

"Okay," she said weakly. He picked her up gently as she gasped in pain.

"I'm sorry," he said.

"It's okay, just go," she said, holding in her pain as best she could. He opened the door and walked into the house, placing her softly onto the couch. He stood back and looked at her. "I'm okay," she said, her tears giving her away.

"Liar," he said and smiled. "I'll be right back with your things from the car. Don't move."

"Not a problem," she said and held a pillow to her chest as she tried to slow her breathing. She looked around at the tastefully decorated room. She sat on a large curved brown couch, very comfortable and plush. She looked at the dining room table and chairs and the large television that was mounted on the wall. There were a few pictures on the coffee table, but she didn't really see who they were.

Tommy came back in with her bag. He put it into the guest room and returned to the family room. She hadn't moved an inch. "Are you hungry?"

"No," she said softly. "I think I would just like to go to go lie down."

"Okay. I can help you get settled if you want," he said.

"Maybe I can use your arm, but walk myself," she said, feeling very vulnerable.

"Okay," he walked over and she reached out for his hand. She wrapped her arm around his and used the cane in the other hand. She leaned on him and slowly made her way to the room. She looked around when they entered and smiled. He had put flowers and chocolate in a basket on the dresser. There was a plate of fruit on the nightstand and ice water in a carafe. She looked into the bathroom, which was connected, and saw a fresh set of towels and toiletries.

"It looks perfect, thank you," she was sincerely touched.

He grinned. "I wasn't sure what you might feel like eating."

She sat down on the bed and he stood back. "I'll leave you alone for a bit, but if you need anything, or want to talk, will you let me know?" he just didn't know what was the right thing to do.

She nodded her consent and he walked out, partially closing the door behind him.

Brittany let her pain come out through her tears after she was alone. She could barely breathe and was exhausted. Everything was running through her head, her attack, Tommy, Jack and Stephanie, Julie and Bill, everything that had happened in such a short period of time. She was having a hard time sorting through it all. She needed to use the bathroom, so she stood up gingerly and made her way to the attached room. She looked in the mirror and touched her face gently, seeing the handprint bruise. She remembered the hit.

Brittany couldn't help it as her tears fell down her cheeks. She was having a hard time holding it together. "I can't sing for you," she said softly. She was stunned as his hand crashed across her face. She almost blacked out.

"You will do as I ask you, or you won't like the consequences," he said.

She picked up her shirt and saw that the bandage on her abdomen had bled through, probably from the exertion of walking. She would fix that in a minute. She looked at the bandages on her arms and sighed. How had all of this happened? She looked at her eyes and saw they were dull and lifeless. She had always loved her eyes and her hair. So many people commented on her beautiful eyes and her thick red locks. She had always felt special; having such beautiful red hair like her grandmother. She had worshipped her grandmother and having this hair made her feel like she was looking back at her. She washed her hands and turned to walk back to the bed, but suddenly felt dizzy. She leaned against the wall outside the bathroom and slowly sank to the floor.

*****

Tommy paced in the kitchen and thought about going in to see her. He must have almost walked into the room ten times before deciding to sit on the couch and wait. He leaned back and exhaled when he heard a noise.

"Tommy?" he heard a tiny voice call him. He walked to the door.

"Red? Are you okay?" he asked.

"Can you help me?" he heard her ask and he walked in. He didn't see her at first so he walked to the bathroom and saw her on the floor outside of the room. She was sitting against the wall, holding her side.

He knelt down next to her. "What happened? Why didn't you call me sooner?"

"I don't know what's wrong with me, you know? I mean, in just a few days I have gone from a self-sufficient woman to a pathetic excuse for a human being," she said, her face showing the pain she was in. She tried to hide it, but her resolve was crumbling and as much as she hated to admit it, he helped her to feel safe; something she desperately needed.

He fought the urge to just hold her and let her get it all out. "I think sitting on the floor is making your sense of reason leave you. How about we get off the floor and talk about what I think is going on," Tommy said, trying a more conservative approach.

"I can't move," she began to cry softly. "Everything hurts, from the inside out," she was panting from the pain.

Tommy felt a sense of protection come over him and he needed to make it better. "I think you have spent enough energy for the day. Now it's my turn to help you."

"You can't touch me," she said. "My stomach is bleeding through," she closed her eyes for a minute.

Tommy felt his heart splinter at her sadness. "Why didn't you tell me?" he walked to the bathroom and took some gloves out of the package he had brought in. He put them on and approached her. He went to move her shirt over and she shook her head and stopped him.

"No, please, I'll do it," she said through her tears. She was having a hard time staying focused.

"No, I'll do it," he said and looked at her. "I am a doctor and you need help."

She touched his hand. "But you have done so much already. You should be free to live your life and not have to take care of me. I'm so ashamed about everything, Tommy. I feel like such a failure," she put her face in her hands.

"That's enough. Come here," he handed her a pillow to hold against her chest to support her ribs as he picked her up. She gasped as the pain shot through her body as he laid her on the bed. He held her while she tried to catch her breath and the pain subsided.

"Oh God," she panted.

"I'm sorry," he said, fighting his own emotions. "I don't want to hurt you."

He walked to the bathroom and gathered the rest of the first aid materials, taking a minute to collect himself. He walked back to the bed and sat down next to her, trying to stay focused. He looked at her and she nodded her approval. His skilled hands gently unbuttoned her shirt from the bottom until he could move the material away from the bandage. She was breathing heavily and her nerves were at their limit. She leaned back and closed her eyes as he moved the fabric from her and saw the bandage was soaked through. He carefully removed the gauze and she let more tears fall. He took the washcloth he had in warm water and squeezed it out before placing it on the wound. She sucked in her breath at the feel of the material on her skin.

"You are doing great. It's just seeping through the stitches, probably because of the stress you put on yourself with walking. I will cover it back up and you need to just rest," he put the cloth in the biohazard bag from the hospital and took out the gauze. He gently covered the gash and secured the bandage. He looked at her. "We need to change your shirt."

She nodded. "Okay."

He looked at her. "Okay," he finished unbuttoning her shirt and she tried to control her quivering chin, as the pain was intense with every move. He was so gentle and so professional that she felt completely cared for despite the situation. He checked the incision from the lung surgery and saw what a mess he had made of her. He finished changing her top and moved to clean everything up. He came back and sat down on the bed. "Do you want to talk about what happened?"

She looked at him. "I don't know how to start."

He took her hand in his. "How about you tell me what you can."

She exhaled slowly. "I thought I was going to die. I thought my life was coming full circle, you know. I figured that since he was able to find me, everything I did to begin again and make a life for myself served no purpose. He would always get to me and never let me go. He has always been in my head, telling me I am so worthless and having this disease, I knew there would be no one else who would want to be with me. He was the epitome of my fears and he won, again," she wiped her face.

Tommy shook his head. "No, he didn't. You got away and you're safe," he needed to ask her something. "Brittany, did he rape you again?"

She looked at him, seeing his compassion and concern and her tears fell. "No," she said almost inaudibly. "But I think he was going to. He wanted me to take my clothes off and put on that dress, and be his bride or something. He had everything planned. He was so angry with me and so violent but I couldn't do what he wanted. I wouldn't."

Tommy felt his anger boil over. "I'm sorry. I don't know what else to say. I am so profoundly sorry about all of this."

She wiped her tears. "Why are you being so nice to me? You don't even know me."

"Because I think you're worth it. I think you're an amazing woman who has survived because of the strength of your spirit. I think I feel things for you that I have never felt before, and I know that you have some feelings for me," Tommy stopped and looked at her.

"I have already told you that I can't have a relationship with you, it wouldn't be fair. I could never be the woman you deserve, Tommy. I am so messed up from everything in my life and I just won't put you at risk for anything," she said. "I just can't do it."

He gently tucked her hair behind her ear. "You could never hurt me," he leaned closer to her. "You just need to learn to trust me, and I will help you to do that."

She closed her eyes. "You are an amazing man, Tommy. I wish I could repay you."

He sat next to her and she ever so gently leaned against him.

"When you're here, my world is a lot less scary."

He smiled. "Well, that's a start," he put his arm around her as she closed her eyes.

Chapter Eighteen:

The doorbell rang and Tommy jumped off the couch to answer the door. Brittany had fallen asleep and he was working on some research for an upcoming case. He opened the door and smiled at Jack and Stephanie.

"Dinner and entertainment have arrived," Jack said as they walked in. He was carrying Chinese food and Stephanie had a bag of things. They put the food down on the living room table and took off their coats. Stephanie looked around.

"She is asleep in the guest room," Tommy said.

Stephanie smiled. "I'll go check on her."

Tommy walked into the kitchen and grabbed some plates and silverware while Jack set out the containers. The men sat down and Jack looked at his friend. "So, how is she doing?"

Tommy exhaled as he sat back. "I don't know. She is in a lot of pain, but she hides it really well. She doesn't want me to know what she went through, but I think it would be better if she did."

Jack picked up a fried noodle and ate it. "Do you think you can deal with what she went through?"

"What do you mean, of course I can," Tommy said. He grabbed a few beers out of the fridge and put them down. "I just want to help her."

Jack nodded. "I know; I just worry about you. You have been through a lot lately, and I don't want you to get hurt."

"Will you stop being my dad?" Tommy smiled. "I know what I'm doing."

Jack smiled. "Sure you do."

"What's that supposed to mean?" he smiled and they both looked up as Stephanie and Brittany walked in. The men sat in silence, both captivated.

Jack stood up and smiled.

"Hi, I hope you don't mind that we're here."

Brittany smiled and Stephanie helped her to sit down, giving her pillows for support. "Of course not, but this isn't my house," she looked at Tommy.

"I tried to kick him out, but Jack is very hard to move," Tommy said. He didn't like how pale she looked, but he decided to let it go for now.

Stephanie walked over and sat down next to Jack. She put some food on a plate and gave it to Brittany. "You really need to eat."

Brittany nodded. "I'll try."

Jack took a plate and put a pile of food on it. Tommy did the same and they all began to eat, except Brittany, who hadn't touched anything.

"So Tommy, Jack tells me you were quite the teachers pet while you were at Michigan," Stephanie grinned.

"Oh really, and what other lies did Jack tell you?" Tommy said as he chewed on a noodle.

"Dude, you were so in the face of every teacher. You were the biggest pain," Jack said.

"Well, not all of us could charm our way through college. Some of us actually had to do work," Tommy said.

Jack snorted. "Right," he put his arm around Stephanie and smiled. "Thomas was at every office hour for Professor Jeannie. The poor woman couldn't eat her lunch without Tommy knocking on her door."

"I needed help with stats, she was nice," Tommy said and blushed.

"And what did she look like?" Stephanie asked with a twinkle in her eye. Brittany smiled at them.

Tommy laughed and Jack joined him. "She was hot, for an 80 year old."

"I swear; I went there every day to make sure she was still alive. If she was late for class, everyone would take bets on what happened. I was just being nice," Tommy took another bite of food.

"She loved Tommy, when she remembered his name," Jack said.

"Okay, so how about we talk about some of your 'issues' while we're at it," Tommy said as he raised an eye at Jack.

"Bring it," Jack challenged

Stephanie looked at Brittany, who was sitting quietly, looking a bit faint. She hadn't touched her food. She saw Tommy and Jack notice as well. "How about you guys go out and get us some ice cream for dessert."

Jack stood up. "Coming right up," he knew his wife wanted to be alone with Brittany.

Tommy shook his head. "I don't know if I should go," he looked at Brittany.

"Come on," Jack patted him on the shoulder. "We'll be right back."

Tommy looked again at Brittany who remained looking down and Stephanie, who nodded for him to go. He sighed and left with Jack.

Stephanie smoothed Brittany's hair from the side of her face and smiled at her friend. "Honey, you need to eat."

Brittany looked at her. "I am so nauseous. The meds are making me feel horrible."

Stephanie nodded her understanding. "I know, but taking them with nothing in your stomach isn't helping. You need to remain strong so your viral load can lower and you can get on with your life."

Brittany looked at her. "What life am I supposed to get on with? What am I supposed to do? The life I worked for is gone and I am back to living in fear. I know I hurt that guy, but I didn't kill him. He will get out again and come after me. Tommy has been so amazing, but that makes it worse. I shouldn't be here, but I don't want to be alone at home. My head is a mess and I don't know how to fix it," she looked at the food and covered her mouth. Stephanie got a bag and handed it to her. She rubbed her friends back as she managed to keep control of her insides. After a minute Stephanie took Brittany's pulse and looked into her eyes.

"I am going to give you some fluids, okay? You seem a little dehydrated," Stephanie said as she got her bag.

Brittany nodded, not having the energy to argue. She stood up to go to the bedroom. Stephanie helped her and started an IV. She hooked it to the bed frame and took her vitals. "I really think you should be back in the hospital," she smiled. "I am also realizing that I am a hypocrite. You know, when I first met Jack, he took me home to stay with him because I kept running from the hospital. He didn't even know my name," she was quiet for a minute. "I was so afraid to let him in," she spoke as she worked, checking Brittany's bandages.

"How did you let him in?" Brittany asked her.

Stephanie smiled. "I didn't have any choice. As much as I protested and tried to put down my worth, he saw inside. He saw the worst of me and he loved me because of it. He made me see my potential and not my pain. He also gave me the gift of a life with love and happiness," she took her friends hand. "Sweetie, you have to stop punishing yourself. Having HIV is a horrible thing, no question, but this disease has taken so much from you, don't let it take your heart."

Brittany wiped her tears away and nodded. "I can't stand the thought of possibly hurting him."

Stephanie knew what she meant. "I know, but you need to understand that you are not the one to make the decisions for anyone else but you. I was afraid to be intimate with Jack because I kept thinking that one day he would have to take care of me in every way, and I couldn't put him through that."

Brittany stopped her. "But Steph, there is a very good chance that you will live a long and healthy life, with no disability."

"I know," Stephanie said as she stopped the IV and bandaged the spot. She disposed of the materials and sat back down. "I also know you and Tommy are at the beginning of getting to know each other. There is no way of knowing what might happen between you. I want you to be looking at it with your heart, and not just your head," she leaned in and gently hugged her friend. "I just want you to be happy."

Brittany hugged Stephanie back. "Thank you for everything."

Jack walked to the door and smiled at them. "Ice cream is in the freezer, are you ready to go?"

Stephanie grabbed her bag and nodded. "See you tomorrow?"

Brittany nodded and watched her leave.

****

"How is she doing, really?" Jack asked Stephanie as they drove home.

"She is a mess. She has a lot going through her head, and she doesn't know how to make heads or tails of it. I think the most pressing issue is Tommy," Stephanie said. She played with Jack's hand, which was on her knee as he drove.

"I wish they would both get out of the way and stop being so stubborn. You and I can see what's happening, why can't they?" Jack asked.

Stephanie laughed. "How quickly you forget."

Jack pulled into the garage and shut the car off. "I didn't forget; I just wore you down until you acquiesced." Smiling, he walked her inside their house and they made their way to the couch.

"I just can't believe how lucky I am to have you love me," she said.

He felt a lump in his throat. "I wish you wouldn't say things like that."

She took his hand in her own and kissed his fingers. "Why?"

"Because I am the lucky one. Stephanie, you have no idea how much I love you and need you. You inspire me every day to be a better man and when I think about what you have to deal with every day, and how you put up with things that would bring another person to their knees, it just makes me love our life even more," he touched her stomach and leaned in and kissed it. "Now we made a baby and that love is going to start a legacy for us. I just feel so incredibly blessed and I don't want to ever lose sight of that."

Stephanie touched his face and leaned into his chest. She had no words that could describe her feelings. She simply wrapped her arms around him and they held each other.

Chapter Nineteen:

Brittany summoned all her energy and walked gingerly into the family room where Tommy was sitting. He stood up as soon as he saw her.

"Do you need something?" he asked as he walked to help her.

"No," she said and let him help her to the couch. "Do you mind if I sit with you?"

He smiled at her and shook his head. "I would love that," he sat back down next to her.

"Thank you again for helping me. I really appreciate it," she said to him.

"You're welcome," he said.

They both sat in silence. "Did Stephanie help you while we were gone?" Tommy asked her, noticing her bandaged arm.

Brittany nodded. "She gave me some fluids which will help."

Tommy turned and looked at her. "You need to eat."

She closed her eyes. "I know, but I am having trouble keeping things down," she looked at him and saw his concern. "It's just because of the meds I'm on; it will get better when my body adjusts."

"Does that happen every time you adjust your meds?"

She nodded. "Pretty much, but the way I look at it is that at least I have meds that I can take. So many people have to fight this disease with no help at all. I know that one day the meds may stop working, so I will be grateful to them while I can."

"I wish you wouldn't talk like that. There is nothing to say you won't live a long and healthy life. You know that," Tommy said.

"Tommy, can I ask you something?" she looked into his green eyes, so compassionate and kind.

"Of course," he had no idea what was coming.

"How did you find me? Why did you put yourself at risk for me?" she really had wondered what happened after she ran.

He sighed. "I got lost in the woods while I was looking for you. The police found the cabin you were kept at and you were gone. They searched, but the storm was coming and it was dark, and I heard them call off the search until morning for safety reasons. I just kept thinking about you out there, alone, and I wanted to help. I didn't think I would find you, but at least if I tried, you would know that someone out there was thinking about you and wishing you were okay," he stood up and walked across the room before turning to look at her. "I couldn't think about what you might have gone through and I had no idea what shape you might be in. I just had to do something," he shrugged.

She wiped her eyes as he spoke, amazed at his words. "You could have been killed. I can't tell you how much that means to me. No one has ever gone out of their way for me and expected nothing in return. I am not used to that kindness."

He felt the familiar tug at his heart that she seemed to be causing him lately. "Can I ask you something?"

She nodded and wiped her tears.

"Will you share some ice cream with me?" he grinned.

"I'll try," she smiled back.

Tommy walked to get the bowls and she watched him, thinking about what Stephanie had said. She wondered if it was possible to be that happy. She sighed and watched him come back and sit down. He handed her a bowl and a spoon and sat down as his cell phone rang. He didn't recognize the number, but he answered.

"Hello?" he spoke into the phone and Brittany tried a bite of ice cream.

"Yes, she is here with me," he spoke and Brittany looked at him. He put his bowl down and listened to whoever was on the other end. "I understand, yes, thanks for calling," he hung up the phone and sat silently for a minute.

"Dare I ask?" she put her bowl down and looked at him.

"That was the FBI," he began.

"And," she prodded.

"Apparently the man who attacked you is no longer under police custody," Tommy spoke quietly.

Brittany felt the blood drain from her face. "What do you mean?"

"He escaped," Tommy said softly, not taking his eyes off her.

"Oh God," she jumped up and went to leave but she collapsed in pain as her foot gave out. She cried out as her side hit the table as she fell.

"Red, stop," Tommy jumped to her and felt sick as she cowered on the floor, shaking and trying to breathe. "Look at me," he spoke firmly. "Nothing is going to happen to you. You are safe with me," he looked at her, but her face was blank again, no expression of contentment or comfort. She was back in her pain.

"I need to go home, now," she said to him, her fear palpable.

"I'm sorry, what?" Tommy asked her. "You're not going anywhere."

She was frantic. "He will find me and if you are there, he will kill you. I don't want him to hurt you," she moved away from him slightly and leaned against the wall, holding her side and closing her eyes for a minute because of the pain.

"Dammit Red, you are the single most stubborn woman I have ever met. What is it going to take for you to realize that I care about you and don't want you to leave? I am not your responsibility to protect. This shithead is out there, so what? Does that mean you go home and wait for him to finish what he started? How about we take the upper hand and live life instead of waiting for death?" he didn't mean to yell at her, but he needed to get through to her.

She looked at him, her chin quivering. "Just because you say the right things, doesn't make them true. You don't know what he is capable of, Tommy. You don't know what he could do to you, just to hurt me."

He knelt on the floor facing her and took her face in his hands. "Just because you think the worst things doesn't mean they will happen, either. What will it take for you to trust me and let me in?"

She looked down and was silent for a minute before meeting his gaze. "I can't. I don't know how," she said softly.

"Then I'll help you. First we need to clean you up and get some food in your stomach. Then we'll go from there," he stood up and picked her up in his arms. She offered no resistance and he walked into the bedroom and placed her on the bed. He went to gather some supplies. He looked in the mirror and sighed at his reflection. He didn't know how to help her and he was beginning to wonder if he could. He picked up everything he needed and walked to the bedroom only to see saw she was gone. He ran through the rooms and called for her, but heard nothing. "Fuck," he swore and grabbed his keys before running out of the house where he saw her sitting on the steps in the cold. He took her arm and she let him help her back inside. They sat down on the couch and he looked at her. "Please don't do this," he said to her as her teeth chattered. "It's like you want to die," he smoothed her hair and wiped her tears. "Do you?"

She shivered and shook her head. "I used to think so. I used to wonder what my purpose was, but now I think I might know," she looked at him. "Maybe there is more to life than pain and loneliness for me. You have shown me nothing but compassion and I have shut you off at every turn. I am a coward, Tommy. I don't know how to let anyone into my life without thinking about pain," she took his hand in hers and smiled a tiny smile. "I don't think that of you at all in my heart, but I don't know how to change what's in my head. I am so scared of hurting you and I am so scared of being alone. I don't know how to figure it out."

He smiled. "That's the problem with you, Red, you think way too much about everything," he leaned in to her and traced a line around her forehead. "Does that hurt?" he asked.

"No," she said softly.

He traced the line to her cheek. "That?"

She shook her head.

He leaned in closer to her and traced his finger across her lips. He took her hand in his and brought it to his lips. He kissed the back of her hand and she felt her tears fall again.

"Did I hurt you?" he asked her, concerned at her tears.

"No," she said. "Not at all."

"Good. How about I help you get warm and cleaned up," he said. He took her into the bathroom and she sat on the closed toilet seat. "You should take your clothes off and put this towel on," he turned to leave, but she stopped him.

"If you just hand me that towel, I would like you to stay. I am not feeling very steady," she said.

He nodded and handed her the towel. Her hands shook as she tried to unbutton her top. He put his hands on hers and looked at her. "Let me help you," he unbuttoned her top and let her put the towel in front of her before he pulled the material off her shoulders. He sucked in his breath as he looked at her back. "I think we should check your platelets. You are bruised worse than before on your back," he helped her wrap the towel around her back and tucked it into the front.

"I fell into the table before I got away and I'm sure that's what it's from. I always bruise easily, I have fair skin and it seems when I bump into something it turns black and blue. We can check, but don't worry," she said.

He helped her stand up while she stepped out of her yoga pants. The towel was long enough to cover her to her knees and she sat back down. Tommy looked at her foot and put on his gloves. "What happened to your foot? Do you remember?" he worked on cleaning around the cuts and swelling. He was as gentle as he could be, but her foot was a mess.

"It was how I got away," she said and he looked up at her. "He wanted me to wear that dress for him, but I put it on over my clothes. I didn't want to take my clothes off, you know? I didn't want," she stopped as the memory came out. Tommy listened with a lump in his throat but let her talk.

"When he came back in, he was really mad that I didn't take my clothes off, so I told him that I wanted to put on a show for him, take my clothes off while he watched," she felt fresh tears fall as she closed her eyes, remembering. "I didn't know what else to do, I was so scared. There was nothing I could find to use, so I had pulled my shoe off, hoping I could hit him with the heel. I had it behind me," Tommy stopped what he was doing and looked at her, wanting her to know she was safe and he didn't feel any pity for her, just admiration. "He seemed really pleased at that and came over to me and held me to him, starting to touch me again," she wrapped her arms around her middle as if to protect herself instinctively. "I grabbed my shoe and hit him with all my might in the head with the heel," she looked at him, her horror mirrored in his face. "He threw me into the table and that's how I cut my abdomen and hurt my back. I just got up and ran as fast as I could. I knew my foot was getting cut up but I couldn't stop, you know? I had to get away from him. I had to get away. I couldn't let him touch me again," she said and looked at him as her tears fell.

Tommy didn't think, he just put his arms around her and held her. She was frozen for a moment, not remembering the last time a man held her. He was strong and protective and she didn't want to stop him. After a few moments she sat back. "Sorry you asked?" she smiled.

He shook his head. "Not in the least. I would just like the chance to kill that son of a bitch," he stood up and grabbed some bandage materials.

"You know, that's why it would be best if I went home tomorrow," she said and he turned again to protest. "It's not that I don't want to be here, but because I am, you are under a lot of stress and you are also in danger. You have a good life here, Tommy. Your sister and brother in law are moving closer and you have a niece or nephew on the way. Your sister was given a clean bill of health and your best friends are going to be parents. I am a complication that isn't necessary," she stood up and gingerly stepped on her newly bandaged foot. She almost lost her footing and when she went to grab the counter her towel fell off. Tommy caught her before she fell, his strong arms supporting her. He helped her sit back down and put the towel back on her.

"Everything you said is true. I have all of those things going for me. But one thing you didn't mention was that none of those things are mine. I don't want to live my life vicariously through everyone else. I deserve more and so do you. I love my sister and I couldn't be happier for her. I adore Stephanie and Jack is like my brother, so I am ecstatic for them, but at the end of the day, I am alone in this world and up until now, I didn't care. Now I do, and you leaving won't take that away," he knelt down and looked at her. "Please let me into your world."

She listened to his words and for a small moment, a tiny piece of her resolve cracked. She leaned in and gently kissed him on the cheek. She leaned her cheek on his and held his face with her hand. She sat back and looked into his emerald eyes. "Okay," she said softly. "Okay."

Chapter Twenty:

"Stephanie, why don't you stay home?" Jack asked his wife as she had another bout of morning sickness.

"For nine months?" she said as she walked out of the bathroom. "Jack, women have worked while pregnant for years, it really isn't a radical concept. Besides, what would I do? Sit home and knit booties?" she ran her hand through his hair.

He smiled. "You can knit?" he ducked when she threw a sock at him. "Okay, I get it, you are woman hear you roar. I just can't help but worry about you. You are my wife, not just any woman. I want to make it better."

She straddled his lap and leaned in and kissed him. "You are sweet and I love you, but I am going to be late for a meeting and then I am going to spend some time with Brittany."

He kissed her and ran his hands up under her shirt. "Are you sure?"

She melted at his touch. "Yes," she spoke into his ear before extracting herself from his grasp. She walked over to the dresser to finish getting ready when Jack heard his cell phone ring.

"Hey Tommy. No, he didn't call me. No, I hadn't heard. Are you fucking kidding me? What the hell are they trying to do to catch him. Fine, I'll go with you. No, I am almost ready to leave. Why don't you pick me up? Okay, bye," Jack hung up and turned to see Stephanie looking at him, waiting for info. "The guy who took you and Brittany escaped," he ran his hand through his hair.

Stephanie couldn't believe it. "Oh God, does Brittany know? She is going to be so scared," she felt terrible for her friend.

"I'm scared, Stephanie. That jackass took you to get to her. Neither one of you are safe," he hated this.

"Jack, look at me. I am safe and so is Brittany, you and Tommy won't let anything happen to either one of us," she touched his chest. "I believe that. Now where are you and Tommy going?"

"To the police station. He wants to know what they are doing to protect Brittany. He told her and she was a mess. I can't say I blame her," Jack sighed.

"Who is with Brittany now?" Stephanie asked.

"Julie and Bill are over. They will stay there until we get back," he grabbed his keys as Stephanie cancelled her meeting.

"What are you doing?" Jack asked her.

"Coming with my family," she said and took his hand as they waited for Tommy.

*****

Tommy and Jack and Stephanie headed into the station to talk to the officer the next morning. They were waiting in the lobby area when the edition of today's paper caught Stephanie's eye. She felt her heart sink as she picked it up. There, on the front page, was a picture of Brittany and the headline 'Teen queen back in the news'.

"Oh no," Stephanie said as read the article.

"What is it? Morning sickness?" Jack asked as he turned to her and immediately saw what she had. "How did this happen? Who could have possibly tipped the news?"

Tommy turned to them and saw they were intently looking at something. "Um, what's going on?" he smiled at them until he saw the looks on their faces. "What is it?" he moved closer.

Jack tried to move the paper but Tommy grabbed it. He felt like he was going to throw up. "Oh God, how did this happen?" he could only think of Red and how upset she was going to be. She worked so long to keep her identity a secret. Would she think he did this?

"I am going to call the paper and see what I can find out. You guys go and talk to the officer," Stephanie said and sat down with her cell phone while the men went into the office.

****

"So all of this was a colossal waste," Tommy yelled as they got into the car. "The police have nothing, and the paper won't give out information on 'anonymous' tipsters. How is it that they can print a picture of someone and expose their life with no proof?"

"I don't know, but I think we need to come up with a better plan. We can't sit back and let everything just happen to us," Jack said.

"What exactly are you proposing?" Stephanie asked her husband.

"I don't exactly know, but we need to do something," Jack said and Tommy agreed.

"Let's grab lunch and figure it out," Tommy said and pulled into a diner. He had gotten off the phone with Julie who said all was going well at home. Brittany had not seen the paper or heard anything. She was resting comfortably.

The three doctors talked and ate, trying to made heads or tails of this recent development.

"At least before, Brittany was able to deal with her attack in private. No one knew who she was, or what had happened to her. But now, there is so much out there that other people will grab onto," Stephanie said sadly.

"What do you mean?" Tommy asked her.

"When Brittany disappeared, no one ever really knew what happened to her, not the details. She was gone and there was speculation, but nothing concrete," she didn't say what she was thinking. "If more gets out, I don't think she can handle that."

"You mean the fact that she is HIV positive," Jack said sadly.

Stephanie nodded. "People can be so very cruel. I just don't think she will be able to deal with that, with what will come along with that."

Tommy smirked. "Well this is just great, isn't it? Two steps forward and 12 steps back. What they hell is she supposed to do? People need to butt out of her life and leave her alone."

Suddenly, a group of men who were sitting near the trio began to laugh uproariously. They were discussing something and began to speak louder. It didn't take the three long to figure out what piqued their interest.

"I would like to help get her over her trauma," one of the men said. He was looking at the picture of Brittany.

"She looks like she needs to be touched up," another man said and they all laughed.

Tommy went to get up but Jack put his hand on his arm. "Don't man, it's not worth it."

"Look at that red hair, I wonder if it's red all over?" a third guy snorted with laughter and Tommy jumped up.

"Hey, why don't you guys show some respect?" he walked over to the men. Jack reluctantly joined him, mostly to keep him out of trouble.

"What the hell is your problem, man? I don't think we were talking to you," the first man said to Tommy.

"I just think you should stop talking about people who you know nothing about," Tommy seethed.

"Oh, the little boy has a crush on the pinup girl. Look dude, she hung in my bedroom, too, but now that she is all woman, I just might try to show her what a real man can do," the man sneered. Tommy jumped at the guy and another man grabbed him. The first man punched Tommy in the face and he doubled over. Jack grabbed at his friend.

"Hey, stop it, now," Jack said to all of them.

"Oh look, your mom is here," one of the guys said to Tommy. He reached over and Tommy shoved him.

Stephanie went to grab help and came back to see an all out brawl going on, with her husband and Tommy in the middle. She went to the side of the bar and grabbed the fire extinguisher. She ran back over and sprayed the pile of men. The fighting stopped, as everyone was stunned. Jack and Tommy looked at her and they both jumped up, grabbed their coats and the three of them quickly left. They jumped into the car and Tommy drove off. They all sat in silence until they were a safe distance away. Stephanie looked at the foam-covered men in the front seat.

"Are you both twelve?" she yelled.

"He insulted my girl," Tommy said lamely.

Jack smacked him. "Next time, man, you are so on your own. I am entirely too old for this."

"Ow, don't hit me. I have bruises on my bruises," Tommy said and smiled. "I feel a little better, though," he said.

"I'm so glad," Stephanie said. "Now this isn't going to be at all suspicious when Brittany sees you," she said sarcastically.

"Shit, you're right. I'll just clean up before she sees me," Tommy said.

Jack and Stephanie grinned at each other. "Good luck with that." They both laughed as Tommy pulled into their driveway.

"I'll call you later so we can continue with the plan," Tommy said as he waved goodbye to them. He drove off towards his house.

When he arrived, Tommy walked into the house, hoping for a quick change before Brittany saw him. Julie walked up to him and crossed her arms.

"What did you do?" Julie asked.

"Nothing. Just had a little issue at the diner," he walked past her. "Where is everyone?"

"Bill had to go to the new house and meet the inspector. He just left five minutes ago. Brittany is taking a nap." Julie eyed her brother. "What was this issue about?"

"Nothing you need to worry about. How did she do today?" he asked.

"She is really weak, Tommy. I think she should be in the hospital, but I know she won't go. She managed to eat some soup and some jello, but to be honest, I don't know if she kept it down. If you have fluids, you should give them to her. I checked on her a little while ago and she was lying down, but I am not sure she was actually sleeping." Julie sighed and then smiled. "I really like her Thomas. Do right by her."

Tommy looked at her. "I'm trying. Thanks, Jules. I am glad you're here," he tousled her hair.

"Stop, I am a married mother to be. You can't treat me like that anymore," she smiled.

"You are my baby sister and always will be and I will do as I please," he moved away from her as she tried to swat at him. "Seriously though, thank you."

She hugged him, wrinkling her nose at the foam on his shirt. "My pleasure. I will call you later," she waved and he walked her out to her car. He headed back into the house and realized he hurt all over.

"Guess I'm not as young as I used to be," he laughed to himself.

"What happened to you?" Brittany asked as she limped out of her room.

Tommy blushed. "Just a little scuffle," he took a towel and wiped off his face. She made her way to him and scrutinized his face.

"Looks like more than a scuffle," she touched the foam on his shirt. "What is this?"

"Stephanie sprayed the fire extinguisher on us," he said in a low voice.

She laughed and held her side. "I'm sorry, what happened?" she hid her smile.

"There were just some guys who needed to be taught a lesson. It was no big deal," he walked towards his room.

"I see, so I am supposed to share everything with you but you can just blow me off?" her tone surprised him.

"No, I didn't mean that," he said and sighed. "I'm sorry," he moved and grimaced at the pain in his side.

"How about you let me help you for a little while?" she asked him. "I am a doctor, after all."

"A gynecologist," he smiled.

"Details," she waved him off. "Come on with me," she walked to her bathroom. Tommy followed reluctantly, knowing he was going to have to tell her what really happened.

"Sit down here," she lowered the seat and he sat down, suddenly nervous. She got the washcloth and filled a small basin with water. She pulled up a chair and sat down across from him. "Can you show me where it hurts?" she asked him.

"My side, a little," he moved to point and grimaced again.

"Can I take a look?" she asked. "Can I pick up your shirt?"

He looked at her and smiled. "I used to be a few pounds thinner. "

She touched his hand. "Are you shy? You have seen me without my clothes on numerous times now."

"But I wasn't looking at that. I mean, it was purely professional, a doctor helping a patient," he looked at her and stammered. "I mean, not that I wouldn't want to look, it was just inappropriate," he looked down, completely embarrassed at his mumbling.

"Are you through?" she asked and smiled at him. He nodded and picked his shirt up for her. She helped him when he had trouble. She pulled the shirt off and looked at his side before putting on gloves. "Tommy, you have a huge bruise here. What happened?" she touched his side gingerly. She took out a stethoscope and placed the cold metal on his skin. "Breathe in," she said. "Again," she leaned in to him and her hair fell over his shoulder. "Your lungs sound good, but your pulse is fast," she said, oblivious to her effect on him.

"I think I will be fine, just sore, nothing broken," he said and she touched his face, looking at his red cheek. He took her hands in his. "You don't have to wear gloves to touch me."

She pulled her hands away and he was immediately sorry. "I have cuts on my hands from before and although they are almost healed, you are hurt. I won't risk any blood on blood contact."

He could have kicked himself. "I don't mean to make you sad every time we talk. I don't think sometimes before I speak."

She smiled. "You don't make me sad, Tommy. I am just sorry you have to think about this, too. It gets to be a pain in the ass."

He grinned. "I'm not perfect, you know. I have a few flaws."

"Oh really? Like what?" she took the washcloth and wiped his mouth. She touched the stubble on his face. "I'm listening."

"Sorry, I was distracted," he said. He felt things happening to him and he knew it was not something she could or should, see. He needed her to leave. "Listen, can we talk in the other room? I think I can take the rest from here."

She felt stung. "Sure, no problem," she threw out the gloves in the biohazard bag and walked out, closing the door behind her.

Tommy turned on the cold water and stuck his face and head under it. He berated himself for reacting to her touch that way. "Get a grip, man," he said and his breathing returned to normal. He wiped his face and looked in the mirror. He could still feel her hand on his cheek. He opened the door and walked out to the family room. She was sitting on the couch. "I'll be right there," he went into his room and quickly changed into a t-shirt and sweats. He walked out to join her. He saw she had been crying. "What's wrong?"

She looked at him, sadness again in her eyes. "Do I repulse you?"

He didn't think he heard her right. "Do you what?"

"Repulse you? I mean, I know it is hard to deal with what happened to me, I still can't even think about intimacy without getting anxious, but you are really nice and incredibly handsome and you always looked at me with respect, until now. Something happened and I made you uncomfortable. I just wanted to apologize," she said and held a pillow to her chest.

Tommy shook his head. "You couldn't be more wrong. What you saw in there was panic at the thought of you seeing just how much you got to me. I am feeling things for you that I have never felt for anyone. I would never want to hurt you or make you think that I expect something from you because I don't and I never would. I just need to figure out how to deal with myself," he sighed.

She felt something change in her at that moment. She felt a pull to him and she tried to stop it, but changed her mind. She moved closer and touched his face as she looked at him. "I would very much like it if you would kiss me," she looked deep into his eyes.

Tommy felt his eyes grow a little wet with unshed tears. He touched her beautiful red hair, long with curls and then he cupped her face in his hands. He smiled at her and she wiped the lone tear that escaped from his eye. "I would like that, too," he said and gently leaned into her, softly brushing his lips on hers at first and then pressing his mouth on hers.

Her lips were soft and full and he felt a rush of warmth flow through his body.

She touched his hair and returned the intensity of the kiss. It was sweet and passionate and full of hope.

After a moment, they broke the connection, both looking at each other. Tommy knew the magnitude of this for them and he just wanted her to be all right with it.

"Are you okay?" he asked her gingerly.

"Better than I have been in a long time," she leaned in to him and rested against him. "Thank you."

He shook his head and wrapped his arm around her. "No, thank you," he knew he would have to tell her about the paper, but that would wait. He needed this moment to be pure and happy for her. If nothing else, that he could do.

Chapter Twenty-One:

Jack waited until Stephanie had a full mouthful of food before he began. "I have a plan," he said the next morning at breakfast.

She chewed her cereal and swallowed. "Is that why you have been staring at me like that while I ate?" she wiped her mouth.

"I think we all need to get away for a while, you and me and Brittany and Tommy. We need to go somewhere warm and tropical, far away from all of this," Jack said. He reached and took her hands in his. "What do you say?"

She smiled. "You're sweet, but how is that going to help anything? Besides, I don't think Brittany is really able to travel. She has a lot of healing to do."

Jack stood up and walked over to her. "I know, and that's why I think it's perfect timing. Think about it, Steph, everything here reminds her of the pain and the fear. She and Tommy need to have time to find each other away from all of this. She is going to see the paper or the news soon enough and then she is going to get bombarded with her past. If we are all together, we can soften the blow and as for her health, we are all doctors, we can handle it."

Stephanie felt a lump in her throat. "You are the sweetest most romantic man in the world. I just worry that this is like running away, and I know from experience that your problems always find you."

"We aren't running. We are taking a break from the harshness and getting back to basics. We will come back, but when we do, it will be to a fresh view of everything," he stood up and walked to the counter. "I know it isn't the most ideal time, but the more I thought about it, the more it seemed right. Will you just think about it?"

Stephanie was quiet for a minute. "Can we all get time off?

"Already thought of that and I put in a request with the chief," he grinned. "So."

She laughed. "You are like a little kid," she walked over to him. "And I love every inch of you and your compassion. I am taking Brittany to her house in a while to get some things and I will feel out the situation. If she is amenable to it, then I think it is a great idea," she stepped on her tiptoes to kiss him.

"I have a surgery first thing and then I will talk to Tommy. I'll tell him what we are doing," Jack grabbed his keys off the counter.

"How about asking him? Telling him might be a bit presumptuous," Stephanie advised.

He waved her off. "Tommy always listens to me. He knows I am always right," he smiled at her and she laughed as he left.

"Good luck Tommy," she said aloud with a smile.

******

A few hours later, Jack and Tommy were in the locker room after both had completed particularly challenging surgeries. Tommy had been a little quiet and Jack was deciding the best approach.

"So, how was Brittany last night? Did you tell her about the paper?" Jack asked as he closed his locker.

Tommy looked at his friend. "She was good," he said, remembering the bathroom moment and the kiss. He had been thinking about her all morning. "But no, I didn't tell her."

Jack ran his hand through his hair and wiped his face. "You need to tell her. She is going to find out and it will be ten times better coming from you."

"I know, but there was a connection last night, and I wanted it to be only that, you know? Every memory she has is always tainted with something horrible. I wanted last night to be good," Tommy caught his friends' gaze and smiled. "What?"

"Connection? What kind of connection?" Jack's eyes twinkled.

"Nothing, it was just nice," he shrugged it off.

"Okay, I'll leave it for now, but only because I have an idea," Jack said.

"Great, you have an idea. How much is this going to backfire?" Tommy said sarcastically.

"Oh ye of little faith," Jack said. "Come on, walk with me while I impart my wisdom," Jack took his coat and walked out with Tommy.

****

"Are you sure you are up to this?" Stephanie asked Brittany as they drove to her house.

Brittany smiled. "I can't wear the same clothes every day, it's not really practical. Besides, this is where I live, this is the home I found for myself and this is where I feel safe in my own skin. Nothing bad has ever touched me here, Stephanie. I need a little normalcy," she pulled her hair up into a twist and Stephanie could see the remnants of the handprint still on her face. Her heart ached for her friend.

"Then I am glad you let me come with you. How did things go last night?" Stephanie asked, trying to gauge if Brittany saw the news.

"Tommy was a mess when he got home, thanks to the fight at the diner. Although I still don't know what caused it?" she thought back and realized he had never told her. "I guess we got distracted."

Stephanie lifted an eyebrow and smiled. "Distracted?"

"It was nothing, just a nice connection. I will have to ask him about the details later," she said, remembering the kiss for the hundredth time.

Stephanie nodded. "Okay," she pulled into the driveway. "Ready?"

Brittany smiled. "Yes," she stepped out of the car and used the cane to walk, Stephanie right beside her. They reached the door and Brittany went to get her key when Stephanie felt the hair on the back of her neck stand up.

"Stop," she said and Brittany looked at her.

"What is it?" she was alarmed at her friends' tone.

"It's open," Stephanie pushed the door and it swung open. Brittany felt her stomach jump as she stepped in and Stephanie dialed her phone.

"Oh God," Brittany said as she walked in. Her house had been ransacked. Everything had been thrown all over. Her books and her pictures were in shambles. She dropped her cane and forgetting about the pain in her foot, she ran to her bedroom. She saw all of her clothes thrown about, cut up. She moved to the one place she held sacred, the one room where she was safe. She collapsed on the floor when she saw it.

Stephanie dialed Jack's number through her shaking fingers. He picked up the phone on the second ring.

"Hi sweetheart," he purred.

"Jack I need you to listen quickly," Stephanie said through her tears.

"What's wrong?" he asked, hearing the panic in her voice. Tommy was with him and picked up on his alarm.

"We are on our way. Did you call the police? Okay. Don't move. I love you," he hung up and ran to his car, Tommy with him.

****

"What the fuck happened? How did he get to her house? Oh God, are they sure he isn't still there?" Tommy was having a panic attack while Jack drove them. He told him what Stephanie had said.

Jack gripped the wheel. "Stephanie wouldn't stay if she thought he could be there. She knows what to do," he tried to convince himself more than anything.

They drove in silence and when they got there, there were police cars all around the house. Jack stopped the car and they both jumped out. The police stopped them.

"You can't go in there, it's a crime scene," the guard said.

The officer who had been helping them at the precinct looked out of the house and told the guard they were safe to come in. They walked into the mess and both Jack and Tommy were speechless. "Steph?" Jack yelled. "Stephanie?"

Stephanie ran down the hall into his arms. He held her tightly and thanked God she was safe. She pulled away and looked at him.

"It's horrible. I didn't know what to do to help. I couldn't think of anything to say. She is just silent. I don't know what to do," she cried and Jack held her.

Tommy looked down the hall and ran toward the bedroom. He saw the cut up clothes and the overturned dresser. He looked in the bathroom and saw her medications all over the floor, but he didn't see her. He ran out of the room and saw immediately where she was. There were officers at the outside of a guest room, quietly talking to each other and motioning inside. He walked to the doorway and looked inside. She was sitting on the floor in the middle of what looked like torn sheets of music. There was a broken guitar at her feet and scores of cd's and awards broken in pieces. He looked up and saw on the wall, spray painted in what looked like blood red, the words, "You will only sing for me." "You are mine." "There is no place to hide."

He held his anger as best he could and walked over to her.

"Red, we need to leave. Let me get you out of here," he reached to her but she moved like he was poison. She held the broken pieces from her guitar in her hands, the jagged wood like a weapon, pointing at her.

He felt his eyes burn with unshed tears. "You need to look at me," he spoke firmly but gently. "Don't do this. Don't let him do this to you again," he reached to her hand and she flinched, but didn't move away. He took the piece of guitar she was holding and put it down. He looked around the room and realized this was her life from before. She had all of her music and all of her accomplishments and all she had hidden for so long. It was all here for her to use and enjoy in the privacy of her home where she could stop hiding. Now it was ruined and it seemed to deflate the last ounce of strength she had.

******

"Jack, I don't know what to do to help her. She just broke, you know? I can't imagine what would happen if that was me," Stephanie cried into his arms and Jack held her protectively.

"Shhh, we will help her. She is not alone and together, we will all show her how much she has to live for," he looked at his wife with concern. "Baby, you need to try to calm down. I am worried about you," he took her small wrist in his hand and checked her pulse. "I don't want you to have a relapse."

She took a deep breath. "I know, and I am trying. I am just so mad."

"I know. How about I take you home?" Jack knew the answer to that. "I know; we aren't leaving without them."

"Family has to stick together," Stephanie said through her tears.

"And that is why I love you," he said and they walked to the room to try and help.

Jack stepped to the doorway and felt the bile rise to his throat when he saw the scene before him. Brittany was sitting in a heap in the middle of the floor and Tommy was next to her, his head in his hands. Stephanie stood silently beside him. He looked to the officers. "Can you give us all a minute alone?"

The officers nodded and walked away. Jack and Stephanie walked into the room. Jack motioned to Tommy and he walked over to them, out of Brittany's earshot, although it didn't appear she was listening to anything. He looked at them with wet eyes. "I don't know what to do," he was fighting his fear and his feelings, trying to stay strong. His quivering chin gave him away.

Stephanie touched his arm. "You can get through to her, Tommy. You just need to show her that you aren't like the rest. With you, she is safe," Stephanie touched his chest. "Talk to her from here."

Jack held his wife to him and they stood back as Tommy wiped his eyes and moved back to her. He sat down opposite her and reached again for her hands. She made no move to resist.

"Red, everything that has happened in the last few days has been real. You are not alone in this. This animal will get caught and you will be free. You and I have something special starting here and you can't give up on me. Please look at me," he touched her face with his hand and tilted it up to look at him. He yelled for Jack and Stephanie.

"Call an ambulance. Get me some gloves," he said as he saw her eyes roll back in her head. She had blood running from her nose and her mouth. He gathered her in his arms and moved her to the one area of the room that was relatively clear. He laid her down and saw a blood spot on her abdomen where her bandage was and her foot was bleeding through. "Oh no, please, Brittany, look at me," he said to her, but she didn't respond. Stephanie handed him gloves and Jack put some on as well. They all worked on her, applying pressure to her wounds and taking her vitals. Stephanie held her friends hand while the men worked on her. She spoke softly to her and encouraged her to hang on.

"I knew I should have checked her platelets. She was bruising and not healing correctly. She should have been in the fucking hospital," Tommy cried.

Jack looked at his friend as he worked on applying pressure to her foot. "Tommy, stop it. You did right by her and you need to stop this. No one could see what would happen and you did what she wanted," he moved as the paramedics came in and hooked her up to oxygen. Jack gave them the details and her medical history. They loaded her onto the stretcher and Jack took Tommy by the arm. "Go with her, we will meet you there."

Tommy nodded and followed them out. Jack stood there and removed his gloves, letting his own frustration come out. He picked up a piece of the broken guitar and flung it against the wall. Stephanie took his hand in hers.

"What kind of person does this? Who is this deranged and sick?" he looked at Stephanie. "Tommy won't be able to handle it if she dies. He can't go through this again. He won't make it," Jack put his hand over his face.

Stephanie smoothed his hair and hugged him. "I am so proud of you. You are a pillar of strength for me and for Tommy. He will get through anything because of your support."

"If it were you, baby, I wouldn't make it," he said softly, wiping his hand over his face.

"Yes you would. It would be your love for me that would help you to pick up the pieces. Love should enable you to withstand the most horrible of situations. You have shown me that. Now let's focus on what we can do right now and help our friends heal. Tommy needs his family now and that's what we will give him. You can lean on me when you need to," she put her arm around his waist and walked out with him, stepping over the mess.

****

Tommy waited outside of the room as they worked feverishly on Brittany. He turned and saw Julie run in and hug him.

"How is she? What happened?" Julie asked. "Why are you in scrubs?"

"I had her blood all over me. I had to change," he said, still looking into the room.

"Are you okay?" Julie asked him. "Look at me, are you okay?" she demanded.

Tommy looked at his sister and saw the fear in her eyes. He hugged her. "I'm fine."

"I am just worried about you. Tommy, what happened?" Julie asked.

"Thrombocytopenia, most likely. She is bleeding internally, probably from her low immune system and a possible infection. I think the shock of what she saw in her house just destroyed her ability to fight," he crossed his arms over his body.

"Then you just have to fix her." Julie said. He looked at her. "What? You don't think you can? I know you, and you can do anything you put your mind to. You are my hero," she hugged him. "And the best big brother in the world."

Tommy wiped his eyes and hugged her back. "Thank you," he kissed her head. "Go home, love your husband and relax. I will call if there is any change."

Julie squeezed his arm. "Bill is bringing dinner and we will be in the waiting room. Wherever you are is where we will be," she turned and smiled as Jack and Stephanie walked in. She went to meet Bill.

Tommy filled them in on what he knew. Stephanie walked into the room to get an update. Jack stood next to his friend. "How are you holding up?"

Tommy shrugged. "I'm great."

"She is going to make it," Jack said.

"Don't think so," he said.

Jack looked at him. "You might want to work on your pep talk," he crossed his arms and sighed. "I know you're scared, man, but you just have to go in there and tell her why she needs to fight," he squeezed his friends' shoulder. "It won't be easy, dude, but love never is."

Tommy looked at him. "Who said anything about love?"

Jack just smiled. "My mistake."

Stephanie walked out to them and sighed. "She is in rough shape. Her platelets are dangerously low so they started steroids and are giving her a transfusion. She is running a low-grade fever and there is probably an infection somewhere. She has lost weight since she was here a few days ago and her electrolytes are out of whack," she looked at Tommy. "She needs you to be strong for her. This is not about what that guy did or what she has been through. This is about where she is in life now and what she is building with you. Tommy, whatever you are feeling, she is feeling it, too," she hugged him. "I just want you both to be happy."

Tommy hugged her back and wiped his eyes. He smiled at them and walked into the room. The nurses were moving away from the bed and Brittany was awake, but sedated. She had oxygen on her face and her blue eyes were red and bloodshot. Her skin was pale and almost translucent. He sat down and picked up her hand. "I'm sorry," he said softly. "I should have taken better care of you."

She looked at him and her eyes filled with tears. She squeezed his hand and then flat lined.

Chapter Twenty-Two:

How many times, as a doctor, had he heard that sound? 'Code blue' 'crash cart'; they seemed like normal parts of the English language. But now, hearing them here, about Brittany, well it seemed like they were speaking a foreign language. He saw Jack and Stephanie rush in and begin working on her, he let himself be pulled away, he saw her eyes still staring at him, but she wasn't there, at least not at that moment.

Jack was working on her, Stephanie was calling out orders, and he was just standing there. CPR was being done. There was a beat, and then nothing. He saw them look at him and look back at her. What was he supposed to do? He was a doctor and he had nothing. He felt like he was in a fog. Maybe he was dying too?

"Tommy, talk to her, dammit. You need to talk to her," Jack yelled at him and Tommy looked at them. He snapped out of his stupor and walked over to the side of the bed. He leaned in and put his hand on her forehead.

"Hey, Red, don't leave, okay? I know it seems like the easy thing to do, but it's not. The hardest thing about going through life is going through life. You know, when I lost my parents, I wanted to die. I didn't know how to go on without them. I was a kid and I had a kid sister and no idea what to do, but I realized something really important then. It isn't about what's easy. I had more to do on this earth and so do you. You have too much to offer the world and it's not fair to leave," he leaned in closer to her. "You can't just start something with me and then leave me alone. I won't survive. I don't care if it's selfish, I need you," he put his head down and kissed her forehead. He sat back and let his tears fall, his head in his hand.

"We have a rhythm," he heard them say. He looked at Jack who was smiling at him with relief. He looked down at Brittany who was struggling to breathe. He rubbed her cheek with his hand and smiled at her. "You came back," he said to her. "You came back," he held her gaze as she looked at him, staying grounded in his eyes.

****

Jack and Stephanie sat in the lounge after working on Brittany. They were both exhausted and lost in thought. Stephanie instinctively reached out to take his hand. "I know," he said to her.

"You were amazing. I almost lost it when Tommy willed her to come back. I just need everyone to be happy and safe," she scooted closer to him and rested her head on his shoulder.

He wrapped his arm around hers. "I know; we all need a happy ending to this horrible nightmare."

****

Tommy sat next to the bed and held Brittany's hand. He was monitoring her vitals and checking her bandages. They had placed a pressure bandage on her abdomen and he knew how uncomfortable that must be. She had been going in and out of consciousness, but she hadn't said anything yet. He leaned closer to her and ran his hand through her hair. He thought about the mess at her house and what that guy did. He thought about the room he found her in and the destruction of her history. He knew they were just 'things', but he also knew how important ties to your past could be. He looked at her and moved closer to her face, so she could hear him over the machines.

"Red, I'm still here with you. I know you are fighting a tremendous amount of pain, but if you can fight your way through to opening your eyes, I will help you do the rest," he traced her jaw line with his fingers. "I am really not very good at this kind of thing, kind of out of my element. But I'll do whatever you need. I'll learn to be the man you deserve." He looked at her and she opened her eyes and tried to focus on him. "Hey, I'm here," he said close to her. "You're okay," he smiled at her.

"Liar," she whispered and closed her eyes again.

He just looked at her. "Can you look at me again? Please?"

She struggled to open her eyes, but finally managed to focus on him. He wiped the tears, which slid down the side of her face. "I'm scared," she said. "I'm cold and I'm scared," she couldn't control the quivering of her chin or the shaking of her body. "I don't want this to be the end."

He felt his heart tearing in two as he looked at her. "Then it won't be. You are going to get through this. This is nothing. You have survived so much, this is nothing," he spoke and tucked the blanket tighter around her.

"It hurts to breathe. It hurts to think. It hurts to be alone," she cried silently, closing her eyes again.

"I know, and that is why we will make sure neither one of us is alone again," he kissed her hand and stood up and moved to the bed. He gently sat on the side and faced her. He placed another blanket on her. "I will help you get warm. I will make you feel safe. I will help you heal," he rubbed her arms as she looked at him.

"What can I do for you?" she asked him through her closed eyes.

He held her hand. "Just live."

******

Jack and Stephanie pulled into their house later that night. Tommy had promised to call if anything changed, but Jack needed to get Stephanie home. They walked into the house and collapsed onto the couch.

"I think I want to sleep for a week," she said.

"I hear you. I can't believe the day we had. It started so full of promise. I was going to convince Tommy to go on a vacation with us, and now he is just trying to convince Brittany to live," he shook his head and looked at her. "Are you sure you feel okay?"

She stretched. "I could use a massage," she said with a grin, "In the bathtub."

Jack looked at her. "Okay, tell me how that goes," he looked down and she tossed a pillow at him.

"If you can't find time to get naked with your wife, than I guess I will have to amuse myself," she stood up and turned to leave. She squealed as he picked her up from behind.

"I was kidding. But now that you said that, can I watch?" he leaned in and nibbled on her ear.

"Only if you do exactly as I say," she said and they walked to the bathroom, shedding their clothes along the way. A few moments they were sitting in the tub, Stephanie's back up against Jack's chest. She was rubbing her hands up and down his thighs. He massaged her shoulders and she melted against him. They were both quiet for a while.

"What are you thinking about?" Jack asked her as wrapped his arms around her chest.

"Nothing, everything. I just keep remembering when it was you lying in the hospital bed and I was so afraid you would leave me. I know I keep saying the right words to Tommy, but in truth, I wouldn't want to live in a world without you," she wiped her face.

Jack turned her slightly to look at him. "That's not going to happen. We have been through so much already, and we survived, it hasn't always been pretty, but there has always been love. I knew from the moment I saw you that my life would never be the same, and it hasn't. It has been monumentally better. He pulled her face to his for a deep kiss.

****

Tommy made his way from the lounge back towards her room. He had gone to get more coffee and to use the restroom. He had been sitting almost all night and she had not been awake at all. Her platelets were a bit higher due to the transfusion, but he knew it might not last. He didn't know what the day would bring for her.

He was almost there when he heard her scream. He ran to the room and saw her thrashing in the bed, screaming for someone to get away. There was a male nurse standing over her with a look of fear.

"I was just going to check her bandage. I moved her blanket and she just flipped out," he said.

Tommy looked at him. "Just go, I'll check her. I thought I made it clear that no men were to examine her without her consent," he was livid.

"I'm sorry Dr. Williams, I didn't know," the nurse stammered and left.

Brittany's eyes were opened and she was very agitated. Tommy sat on the bed and took her hands in his own. "You're okay, you're safe," he repeated calmly.

She looked at him and his mere presence seemed to calm her down. "I don't want anyone to look at my body. I don't want anyone to touch me," she said and closed her eyes, breathing heavily. "I still smell him on me. I feel so dirty," she pulled the blanket up

"You're not dirty. No one will touch you, Red. I'll make sure of it. Can you look at me?" he pleaded with her, his neediness in his voice.

She opened her eyes and looked at him. "I won't hurt you, ever. Do you trust me?" he asked softly.

She nodded.

"Then let me help you. Can I check your bandage?" he asked, never taking his eyes off her. "You know it's important to make sure it's okay."

She nodded again, although a few tears escaped. He wiped them away and she touched his hand. He swallowed and nodded, putting on gloves. He moved her blanket and she closed her eyes as he gently lifted the hospital gown to look at her abdomen. He checked the pressure bandage and saw it seemed to be holding. He hoped they could remove it later, as it had to be uncomfortable. He checked all around and put the gown back down and then covered her with the blankets. He looked at her, her eyes still shut.

"Brittany, please look at me," he took off the gloves and touched her face. "All done, everything looks great," he smiled. "You're going to be fine."

She looked at him and didn't say anything. She just took his hand in hers and held it to her heart.

******

Jack walked in to see Brittany the next morning and saw Tommy sprawled out on a chair, asleep. He smiled as he walked over and put the coffee he had brought for his friend on the table. He looked at Brittany who was also asleep. He checked her vitals and sat down next to the bed. He looked at the scene and remembered the past, when he sat with Tommy after his parent's car accident. The situation was different, but Tommy still looked like that same 18-year-old boy who had to grow up so fast. Julie had only been 12 years old. Jack remembered how he admired his friend. He seemed to be able to transition from a high school graduate now in the middle of his first year of college to a father to his sister and the man of the house.

"How long have you been sitting there?" Tommy said as he rubbed his eyes.

"They called me to come in because your snoring was keeping the whole floor awake," Jack said with a smile.

Tommy gave him a look. "I don't snore."

"Sure, and I am not devastatingly handsome," Jack quipped. He stood up and handed Tommy the coffee from the table. "Here, drink this before you scare someone."

Tommy took a sip of the hot liquid and exhaled, looking at Brittany. "I wish she would stay awake for more than five minutes at a time."

Jack nodded. "You know that sleep is the best way for her to heal," he said. "Has she said anything to you yet?"

Tommy shook his head. "Not really. She has been having nightmares, I can only imagine what about, but she won't talk about it."

"She will, just give her time. Sometimes the heart can only deal with one thing at a time," Jack said. "Trust me, I am the best cardiac surgeon there is."

Tommy snorted. "As named by yourself," he stood up and stretched. "As a fellow, less narcissistic surgeon, I agree."

"Good. How about you go home for a bit. I will stay here with her," Jack said.

"I don't want to leave. She had a rough time when a male nurse came in to check her bandage and I promised no one would touch her," he sighed. "You should have seen the fear in her eyes, like she was going to be attacked all over again."

Jack nodded. "How about you go lay down in one of the on-call rooms and I'll page you if she needs you. You won't be any good to her if you pass out from exhaustion. I'll make sure no one touches her."

Tommy looked at her and then at Jack. "Okay, I'll be down the hall, but call me if there is any issue."

Jack assured him and Tommy left. Jack sat down next to the bed and sighed. He had watched Stephanie for many an hour just like this, during a particularly aggressive exacerbation. He knew the turmoil Tommy must be going through. He saw her open her eyes and he smiled at her. "Hey, how are you doing?"

Brittany smiled at him. "I'm okay. It's good to see you."

Jack laughed. "After looking at Tommy for so long, I can appreciate the sentiment."

"Where is he?" she asked him.

"He went to take a nap in an on call room. Do you mind that I'm here?" he wanted to make sure she was comfortable.

"Of course not. I am very glad you are here and that he took a break. He's exhausted," she closed her eyes. "It will also give me a chance to talk to you."

He looked at her. "Of course, do you need something from me?"

She took a deep breath. "Kind of. I need you to help Tommy when I'm gone. He doesn't want to admit what we all know."

Jack looked at her. "And what's that?"

"I am probably not going to get out of this, Jack," she said softly.

"You don't know that. You are such a strong and capable woman, Brittany, don't give up on yourself," he couldn't help but see Stephanie in her position.

"Besides, I am going to be a father and there is only one person Stephanie and I want to help bring our child into the world."

She sighed. "There are plenty of Obstetricians on staff. I am just worried about how Tommy will get by. I need you to promise me you will help him. You need to make him move on with his life. I need to know you will do that for me."

He swallowed a lump in his throat. "Tommy and I have always had each other's backs, and now is no different. I don't want you to give up, Brittany, but if the worst happens, then I will be there for Tommy."

She smiled. "Good, thank you," she closed her eyes.

Chapter Twenty-Three:

Stephanie came by Brittany's room when she was finished for the day and saw Jack sitting there. She walked in and smiled at her husband. Brittany was sitting up and Jack was asleep in the chair. She grinned at her friend and walked over to Jack. She touched his cheek and he sat up quickly.

"What's wrong?" he asked, startled until he saw her. "Oh, I was just keeping Brittany company while Tommy slept."

Brittany stifled a laugh along with Stephanie. Jack looked at them. "What? I just closed my eyes for a second," he smiled a dimpled grin.

"Why don't you go home and I will hang out with Brittany for a bit," Stephanie said as she ran her hand through Jack's hair.

"I am okay alone. You guys don't need to baby-sit me," Brittany smiled.

Jack looked at her. "Tommy will kill me if you are left alone. Besides, we like you," he said simply.

"I want some alone time with my doctor. We will be fine," she leaned in and kissed him.

"Okay, but call me if you need anything," Jack returned the kiss and smiled at Brittany before leaving.

"Finally," Stephanie smiled and came over to sit on the side of the bed. "I was so glad you had me paged. Are you really feeling better?"

Brittany smiled. "I am feeling stronger. I need to apologize to Jack for my state earlier. I was feeling less than optimistic and I think I was a little depressing. I told him to take care of Tommy if I didn't make it."

Stephanie took her friends hand. "I understand why you feel the need to protect Tommy, but you need to just concentrate on getting better. It is hard to admit this as a doctor, but there is a lot more than medicine that you need to get better. You need faith and you need family. I know how important both those things are."

Brittany shook her head. "I am beginning to realize that. That's why I wanted you to help me," she smiled and told Stephanie what she wanted to do.

****

Jack took Stephanie's hand as they sat at a table in their favorite Italian restaurant later that evening. He gazed into her eyes and she smiled. "I think this dinner is exactly what we needed."

"I am just glad we had a calmer day today. Brittany really seemed to be better and I only hope she continues on the path to recovery. I would love to be able to go away with them like you wanted. I think we all need the break," Stephanie took a sip of her water.

"What did she want to talk to you about? Is everything okay?" Jack ate some bread.

"She wanted to do something for Tommy and she needed some help," she sighed.

"What is it?" he asked.

"She just won't talk about what happened at her house. I wonder if she blocked it out or something. It's like she is just avoiding dealing with it. I wonder if I should have pushed it," Stephanie took a bite of her salad.

"I think that right now she just needs to get stronger. She will have to face everything in time. I just hope she doesn't shut down on Tommy or us. If I have learned anything from you, it is the importance of family. Brittany will see that, too. She will see she is not alone. Stephanie, that is a powerful feeling, to belong to something, be connected to someone. I am so grateful you have shown me that," he spoke from the heart.

"No, Jack, you showed me that. You wouldn't let me fall apart. You made me walk back into my life and it was the greatest gift I have ever received. Now we are going to show our child the same thing," she reached out and took his hand in hers. "We are the luckiest family."

****

Tommy walked back toward Brittany's room, feeling much better after sleeping in an actual bed. He showered, but didn't shave, so he was sporting a nice five o'clock shadow. He made a mental note to get rid of that later. He walked to her room and stood at the door, shocked at what he saw. She was sitting up in bed, with a fancy blue hospital gown on. Her hair was loosely piled on her head with strands of curls framing her face. She had some lip gloss on which brightened her complexion and there was a table set up next to the bed with a small tablecloth and two covered plates. She smiled when she saw him.

"Hi," she said shyly.

Tommy walked in. "Hi. What's all of this?"

She smiled. "I thought we could have a thank you dinner. We have never really had dinner together, and I know it's not much, but I wanted you to know how much I appreciate what you have done for me," her eyes shined with unshed tears of appreciation.

He swallowed the lump in his throat and sat down next to the bed. "You don't have to thank me for anything."

"But that's where you're wrong," she sighed. "I'm not going to lie, Tommy, I don't know if I will recover from this," he began to interrupt her but she stopped him. "I am just being realistic, not fatalistic. All I know is that since I met you, my life has become infinitely better than it was before. I have a reason to fight for my life now and you gave me that reason. I don't mean to make you uncomfortable or make more out of what we have than you feel, but the more I think about it, the more I see that the way I viewed my life was wrong. Maybe I don't have to be alone. Maybe I can offer something to a relationship. Maybe I can learn to trust that something extraordinary is possible," she looked at him.

"I don't know what to say. I don't know how to thank you for that. You are not making me uncomfortable. You are not making more out of what I feel. I am grateful that you trust me enough to let me take care of you. I am thankful you are giving yourself a chance to see where this might go and I am amazed at the amount of strength you have. I am honored to be someone you feel is worth taking that risk," he took her hand in his and held it before they ate.

She looked at him after they were finished. "I need to talk to you about something, not to ruin the mood, but it's important."

"Okay, I'm listening," he said.

"My health is precarious at best. There is a chance that my immune system won't be able to recover from this and I could develop AIDS. " She looked into his eyes. "You don't need to see that. You don't need to be a part of that. I understand what I will be facing, but I don't want you to have to watch me go through that."

Tommy looked at her and smiled. "If I was diagnosed with cancer, would you leave me to suffer alone? If I became paralyzed or somehow incapacitated, would you run away?"

She nodded, "No, of course not."

"Than why on earth would you think I would let you be alone? Do you think I'm that shallow that I wouldn't want to see you through something like that? I know you are HIV positive. I also know that you are more than that. If there comes a time where your immune system fails, then we will deal with it together. I am not leaving. You're stuck," he smiled.

"I'm sorry, I don't think you're shallow, it's just that it's an ugly disease and I want you to look at me with your eyes open," she said.

He leaned in to her and touched her face. "I see you for who you are, Red, and I wouldn't change a thing."

She touched his hand. "Okay," she leaned back and closed her eyes, suddenly exhausted.

"Are you okay?" he asked, looking at her vitals.

"Yes, just tired," she opened her eyes and looked at him. "You never told me why you and Jack got into a fight with those guys at the diner."

Tommy sighed. "It's not important right now. Why don't you just rest?"

She looked at him. "I can't sleep. Every time I close my eyes I see my house and what he did," she felt fresh tears fall. "Every time I see someone come in to check my bandages I feel dirty. I am a mess of emotions and although I understand what's happening, I can't stop the fear from creeping in."

He held her hand in his and rubbed her arm. "I know, but we are going to work on that."

"I just want to go home, but now, I don't really have anywhere to go," she looked at him. "You know he will find me," she closed her eyes again.

Tommy felt his anger rise. "Over my dead body."

Chapter Twenty-Four:

Brittany had finally fallen asleep after having another nightmare. Tommy was going to check on some of his charts when he heard the commotion outside. He went to see what was going on and saw the hospital police trying to remove a bunch of what appeared to be paparazzi from the hall. He made his way to the nurse's station and inquired about the mess.

"Apparently there is an unnamed singing sensation in the hospital somewhere. We don't know who or where, but I know it has to be huge if they are here to get a scoop. Do you know anything?" the nurse smiled at Tommy.

He didn't say anything, just turned and walked down the hall to the group of reporters. He stayed back and listened to them ask about Barbara Rose. They had gotten a scoop that she had been found after all of these years and was injured. They wanted a statement. The police were keeping them at bay, but Tommy knew it was only a matter of time before they found her. He turned to go back to the room when he saw Dr. Lacey walk by. He knew she was a coworker of Brittany's, so he smiled as he walked by. He heard her talk to the nurse about Stephanie and he stopped.

"Is Dr. Stephens here?" he asked.

"Hi Dr. Williams. Yes, she and Jack are down in room 1405," she saw his concern. "She is okay, you can go see."

"Thanks," Tommy said. He looked towards Brittany's room but decided to go make sure Jack and Stephanie were okay. He walked past the cameras and down to the room. He knocked on the open door and saw them sitting on chairs.

"What happened? Are you okay?" Tommy asked.

Stephanie smiled. "I'm fine and the baby's fine. I just got a little light headed and Jack made me come in. Everything looks perfect."

"She almost fainted after we ate," Jack said as he kept his arm protectively around her. "How did you know we were here?"

"I saw Dr. Lacey in the hall and she told me you were here. She didn't say why," Tommy said. "Are you sure you're okay? Can I do anything?"

Stephanie stood up and hugged him. "I am fine and we are going to go home," she looked at Jack and he nodded.

"Walk with me, okay?" Jack said to Tommy.

"It's okay, I know what you want to talk about. I saw the cameras," he sighed. "I don't know what to tell her. I wish I could take her out of here, but she is too weak and she needs care. I am open to ideas," he smiled sadly.

Stephanie looked at Jack and he returned the knowing look. "Do you think three doctors could handle what she needs?"

Tommy looked at each of them. "What are you two talking about?"

Stephanie grinned. "This was all Jack's idea, and before everything happened with Brittany's house, we were going to talk to you guys about it. We want to go away for a while, the four of us. A chance to leave all of the pain and the memories here and just heal. We all need the break. What do you think?"

Tommy shook his head. "It sounds wonderful, but I don't think she will want to go. I don't know how she is going to react to the people here."

"I think you should bring it up and see what happens. Brittany is a lot stronger than I think we have been giving her credit for. She is also falling for you, Tommy. You would be surprised what someone would do for those they care about," Stephanie yawned.

"I am going to take Stephanie home. How about you see if she is open to the idea," Jack said.

"Okay, thanks. I'm really glad you're okay, Stephanie," he said and turned to go back to Brittany. He would love to get her out of here. They all could use the distraction, and he wanted her to be able to let loose and just relax. He put his head down as he walked past the reporters still milling about. He walked into her room and she was sitting up, brushing her hair. She smiled when she saw him.

"Hi," she said. "I though maybe you went home."

"Nope, just went to see Stephanie. She had a fainting spell and Jack brought her in to be checked out."

"Oh no, is she okay? I should go see her," she said.

"She is fine, already released. Her pressure was normal and they are running a full panel to check everything. Dr. Lacey checked her out," Tommy smiled. "You need to relax, although I am happy to see you awake and alert."

"My platelets are almost in a respectable range. I am feeling better than I have in a while," she pulled her hair up into a twist. "I want to get out of here. I really don't want to stay in the hospital."

Tommy was silent for a moment. He didn't know what to say first. "I need to talk to you about something," he said softly.

"Okay, but I feel like I'm not going to like this," she said. "Stephanie is okay, right? You told me the truth?"

"Of course I did. I wouldn't lie to you," he said.

"I know that. I just don't want you to hide anything from me, because you think I can't handle it," she said.

He nodded and stood up to move closer to her when the commotion that had been kept at bay, came all the way down the hall. There were yells from the police and the journalists and cameras flashing into the rooms. Before Tommy could do anything a photographer stood in the doorway and flashed the camera in Brittany's face.

"I got her! This has to be her," the man yelled before the police tackled him. They cuffed him and placed him under arrest for intimidation and trespassing. The cop nodded his apology and reached in to close the door to the room.

Tommy looked at Brittany. She was sitting in her bed with her eyes wide. She looked at him. "This isn't real. This can't be happening," she said to herself.

He walked to the bed and sat down. "It's okay, we can deal with this. No one has to know anything you don't want them to know."

She looked at him. "You don't understand," she had a cold look on her face, almost detached. "I think I want to be alone for a bit, if you don't mind. I am feeling better, so you don't have to worry so much. Why don't you go home, have dinner with Julie and Bill and relax."

"I don't want to leave you," he said simply. "Why can't it be what I want? You know, you're all cryptic about your life and what you've been through, but you're not the only one who has a past. I may not be famous, but I have had a hell of a lot to deal with in my life, too. You act like I can't possibly understand what you are going through, and maybe you're right, but you also don't know what I go through. I am not even sure you care," he paced around the room. "You know what? You're right; I am leaving. I am going to go home and spend a nice quiet evening away from all of things that I can't 'understand'," he turned and stormed out of her room, slamming the door behind him.

****

Jack tucked Stephanie into bed and sat on the covers next to her. He traced a line up and down her arm as he looked at her stomach. He rubbed a circle on her sweater and she played with his hair.

"Hi baby, it's daddy and mommy. You gave us our first scare tonight. I know we signed up for a lifetime of scares, but we were hoping you could wait until you could look at us, face to face. We have a few ground rules that are really important, and we think it's time you heard them," he leaned in and kissed her stomach. "First of all, never go to bed angry. My mom used to always tell me that. You never know what the next day will bring and you always need to keep those you love in your heart in a positive light. We can get angry and mad, but if we love someone, we have to let them know that," Stephanie put her hand on his hand and closed her eyes. "Also, your mom has this habit of snoring sometimes," he felt her swat his head. "She is kind of sensitive about it, so I try not to bring it up," he smiled at her and looked back at her stomach. "Anyway, we know you are working hard at growing and we just want you to know how much we love you and how much you are wanted," he laid his head on her stomach and she smiled in contentment, hoping Tommy was able to talk Brittany into going away with them.

Chapter Twenty-Five:

"So, where should we go?" Stephanie asked as she looked on her laptop the next morning. "Somewhere warm or cold?"

Jack was sitting next to her on the couch, staring at her. "Somewhere warm would allow for a skimpy bikini," his eyes twinkled at her.

She smiled. "But somewhere cold would allow for a secluded cabin with lots of snuggling."

He leaned towards her. "You're right. But we could snuggle in the tropics as well."

"Yes, but if you are newly together with someone and you want more chances to need to be close, perhaps the cabin idea is better," Stephanie said slyly.

"But we aren't newly together," he said and then smiled. "Why Dr. Stephens, you are a little matchmaker."

"I just want them to get out of their own way and sometimes circumstances can help," she shrugged. "I'm just saying."

He leaned over and kissed her. She pulled him to her for a longer kiss, but the doorbell interrupted them. Jack looked at her. "Did you order a pizza?"

She swatted at him. "No, just because I'm pregnant, doesn't mean I am always hungry," she laughed. "But now that you mentioned it, I could eat something."

He laughed and went to see who it was. He looked through the peephole and opened the door. "Hey, come in," he said to Tommy who was standing there, looking forlorn.

"Hi Tommy," Stephanie said as she closed the laptop and put it aside. "Do you want something to drink?"

He shook his head. "No thanks," he said.

"Come in and sit down," Stephanie said and smiled. Jack walked over and sat down next to her. Tommy sat in the chair across from them.

"So, what's up?" Jack asked him. "Things didn't go well?"

Tommy looked at them. "I think I screwed up big time."

Stephanie looked at Jack and he smiled. "I doubt that. Tell us what happened."

"I yelled at her last night and then stormed out of the hospital," Tommy said and crossed his arms. "I am an idiot."

Stephanie looked at him. "What happened?"

Tommy relayed the story about the photographer and Brittany's reaction. He then told them how he exploded at her and left. Jack shook his head. "Dude, that's not so bad."

"Tommy, why don't you tell her why you're afraid for her, show her that you value her feelings and aren't going to be turned away by them. She also needs to understand where you are coming from. Why don't you tell her some of your story?" Stephanie looked at him. "I think some of this is hard for Brittany because she feels like no one understands what she has been through, and therefore, no one can help. I used to feel the same way. It took someone who cared about me enough to push me on my issues. Jack didn't let me run and hide anymore. He made me face life and I discovered that what I was hiding from was the very thing I needed more than anything. Tommy, you have suffered extraordinary loss in your life and I think if you open up a little to her, she just may realize how much you can understand."

Tommy was touched by her candor. He looked at her. "How do I know if she even cares?"

Jack looked at his friend. "I think the fuzz on the floor knows she cares."

Tommy rolled his eyes at him and Jack laughed. "We can all see it, Tommy. She cares. I think it's more than cares, actually, but that's just me. You only need to decide if you care."

Stephanie stood up. "I am going to call the hospital and see how Brittany's doing. I think we should all go and have lunch with her. Maybe we can help," she walked into the other room and made the call.

"Your wife is something else," Tommy said. "How did you get so lucky?"

Jack shrugged. "I ask myself that every day," he looked at Tommy. "We both just want you to be happy."

Stephanie came back in and sighed. "We might have a problem."

Tommy felt his stomach lurch. "What is it? What happened?"

"Brittany checked herself out of the hospital last night," Stephanie said.

Tommy sighed dejectedly. "Of course she did," he ran his hand through his hair. "This is all my fault. I knew how upset she would be about the press and what the fuck did I do? I yelled at her and stormed out like a child. Why would she trust me? Why would she even want to see me?" he stood up and paced around the room. "What if they followed her? She isn't ready to be out of the hospital. She is probably going to need another transfusion to keep her platelets up. Just because she feels better doesn't mean she is better," he realized he was rambling and turned to look at them. "What do I do?"

Stephanie looked at Jack who nodded. "Where do you think she would go?"

Tommy looked at him. "I don't know."

Stephanie walked over to him. "I think you do."

Tommy nodded. "I'll let you know what happens."

Jack let him out and turned to Stephanie. "Should I go with him?"

"No, he needs to do this on his own," she put her arms around his waist and hugged him to her. "I can't imagine the fear she must be feeling. Brittany has to deal with this entire trauma while trying to hide from everyone for fear that her secrets will be tabloid fodder. I don't how she deals with that."

Jack rested his cheek on her head, a position he loved. He breathed in her shampoo scent and closed his eyes. "I love you."

She rubbed his back. "I love you more."

*****

Tommy pulled up to Brittany's house in the bright sunlight of the day. He didn't know if she was here, but he figured it was his best bet. He went to the door and knocked, but the door was still broken. He opened it and stepped over the caution tape. "Red?" he asked as he walked in. He looked around and saw the mess as they had left it. He walked down the hallway and looked in the room he had found her in before. She was sitting in the middle of the room again, trying to piece together some of the music. He knocked on the door and she looked up, her blue eyes a bit brighter than before. "I knocked, but you didn't come out. I hope it's okay that I came."

She nodded. "Of course, but I didn't think you would want to see me anymore."

He walked over to her. "Why not?"

She shrugged. "You're right, you know. I am selfish. I guess I have been alone for so long I don't know how to let people in. I also don't know how to listen," she looked at him. "I want to know more about you, Tommy. I want to know what you've been through. I want to help, but I think everything just got so messed up."

He smiled as he joined her on the floor. "I don't think you're selfish. I think you're amazing. I think I acted like a child last night," he looked at the walls and then at her. "Why did you come back here?"

She smiled sadly. "This is my home. I didn't know where else to go."

He took her hand in his. "You should be in the hospital."

She looked at him. "I couldn't stay there. I need to protect myself and I just couldn't stay there," she fingered the torn papers in her hand.

"What is this?" he asked her, touching the music.

She smiled. "This was the first song I ever wrote. I had always kept it with me to remind me where I started. I guess it was kind of a security blanket," she put it down.

"Maybe we can fix all of this?" he stood up and walked around the room. He picked up a broken frame and saw there was a platinum record broken inside. "Oh Red, I'm so sorry this happened," he said to her. This room was her only tie to her past and it was truly in shambles. He couldn't imagine if this had happened to his parents' things. He would be destroyed.

She stood up and limped over to him. "Tommy, I really am sorry for how I have treated you. You deserve a lot more."

He put down the broken frame and touched her face.

"You have nothing to be sorry for," he pulled her to him and hugged her. She let him hold her and she rested her head on his chest. She felt her heart beat faster and felt a sense of comfort that only he seemed to bring to her. She pulled away and looked at him.

"What do we do now?" she asked him.

He brushed her hair behind her ear. "Well, we survived our first fight, so I think we should celebrate," he smiled at her.

"Oh really? What do we do to celebrate?" she asked him with a smile.

"I think a trip is in order," he blurted out, not meaning to bring it up like that, but now that it was out, he went with it. "What do you say? Will you go away with me and Jack and Stephanie?"

"I'm sorry, what did you say?" Brittany said as she backed away from him slightly.

Tommy got nervous that maybe it was not the right thing to do. "It was actually Jack's idea. He wanted to take Stephanie away for a vacation and they both thought it would be nice for us to get away, too," he moved closer to her and took her hands in his. "I am not trying to be too forward, and I hesitated at first, but I think it's a good idea. We met under the worst of circumstances and we have grown closer because of it. I think if we had the chance to get away from the constant reminder of the sadness here, maybe we could see something else in each other," he was putting it all out there.

She rubbed her arms and turned away from him. "I don't know, Tommy. I don't want you to be disappointed."

He turned her back gently to look at him. "Why would I be disappointed? I am not asking anything of you other than to take a leap of faith and have some fun with friends."

She shrugged. "I don't know; it's just not that simple. Besides, I am not in any condition to be away from medical help. I certainly don't want to go away and end up spending time in a clinic somewhere."

He nodded. "I know, but I think with all of us being doctors, we should be okay. We know what we are up against with your injuries and I know we can take care of you," he felt her closing up and he spoke from the heart. "Look, I am out of my element here. I have grown up in the shadow of Jack for a long time. He is handsome and debonair and brilliant and the women have always loved him. I have been a great wingman, but I have never given my heart to anyone. I have always been in the background and I haven't minded, but now, I want more. I see what Jack has found with Stephanie and it makes me want to find that, too. I am scared of being too pushy with you, and I don't want to pressure you, but I also don't think I like being without you."

She felt tears in her eyes as she looked at him. "Is that what you're doing? Are you giving me your heart?"

He blushed. "I don't know. I don't know how to answer that. I," he stopped talking when she touched his cheek. She looked into his eyes and pulled him to her for a kiss. He stopped just before their lips met and looked into her ocean colored eyes. He saw what he needed there, yearning and compassion. He pressed his lips to hers and she wrapped her arms around his neck. He deepened the kiss and she opened her mouth, allowing him access to her tongue. They were lost in the kiss until she finally broke the connection. She cupped his face in her hands and pressed her forehead to his.

"A leap of faith, huh?" she said softly.

He nodded, unable to find his voice.

"Okay, if you leap with me, I'm game," she said and he held her to him.

Chapter Twenty-Six:

Stephanie was so excited. She ran into the room to find Jack. He was on the floor trying to fix the garbage disposal. He sat up and wiped the grime from his hands. "You would think that someone who is so good with their hands could fix the stupid disposal," he realized she was grinning.

"What? Do I have food in my hair?" he stood up.

"She said yes," Stephanie squealed. "Tommy just called and told me Brittany said yes."

Jack swooped her up in his arms and they danced around the kitchen. They laughed as Jack sat down on the chair and she plopped on his lap. "I love it when you're so happy," he said, smoothing her hair behind her ear.

"I just want something good to happen for all of us. We have all had enough sadness to last a lifetime. I think this could be a fresh start for us and a new beginning for Tommy and Brittany," she was quiet for a minute, her mind running. "We need to make reservations."

Jack smiled. "Did he say where she wanted to go?"

Stephanie shook her head. "Brittany shouldn't fly, and I probably shouldn't either for that matter, so I think it might have to be a cabin. We can go up to the Catskills, or the Hamptons, or somewhere else, I just don't know. That might be kind of a long drive."

He looked at her and his eyes were sad. "Not the Hamptons."

"Why not?" she asked.

"That's where Tommy's parents were killed. They were vacationing in the Hampton's when they had their accident," Jack said sadly.

Stephanie covered her mouth. "Oh no, I am so glad I didn't mention that to him. Maybe we should go somewhere else all together."

Jack thought for a moment. "Let's go look for some romantic cabin getaways. Maybe the Pocono's?"

She looked at him with her eyes wide. "I love it and Pennsylvania is much closer! Let me go online and look," she jumped up and ran to the couch and to her computer. Jack watched her and his heart swelled at her happiness. This was going to be a trip of a lifetime.

****

Tommy was sitting in Brittany's living room while she gathered some things into a suitcase. He was giving her some privacy, but he wasn't far out of earshot. He was so incredibly happy she was going to give this a chance. He thought of their kiss and he knew he was in trouble. He heard a crash and jumped.

"Red, you okay?" he walked to the room. He saw her throw a drawer across the room in anger. "Hey, hey, what's wrong?"

She looked at him, anger flashing in her eyes. "All of my lingerie is gone. That fucker took my underwear. Who does that? When is it enough?" she screamed.

Tommy felt sick as he walked over to her. "Come on, we need to leave. There is no reason for you to go through this," he tried to take her hand but she was on a roll.

"What will it take for him to stop?" What can I do so he will leave me alone? Should I make myself look ugly to him?" she walked over and grabbed a pair of scissors from the desk. She took a handful of her hair and went to cut it off. Tommy jumped and grabbed her hand.

"Stop it," he said. "That's enough."

She looked at him and burst into tears. "I have to do something, Tommy. I just let him win every time. He will never stop until I'm dead. I can't do this anymore. This was my home, my sanctuary," she looked at him. "I know I haven't been here for long, but it was mine. I painted each room, you know. I decorated and I felt safe here. I was the real me when I was here. Nothing touched me from before. Nothing got inside and now, it's all corrupted. I feel like I will never be free."

He shook his head. "I am going to say something that is very cliché right now, but I think it's true," he took a deep breath. "When my parents died, I was afraid to put anything away. I kept their things exactly as they were for the longest time because I felt like if I packed things or removed their toothbrushes and personal items, then I was losing them from my life. I was erasing them from what they had built and I was dishonoring them. I didn't want to make it like they had never existed, but I also couldn't come home and look at their things and know they were never going to use anything again. I look at this house as something similar. You can't look at this place without seeing all of the sadness, but that is something that can be fixed. This home is what it is because you made it that way. It is because of you that it was a safe place. It isn't this house; it's what you made of it. You can do that again. If it isn't here, it will be in a new house, but it will be just as safe and just as 'you'. We can fix this. You can win, Red. I learned that and I will help you learn that, too."

She looked around the room and then at him. "I think I have a lot to learn from you," she took his hand. "Thank you."

Chapter Twenty-Seven:

"Are you sure you have everything?" Jack asked Stephanie for the millionth time as they pulled away from Tommy's house. Tommy grinned at them.

"Jack probably left all of his things at home and will no doubt blame me," Stephanie smiled.

"I am just trying to avoid a freak out when we get there," he said.

Stephanie rolled her eyes. "Right."

Jack looked in the back. "Are you sure Brittany will be ready to go?"

Tommy nodded. "I told her when we would be there and she said she would be. I didn't tell her that Julie and Bill were going to be there, too, but I don't think she will mind."

"I can't believe your sister is coming. Was she surprised when you told her we were all going on vacation?" Stephanie asked.

"She was," he nodded. "She was so excited that Bill had planned this trip for them to get away before he starts his new job at the Precinct and it was just a coincidence that they picked the same resort we did. They should be there a few hours before us."

"Were you able to get the gift into their trunk?" Jack asked.

"Yes, but I still don't know if I should give it to her. I just don't know how to proceed with that. I guess I will just wait and see how it goes," Tommy said.

Stephanie looked at them. "What gift?" she asked.

"Just something I did for Brittany," Tommy said and smiled.

Jack pulled up to the Holiday Inn. Brittany had been staying there for the last week while she recuperated. Tommy had wanted her to stay with him, but he respected her choice to be on her own. It didn't mean he hadn't been there each day. Jack stopped the car and Tommy got out to help. He walked into the lobby and saw her sitting there with a suitcase. She was all covered up, wearing sunglasses and a hat. He knew she was just trying to prevent anyone from noticing her. She smiled when she saw him and stood up. He came over and picked up her suitcase and she grabbed her cane. She was walking much better, but her balance was still a little off.

"Are you ready to go?" Tommy asked.

She nodded. "I think I am," she said as they headed out.

****

An hour into the drive, Stephanie looked in the back and smiled at her friends. Tommy was looking at Brittany who had fallen asleep. She was exhausted and they all knew that even though this was going to be a fun vacation, she still needed time to heal. They all kept quieter as she rested. Jack let the soft music from the radio play as they drove, everyone lost in their own thoughts. It wasn't long before they pulled into Pennsylvania and made their way to the resort. Tommy thought about what a big step this was for them and he was truly excited.

"I can see it," Stephanie said with excitement as they pulled onto the road. She was so happy to finally get out of the car and be alone with her husband. They pulled up to the beautiful resort main building and Jack and Tommy got out to check in and find out which resort cabin was theirs. Stephanie turned around in her seat to look at Brittany.

"How are you doing?" she asked with compassionate eyes.

"I'm okay. I'm kind of nervous. I just don't want to disappoint Tommy, but I am not sure what kind of company I will be," she smiled. "I am just so exhausted all the time."

Stephanie nodded. "You are still recovering from a major ordeal and your platelets need to keep replenishing. Fatigue is totally expected. As for Tommy, I think he is simply happy to get away and wants you to have some time to just relax."

Jack walked back to the car and sat down. He looked at Stephanie. "We might have a small problem.

"What is it? Where is Tommy?" Stephanie asked.

"He is waiting for the manager," Jack sighed. "Apparently they made all 3 reservations in the honeymoon suite. The whole facility is booked and they don't have another cabin. Tommy is pitching a fit because he was supposed to have the two room cabin," he looked at Brittany and sighed. "I'm sorry, Brittany, this is all my fault. I promised Tommy I would set this up and I didn't check the reservation like I should have," he ran his hand through his hair. "The good news is that the rooms are all in the same area, so we are all next to each other."

Stephanie looked at Brittany. "Are you okay?" she asked.

Brittany shrugged. "It doesn't sound like there is any other option."

Tommy walked back to the car. He sat down and looked at Brittany. "I'm sorry, I didn't plan this. I was able to get a cot delivered to the room so we will have separate sleeping areas. It was the best they could do."

Brittany nodded. "It's okay, we will be fine," she said and looked out the window.

Tommy felt terrible. This was not starting off on the right foot at all.

*****

Jack opened the door to the cabin and walked in. He smiled when he saw the scene before him. "Oh my," he said.

 Stephanie put down her purse and walked up to her husband. She looked around and joined him in her awe. "Is that what I think it is?"

"A champagne glass hot tub nine feet in the air? Why yes it is," he said and grinned.

"And a satin covered heart shaped bed," she laughed. "Oh, but Jack, look at the fireplace," she ran over to it and sat down on the plush comforter, which lay before the fireplace. She felt the squeak of plastic and laughed. "I guess it's good they give a fresh comforter to each guest," she opened the package and uncovered the soft fabric.

Jack grabbed the sparkling cider, which was chilling and brought it over to her. He sat down next to her and started a fire. She leaned in to him and sighed. "This was such a beautiful idea. I am so happy we're here and all of our friends are here, too."

He looked at her. "I still hope Brittany is okay with the room. I really didn't mean for that to happen. I would never do that to make her intentionally uncomfortable," he frowned.

Stephanie turned to look at him. "She knows that and Tommy will do whatever he needs to do to make her comfortable. I bet he would sleep in the bathroom if she asked. My guess is that this may turn out to be a blessing for them. It will force some issues out that need to be talked about," she got on her knees and faced him. "I don't want to talk about anyone else right now. We have some time to kill before we all meet for dinner and I intend to use that time to my advantage."

Jack grinned. "What did you have in mind?"

"I want to show my husband my appreciation for his big, um, heart," she moved closer to him and pulled his shirt up and over his head. She gently pushed him down onto the blanket and straddled him. She reached over and grabbed her bag, which she had placed near them. She pulled out some massage oil and looked at him. She licked her lips and squeezed some oil on her hands. She placed her hands on his torso and began to massage his chest. She moved her body with each stroke of her hands and she could feel his hips begin to press against her. She leaned down and moved to kiss him but teased him and stopped before making contact with his mouth. She took one of his arms in her hands and began to massage his bicep and she took each finger in her mouth and sucked on each digit. He moaned in pleasure and she moved to do the same with the other arm.

"Steph, you're killing me," he said through eyes that were dark with desire. She moved and looked at him. "I'm just getting started," she said.

He looked at her and his heart filled with love for his beautiful wife. She moved her hands to his waist and leaned down to unzip his jeans. She pulled them down and felt her heart beat faster at the sight of his bulging briefs. She pulled the pants off and tossed them aside. Looking into his eyes, she ran her hand over his briefs. He thought he was going to lose it right then, but she stopped, sensing his brink. She leaned into his face and once again went to kiss him, but teased him and whispered an inch from his mouth. "Not yet."

He tried to hold it together when she stood up and undressed in front of him. She was completely naked and she took the oil and put some in her hands. She rubbed herself down, paying special attention to each breast. She gave him a show as she ran her hands over her body. She watched him as he watched her and he licked his lips in anticipation, enthralled at her beauty.

"Stephanie, please, let me do that. Let me make love to you," he begged.

She smiled as she saw what she was doing to him. She sat down next to him and took his waistband in her teeth. She pulled it down and used her hands to pull the garment off completely. He didn't want her to tease him anymore. "Please," he said as she crashed her mouth down onto his and he moaned in contentment, as he was able to finally taste her. He pressed his tongue into her mouth as he wrapped his arm around her and flipped them both over so he was hovering above her. He looked into her deep brown eyes and she touched his face.

"Love me, Jack, I need you now," she said.

He put his arms under her back and propped her up into a higher position. He teased her before finally making love to her like it was the first time. He collapsed on top of her and she relished the feel of his body on her own. She would never get tired of that feeling. His naked body was all hers and she loved every inch of him.

He rolled them over and covered them with the blanket. She traced her finger across his torso and he rubbed her back. "I love you," he said.

"I love you. I just wanted you to know that," she said as she looked into his eyes.

"I do know that and I am the happiest man in the world," he said and they both closed their eyes, exhausted."

Chapter Twenty-Eight:

Tommy opened the door to the suite and walked in, putting their bags down. He turned to help her and closed the door behind them. They both stood in silence, surveying the room before them. There was a heart shaped whirlpool in the middle of the room and a beautiful fireplace surrounded by pillows and wrapped blankets. There was a huge bed in the shape of a circle with red satin sheets and a sign that read 'blush bed'. There was a large basket with honeymoon items on the counter and champagne chilling on ice. There was a long couch that curved across the room. There were bathrobes hanging with his and hers printed in pink letters.

Tommy was so embarrassed. He turned and looked at her. "I am going to kill Jack," he said. He ran his hand through his hair. "I think we should just take the car and go back to Michigan. I'll send a cab for Jack and Stephanie later in the week."

Brittany looked at him. "Do you want to leave?"

He didn't want to leave, but he didn't know how to answer. "Do you want to stay?"

"Well, I am tired, and it has been a long drive. I don't think Jack meant to do this, and I think it might be rude to just leave. Maybe we should try it for a little while?" she walked past him and sat down on the side of the bed and smiled. "It's cushy."

He looked at her, amazed by her attitude and her willingness to try. "Okay, we can try it for a little while," he walked over to start a fire. He was happy she was giving this a chance. He looked and saw a basket next to the fireplace with a covering on it that said. *"For all of your erotic honeymoon needs."*

No, Jack was a dead man. He turned to see if she had noticed it, too and saw that she had fallen asleep. He smiled and walked over to her. He gently removed her shoe and covered her with a blanket. He went over and sat down on the couch, exhausted himself.

*****

Later that evening, Jack and Stephanie were waiting in the restaurant lobby with Julie and Bill. They had reservations and were waiting for Tommy and Brittany to arrive. Jack couldn't keep his hands off of Stephanie and she kept swatting him away. "Later," she giggled.

Bill was holding Julie to him as they waited. He nibbled her neck and she grinned. She looked at him and whispered in his ear and they both smiled.

"So, what do you think happened with your brother and Brittany?" Stephanie asked Julie.

"If Tommy really had to stay in the suite you said, he will be out for blood. My brother is nothing if not shy about certain things. He is going to be beyond embarrassed, but I hope it opens his eyes up to what fun he could be having," she smiled at them.

Stephanie hugged Jack's arms around her. "Look, here they come."

Tommy and Brittany walked into the lobby and smiled at them. Tommy gave Jack a look and Julie and Stephanie both went and greeted Brittany.

"A freaking honeymoon erotica suite?" Tommy hissed to the men.

Jack laughed and then tried to stifle it.

"What do you mean erotica? I don't think mine is erotica." Bill said with a smile.

"You know I'm sorry, man. I really didn't mean it," Jack said sincerely.

"I know, it's just not shaping up to be a very relaxing trip," Tommy sighed. "I feel like a moron."

"You should be used to that by now," Jack said and Tommy glared at him. "I'm just kidding. I have a feeling once you have time alone and talk and maybe give her your present, this might not be such a bad trip after all."

The ladies joined them and they all walked into the restaurant. The tables were filled with couples all over each other. Tommy and Brittany walked in and sat down on the outside part of the curved booth. "Don't people need to breath? Why is everything so smushed?" Tommy asked.

Stephanie laughed. "It's romantic."

Brittany smiled. "I think it's sweet."

Tommy looked at her. "You do?"

She nodded.

"My brother is so old fashioned," Julie said. "Do you remember when," she began but Tommy stopped her.

"Okay, time to order," he said and everyone smiled, even Brittany. He noticed a little light was back in her eyes. She was really so beautiful.

They ordered and the dinner went on and ended up being very nice. The food was great and the talk was filled with laughter and stories from Tommy and Jack and Julie. The other three relished hearing everything and it really seemed as if everyone was finally beginning to relax. The restaurant had a beautiful dance floor and after they ate, the music began to flow. Couples all made their way to the dance floor and swayed. Bill took Julie and Jack took Stephanie. Tommy sat next to Brittany and smiled. "Are you glad we decided to stay?"

"I am. This is nice," she said, watching the couples move together.

Tommy cleared his throat. "Would you like to dance?"

She blushed. "I am not sure I am all that steady on my feet. The last thing I want is to draw attention to myself."

He leaned in closer to her. "I won't let you fall," he stood up and held out a hand. She looked at him and smiled. She took his hand and they walked to an empty spot on the floor as a new song began. The lyrics couldn't have been more appropriate. Tommy wrapped his arm around her waist and held her protectively to him. He took her other hand in his and held it to his chest. She leaned her head on his chest as they slowly moved to the music. It seemed as if they were suddenly alone in the world.

They were completely lost in the moment and when the song ended, Brittany felt overwhelmed by her emotions. All of this was too fast and she didn't know how to respond. He felt her tense up a little and looked at her. "What is it?" he asked.

"Nothing, would you mind if I went back to the room? I think I need to lay down," she didn't wait for a response; she just turned and left, grabbing her cane on the way. Tommy felt deflated and walked back to the table.

"Where did she go? It looked like you had a nice dance," Julie asked.

"I thought we did too, but she wanted to go back to the room. I think this might be too much for her," he said softly.

Stephanie shook her head. "No it isn't. She is scared of her feelings and she is trying to run from them. You need to help her feel them. I know from experience how intense love can be, but you need to allow it to come in or you may lose your chance."

Jack looked at her with love in his eyes.

"Who said anything about love?" Tommy said again.

Stephanie's eyes twinkled. "My mistake," she turned and looked at Jack.

Tommy could see both couples had other things on their minds so he stood up, shaking his head. "I'll see you all tomorrow," he said and left, realizing they were all lost in each other. He made his way back to their suite when he saw a television running with the weather forecast on. It looked to be a major winter storm coming tomorrow. Great, he thought, just what they needed, to be stuck in this situation longer. He shook his head and walked to the room. He wondered if he should knock or just go in. He put in his key and opened the door, walking in and putting his key on the table before seeing her sitting in front of the fire, wearing an oversized pajama top and bottoms. She turned to smile at him. "Want to join me?"

He nodded. "Let me change out of this suit," he grabbed his sweats and went into the bathroom. He changed and cleaned up and went out. He sat down next to her on the plush comforter and she handed him a glass of champagne. He took it and looked at her. "What's this about?"

She sighed. "I have had a lot of time to think lately, Tommy, and I am unsure about a lot. I don't know where I am headed, if I can go back to any semblance of normalcy or if my life is about to be on display. I am not sure how much of that I can even control," she looked at him and smoothed his hair, which was sticking up. "What I do know is that something has happened to me. I am a different person when I'm with you. I feel alive and I think about a future that I never would have even considered before. You do something to me that excites me in ways that I don't know how to handle. It's just that I don't want to lead you on or make you think there's something happening that just can't." She looked down. "This isn't coming out like I planned."

He listened to her and let her get it all out. He put his glass down and took hers and placed it down as well.

"Can I ask you something and have you be completely honest with me?"

She nodded. "I'll try."

"Why can't something wonderful happen? Are you afraid I might hurt you?" he asked her softly.

She shook her head. "No, of all the things I feel for you, fear is not one of them. It's just that I have so many issues with intimacy, Tommy. I am not ready to go there yet and I'm afraid that I might never be. You deserve someone who can satisfy all of your needs and I am afraid that you might be wasting your time. Why would you want to be with someone who is such a mess? You shouldn't have to take care of me all the time. It isn't right," she wiped her eyes.

Tommy smiled at her. "I don't think any of that is for you to decide," he touched her hand and kissed it. "You worry about things that we all worry about. I look at you and I think how beautiful and how far out of my league you are," he stopped her when she began to interrupt him. "I don't mean to put myself down, I am just being honest. You aren't the only one with insecurities. I am here for the journey wherever it may lead. If it goes somewhere that we both feel comfortable with, then we will take that road. If it doesn't, then it was fun while it lasted. You are putting so much pressure on yourself and you shouldn't. We just need to live each day and see what happens. I am not expecting anything from you and I don't want you to feel like you should be doing anything more than you already are. I just want you to be honest with me and try not to run from your feelings," he looked at her beautiful blue eyes. He handed her the champagne and took his. "I would like to propose a toast to us and the most awkward first vacation atmosphere ever, but hopefully the most amazing trip will unfold," he smiled and clinked her glass. They both took a drink and put the glasses down.

Brittany looked at him and felt her heart swell. She moved close to him and he put his arm around her. She leaned in to him and rested against his chest, both of them watching the fire burn.

Chapter Twenty-Nine:

"So, what should we do tomorrow?" Jack asked Stephanie as they sat together on their couch in the room.

"There is supposed to be a huge snowstorm, so I think a walk in the snow will be warranted and then we will have to somehow warm ourselves," Stephanie said.

"Right, but when can we use the hot tub?" he looked up at the champagne glass tub. "Do you think if you sit in it up there I can see through it down here?" he smiled a dimpled grin at her.

"I don't know, but it would be much more fun if we were both in there together," she said as she eyed the glass tub.

He nodded. "I think we can do both," he looked at her and she turned to face him.

"What is it?" she asked, touching his chiseled jaw line.

"I have something for you," he said softly.

"Jack, you don't need to give me anything. This vacation is the best thing ever. We are together and it is the most romantic, albeit cheesy resort I have ever seen. All I need is you and my world is complete," she kissed him.

"I know that, baby, but I need to share something with you," he said, suddenly serious.

She nodded, "okay."

He stood up and walked to his bag where he took out a small box and came back and sat down. He looked at her with his eyes wet.

She smiled. "What is it?"

He smiled. "I don't know why I'm getting all choked up, I didn't mean to," he said. "Do you remember our first real kiss?"

She smiled. "How could I forget?"

"It was the first time I was ever at a loss for words," he said. "That kiss came out of a passion and intensity that I had never felt before and you have continued to bring that intensity out in me every day. I remember thinking about all of the time I spent alone in my life and how empty everything felt to me. You make everything so electric, so alive," he put his hand on her stomach. "And now, we are having a baby," he let a tear escape and she brushed it away. "You have made every part of this world better for me. I just feel so lucky and so blessed to be who you love and I want you to know that for ever and always, I will be the man you deserve," he opened the box and there was a beautiful gold charm bracelet inside. He picked it up and held it for her. He fingered the first of 3 charms. "This is a heart that is shaped out of brittle crystal pieces. It represents my life before I met you and how there was nothing holding my heart together. This next charm is a heart made of solid gold, but it's missing a piece. This is how you were when we met, so full of sadness at the losses you had suffered, but your strength of spirit held you together. This last charm made of gold and diamonds is solid and strong. It represents our love and our future. We are strong individuals, Stephanie, but we need to remember how much stronger we are as a unit. I want you to look at this bracelet and feel that strength for our baby and for you whenever you may need it."

She looked at him as he placed it on her small wrist. It was beautiful and it sparkled in the light from the fireplace. "I don't know what to say," she said as she fingered the gold. She looked up at him. "Thank you," she pulled him to her for a kiss, holding his face with her hands and then wrapping her arms around his neck, deepening the kiss. She broke the connection and sat back, overcome with emotion.

"Are you okay?" he asked her.

"Yes, just happy. I don't know what I did to deserve you," she said.

He gathered her in his arms and carried her to the bed. "You deserve so much more. Just let me love you."

*****

Tommy went to take a shower and Brittany decided to get into bed. She had been feeling so tired again and she worried about her platelet count, but she had the medication with her to help. She needed to check the incision on her abdomen. She took her bag of supplies and limped to the table. She unbuttoned her shirt and moved the fabric aside to check but began to feel lightheaded, so she put the pills down on the table and went to move to the chair but she lost her footing and crashed to the floor.

"Ouch," she cried loudly as the chair crashed onto the floor with her.

Tommy ran out of the bathroom, soaking wet with a towel hung loosely around his waist. He saw her on the floor, her shirt open. He was at her side in an instant. "I heard a crash! What happened? Are you okay?"

She sat still for a minute. "I think so, I just need the room to stop spinning," she smiled. "It's okay, I'll be fine."

He made her look at him. "Let me see your pupils. He took the pen light she had in her bag and checked her pupil response."

"I'm okay, really. I just lost my balance," she was keenly aware he was only wearing a towel and he was dripping wet.

"I am a doctor, humor me," he checked her pulse and realized her shirt was half off. He also suddenly felt a breeze and remembered he was wearing a towel, only a towel. He didn't care at the moment; his only concern was her well-being.

"How long have you felt dizzy?" he asked her.

"Tommy, stop. Look at me," she took his hand. "I'm okay."

He put his head in his hand. "I'm sorry. I'm just worried."

She smiled. "I know. Maybe if you just help me up, I can finish changing my bandage and get some sleep."

"Okay, I can do that," he said and helped her stand up slowly. She held onto him tightly until she felt sure on her own. She was intensely aware of his bare skin on hers. The hair on his chest made her heart race. He helped her to sit on the bed and she took a few deep breaths.

"Will you let me help you?" he asked her.

She was a bundle of raw emotions and feelings. She wanted to run her hands over his chest. She wanted to lie in his arms. She was so confused.

"I just need to take care of the area where the pressure bandage was. I had a bit of a reaction to the material and it is a little painful. I guess that's the price I pay for having such a pale complexion," she laughed it off, but it was really sore. "I have the things I use in the bag on the table."

He walked over and grabbed the bag and went to sit down on the opposite part of the bed to lay out the materials. His towel acted like a sled on the satin and he slid right off the bed and onto the floor.

Brittany moved to the edge. "Are you okay?" she stifled a laugh.

"Just hurt my pride," Tommy stood up and held the towel in front of him. "I am going to go put some clothes on. Don't move," he grinned and went into the bathroom before he died of embarrassment.

Brittany smiled. He was so handsome, and he had some amazing muscles. She was lost in thought when he came back out, wearing pajama bottoms and a t-shirt. He walked to the bed and sat down carefully. He put on the gloves and moved the bandage away. There was bruising all around the area the pressure bandage had been and he could only imagine how uncomfortable that must be.

"I'm sorry, Red. This has to hurt," he gently cleaned the skin where the bandage had reacted.

"It's not so bad," she said. "You have the hands of a surgeon, gentle and precise," she leaned back while he covered her back up.

He looked at her. "What's next?"

"I need my meds for the night. I can take them if you just hand me my bag," she said and he did. She put the bag down when she was done and looked at him. He was gathering some blankets and going to the couch.

"What are you doing?" she asked him.

"They never brought the cot up, so I am just going to sleep on the couch," he said. "I will find out what the deal is with the cot tomorrow."

She was quiet for a minute. "Tommy, this is a really big bed and I think it's silly for you to be uncomfortable. I don't mind if you join me," she said and then realized he might not want that. "If you want to, I mean, it's okay if you would feel more comfortable on the couch. Actually, I could sleep on the couch if you want the bed alone," she started to get up.

He laughed. "Don't you go anywhere. I appreciate the offer and I will be sure to stay on my side."

"Good," she said. "That you will share, not that you will stay on your side, but that's okay, too," she rubbed her face. "I am going to shut up now," she said with a smile.

"Goodnight Red," he said and made sure there was enough space between them.

"Goodnight Tommy," she said and turned to face away from him as she lay down.

****

"Hi honey, I'm home," the man said to her. He moved a chair closer to her and sat down facing her. "You were really hard to find, you know that? But so worth it, Barbie."

Brittany felt her stomach churn as he spoke and the memories of such a terrifying and painful moment in her life came flooding back. She fought back tears, not wanting to show him anything. She looked away from him but he grabbed her face roughly and jerked her back toward him. Her neck strained and a shooting pain went through her body. She sucked in her breath.

"You will look at me when I talk to you. That's what's wrong with people these days; they don't maintain eye contact," the man sneered at her. "Now, how about some dinner?"

Brittany stared at him, not saying anything. She couldn't imagine eating anything.

He opened the package he had brought in and pulled out something that smelled worse than he did. "How about some dinner music before we eat?" he said to her. He walked over to his small tape player and brought it over. "I have waited for a long time to hear this again. I know why you never sang again after our last meeting. It was because you missed your inspiration, you missed me."

Brittany couldn't help it as her tears fell down her cheeks. She was having a hard time holding it together. "I can't sing for you," she said softly. She was stunned as his hand crashed across her face. She almost blacked out.

"You will do as I ask you, or you won't like the consequences," he said.

Brittany screamed as her nightmare continued and she felt strong arms around her. She thrashed and tried to move until she realized she was dreaming. She opened her eyes and saw Tommy next to her, trying to wake her up. She had a hard time focusing and finally she saw where she was. She looked into his eyes and saw compassion, but she felt sick. She got up and ran to the bathroom, ignoring the pain in her foot as she closed the door behind her. She emptied the contents of her stomach and sat down on the floor. "What am I going to do?" she said to herself. "When will this be over?"

There was a soft knock at the door. "Are you okay? I mean, obviously you aren't okay, but can you come out? Do you want me to go get Stephanie?" Tommy spoke through the door.

She sighed and stood up slowly. She opened the door and saw him standing there, hair disheveled, nothing but concern on his face. She looked at him. "Any chance you can just forget the last half hour happened?"

He smiled. "I will when you will," he said and she walked into his arms and cried.

Chapter Thirty:

"Have you seen my scarf?" Stephanie asked Jack as she zipped up her coat. She was bundled up and ready to go out in the snow.

"No, but maybe we should take off all of your clothes and see if it's under anything," he nibbled on her ear.

"Stop it or we are going to be late," she pushed him playfully off her neck. "We are meeting everyone in the lobby in 10 minutes."

"I know," he smiled and walked over to the couch. He picked up her scarf and handed it to her. "I wish we were back already so we can go hot tubbing."

"Just think; it will give us something to look forward to," she patted his behind and squealed as he chased her out.

Julie and Bill were in the lobby waiting when Jack and Stephanie got there. The four greeted each other and turned to looked outside. "It looks like we got two feet of snow out there!" Bill said.

"I think it's more like three," Tommy said as he and Brittany arrived. Everyone was bundled up and Brittany joined Stephanie and Julie. They all walked outside and Stephanie grinned.

"It's so beautiful. Look at the blue sky and the white snow," she looked at the sky and a snowball smacked her from behind.

"Oh no you didn't!" she looked at Jack who grinned at her.

Stephanie gathered a large snowball and threw it at him, but he pulled Tommy in front of him and it hit him square in the face. "Oh, Tommy, I'm so sorry," Stephanie said with a smile.

Tommy turned and looked at Jack. "Really? Really? Are you five?" he wiped his face off and looked at Stephanie. "He needs to pay."

Stephanie laughed as Jack tried to run away from them but lost his footing in the snow. He fell down and Tommy pummeled him with snowballs before falling himself. The women laughed and looked to see Bill and Julie sitting in the snow kissing each other.

Brittany laughed at the scene in front of her and realized she was truly having fun. She turned to watch the other couples walking and frolicking in the snow and suddenly felt a snowball smack her arm. She turned to see Tommy shrug and smile at her. "It slipped," he said.

"It's on," she said and all four of them threw snow at each other like they were in grade school. They all were red from the cold and the snow and tired from the exertion when each couple split into their own group. Bill and Julie walked back to the cabin and Jack pulled Stephanie down into the snow with him. He looked at her dancing eyes and her flushed cheeks and he couldn't help himself. He pulled her on top of him and kissed her passionately.

"I think we should go back to the room before something indecent happens," he said.

"Why Jack, how can you get so hot when it's so cold out?" Stephanie reached down and ran her hand over his groin.

"Stop that, or it will get really indecent," he said. She stood up and he stood up with her. They walked quickly back to their room. As soon as they got inside, Stephanie turned and pressed him against the door. She threw her coat on the floor and removed his coat. She fumbled with her scarf and he pulled it off, pulling her face up to his. He pressed his mouth to hers and she opened her mouth for his tongue to play with hers. She reached for his pants and unzipped them, not wanting to wait. He moaned into her mouth as he feasted on her neck. He moved her into the room and pulled her shirt over her head, her hair falling all around her shoulders. He removed her bra and looked at her.

"To the tub?" he asked her.

"Yes, now," she said. She looked up to the glass. "How do we get there?"

"Come on," he picked her up in his arms and he walked up the stairs which led to the top of the champagne glass tub. He turned on the jets and watched as the bubbles formed. He stood her up and she removed the rest of her clothes.

He turned and looked at her and stepped out of the rest of his clothes. "Are you sure it's safe?" she giggled.

"I think so," he smiled. "I'll be right back, I have to get something."

She smiled and stepped into the tub. It was warm and inviting. She looked down and saw him. "So, can you see anything?"

He looked up and grinned. "Everything," he smiled.

"No you can't," she grinned. "Come here, right now."

He jumped up the stairs and stepped into the water and she moved to him. She wrapped her arms around him and he held her to him. He kissed her and ran his hands all over her body. The water jets were making the intensity of all of their feelings so much more pronounced. She leaned back against the side of the tub and he began to massage her body. He ran his hands over her breasts and leaned in to her, pressing his mouth to hers as she wrapped her legs around him and sank onto his shaft.

"Oh God, Jack," she cried. He wrapped one arm around her and she moaned against him and he continued to kiss her. She reached down and moved her hands all over him while he kissed her neck and continued to love her.

"I love you so much," he said to her as he searched for her mouth.

"You are my whole world, Jack," she said. She ran her hands across his chest and clenched her fists as the waves of pleasure took over. She looked at him through half closed eyes and pulled him in closer. She leaned her head on his chest and he moved to a sitting position. She straddled him and moved her body to continue to control their movements. He was at her mercy and he looked at her, complete trust and love in his eyes. She smiled at him and moved off of his body, stood up and got out of the tub. She laid the towel down and reached for him and he came out and lay down on the towel.

"Are you okay?" he asked her, noticing her flushed face. He knew how the heat aggravated her Multiple Sclerosis and he should have remembered that.

"I think I have had enough of the heat, or else this night will be over way too fast," she smiled as she pulled him to her and guided him back to enter her. He moved slowly and sensually and she held him while he exploded inside of her.

A little while later, they sat on the plush blanket, her back against his chest and his arms around her waist. She played with his hands and leaned back into him. "Are you okay?" she asked.

"I am better than okay," he said as he held his hands to her stomach. "What are you thinking about?"

"Nothing, everything, how happy you have made me," she said. She felt a tear fall and she wiped it off. He moved her so he could look at her.

"What's going on? Talk to me," he said.

She shrugged. "I don't know. Sometimes it gets overwhelming," she brushed her tears away. "I am so happy, you know? Everything that I ever wanted is happening and I guess I just can't help but think that it won't last."

He cupped her face in his hands and brushed her tears away with his thumbs. "I understand your fears. You have been through so much in such a short time and it is hard to just let yourself be happy. I get that, but I also know that I am not about to waste one single minute of our life worrying about what we can't control. We are going to be smart, take care of ourselves and love each other. The rest will work out as it should. We are going to come back here to this very room on our 40th anniversary and laugh at our remarkable life together."

She hugged him. "Promise?"

"I promise. Now tell me how you think it's going with our friends. I think I saw Tommy actually relax for a minute," Jack laughed.

Stephanie appreciated him taking her mind off her fears. "I think the room mix up might just work in their favor. Brittany will fight it all the way, much like I did, but I know her heart and her compassion. She is falling hard for Tommy and she isn't going to be able to run forever."

"You did fight it, but I won," he grinned at her.

She touched his chest. "You are wrong. I got the best prize," she leaned in and kissed him.

"Round two?" he asked with a grin.

"I'm ready if you are," she said and they met in a passionate kiss.

Chapter Thirty-One:

Tommy looked at Brittany after they watched both couples leave. "Well, that was subtle," he said.

She smiled. "Come on, let's go inside. I'm cold."

He nodded and looked at her. "How is your foot?"

"You wrapped about a pound of plastic around it. I think it is the only part of me that is still dry," she looked at him. "Thank you."

"For what?" he asked.

"For making me laugh, for putting up with my issues, for thinking that I'm worth the effort," she said and looked at him, her nose red and her cheeks flushed. She had earmuffs on her ears and her hair framed her face. He put his arm around her shoulders and smiled. "Let's go in. I have something to show you."

Tommy opened the door and they walked into the room. "Do you want to change while I order us something to eat?"

She nodded. "I want to take a quick shower while my foot is still wrapped."

"Okay, I'll be out here if you need anything," he said.

She smiled and walked into the bathroom. She closed the door and looked in the mirror. She didn't know what was happening to her. Maybe it was the atmosphere or the people all around, but she was beginning to think there could be more to her life than just work. Maybe she could have a relationship with Tommy. She took her clothes off and stepped into the shower. She washed her hair and cleaned up before turning the water off and stepping out of the stall. She wrapped her hair in a towel and put on her yoga pants and a t-shirt. She opened the door and stepped out of the bathroom. She saw Tommy sitting on the bed, looking at something. She took the towel off her head and her wet hair fell down around her shoulders as she walked over to the bed. "What are you looking at?"

He looked up at her and smiled. "I just found something in my bag that I didn't know was there. I had packed this bag for the trip because my other suitcase was at the hospital in my office. I don't think I have used this bag in years. I was looking for something and I found this," he held out the piece of paper he was holding. "My mom wrote this note to my dad. He kept it with him all the time and after their accident, I was sitting with him in the room right before he, well, he wanted me to keep it," he wiped his eyes and smiled. "Sorry, I don't know why this is getting to me right now."

She sat down next to him. "Can I see it?" she asked him softly.

He looked at her and handed it over. She fingered the crinkled sheet and read the words.

My dearest David,

As I sit here and watch you as you are on the phone with your mom and you are trying to chase Tommy around the room and Julie is hanging off your leg, I am reminded how much I love you and our life. I know things have been stressful lately and that you worry about how we will get by financially, but as I watch you, my heart swells with the love and the faith that I have in us. I know you may think it's kind of hokey, but I am reminded of the song Tommy makes us sing to each other and I think it speaks to what we are. Do you remember how it goes? When the rain is blowing in your face. And the whole world is on your case. I will offer you a warm embrace to make you feel my love. When evening shadow and the stars appear. And there is no one to dry your tears. I could hold you for a million years. To make you feel my love. Just know how much I love you, today and for always.

My love,
Julianna

Brittany looked at him after she finished reading the letter. She handed it to him and smiled. "You made them sing that song?"

He grinned. "I loved Dylan when I was a little kid and one evening I walked in on them dancing to it. I was a bit of a pest and I made my mom play it all the time. I guess I loved seeing them so happy in that moment, I just hoped it would keep that feeling going," he ran his hand through his hair. "After the accident, when my dad was in the ER, he pulled it out of his shirt pocket and told me," Tommy stopped talking for a minute, his emotion getting the best of him.

Brittany took his hand in hers. "What did he tell you?"

He looked at her. "He wanted me to know what real love was. He knew how much Julie and I needed him, but he knew that he wasn't going to make it. After he learned my mom died at the scene, he didn't, or couldn't fight; he just couldn't be without her. He told me to take care of Julie and teach her about love and trust. He wanted us to see the love in that letter, and whenever we felt alone, we should read it and know they were there with us."

Brittany felt a connection to him that she hadn't before. She wasn't the only one who had suffered a loss in life and she was ashamed at not having seen his pain sooner. She touched his face and put her hand on his chest. "You have made your parents so proud. Julie is happily married to Bill and expecting a baby. She seems to be truly happy and for someone to lose his or her parents at such a young age, she is a remarkable young woman with a strong sense of right and wrong. That is because of you. Your heart enabled her to have as normal a childhood as she could. You have done your job, Tommy, and it's time for you to let yourself off the hook. You will always be there for Julie and you will always make her a priority in your life, but you don't have to live just for others. You need to live for you. You deserve to be happy."

He looked at her. "I am not sure I know how to do that. I have lived my life the only way I know how," he looked down and then back at her. "Do you know I have never told anyone about that night? I don't know why I haven't, I just didn't."

She smiled. "Then I am honored to be the first," she went out on a limb. "Maybe this is the first of many things to come."

Tommy looked at her and took a deep breath as he put the note away. "I have something I would like to give you."

She was surprised. "Why? I mean, what's the occasion?"

He sighed. "There isn't a lot I know about your past, other than the parts that were really horrible. I know what I've learned from the articles written and the tidbits Stephanie has told us. I know you ran from that life with good reason, and to be honest, I don't know if I could have survived what you have been through," he didn't mean to ramble.

"What I am trying to say, is that over the last few months, I have come to know you as a wonderful woman with strength and honor and the fact that you have started a life again while dealing with your past is admirable to say the least. I didn't fully understand the connection until I saw you sitting in the middle of your music room in your home. All you have hidden from the world has never been hidden from your heart. You were free to be who you wanted to be while in your house and I think you relished that. When I saw the destruction of all you held so dear to you, well it made me want to do something. I know I can't fix your pain or take the stain of him being in your house away, but I thought I could maybe do this."

He walked to the closet door and pulled out her guitar, fully restored to its previous form. He brought it to the bed and placed it down in front of her. "I just wanted something to be able to be fixed," he sat down facing her, the guitar between them.

She looked at the guitar and ran her hands over the beautiful wood. She grasped it and picked it up, looking at it from all sides. She put it down and looked at him, tears in her eyes. "I don't know what to say."

He smiled and raised his eyebrows. "Is that good or bad?" he wasn't sure.

She shook her head. "It's amazing, Tommy. I don't know how to thank you," she looked down at the instrument. "This guitar is very important to me. It was the last thing my dad ever gave me. It was where I learned to appreciate music. It is a tie to my past and I thought it was gone forever," she closed her eyes for a minute and remembered. "My dad loved music. He would always quote his favorite Shakespeare line. 'If music be the food of love, play on,'" she looked at him. "You don't know what you've given me," she smiled. "You have given me a glimpse of hope," she moved closer to him. "Thank you," she said as she touched his face and took his hand in hers. She brought it to her lips and kissed the back of his hand. He felt his heart skip a beat as he took his other hand and moved her still wet hair over her shoulder. She looked at him as he moved closer to her and pulled her to him for a kiss. His mouth found hers and he wrapped his arms around her. She held onto him as the kiss deepened and he stopped, not knowing how far to go.

He looked at her. "Are you okay?"

She nodded. "I am," she touched his shoulder and went to run her hand down his arm but pulled away.

"You can touch me, Red. It's okay," he said softly.

"No, it's not. I don't want to lead you into something I can't finish," she said and looked at her hands.

"How about we just get used to each other a little, nothing more," he said.

She nodded at him. He took her hand in his and put it on his chest. She moved it to his arm and he leaned in again and she let him find her mouth and their lips met as he moved closer to her. She inched closer to him and touched his forehead and traced a line down his cheek and his jaw. He looked into her eyes and she smiled at him. "What's happening to us?" she asked him.

He cupped her cheek in his hand.

"Something amazing," he said and kissed her again.

****

"You can survive a few hours without me," Stephanie said to Jack after they got up from their nap. "Besides, I think we both need time to recover after our champagne excursion," she smiled at him.

"But won't you miss me?" he whined.

"Of course, but think how happy I will be to see you later," she put on her lipstick.

"Who are you putting on makeup for?" he asked as he watched her.

She laughed. "A woman never goes out without putting on her face." She looked at him. "You're cute when you're jealous."

He pouted. "You don't see me putting on makeup," he said and she looked at him.

"I should hope not," she walked over and sat on his lap. "Brittany, Julie and I are having a girls afternoon at the spa. We will all be spending the evening with our men, so you and Bill and Tommy should prepare for some well rested and pampered ladies."

He smiled at her. "We are going to do some fun things while you're gone, too."

"Oh really, like what?" she asked as she picked up her purse.

"I don't know, but it will be great," he grinned. "Actually, I think we are just meeting in the bar and playing pool."

"Well play nice and have fun. I'll see you in a few hours," she kissed him and left.

****

Stephanie, Julie and Brittany walked into the spa lobby and were immediately whisked away into a dreamlike room. The spa attendants came to take each woman to their own appointment. Julie and Stephanie were having the 'mommy and me' pregnancy massage and Brittany was going to have the 'warm essential oil body wrap'. They were all going to be in the same area and the attendant was already notified of Brittany's injuries, so they were prepared to work around them. The three women were pampered and lavished with wonderful attention and they all were more relaxed than they had been in a long time. The next stop was shopping for outfits and then hair and make up. Stephanie found a beautiful red dress, which clung to her body and accentuated her curves. Her newly rounded breasts were more pronounced and she smiled. "Well that's new," she said and they all laughed.

Julie found a long purple dress with a beautiful black satin drape for her shoulders. It fit her beautifully and she twirled in the mirror. "Bill is going to flip," she said with a grin. The two women looked at Brittany. "Your turn."

"Oh, no, I don't think I need a new dress. You guys know that Tommy and I aren't like that," she blushed.

"Brittany, you asked us to help you set up your room tonight for a surprise and if you think we are going to let you go back up there wearing that, well you are sadly mistaken," Stephanie smiled at her.

Brittany smiled. "I guess I could get a little something new," she said and they pulled her to the racks. The women fumbled through the dresses until Stephanie pulled one out.

"This is it," she said as she held up the gown. It was emerald green and sleeveless. It had beautiful ruffles around the top and the bottom. Brittany looked at it and smiled.

"It's beautiful," she said and fingered the fabric.

"Try it on," both girls said to her.

She grinned and walked into the dressing room. She put the fabric on and it fit her like it was made for her. She felt tears come to her eyes as she realized she hadn't dressed up like this since she was performing.

She heard Stephanie's voice from outside. "Are you okay Brit?"

She opened the door and walked out. Both Stephanie and Julie smiled at her. "My brother is going to shit," Julie said.

All three women burst out laughing. "What?" Julie said and shrugged while they all laughed harder.

****

Jack looked at his phone as the three men sat in the bar. They had played pool and darts and all of them were sorely missing their ladies. Jack looked at Tommy who appeared to be lost in thought. He winked at Bill. "So, how are things going for the newlyweds?"

"Amazing. You wouldn't believe some of the things Julie can do," Bill said, his eyes twinkling.

Tommy looked at him with disgust. "Dude, that's my sister," he said and then saw the two men laugh at him. "What, I just have things on my mind," he blushed.

"Certain tall redheaded things?" Bill asked him.

Tommy took a drink of his beer. "Something like that."

Jack grinned. "So, how has it been going in the erotica suite?"

Tommy glared at him. "You know, there will be payback and it will be nasty."

Jack laughed. "I'm shaking in my boots." His cell phone buzzed and he looked down and smiled. "Okay boys, we have a directive. Put on a suit and tie and meet in the lobby in an hour. Tommy isn't allowed to go to his room because the girls are getting ready there."

The men all looked at each other and smiled. This was going to be an interesting evening.

****

"I think he will love it." Julie said as she and Stephanie finished helping Brittany get the rest of her surprise ready.

Stephanie smiled at her friend and looked at her. "Are you okay?"

Brittany sighed. "I am, just nervous. I haven't done this in a really long time."

Stephanie hugged her friend. "I am so proud of you."

Brittany smiled at them, She only hoped she could finish what she started.

Chapter Thirty-Two:

Jack, Bill and Tommy stood in the lobby at the appointed time and waited. The three of them were a sight to see, all incredibly handsome. They were garnering looks from those around them and they knew it. The elevator opened and Julie came out. She smiled brilliantly at her husband and Bill walked over to her. "You look amazing," he said and pulled her to him in a hug. The two of them were oblivious to the rest of the people in the room and soon they headed to their private dinner.

Jack looked at Tommy and smiled. "Don't worry, I'm sure he will be very respectful," Jack said and tried to stifle a laugh.

Tommy smirked at him. "Shut up."

Jack was about to say something else but the elevator opened and Stephanie stepped out. He really felt his jaw drop. She was the most beautiful vision he had ever seen. She walked up to him and he smiled at her. "You are so beautiful. I missed you," he said and pulled her to him for a deep kiss. She wrapped her arms around him and they broke apart.

"You look so handsome," she said and smoothed his hair. Her heart jumped at the sight of his dimples. "Let's go start our evening," she said.

He grinned. "My pleasure."

They smiled at Tommy and walked away. He stood there alone, feeling more than a little silly. He put his hands in his pockets and loosened his tie. He hummed to himself, wondering if maybe it was supposed to be just the two men, and not him. He scratched his chin and turned to walk toward the elevator when he saw her. He almost lost it. She was standing in the hallway, fixing her bracelet and didn't see him at first. She was wearing the most beautiful emerald green dress that made her red hair stand out. It was sleeveless and low cut. She had part of her hair loosely piled on her head and there were curls hanging to frame her face. He walked towards her as she looked up.

"Oh, I was supposed to make an entrance. I think I got turned around," she smiled at him. He was a sight, handsome and strong and he seemed to only be able to look at her.

"You look absolutely stunning," he said softly, almost speechless.

"I feel a little uncomfortable. I didn't think this dress was really necessary," she smiled. "They talked me into it."

"I will have to thank them," he said. He noticed a few guys staring at her and he moved closer, protectively. "Shall we go?"

She nodded. "I have something for you upstairs," she hooked her arm in his and they made their way, riding the elevator in silence, both lost in thought. When they got to the room she opened the door and walked in, Tommy right behind her. He looked around and smiled at the beautiful setting. There were flowers in vases all over and a plate of fruit and cheese set up on the table by the fire. There was a chair set up in one area and she walked him to the couch. "Will you sit there?"

He nodded and sat down, unable to take his eyes off of her. He watched her as she moved next to him and sat down, taking his hand in hers. "Tommy, I need to tell you something important, and I need you to let me get it out," she said and smiled.

"Okay," he said and waited.

"My life before the attack was so very different. I was someone who looked at the world like it was mine to tackle. I thought I was infallible and everywhere I went and everyone I knew reinforced that idea. I felt like nothing could touch me and when I sang, I was free. I never thought about the world being bad or the people out there wanting anything from me other than my music. I loved to sing and the fact that other people liked it too, well that was just icing on the cake," he saw a sadness come over her face.

"The day I was attacked, everything changed," she looked down. "I don't just mean the actual attack, but I changed. I went from someone full of life and hope to someone who was all alone. Most of the people who I thought were my friends left after that. It was like if I didn't sing, then I wasn't good for anything else. The attack took so much from me, but the worst thing was the fact that I never sang again. I couldn't look at music without thinking of what it cost me, and how everyone left when I stopped performing. I lived to sing and I just couldn't do it anymore" She put his hand down and smiled a small smile. "But now, because of you, I am starting to remember the good that life can be. You seem to like being with me, not for what you can get, but for who I am. You challenge me to fight for my happiness and I wake up in the morning a little happier each day. I am stronger than I have been in a long time. I want to thank you, so I hope you'll let me."

She stood up and walked to the chair across from him. She picked up the guitar, which was on the floor and put it in her lap. She began to strum the chords. Her dress was draped across her legs as she propped one knee higher and looked at him. She sang the song his parents loved and the emotion in her voice matched the emotion in his heart.

She strummed the last chords and her tears fell down her cheeks. It was a profound moment for her and he knew it. He walked over to her and knelt before the chair, taking the guitar from her and putting it down. He touched her face and pulled her to him in an embrace, holding her and letting the moment take over. He had never heard anything so beautiful. Her voice was clear and throaty and pure magic. He sat back and looked into her eyes. "Thank you."

She wiped her face. "No, thank you. I have been so lost, Tommy, for so long, and now, well, I don't feel so alone," she stood up and smoothed her dress. She touched her face and wiped her eyes again. "This wasn't supposed to happen. I am probably all blotchy now," she laughed.

He looked at her, his face serious. "Can I tell you something, too?"

She saw his expression and nodded. "Of course."

He led her back to the couch and they sat down. He looked down at his hands and then back up at her. "You know, I use my hands to perform miracles at work. I try to fix things that make people sick and watch them go home whole and happy. I love my work and it makes me feel like I am contributing something to the world, something extraordinary. But when I met you, I felt like my hands were useless, you know? I couldn't help you through the pain and the sadness. I couldn't do anything to fix it and it humbled me in a way that has changed who I am. I learned that sometimes it's okay that things can't just be fixed because it is a journey to discover that maybe the solution isn't a repair, but a new beginning. You have given me that new beginning, and I am scared to death that you are going to realize soon enough that I am not worthy of your admiration," he sighed and she took his face in her hands.

"Tommy, you are worthy of so much more," she said and pulled him to her and his mouth crashed onto hers. He stood up and pulled her up with him and wrapped his arms around her. She wrapped her arms around his neck, deepening the kiss and relishing the feel of his mouth on hers. He broke the kiss and stepped back, looking at her flushed face and swollen lips. He saw the fear creep into her expression.

"What is it? Are you okay?" he asked her as she sat down.

"I'm sorry, Tommy, I am just not sure I am ready for this. I don't think I can be intimate with you, yet. I don't know if I will ever be ready. I'm so sorry," she said and stood up. "I think maybe I should go."

He smiled at her. "Come here," he said.

She sat down but wouldn't look at him.

"If you think that the only way for you to make me happy is to sleep with me, then I have done a really crappy job of letting you see who I am. Do I want to make love to you? Of course I do, but not until you want to make love to me," he tilted her face to look at him. "I am not pushing you into anything, and to be honest, I am not all that ready myself. I think we need to get used to each other in an intimate way and then see how things go. I think you need to see what it means to be loved, Red, and that it doesn't have to be sex," he smiled at her. "Let's just get used to each other."

He stood up and removed his jacket. He pulled off his tie and unbuttoned his shirt. She stood up as he moved the fabric away, revealing his toned chest. She took a deep breath and moved closer to him. He took her hand in his and placed it on his chest. He didn't move, but let her explore his torso, and be comfortable. She looked into his eyes and swallowed. She took his hand in hers and placed it on her shoulder. He moved it back and looked at her. "I don't want to hurt you,"

She smiled. "I want you to touch me. I need that," she said.

He moved his hands over her shoulders and down her arms. She was so beautiful. He pulled her to him gently and softly found her mouth with his. He reached up and took the clip out of her hair, letting her long red locks spill over her shoulders. He walked over the radio and turned on his ipod.

"Can I have this dance?"

She nodded and felt the lump in her throat beginning to disappear. The beautiful music flowed and he pulled her into his arms. She laid her head on his bare chest and he wrapped his arms around her.

When the music ended, Tommy didn't want to let her go. He felt her hold onto him a little tighter and she whispered. "I think I need to sit down."

He helped her to the couch and held her hand. "Are you okay?" he asked her, smoothing her hair behind her shoulder.

"I'm just tired. I am always so tired. I really hope that gets better soon," she said.

"Maybe we should check your blood levels?" he said, concern in his voice.

"Stop being so romantic," she joked. "I have just had a long day. Stop being my doctor and just be with me, here, in the moment," she said.

He sighed and held her, "I just worry about you. You don't need to push yourself for me. I'm here for the long haul."

She closed her eyes and smiled. "Promise?" she whispered.

"Cross my heart," he said and held her.

"Can I tell you something shallow?" she murmured, half asleep.

He laughed.

"Of course."

"I think your hairy chest is incredibly sexy," she said.

He grinned and simply held her tighter to him as her breathing slowed and she was asleep.

*****

About an hour later, there was a knock on the door and Tommy woke up with a start. Brittany moved from his arms, both of them having fallen asleep on the couch. He made his way to the door and opened it to see Julie.

"Hey, what's wrong?"

"Is Brittany awake?" she asked. "We were in the lobby and there is a woman there who is like nine months pregnant and her water broke and they can't get an ambulance through the snow yet. They asked for a doctor. Do you think she can help?"

Tommy knew she was exhausted but when he turned around he saw her grabbing her bag. She piled her hair onto her head and clipped it. She slipped on her shoe and her boot and walked to Julie. "Come on, let's go," she said.

"Are you sure you are up to this?" Tommy asked.

She smiled. "It's what I do. Put a shirt on and come join us."

He nodded and watched them leave.

Brittany made her way to the lobby with Julie. She saw Jack and Stephanie sitting with the worried couple. "How come you came?" she asked as she walked up to them.

"Apparently the resort looked to wake up every doctor staying here in hopes one could help," Stephanie smiled at her.

Jack smiled. "We figured this was more up your alley."

Brittany sat down and looked at the woman. "Hi, I'm Dr. Anthony. I am an Obstetrician. Tell me how far apart your contractions are," she spoke soothingly to the woman.

"See babe, they have an OB here. You're going to be fine." The gentleman with the woman said. He was sweating and obviously nervous. "I told her we should have never gone on this trip," he said.

The woman glared at him and then at Brittany. "About three minutes. Oh," she screamed.

Brittany held her hand as Tommy came in. He walked over to Jack and Bill. "What's the story?"

"Apparently she is nine months pregnant and her water broke. The ambulance is stuck a half hour away and they don't think she can wait," Jack said as he looked at Tommy. "How did things go upstairs?"

Tommy smiled. "Wouldn't you like to know?" he walked to Brittany. "What can we do to help?"

She looked at the woman. "What is your name?"

"Rachel, and this is my husband Simon," the woman said.

"Hi Rachel. I would like to move you to a bed and check your cervix. I need to let you know that I am HIV positive, but I will take all of the necessary precautions to ensure there is no contamination," Brittany said quietly.

Tommy hated that she had to do this each and every time she treated someone. He touched her shoulder.

The woman smiled. "I am a nurse and I have no problems with that. Please, do whatever you can to deliver my baby healthy."

Brittany smiled. "Okay," she looked at Tommy. "See if anyone has any kind of lubricant, and have someone help move her to a room with a sterile setting if possible and maybe the warming lights from the spa," she grabbed her gloves and her bag and stood up. "Okay, let's go have a baby," she smiled.

A few minutes later the woman was in the bed and Stephanie stood with Brittany, helping her. Tommy came in with a pile of lubricants. Stephanie looked at him and smiled.

"What, it's a honeymoon resort," he grinned. "Let me know if you guys need anything."

Stephanie smiled. "I will. Now why don't you take Simon out for a minute while we see what we have? He looks like he is going to faint."

Tommy nodded. "Come on, man, let the women do their work. We promise, you won't miss anything." The man nodded and kissed his wife before walking out.

Brittany checked the woman and sighed. "You are fully effaced and dilated, but the baby is in a bad position," she looked at Stephanie. "I think we need to turn the baby."

Stephanie nodded. "I will go explain what's happening to Simon."

Brittany looked at Rachel. "Rachel, your baby is in a breach position. It is not recommended to deliver this way, but since we can't perform a Cesarean here, I am going to attempt to turn the baby. I will apply pressure to your uterus from the outside while trying to turn your baby from inside. It is going to be a little uncomfortable, but it is the best chance we have," she smiled. "You are going to be okay and we are going to deliver your baby safely."

Rachel panted as she fought through another contraction. "Okay," she said as she squeezed the sheets below her.

Stephanie came in with Simon and Jack and Tommy. Brittany smiled at Rachel. "We are all doctors, Rachel, and they will be here if I need an assist with anything. Is that okay with you?"

Rachel nodded. "Fine, just make it stop," she screamed again and Tommy pushed Simon to her.

"Go help your wife. Hold her hand, be with her," he said.

Simon looked at him like a deer in headlights. "Okay," he said and walked to her. "I love you, Rach, you can do it."

"Shut up," she said and screamed. Stephanie smiled at Simon. "It's okay, pain makes us say things we don't mean."

Simon nodded and just held her hand.

Brittany stood up to get better traction and began to expertly turn the baby. She was struggling with the exertion, and Tommy was worried, but she shrugged him off. "I need to help her," she said.

Jack pulled Tommy back. "Let her do her job," he said.

"She can barely stand. She is going to hurt herself," Tommy said.

"It will hurt her more if you try to stop her," he said. "It's okay," he patted Tommy's shoulder. "That dress is beautiful," he said.

Tommy smiled. "Yes, it is," he watched her work.

Brittany sat down and motioned for Stephanie to get some towels. "Okay, Rachel, I think we are good. Now when I tell you, you need to push."

"I can't," Rachel said.

Stephanie smiled at her. "Yes you can. You are a mom now and you will do whatever you need to do for your baby. It's remarkable the strength we never knew we had."

Rachel looked at her with sweat trickling down her eyes. "Okay."

Brittany looked at her. "Push now," she helped to guide the baby's head. "You're almost there, sweetie. Now push again."

Rachel pushed harder and Brittany delivered the baby. She reached for her towel and held the infant in her arms. She suctioned the mouth and nose and rubbed the baby as it took its first breath. The wail of the infant filled the room and everyone cheered. Brittany looked at the couple. "You have a beautiful son," she said. "Would you like to cut the cord?" she asked Simon.

He walked over and Brittany showed him where to cut. She wrapped the boy in the blanket and handed him to Rachel. She sat back down to finish the placenta delivery.

"Everything looks great," Brittany said just as the paramedics got there. She moved aside as they came in to help. Tommy and Jack stood back and both were silent, lost in thought. They walked into the other room as the gurney came through.

Rachel reached out to Brittany and Stephanie. "Thank you so much. I don't know what I would have done if you hadn't been there. We might have lost our boy," she cried.

Brittany touched the woman's hand. "Don't worry about what if. You have a beautiful family and that is all that matters."

The paramedic looked at Brittany and smiled. "You look familiar. Hey, aren't you that singer that was just found?"

Brittany turned and picked up her things. Stephanie walked quickly to get the men. "Hey, are you her?" the paramedic touched Brittany's arm.

Tommy moved to the paramedic. "Don't you need to get to the hospital?" he stood between the man and Brittany.

The paramedic raised his eyebrows and nodded. "Okay, come on," he said to his partner and they all left. Finally it was the six of them alone in the room.

Tommy turned to Brittany. "I think I need some help," she said before passing out.

Chapter Thirty-Three:

"Hey, Red, Hey," Tommy held her as she sank to the ground. He laid her down and Jack and Stephanie rushed to her side, Bill and Julie stood back. "Shit," Tommy said.

Jack took his stethoscope out and listened to her chest. Her pulse was steady and he looked at Tommy. "What has she eaten today?" he asked.

"I don't know; nothing with me," he looked at Stephanie. "Did she eat with you guys earlier?"

Stephanie nodded. "We had some sandwiches at the spa. I think she ate, but I don't know for sure. The meds are so hard to take, and she is probably struggling to keep anything down."

Jack looked at them and nodded. "I think she is just exhausted and dehydrated. I don't see any new bruising, so her platelets should be okay. Do you have the fluids we brought?"

Tommy nodded. "They are in our room."

"I think you should give her the fluids and let her rest. That should be fine for tonight," Jack looked at Tommy, who seemed ready to lose it. "Come with me for a minute, Stephanie will stay with Brittany," he smiled at his wife who nodded.

Jack led his friend out to the hall. "Tommy, what's going on with you? Are you okay?"

Tommy wiped his face. "I'm scared, Jack. I can't handle it if something happens to her."

Jack smiled. "You know, she knew you would say that."

Tommy looked at him. "What do you mean?"

"When she was in the hospital, we had a talk and she promised me to make sure you were okay. She was so worried that if something happened to her, you would be alone. I told her I would help you and now I am. You can do this, Tommy. I know you better than anyone and you never walk away from a challenge," he put his hand on his friend's shoulder. "Whatever happens, you need to be with her. Don't expect the worst, but if it happens, be there with her. Every minute you have together is precious. I predict a long life, and that's what you need to believe," Jack smiled as Julie walked up to them. She hugged her brother tightly and rubbed his back.

"Listen to Jack, he's right," she said.

Tommy nodded. "Okay."

Julie looked at him. "Tommy, what did the paramedic mean when he said he recognized Brittany? What's going on that you aren't telling us?"

Tommy looked at her. "I'll tell you everything, I promise, but not right now."

Jack looked up as Stephanie motioned to them.

"She woke up," Stephanie said.

Tommy hugged Jack and Julie. He walked back to Brittany and Jack walked to Stephanie. "Let's help them get back to their room," Jack said and Stephanie nodded. She gathered their supplies and Tommy picked Brittany up in his arms. He began to follow Jack and Stephanie to the elevator.

"Can you put me down? I want to walk," she said weakly. "Just help me stand with you. I don't want any more stares."

He nodded, placing her down gently, but keeping his arm protectively around her. They arrived at their room and Tommy nodded to Jack and Stephanie and Bill and Julie that he was good from there. They walked to their room. Tommy opened the door. He led her to the bed and she sat down. He sat next to her. "I need to give you some fluids, okay?" he said. "You need to make sure your electrolytes are replenished," he tried to keep busy, not allowing his fear to creep in.

She nodded. "I need to change," she said.

He nodded. "What do you want to put on?"

She looked at him with tears in her eyes. "I don't know," she started to cry. "Tommy, I'm so sorry. This is so ridiculous, I'm sorry."

He went and grabbed one of his t-shirts, which was close by. He put it down and moved to get the fluids. She slowly unzipped the dress and pulled his shirt on. She barely had the energy to move. He came back to the bed and put the supplies down. He sighed and looked at her. "I need you to stop apologizing. I can't do this if you keep saying you're sorry," he wiped his eyes.

"Okay," she said. She went to stand up to take the rest of her dress off but she couldn't. "Can you help me for a minute?"

He nodded and pulled the dress the rest of the way off her body, putting it down. He took off her sock and the boot covering her foot. He removed the clip from her hair and let the locks fall down before helping her sit up against the pillows and he took her hand in his. "I am going to put in the IV," he said and put his gloves on while she closed her eyes from exhaustion. He worked, trying to keep his emotions in check. He hooked the bag up to the bedpost and went to change.

He came back in his pajama bottoms and saw her eyes were still closed. His t-shirt looked so huge on her. He moved the covers and helped position her underneath and made sure her arm was still in a good position while the fluids were running. She looked at him. "Tommy," she said as her tears fell down the side of her face.

"I know," he said and held her hand as the fluids ran down into her arm, replenishing her body. She closed her eyes and he let her rest. After enough of the bag was emptied, he removed the IV, wrapped her arm and disposed of the materials. He came back to the bed and sat down next to her. She moved closer to him and rested her head on his chest. He pulled the covers over them and wrapped his arm around her, sitting in silence until he heard her breathing slow. He figured she was asleep, but he checked. "Are you awake?"

She made no move or response to him. He ran his hand over her hair. "You know, you can't do this to me. You can't make me fall in love with you and then leave me. I'm not strong enough. I won't survive," he leaned in and kissed her head. "I need you to get better. It's simple; you just need to get better."

He closed his eyes and prayed.

******

Jack walked into their room and Stephanie went into the bathroom. He started a fire and took his suit off. He pulled on his pajama bottoms and took out some grapes from the mini fridge. He looked at his phone, making sure Tommy hadn't called. He looked up as Stephanie came out. It was clear she had been crying.

"Hey, come here," he said and she moved to him. He helped her out of her dress and she pulled on his pajama top. He sat down in front of the fire and she joined him. He faced her and took her hand in his, bringing it to his lips for a kiss. "Tell me what's on your mind."

She smiled at him and sighed. "I just feel so bad for Brittany and Tommy. It so easily could be you and me," she said and Jack instinctively pulled her close to him.

"Why do you say that?" he asked.

"I am so lucky, Jack, in so many ways. I have had it relatively easy, managing my MS. I found a man who loves me, and now I am pregnant," she looked at him and touched her stomach. "But I worry a lot about when that luck runs out. What if our child is born and I get worse. What if I can't take care of our baby? I just hate every way that this disease creeps into our lives."

He nodded. "I agree that I hate this disease, Stephanie, but you need to stop looking at it like that. We can't change the fact that you have Multiple Sclerosis. We can't make everything better just because we want to, but we have the power to do amazing things. You struggle with your health every day and the fact that you continue to put the needs of others above your own is a tribute to your big heart. The best thing we can do for our baby is to love each other the best we can. We will show our child that it isn't important the things we carry with us, but how we deal with the things we are given," he leaned in and kissed her cheeks. "We have been given an amazing gift, Steph, and sad or happy, we need to nurture and respect each other. I love you so much, and I need you to always remember that."

She kissed him softly and ran her hand through his hair. She looked at his face like she was studying it and then put her hand on his chest. "You are my heart and soul. I love you," she pulled him to her and kissed him again, wrapping her arms around his torso. She leaned in to him and rested her head on his chest.

He put his hand on her hair and hugged her to him. He knew what his friend was facing, and he knew he needed to be strong for all of them, but he also knew that if he lost Stephanie, he would be destroyed. He closed his eyes and prayed for all of them.

Stephanie looked over at the grapes. "I think we need some fruit," she said with a smile. He reached over and grabbed the dish. She took a grape and popped it into her mouth. She grabbed another one and dropped it purposely on his lap. "Oops," she said.

He smiled at her. "Nice," he said. He picked up the bowl and dropped them all on his lap. "Oops," he said with a twinkle in his eyes.

She sighed. "Well, it looks I have my work cut out for me," she grinned as she pushed him down on his back and began to collect all of the grapes.

****

Tommy felt something heavy on his chest and opened his eyes. He realized Brittany was sprawled half on him, her arm across his waist and her head on his chest. He smiled and closed his eyes again. He didn't want to move. He didn't want her to leave. He realized her leg was over his and her knee was precariously placed on his upper thigh which made his heart beat faster. He thought about everything that had happened the day before, from the song to the intimate talk they had to the baby delivery. He knew she was far from being okay, but for this moment, everything was as it should be. He kept his arm around her and drifted off again.

Brittany hadn't slept this well since, well, she couldn't remember. She opened her eyes and realized quickly that she was totally not on her side of the bed. She moved her plastered hair from her face and saw Tommy sleeping, seemingly unaware of her intrusion.

She watched him sleep for a minute, resisting the urge to touch his mouth. She gently extricated herself and swung her legs over the side of the bed, taking a moment to make sure everything was steady before she stood up. She realized she was wearing his t-shirt and she felt warm all over. She walked slowly to the bathroom, looked at herself in the mirror and frowned. Her skin was so pale and she looked like she hadn't slept for a week. She took off the bandage, which was on her arm and remembered Tommy giving her the IV. There was a nasty bruise from the needle, and she knew her platelets were probably low, although she always bruised easily. She ran her hand through her hair and sighed. She was still a little dizzy, and knew she shouldn't stay on her feet too long. She needed more time to recover from the last day, and she needed more fluids. She wanted to take a shower, but she wasn't sure she was steady enough. She cleaned up as best she could and walked out.

Tommy woke up and quickly realized she was not in the bed. He sat up and saw she was sitting on the blanket by the fire. He got up and walked over and sat down next to her. She was staring into the fire her hands under her knees. She turned and looked at him. "Did I wake you up?"

He shook his head. "No. How come you aren't sleeping? Did you have another nightmare?"

She shrugged. "No, I just have a lot on my mind. I can't seem to stay asleep for very long, even though I know I need it," she looked at him. "The fluids helped a lot, I really do feel better."

He nodded. "Liar," he said and smiled when she smiled at him. "Since we're both up, do you want to talk about it?"

She looked into the fire and hugged her legs to her. "What happens when we go back home?"

He brushed her hair behind her shoulder; an intimate gesture that she found warmed her heart. "What do you mean?"

She turned and looked at him. "You never told me why you got into that fight at the bar. It was about me, wasn't it?"

He looked at her, unable to lie. "Yes, but so what? I shouldn't have let the guy get to me, but I did."

"What did he say?" she asked.

"It doesn't matter, he was an asshole," Tommy said, looking at the fire.

She turned and looked at the fire, too. "It will follow me everywhere, and if you are with me, it will follow you, too. That fight was just the beginning," she wrapped her arms around herself. "He is still out there and he knows where I live and where I work. I don't know if I can even go back to work, or if I will be too much of a distraction," she looked at him. "People don't want to come for their ultra sound and have to dodge the paparazzi."

He sighed. She was right, but he didn't know what to tell her. She turned back to the fire, a profound sadness in her voice. "The worst part is still to come."

"What's that?" he moved closer to her.

"When they find out I am HIV positive," she said softly and wiped at her eyes. "What then?" she was quiet for a minute before turning to look at him, her eyes bluer than he had ever seen. "See, I told you I had a lot on my mind."

He nodded. "You're right. There is a long road ahead of you. There are questions and answers we don't know. I realize you have all of this on your mind, but if you don't get stronger and let yourself heal, none of it will matter. We are here, now, and this room is beautiful and romantic and safe. You have nothing to worry about except how much I am bothering you," she smiled at him and he touched her cheek. "The problems will be there when we go home and we will deal with them, together. I'm not going anywhere, but I need you to promise me the same."

She looked at him and saw the fear in his eyes, not for what she said, but for her. She knew how scared he must be. She moved closer to him and held his face in her hands, smoothing the imaginary lines of his forehead. "You're right," she said and put her forehead to his.

He looked at her and smiled. "Tell me what I can do for you."

She sat back and stretched. He saw her arm and was horrified. "Oh God, did I do that?" he looked at the bruise she had from the IV.

"No, I told you I bruise easily. It's fine," she said and sighed. "I really am okay, I just need to take some time and relax. I think I will take a shower and then go back to bed. I need to clean up after all of that makeup and then the baby; I just think it will help my muscles if the water falls on me."

"I don't think that's a good idea. You aren't ready to stand in a shower. I'll tell you what. There is a huge hot tub in the room that we haven't used. I can help you sit in the tub and that way you won't hurt yourself," he said. "I promise, strictly professional."

She smiled. "Maybe only slightly professional?"

He grinned. "You got it."

****

Tommy waited while Brittany got into her bathing suit in the bathroom. He put some candles next to the tub and turned as she came out. He caught his breath in his throat when he saw her. She was wearing a one-piece white swimsuit that was very low cut. She crossed her arms around herself as she walked to a chair and sat down. "I had to buy a new suit when we were shopping because mine was ruined. This was the least provocative one they had," she blushed the color of her hair.

He smiled. "I think it's beautiful," he looked at the tub. "It's ready for you."

She smiled. "Okay, I'm just going to sit for a minute, get my legs under me," she was so unsteady; it worried her, but she didn't want him to worry.

He walked over to her. "Not feeling strong enough?" he asked her as he knelt in front of the chair.

She sighed. "I just lose my momentum pretty fast," she smiled. "I guess putting on a bathing suit is my workout for the moment," he grabbed the plastic and covered her foot until he was satisfied it was protected.

He took her hand in his. "This is where I come in," he said.

She looked at him. "You don't have your bathing suit on," she said, referring to his pajama bottoms.

"I wasn't sure if you wanted me in the water," he said.

She touched his face. "My stomach is healed enough and I made sure to wrap the waterproof bandage around my middle just in case. I don't want you to worry about any contamination. If you want to, I would like you to come in with me."

He stood up and removed his pajama bottoms, revealing his swim shorts.

"Ready?"

She laughed and let him pick her up in his arms. He walked to the tub and put her down, letting her go in herself. She walked in slowly and sat down on the step. He made sure she was okay and stepped in himself. He moved to the step and she smiled at him. "Come here."

He moved closer to her and she faced him, the water flowing around them. "I am so thankful for you, Tommy," she began. "I just never thought there was someone out there who would treat me the way you do. I don't know why, I just thought I wasn't meant to have this."

"To have what?" he prompted.

"I don't know, happiness maybe?" she said.

He reached for her and she moved into his arms. He held her to him and he melted as she rested her head on his chest. "Is that what you are now? Happy?"

She reached up and touched his face. "Yes," she said as she pulled him to her for a kiss. His mouth fell on hers and he ran his hand up under her hair. He pulled the sponge from the side of the tub and moved so she was sitting with her back against him. He put the sponge in the water and let it run over her arm. He did the same for her other arm. She leaned her head back and closed her eyes. They were silent for a few minutes before Tommy began to worry about her shivering.

"I think we should get you back to bed," he said. She was exhausted and nodded; the water seemed to have the desired effect on her.

He moved out of the tub and grabbed a large bath towel. He helped her stand up and she slowly moved out of the water. He wrapped the towel around her and she turned to walk. He grabbed another towel and saw she was in trouble. "Red," he moved to her as she faltered. He picked her up and walked to the fire, placing her down on the blanket and took her face in his hands. "Talk to me, tell me what you need."

She smiled. "I just need you here with me, nothing else," she lay down on the blanket, falling asleep almost instantly.

He exhaled. "Okay," he figured it would be enough for now. He removed the plastic from her foot and lay down behind her, pulling the blanket over them, as they were both still in their suits. He smoothed her hair as she slept and he closed his eyes, wondering what the new day would bring.

Chapter Thirty-Four:

"I can't believe it's our last day here," Stephanie said as they got dressed the next morning. "I don't want to go home tomorrow."

Jack sat down and nodded. "I know, but we can't stay forever. Besides, from how Brittany and Tommy seemed together, I think our trip had the desired effect," he smiled.

"Do you think so? I mean I know they seem really into each other, but I worry about Brittany. I know what it's like to always doubt your ability to be an equal in a relationship. I think she fears that Tommy will grow tired of her," Stephanie said.

Jack looked at her. "You don't think that about me, do you?" he took her hands in his. "I could never get tired of you or of our love and life together."

She touched his face. "No, I don't think that, but I used to be where she was. I think when you are alone for so long, and in a state of constant fear about your life being exposed for something it isn't, I just think she is not going to be able to let down her guard so easily. I worry about what happens when we are home and away from this safety zone."

Jack walked over to the counter and grabbed a glass of orange juice for her. "Here, let's worry about tomorrow when it comes. Today is about us and our friends and making the most of our last day in cheesy paradise," he handed her the glass.

She grinned. "It is cheesy."

"A little cheese is good every now and then," he smiled at her.

"So what are we going to do today?" Stephanie asked him after she finished her juice.

Jack looked at his phone. "I am waiting to hear from Tommy before I know. Brittany was truly out of it last night and I know he was really concerned. I think it might be a good idea to stay close to the room today. I don't know if she will want to go out anywhere," he ran his hand through his hair. "There was also the small matter of the paramedic."

Stephanie sighed. "He recognized her, didn't he?"

Jack nodded. "I only hope it ends there."

Stephanie looked at him. "Can you come here for a minute?" she asked him.

He looked at her, concerned. He moved to her. "What is it?"

"You were too far away," she said and pulled him in for a kiss.

He could never get enough of her, his beautiful, amazing wife.

****

Tommy woke up and took a minute to realize where he was. He was still in his swimsuit and the image of the evening before came flooding into his mind. He looked and saw her turned toward him, her face on his chest. Her bathing suit had moved down and the top of her chest was almost exposed. He smoothed her hair from her face and she stirred. She opened her eyes and squinted up as she saw his beautiful green eyes looking at her.

"Sorry," she smilesd as she moved away from him, straitening her suit as she did.

"Why are you sorry?" he asked her as he realized his suit was precariously positioned as well. He moved the blanket over his waist and blushed.

"I kept you up last night," she moved to look at her foot and sighed when she saw the swelling. She smoothed her hair down. "I think I need to get out of this suit," she smiled. "Not the most conducive sleeping attire."

"Agreed, but you will let me know if you need anything?" he asked as she stood up slowly and limped to the bathroom.

"I will," she said softly.

When she was safely in the bathroom, Tommy stood up and fixed himself in his suit. He moved to his bag and grabbed his clothes, waiting for her to finish so he could go in. He sighed as he thought about their evening. This was quite the vacation, he thought, but tomorrow, it all changes. He looked up as she walked out, dressed in a t-shirt and yoga pants. She had pulled her hair up into a ponytail and she carried her first aid bag with her.

"I didn't want you to have to wait. I'll fix my foot out here," she smiled at him.

He smiled and walked into the bathroom. He pulled off his suit and jumped into the shower. He let the water run over his back and his face and he thought about her. His heart beat faster as he remembered the feel of her on his skin. He was in trouble, real trouble. He finished his shower and dried off. He put his clothes on and finished getting ready. He towel dried his hair, combing it down and walked out of the bathroom.

"Feel better?" she asked him with a smile.

"Yes, refreshed," he said and walked to sit down across from her. He saw she had fixed her foot and covered it with a sock. "How is your stomach?"

She smiled. "I'm good, no worries," she stood up and walked to him. "What are we doing today?"

He reached up and touched her hair. "I don't know; what do you want to do?"

She shrugged. "I don't know, maybe we can have a nice lunch, all six of us, and then we can spend some time relaxing up here."

"Sounds good to me," he said and dialed Jack.

****

Stephanie and Jack walked down into the main lobby of their resort and waited for their friends. He had his arm around her and they walked by a store. Stephanie looked at the baby clothes which hung in the storefront and Jack stood behind her and wrapped his arms around her.

"Should we buy it?" he asked.

She laughed. "No, I think I should be in the second trimester before we begin to buy clothes. She turned in his arms and reached up to kiss him. He lingered over her lips and smiled.

"Maybe we should skip lunch," he said and kissed her again.

She wrapped her arms around him. "We will have our time later tonight. One last night of wild and reckless abandon," she said as she ran her hands over his behind and he grinned.

"Promise?" he asked her with a wicked smile.

"Oh, I promise," she said.

They parted a little, not wanting to start something they couldn't finish and Jack turned in time to see Julie and Bill come in. He smiled at them as they walked up.

"I'm glad Tommy and Brittany are joining us. Did he say how she was feeling?" Julie asked them.

"He just said she wanted to have lunch together. I think it will be a nice distraction for them," Jack said. He looked at Stephanie and she nodded. "Let's get a table."

The four walked into the restaurant and were having a nice time talking and laughing when Tommy walked in with Brittany. They joined the table and everything seemed to be going great.

"So, Julie, have you guys thought about names for the baby yet?" Stephanie asked her.

Julie held Bill's hand in hers and looked at him. "A little, but we have to decide for sure."

Bill smiled. "I think we will go with David if it's a boy and Juliana if it's a girl," he squeezed his wife's hand.

Tommy felt tears fill his eyes. "I think they would be honored," he looked at his sister.

She wiped her eyes. "I think so, too."

Stephanie looked at Jack with a question in her eyes. He smiled at her. "David and Juliana were Tommy and Julie's parents." He looked at Julie. "You are going to be a great mother."

Julie grabbed a Kleenex and wiped her face. "Well now I feel a little silly. I swear; these hormones have me acting all sorts of weird."

Stephanie smiled. "Yes, I have noticed some strange hormonal urges myself," she reached under the table and squeezed Jack's thigh. He cleared his throat.

"Maybe we should order," he motioned to the waiter.

They all ate and had a really nice time. Brittany was able to finish her oatmeal and even managed a few bites of fruit. She had a little more color in her cheeks and Tommy caught himself staring at her. She reached up onto the table and covered his hand with hers, a gesture no one at the table missed. They all finished their lunch and got up to go their separate ways.

Jack and Stephanie made their way to their room and once inside, Jack's cell phone buzzed. He looked down and saw he had missed a call.

"I guess I had it on silent," he said and looked at the number. He didn't recognize it, but listened to the message as Stephanie went to change. She went into the bathroom and when she came out, she saw he was standing by the window, looking out.

"Who was on the phone?" she asked him as she walked to join him.

He turned to her. "My dad. He is coming back to Michigan to have surgery," Jack's dad Ron had been absent from his life for the past 15 years, since his mother died. He was an alcoholic and no matter what Jack tried; he couldn't help him. They had reconnected a few months before when Jack found out his father was suffering from liver cancer. He was also remarried. Jenny was a burn specialist who helped him get clean.

She smiled at him. "That must mean the tumor has shrunk enough to be removed. That's good news, right?"

He crossed his arms over his chest. "Yes, but."

"But nothing," she said as she hugged him. "He will be fine and we will be there to help him with his recovery. You know the only cure for liver cancer is surgery and now that he is eligible, I choose to think of that as a sign that we are all destined to be happy."

He smiled at her. "I'm so glad you're here."

"Good because I love you," she pulled his face down to hers for a kiss.

Chapter Thirty-Five:

Tommy and Brittany walked into the room and she went and sat down on the couch, pulling her hair out of the ponytail before leaning back on the pillows.

"Tired?" Tommy asked as he sat down across from her on a chair.

She looked at him. "A little, but not as much as before."

He smiled. "That's good, right?"

She nodded. "That's very good," she turned to face him. "I think it is really nice that Julie and Bill want to honor your parents with naming their child after them."

Tommy felt the lump in his throat come back. "Yes, she is an amazing woman. I don't know how she managed to turn out so well."

Brittany stood up and walked over to where he was sitting. She knelt down in front of him and took his hands in hers. "Tommy, she is the best of you. You took a horrible situation and made it livable for her. Most people who have lost a parent, let alone both would fall apart at the very least. Tommy, you gave Julie the best, most amazing gift. You gave her a life with love and family. You showed her that the bond your parents instilled in you could survive such a loss and that the best tribute to their lives was to live yours with honor and integrity. You have such a huge heart and I am honored to know you."

He felt a huge lump in his chest as he looked at her. "Wow," he said softly.

She stood up and smiled. "What?"

He shrugged. "I don't know, no one has ever said anything like that to me," he cleared his throat, got up and walked across the room before turning to look at her. "What's happening here?" he wiped his face. "What are we doing?"

She walked over to him. "What do you mean?"

"I don't know; I just feel like something important is happening, and I don't want to let it pass us by," he said, not even knowing himself what he meant.

She put her hand on his chest and smoothed an imaginary wrinkle. "Tommy, I don't know what to tell you," she looked up into his eyes. "I am HIV positive. That has to matter," she turned to look away when he gently pulled her to him and looked into her eyes.

"It matters, but not in the way you think. When will you stop punishing yourself? You are entitled to be happy. You are entitled to find love and you are entitled to want more. I don't know how to make you see that," he said, as his eyes grew wet.

She didn't care that her tears fell. "Tommy, I can't risk infecting you. I just won't."

He sighed. "So you will just crawl into a hole and hide? Is that it? You are going to live a life of solitude and let the horrific actions of a deranged lunatic end any chance you have at happiness?"

She looked at him, her eyes blazing. "You act like I like this. You act like my fear of passing my HIV to you is silly and irrational. You don't know what I feel. You don't know how much I wish I could make love to you and just give in to my feelings. You don't know how hard it is to see you and not want to feel your hands on me, holding me and loving me," she let her anger come pouring out. "You think I'm flippant about this, but I'm not. God, Tommy, I have never wanted anything more, but not at the risk of infecting you. I'm not worth dying over."

He didn't say anything; he just pulled her to him and pressed his mouth on hers. He felt her melt against him and she wrapped her arms around him. He picked her up and carried her to the blanket, placing her down gently as she pulled him onto her, kissing him and slowly moving her hands down his arms. He moved his hands to her torso and when he touched her stomach, she pulled back, pain ripping through her body. "Oh," she cried.

Tommy sat back, feeling like a complete idiot. "Oh Red, I'm sorry," he said.

She closed her eyes, trying to control her breathing. "No, it's okay."

He shook his head, "No, it's not. It's not okay at all."

She lay back on the blanket; he sat on his knees and brushed her hair off her shoulders. He went to move her hands away from her side, but she stopped him. "No, enough taking care of me," she looked at him and spoke through her quivering chin. "This is what's so wrong, Tommy. You can't touch me without gloves and

I can't take it anymore. I don't know what to do," she sat up and gingerly moved away from him. "I'm so sorry," she stood up and walked to the bathroom, leaving him speechless.

****

Jack was lost in thought when Stephanie came out of the bathroom. He turned and looked at her. "Are you okay?"

She nodded. "I think my morning sickness has kicked in again," she sat down and smiled when he handed her some crackers. "I'm sorry, not really a romantic last day."

He pulled her feet onto his lap and began to massage them. "I think watching you get sick while sitting in a honeymoon suite is beyond romantic," he grinned when she rolled her eyes at him.

"We need to talk about your ideas of romance," she sighed. "I am feeling better, though, so maybe tonight I will be up for a more fitting farewell to our room."

He smiled at her. "Why Dr. Stephens, what did you have in mind? I think we did everything the room advertised."

"I have some ideas, but right now, I just want to rest for a bit," she yawned.

He moved so she could crawl into his arms, she rested her head on his chest and he wrapped his arms around her. "I love you," he whispered.

"I love you more," she said as she closed her eyes.

A few minutes later there was a knock at their door. Stephanie looked at Jack who shrugged. He stood up and went to look. He opened the door to Tommy, who looked like he just lost his best friend. "Hey, come in," Jack said. Stephanie sat up and smiled.

"I'm sorry if I'm interrupting," Tommy said with his arms crossed in front of his chest.

Jack could tell something was really bothering him. He shook his head. "Of course you're not interrupting, come in."

Tommy lingered by the door and looked up at the champagne glass tub. He looked at Jack and smiled.

"What? Doesn't everyone have a six foot champagne glass tub in their room?" Jack grinned at him.

Tommy laughed and looked at Stephanie who stood up. "Is Brittany in your room?" she asked softly.

He nodded.

"I'll go see how she is doing," Stephanie walked up to Jack and kissed him, giving him a look that said what she was thinking.

She smiled at the men and walked out.

"So, want to tell me what happened?" Jack asked him. He walked over and sat down on the couch. Tommy sighed.

"If I knew what happened, I would feel better," Tommy said.

"Ah, one of those moments," Jack smiled. "You know, a relationship is a lot of work, and starting it off the way you both have is even harder."

Tommy didn't argue with the relationship word. He looked at him. "She is scared of hurting me," he said quietly. "That sick fuck took everything from her and she continues to let him hurt her."

Jack sighed. "She doesn't want to infect you, Tommy; it is a real fear for her. You need to look at it from her point of view."

"I try to, but there is no opening, no way for me to show her that I am not scared of her hurting me. She just doesn't want to try," he walked to the chair and sat down.

Jack stood up and walked to his friend. "Look, as a doctor, I know you get it, but Tommy, Brittany isn't the same. She is fighting this disease and it has, up until now, been winning. The fact that you can see past it isn't so easy for her to handle. She has to deal with the what-ifs and no matter what you tell her, she feels it is ultimately on her. What this guy did to her was not only destroy her faith in man, but destroy her ability to recognize love before it even started," Jack walked over and grabbed two bottles of water from the mini fridge.

"When did you become Dr. Phil?" Tommy asked with a smile.

"So, do you want to tell me what happened?" Jack handed him a bottle of water and sat down with a grin. "The office hours begin now."

******

Stephanie smiled at Brittany when her friend opened the door for her. She could see that Brittany had been crying. "Want to talk about it?" she asked as she hugged her friend.

Brittany wiped her face and sighed. "I don't think there is anything to talk about."

"After seeing Tommy's face, I beg to differ," Stephanie said as she walked into the room.

"Was he okay?" she asked as she sat down on the couch. She picked up the blanket and began to play with the fabric.

"He looked like you do, like you lost your best friend," Stephanie sat down next to her. "Tell me what happened."

Brittany looked at her friend. "I think I'm falling in love with him, Steph."

Stephanie smiled a huge smile. "Britt, that's wonderful," she looked at her friends' expression. "That's not wonderful?"

Brittany shook her head. "I can't offer him anything. I can't be with him."

Stephanie was at a loss. "Why? Because you're HIV positive?"

Brittany looked at her hands. "Because I am damaged. Having HIV is just a reminder of that damage," she looked at her friend. "I look at you and Jack and I see what could be. It's a fantasy life that I can't have. I have a viral load that fluctuates because of the damage to my body. I could not only infect Tommy every time my platelets get low, but I could put him through something so much worse."

Stephanie knew what she meant. "Brittany, you don't have AIDS. He won't have to watch you die."

Brittany wiped her tears. "He has suffered so much loss, Stephanie. How do I go into a relationship knowing I will most likely contribute to that loss? I can't do that to him."

Stephanie looked at her and felt her own memories creep up. "I was able to open my heart because I met someone like Jack who showed me that I was worth it. He was so amazing because he took the time to let me see that what I thought about my life and what I 'deserved' was so wrong. I am worth love and I am worth respect and so are you, for as long as that may be. Tommy is a wonderful man and he loves you, whether or not he has said it. He is scared of hurting you and pushing you, but I can tell you from experience, you will find something that is so much more powerful than the fear. If you let him love you, everything else will make sense in a way you never thought possible," Stephanie smiled as she thought of Jack. "I know you're scared, but so is he. Maybe if you let him in a little at a time, you both can find something amazingly wonderful," she stood up, wanting to see Jack, to thank him, to love him. "Just think about it, okay?"

Brittany nodded as she walked Stephanie to the door. "Thank you; and thank Jack, too."

Chapter Thirty-Six:

Stephanie came in to her room and saw Jack was asleep on the couch. Tommy must have left. She smiled as she walked over to him and sat down on the floor near his head. She watched him sleeping and put her hand on her stomach. She was so proud to be his wife and to be carrying his baby. Being with Brittany and Tommy made her appreciate everything she had built with Jack. She knew how precious their love was and she never wanted to take it for granted. She smoothed his hair away from his eyes and he began to stir. He smiled before he even opened his eyes.

"I missed you," he said as he woke up, looking at her.

"I missed you more," she said softly.

He sat up and pulled her to him. She sat down on his lap. "How did your talk go with Tommy?" she asked him as she played with his hand.

"I don't know," he said. "I tried to get him to see her fears, but he is so damn stubborn," he looked at her. "How about Brittany? Did you get through to her?"

Stephanie rested her head on his shoulder. "I just love you," she said, not answering his question.

He tilted her head up to look at him. "I love you too. What's going on in your head?"

She shrugged. "I don't know, I just wonder why I am so lucky. I mean, I just look at Brittany and her fears and her doubts are so palpable. I wonder why I am able to live my life with such good health and happiness."

He sighed, "I wish you wouldn't apologize for being happy and healthy. I am your husband and you are my life. If you got sick, I don't think I would make it, and to hear you talk like this, it breaks my heart."

She touched his face. "I'm sorry, I don't mean to dwell on it, I really don't, it's just that Tommy and Brittany are having such a hard time, that I guess it's just bringing up a lot of my issues."

He looked at her. "I get it, Stephanie, I do, but I will never apologize for being happy or for you being healthy."

"I would never want you to. I am so happy, Jack. I have everything I ever dreamed of. I am sorry I am making our last day such a downer," she smiled at him. "Can I make it up to you?"

He grinned. "First of all, you are not being a downer. Second, you never have to apologize to me or hide what you are feeling, and third, yes, you can make it up to me."

She smiled. "Good, because I have a special outfit I have saved for tonight."

He raised his eyebrows. "Really? Does it look good on the floor because that's where it's going to be?"

She laughed. "Nice," she said as she leaned in to kiss him.

*****

Tommy made his way back to the room after taking a long walk. He needed to clear his head and think about everything that had happened. He walked into the room and saw she wasn't there. He checked the bathroom, but it was empty. He ran his hand through his hair and went down to the lobby. Walking through the restaurant, he looked out the window at the enclosure where they had been the other day, playing in the snow and saw her standing by a tree, her red hair clearly visible under a hat. She hugged her coat around her and was looking at something in her hands. He walked out into the cold.

"Penny for your thoughts," he said as he walked up to her.

She turned and looked at him. "Hi."

"Hi yourself. It's cold out here," he said.

She nodded. "It is."

He looked at what she was holding. "What's that?"

She looked down and handed him the paper. He looked at it and his heart sank. It was a story about a Barbara Rose sighting at the resort. "The paramedic?"

She nodded. "I guess, but who knows. It doesn't matter. It's out now, so I should just get used to it," she turned and looked at him. "I am going to take a cab and head back tonight. I think it's best that my vacation ends," she walked back inside, leaving him standing in the cold.

Tommy stood still for a minute before following her back into the resort, making his way back to the room to talk to her. He walked in to find her packing her things. "So that's it? We get too close and you bolt?"

She kept packing. "This isn't about you, Tommy. This is about me and what I need to do to live my life."

He nodded. "Okay, so I don't matter at all. Everything we have been through, it all meant nothing. You are just going to go back and pretend like what, nothing happened?" he spoke with anger and fear.

She calmly closed the suitcase and turned to look at him. "It's better if that's what happens. You can just spend the evening getting a good night's sleep, which I am sure you haven't had since I've been with you. You can relax without worrying about what crazy reaction I might have to something you do or say. You can eat and laugh with your friends without watching me and making sure I'm okay. What could possibly be better than that?" she couldn't help the biting sarcasm that came out in droves.

Tommy looked at her. "Are you through?" he crossed his arms in front of him. "I think you're right. You don't have any idea of what it means to be in a relationship. People don't leave when things get rough. They don't look at the other person as a burden, or an obligation. You don't get to tell me how things will be."

She looked at him, her eyes blazing. "Why not? Why can't I do something for you? Why can't I leave now, before we get in too deep and save you from the hurt you will undoubtedly suffer because of me?"

He wanted to scream at the top of his lungs. "You are the single most stubborn, aggravating, infuriating woman I have ever met. You are the most thick headed, arrogant human being I have ever known."

"Then why do you care if I leave? It should be easy for you to let me go. Why can't you just let me leave?" she asked him, her resolve crumbling.

"Because I love you, and I want you to stay."

She stood there for a minute, not sure she heard him correctly. She shook her head. "No, Tommy, you don't mean that."

"Like hell I don't. Look, I am not really sure why I love you, because God knows you are driving me crazy, but I do, nonetheless. If you can just walk away from this, from me, then I am the biggest sucker of them all," he said emphatically.

She stood, rooted in place, looking at him. "Why?"

"Because for my whole life, I have been asleep. You woke me up, Red. No, you didn't just wake me up; you poured a bucket of ice onto my life. "I like who I am when I'm with you, and when I look at you, I just want," he stopped for a minute.

"You want what?" she asked him softly.

"I just want you," he said simply.

She knew he was standing there, exposed. The next move was hers, and she didn't know if she had the courage to take it. She walked over and faced him, looking into his eyes. She put her hand on his chest and squinted as she studied his features.

He felt so bare, so vulnerable by the way she looked at him, but he held her gaze. She moved her hands to his face and blinked, letting the unshed tears in her eyes fall down her cheeks. She took a deep breath. "I don't see it," she whispered.

"Don't see what?" he asked her, almost holding his breath.

"There's no sadness or pity, no regret or remorse. I just see the man I am completely in love with," she spoke softly and finally, a small smile broke out across her face.

He shook his head. "Did you say you loved me, too?" he put her hands in his.

She nodded, tears falling from her eyes. "I did. And I do. I love you."

He pulled her to him and she met his lips in an intense and passionate kiss. He held her tightly, not wanting there to be any doubt in her mind at all of his feelings. They held that pose for a long time until she broke it. She felt light headed, but she knew why this time. He took her breath away. She wrapped her arms around him and put her head on his shoulder. He held her, not wanting the moment to end.

Brittany backed away from him after a moment. She walked to the couch and sat down. He walked with her and knelt down in front of her. "Are you okay?" he asked her.

She nodded and smiled. "I guess I am a bit overwhelmed by everything," she looked at him. "But

Tommy, this doesn't change what I'm facing, and it just makes it harder."

He looked at her and smiled. "Why would love make it harder?"

She ran a hand through her hair. "Because now, it opens you up to so much. I don't want you to get hurt. I don't want what has touched me, to touch you or anyone you love."

He shrugged and sat down next to her. "But don't you see; it already has. I'm involved now, and you can't just change that, no matter how much you might wish you could."

She put her hand on his thigh. "I don't wish I could change it. I don't want to be without you," she looked at her hand.

He turned and cupped the side of her face in his hand. "I'm so glad you finally came to your senses," he smiled when she smiled. "Now can we just enjoy our last evening here tonight? I wish you would just let me keep your mind off of everything else for a little while."

"Okay, I'll try," she said.

"Okay, I'll take that," he pulled her to him for another kiss.

Chapter Thirty-Seven:

"So where is Brittany going to live after we get back? Do you think we can get her place cleaned up?" Stephanie asked Jack, as she got ready for their evening.

"I don't see how she can go back to her house while that pervert is still free. We need to make sure she is kept safe. Plus, I don't know how she will feel about going back there," he said as he straightened his tie.

She was quiet for a minute. "Do you think she can ever go back to her life?"

He shrugged. "I don't know. So much has to be determined. Will people leave her alone or will she be bombarded with her past. I am just not sure what to expect. I do know that I would love to hear her sing."

Stephanie smiled. "Jack, she has the most beautiful voice. It was so special and so pure. I hope maybe one day, she will share that gift again."

He walked up to her and wrapped his arms around her from behind. "Are you ready for dinner?"

"Yes, but you still didn't tell me where we are going," she turned around in his arms.

He looked out into the main room of their suite. "Right there."

She looked out and then looked at him. "We are going to the table in our own room?" she was confused.

"Yes. I want to have a romantic dinner with my beautiful wife in the privacy of our room where we can do anything we want," he nibbled on her ear.

She smiled at him. "I think that's a wonderful idea."

The room bell rang and he grinned. "Dinner is here," he walked to the door and opened it. The concierge brought in a table, decorated beautifully with two covered dishes on it. He brought it to the middle of the room and Jack tipped him as he left. He walked over to her. "Shall I escort you to the table?"

She took his hand. "Why that would be lovely."

They walked to the table and he moved her chair for her. He took the napkin and placed it on her lap before filling her glass with sparkling cider. He did the same for himself and then sat across from her. He picked up his glass and she did as well. "A toast to my beautiful, intelligent, sexy, amazing and incredibly talented wife and soon to be mother of my child. I am so blessed to be sharing this amazing journey with you and from today forward, I want to make each and every one of your days the best it can be. I promise you I will never give you reason to doubt my love for you. You are my heart and my hero," he clinked her glass and they took a drink, Stephanie trying to keep her emotions in check.

"You are just amazing," she said. "I don't know how you do it."

"Do what?" he asked her, his dimples showing as he looked at her.

"Make me love you even more than I already do. I wish you could see it," she said.

"See what?" he asked, confused.

"My happiness, my joy, my love. I just feel so full of everything, Jack. I can't find the words to describe what you do to me. I just want you to always remember that," she said through shining eyes.

He walked over to her and knelt in front of her. "I don't need to remember it, because you are going to show it to me every day," he picked her hand up in his and brought it to his lips.

She smiled. "I like that plan."

"Me too. Shall we eat?" he stood up and walked back to his chair.

She nodded and they opened their food.

******

Tommy and Brittany sat in front of the fire, both lost in thought before Tommy spoke up.

"Are you hungry?"

She looked at him. "Maybe a little."

"We can order something to eat if you want," he said.

She looked at him and took a deep breath. "How about if we go downstairs and eat in the restaurant we saw the first night we were here."

"With all of the couples squished in tiny booths?" he asked her.

"Yes, with all of the couples squished in tiny booths," she smiled at him.

"Okay. Let's go," he said and stood up, helping her up with him. They headed out to the restaurant.

****

"So, where is the outfit you were going to show me tonight?" Jack asked Stephanie as they stood at the window, looking out into the darkness after they ate.

She looked at him. "I'm wearing it," she pouted.

He looked flustered. "Oh, it's great, I mean, I didn't realize that, but it's nice."

She grinned. "Just kidding."

He pouted. "Don't do that to me. It's mean."

"Are you ready for dessert? I will have to change for a minute," she said. "Don't pout."

"Hurry back," he said and went to get his surprise for her.

A few minutes later, Stephanie walked out of the bathroom wearing a bathrobe. She looked to see him lying on the bed. He was also wearing only a robe, but he looked very uncomfortable.

She walked over to the mini fridge and grabbed the can of whipped cream and walked to the bed. "What's wrong?" she could tell he looked strange.

"I got you a present, but I don't think I put it on right," he squirmed.

She laughed. "Where is it?"

He opened the robe and she almost squirted the whipped cream all over. He had on a g-string that was made out of something unique.

"It's chocolate," he said. "They said you would love it, you know, penis and chocolate."

Laughing, she said, "I think the phrase is peanuts and chocolate," she stared at the mound of chocolate, which sat covering his groin. "Is it supposed to look like that?" she stifled another laugh. "Maybe you needed a bigger size," she smiled at him.

"Can I move it now?" he asked, laughing with her.

"No, let me," she put the whipped cream down and stood before him. She dropped her robe and he dropped his jaw. She had on a body suit with openings between her legs and for her breasts. She walked over to him and leaned down to inspect the chocolate. "I think we might need surgery here," she looked up at him through her long hair and gently bit a piece of the chocolate. She stood up with the chunk of fudge in her mouth and proceeded to savor it between her lips. The piece began to melt and she leaned in to him. "Can you help me with that?"

He reached up and licked the chocolate from her chin. She stood back up and swallowed the delicious dessert. She leaned back down to his waist and he thought the chocolate would pop off on its own any minute. "Careful, there is more under there than before," he said, mesmerized by her outfit.

"Well, this isn't my area of expertise, but now that I think of it, I do work with bones," laughing she winked at him and continued to inspect the chocolate. "But I have been known to extricate a few things in my career, especially when it will benefit me. I promise I'll be very delicate," she straddled his waist, her back to his face, giving him a perfect view of her outfit. She ran her hands down his waist and gently ran her hands under the chocolate, pushing up and releasing the chocolate mound. She leaned down to inspect the damage. "I think we may need some intensive care," she reached over and grabbed the whipped cream. She moved to face him, sitting on her knees next to him on the bed. She sprayed the whipped cream onto him, the cool sensation made him shudder as she looked at him. "Let me make sure everything is working correctly," she leaned down and gently ran her hand over his thighs, paying careful attention not to touch the whipped cream. "Here is some chocolate," she leaned in and licked a piece off of his thigh.

"Mmmm," she said with her lips on his skin, making the sensation of her vibrating voice drive him wild. She looked at him, his eyes almost black as he watched her take him in her mouth and clean off every bit of whipped cream,

"Stephanie, come here," he said in a sultry voice. She looked at him and crawled towards him. He picked up the whipped cream and sprayed some on each of her breasts. She leaned back on the bed and he devoured the cream and her flesh. She arched her back as she ran her hands through his hair. He sat back and looked at her. "You are so beautiful."

She sat up and wrapped her arms around him. "You make me beautiful," she smoothed imaginary lines on his face and got on her knees to be his height. "You have made this vacation the most amazing thing I have ever experienced."

He tucked her hair behind her ear. "That's because we are together, Stephanie. My love, my life," he leaned her back onto the soft sheets. She sucked in her breath as he filled her so completely. She moved a little and he looked at her. "Are you okay?" he whispered to her.

"I am more than okay. Just love me," she said as they both lost themselves in their feelings of love and fulfillment. Later, as they both lay there, Stephanie sat up suddenly. Jack sat up and looked at her.

"What is it? Are you okay? Did I hurt you?" he looked at her face, at her tears. "What's wrong?"

She looked at him. "I know it's early, but I think I felt the baby move," she smiled as her tears fell.

"Really? It really moved?" he was so excited.

"I think so, I mean, I have never felt it before, so I don't know, but I think maybe," she looked at him, her eyes shining.

Jack looked at her. "Do you think it knows what we just did?" His eyebrows shot up and Stephanie laughed.

"No, I don't think we need to hide anything just yet," she smiled and he pulled her into his arms.

"Thank you for this life," he said to her as they snuggled for their last night in paradise.

Chapter Thirty-Eight:

Tommy and Brittany sat in a small half moon shaped booth in the back corner of the restaurant. He was staring at her as she nursed her hot chocolate.

"What?" she asked.

He shook his head. "Nothing, I was just thinking."

She smiled. "Care to elaborate?"

He shook his head again. "No," he said with a smile.

"I see. So you're just going to stare at me?" she looked at him, her eyes twinkling.

"Maybe, what are you going to do about it?" he challenged her, fun in his voice.

She turned and waved to the server. He came over and she whispered something in his ear. He smiled and nodded, walking away.

Tommy looked at her. "What was that about?" he asked.

She shrugged. "Nothing," she said smiling.

They sat in silence for a minute when the DJ spoke through the crowd. "This next song is for Tommy from Red."

Tommy looked at her, surprised at the very least. She stood up and walked over to him. "May I have this dance?"

He took her hand. "I would be honored," he walked with her to the dance floor, overwhelmed that she felt comfortable enough to be this bold in public. He listened to the song and grinned. "Air Supply?"

She wrapped her arm around him and took his hand in hers. "The words seemed fitting," she smiled as she rested her head on his chest. He held her close as they moved to the music.

The music ended and they broke apart. She looked into his eyes and touched his face, pulling him to her lips. He kissed her softly and for that moment, the only that mattered was each other.

******

"I think I got a rash from that outfit," Stephanie said as they walked into their house after driving back from Pennsylvania. She scratched her back.

"It was worth it," Jack said as he put down their bags. "I don't know about the chocolate, though."

"So worth it. I won't be able to eat chocolate and peanuts again without that image," she giggled.

"Good, I should always be on your mind when you are enjoying chocolate and peanuts," he wrapped his arms around her and leaned in to kiss her.

"Mmm, so what's on tap for work tomorrow? How come we have to go back to work so fast?" she walked over to the counter and looked at the mail they had picked up.

"I think Tommy and I have some consult to go to, and after that, I don't know. I am sure we will find out what colossal event has occurred in our absence," he said.

She nodded. "When is your dad coming in?"

He looked at her. "Tomorrow I think. Jenny emailed me their flight plans," he sat down and sighed.

She walked over to the couch. "What is it?"

He ran his hand through his hair. "I don't know; it's just a really dangerous procedure for him to go through. I can think of numerous ways this could go wrong."

She smoothed his hair after he ran his hand through it. "That's the problem with being doctors. We always look at the worst case; but Jack, your dad has defied the odds so much already. He is destined to be with you for a long time."

He looked at her. "I know, but he has to be in rough shape from the treatment. I wish he would wait longer."

Stephanie thought about it for a minute. "If he waits, the tumor could probably begin metastasizing again. The treatment was very localized and he said that he felt great throughout. I think we need to trust what he says and just be there as his family, not his doctors."

He shook his head. "I don't know how to do that."

"That's why I'm here," she grinned. "I will rein you in when you swim out too far."

"Promise?" he asked her. "You will be my life preserver?"

"Always," she said and pulled his face to hers.

****

"So you're sure you are okay staying there alone?" Tommy asked Brittany as they spoke on the phone after they all arrived back home. He had wanted her to stay with him, but she refused, deciding to stay in the hotel for the time being.

"Yes, I am fine. Everything I need is here, and if not, I can call room service. I will be okay, Tommy," she smiled into the phone. "You should go to bed; you have a big day at work tomorrow."

He sighed. "I don't want to go back to work."

"I know, but a little normalcy will be good for everyone," she said. "We can have dinner tomorrow if you want."

He smiled. "I would like that. You'll call me if you need anything? Even if it's the middle of the night and you need to talk, I'll be here."

"I know. I'll see you tomorrow," she said softly.

"Goodnight," he said.

"Goodnight Tommy," she said and they hung up. Brittany sighed and went to take a shower and try to sleep.

****

Tommy tossed and turned, not able to fall asleep. He had grown accustomed to having her near him and now, he felt an emptiness in his bed. He was also worried about what was going to be at the hospital when they got there. He got out of bed and walked to the guest room where she had stayed. He hadn't changed anything yet, hoping she may decide to come back. He sat in the bed and felt a little closer to her.

Brittany picked up the phone to call Tommy for the third time, but again decided against it. He needed his sleep and she needed to be able to get by on her own. She felt like a teenager, missing him after only a few hours. She smiled as she thought of their vacation. She was so glad she decided to go with them. She really felt like things were finally looking up.

****

"I can't believe the craziness here today, I will be very glad to get home," Jack said to Tommy as they sat in the locker room after finishing their last procedures for the day. Jack closed his locker and smiled at Tommy. "Have any plans for the night?"

Tommy looked at him. "Nope, just a relaxing evening at home."

Jack smiled. "Alone?"

The men exchanged looks. "Maybe, maybe not."

They both laughed. "Did you go by Brittany's office? Any reporters?" Jack asked him.

"No, it was relatively calm, and I hope it stays that way. I know she is going to want to come in and start doing paperwork soon, and I just hope things stay quiet," Tommy sighed. "I know that's probably wishful thinking."

Jack looked at his friend. "It didn't seem like they knew she worked here, just that she was a patient, so maybe the trail is cold?"

Tommy nodded. "Maybe," he closed his locker and grabbed his bag.

Chapter Thirty-Nine:

Stephanie and Jack waited for Ron and Jenny at the airport. Stephanie saw them as they got off at the gate. She waved and walked to Ron who gave her a big hug.

"Stephanie, I'm so glad to see you, you look wonderful."

Jenny hugged her after. "It's so good to be back home," she said.

Jack stood back a little, checking out his father. He still couldn't get used to the fact that he was back in his life. He wouldn't admit it, but he couldn't lose him again. Ron walked up and looked his son in the eye. "Jack?" he said. Stephanie motioned for him to hug his father.

Jack pulled him into a hug. "Hi dad," he said.

Ron smiled broadly at his son. "I'm so glad you came to get us."

Stephanie walked up to Jack and took his arm. "We couldn't let you take a cab. Besides, we figured you might want to have dinner and we could talk."

Jack smiled at her. Subtlety was not her strong suit. Jenny smiled at them. "I am famished," she linked arms with Ron and the four walked to baggage claim.

A while later they all sat in a nice diner, enjoying some soup while waiting for their meals. Ron looked at Stephanie. "You look different, somehow. Well rested maybe?"

Stephanie smiled and looked at Jack. He nodded and she turned to them. "I was going to say the same thing to you, grandpa."

Ron looked from his son to Stephanie. "Are you guys pregnant?"

Stephanie nodded and Jack smiled a huge smile. "We are. We are going to have a baby."

Ron stood up and pulled Jack into a hug. He slapped him on the back, and Jenny went and hugged Stephanie. "That is the best news I have heard in a long time."

They all sat down again. "Grandpa, wow," Ron said.

Jack looked at him. "I am counting on you being here for a long time, dad," he said to him.

Ron took the look from his son and nodded. "I intend to, son."

Stephanie smiled at them with tears in her eyes. She knew how much his dad meant to her husband and how scared he was to lose him. She prayed everything would work out for them.

*****

Brittany waited in the exam room for the results of her follow up appointment with Dr. Schmidt the next morning. She had dinner with Tommy last night, but didn't tell him she was going in because she hoped to surprise him with a good report. She was feeling much more like her old self and she knew a lot of that was because of him. She smiled as the doctor walked in.

"So, tell me the damage," she said in a playful tone.

Dr. Schmidt sat down and looked at Brittany. She began to get a little nervous. "Brittany, you suffered a severe blow to your immune system with the attack, and although I am happy to see some of your numbers come back, your viral load remains higher than I would like. I want to try a slightly different drug cocktail and see if we can't lower it," he sighed at her crestfallen look. "I know that this means you are going to feel worse for a while, but we need to be a little more aggressive with your treatment. We will also have to wait on your foot surgery until your numbers are stable," he smiled. "The good news is that your platelets are holding their own, and your counts aren't worse, so whatever treatment you had while you were away seems to have done wonders for that."

She nodded. "Okay, I'll do whatever you think is best."

He stood up and touched her arm. "Brittany, you have been fighting this disease like a champion for many years, and this is no different. You need to believe you can win. I believe you can win."

She smiled at him. "Thanks Matt. I appreciate all you have done for me."

"I'll order the new cocktail and you can pick it up later tonight," he said. "You'll call if you need anything?"

She nodded. "I will." She watched him leave and put her head in her hands. She knew what was coming, and it wasn't going to be pretty. She thought of Tommy and her heart sank. She couldn't tell him. She couldn't make him go through this. She didn't know if she could go through this again. She stood up and picked up her purse, not really sure where she was headed.

****

"So tell me again when you go in?" Jack asked Ron as they sat in the hospital cafeteria the next afternoon. Ron had come in for his pre-op blood work and had met Jack between surgeries.

"I go in on Wednesday and hopefully, I will only have to stay a week at the most. It all depends on how quickly the hepatic artery resumes function." Ron said. "Hopefully it will be sooner."

Jack sighed. "Are you sure this is the right time for surgery? I mean did they check everything? What are your bilirubin levels?"

Ron smiled at his son, knowing he was asking these questions out of fear. "I am going to get through this and be able to annoy you for years to come."

Jack brushed off his attempt at analyzing his fears. "I just want to make sure you checked all avenues."

Ron nodded. "Jenny and I are doctors too, you know, and believe me, Jenny has used every resource she has to make sure I was seen and treated by the best. I know what I'm doing and what the best course of action will be for me," he sighed. "Look, Jack, I have no one to blame for my condition other than myself. I am an alcoholic, and although I have been sober for years, the damage I did can't be reversed, and I don't just mean to my body. Son, I'm sorry for abandoning you the way I did and for leaving you to deal with so much on your own. I can't take that back, but I can make better choices today and be here for you now."

Jack felt his hard exterior soften a little. "I appreciate that," he said quietly.

"So tell me, how is Stephanie doing with the pregnancy? I remember with you, your mom was sick as a dog. She yelled at me daily for doing this to her," Ron laughed and his eyes crinkled.

Jack smiled. "She is amazing, dad. The morning sickness has been minimal, but I know she has suffered more than she tells me."

Ron grinned. "Sounds like Stephanie. Do you know what you're having?"

Jack shook his head. "No, and I don't think we will find out ahead of time. It doesn't matter, as long as we have a healthy baby," he looked at his watch and sighed. "I have to go; can I see you before you go in tomorrow?"

"Of course; I will be here at 7am and the surgery isn't scheduled until 10," Ron said to him.

"Okay, then I'll check in on you before you go in," he said.

"I'll count on it, son." Ron said and Jack left.

Chapter Forty:

Tommy tried her cell again and got no answer. He tried to calm his fears and not imagine all of the horrific things that may have happened. Maybe she fell asleep? Maybe she was in the shower? She knew he was going to be home early today and he wanted to talk to her.

He picked up his cell phone to try again and saw it was ringing.

"Hello?" he said, not looking at the number.

"Hi Tommy" Brittany spoke softly into the phone.

"Red, where are you? What happened? Are you okay?" he was so relieved to hear from her.

"Yes, I'm okay. Can I come over?" she asked him.

He smiled into the phone. "Of course you can come over, you don't need to ask."

"Good, I'm in your driveway," she said and he smiled.

He opened the door to greet her. "Hi? You scared me to death. You can't be unreachable when there is a psycho after you," he said emphatically.

She knew he was right. "I'm sorry, I just needed to figure something out."

He could see she had something big on her mind. They walked into the house and she sat down before looking at him. "I was going to leave," she said.

"Leave where?" he sat down, confused.

"I had a follow up with Dr. Schmidt this morning and I've been driving around since," she said, looking at her hands.

Tommy felt his heart lurch. "Why didn't you tell me? I would have gone with you."

She smiled. "I thought I was going to be able to surprise you. I thought I was going to get a clean bill of health and we could celebrate. I had been feeling better, you know."

He took her hands in his. "Tell me what he said."

She met his gaze, disheartened. "My viral load is still high, Tommy," her voice was soft. "He wants to try another drug cocktail."

He pulled her to him and held her, knowing how this scared her. He sat back and touched her face. "You can fight this, I know you can."

"Liar," she said and brushed her tears away. "I am not sure your faith in me is warranted this time."

He shook his head. "You are so wrong. You are the strongest person I have ever met."

She looked at him. "I wasn't going to tell you, Tommy. I wanted to run, to let you move on with your life and not have to deal with all of this."

"What made you call me?" he asked.

She shrugged. "I love you and I need your strength to help me," she looked at him. "For the first time in my life, I don't feel so alone."

He touched her hair, smoothing it down her shoulders. He was at a loss for words. "You can have all of my strength," he said and pulled her to him.

Later that evening, they lay together on the couch, Tommy running his hand through her hair. They had the hockey game on TV and were just relaxing. He spoke after a while. "Why don't you stay here while you adjust to your meds?"

She sighed. "I don't think that's a good idea. It won't be pretty."

He smiled at her. "I'm a pediatric surgeon in Oncology, it won't be the first time someone has thrown up on me."

She looked down. "This is different, Tommy."

He tilted her face up at him. "It doesn't have to be. I want to help you through this, will you let me?"

She smiled at him. "How about if it gets to the point where I feel like I need help, you will be the first one I call."

He didn't want to push her on it, so he agreed and she snuggled up to him, content for the moment.

******

The next morning, Tommy met Jack and Stephanie for Ron's surgery. "They should be starting the procedure now. I'm glad you decided to wait out here instead of the observation room," Tommy said to Jack.

"Stephanie wouldn't let me stay up there. She can be persuasive when she needs to be," Jack smiled while he looked at his wife. She was sitting with Jenny, and he knew she was trying to distract her from worrying. Jack crossed his arms in front of his chest.

"He's going to be fine, Jack. Try not to worry," Tommy said.

Jack ran his hand through his hair. "I know, I know," he said and smiled as Stephanie came up to him and wrapped her arms around him from the side. Tommy smiled at her.

"How are you feeling?" Tommy asked her.

Stephanie beamed at him. "Fat and amazing," she laughed when Jack looked at her like she was crazy.

"You are not fat. You are carrying my seed and you look radiant," Jack said and Tommy and Stephanie burst out laughing.

"Your seed?" Stephanie said between laughs.

Jack looked hurt. "What? It's true."

She leaned up and kissed him. "You manly man, planting your seed in your woman," she giggled.

Tommy rolled his eyes at them. "You guys are something else."

Jack smiled as he looked at Tommy. "Hey, how is Brittany doing? I thought maybe she would come."

He shook his head. "I didn't want to say anything, but her last blood test wasn't great. Dr. Schmidt is changing her cocktail."

Stephanie sighed. "She needs to be home and near a bathroom. I am so sorry, Tommy, this has to be scary for you," she hugged him.

Jack felt a familiar pang in his heart when he heard Tommy's news. Although it wasn't the same, he remembered how Stephanie felt when she had to begin her injections. It was a helpless feeling and he didn't envy Tommy. He shook his head and looked at his friend. "Why don't you go be with her?"

He smiled. "I will, but I wanted to be here with you."

"She wouldn't let you stay, huh?" Jack said.

Tommy blushed. "She kicked me out and told me to be here. I am to report back with any news."

Stephanie smiled at the two men. She and Brittany were so lucky; they were the best there was.

Jenny stood up as the doctor came out. Jack walked up to her and Tommy and Stephanie followed. "He did great, came through the surgery just fine."

"Oh thank God," Jenny said and Jack hugged her. He looked at the surgeon.

"How did the rest of the liver look? Were you able to save enough of the lobe after removing the tumor? Was the hepatic artery compromised? How about the bile ducts?" Jack asked all he could think of.

Stephanie looked at him and smiled. "Your dad made it, the surgeon said it was successful, let's just bask in that for now."

He nodded. "Sorry, I just."

"Think of all of the complications," the surgeon finished for him. He smiled. "I gave you full access to his chart and you are welcome to review any and all findings and results," he looked at Jenny. "I'll take you to recovery."

Jenny smiled at them before walking with the doctor. Stephanie turned to Jack and he pulled her into a bear hug. He let out a huge sigh of relief. "Wow, unbelievable," he said.

Stephanie ran her hand over his chest. "No, not unbelievable, you and Ron deserve a relationship that will grow and flourish. Our child needs to know its grandpa Ron and he is going to dote on him or her. I think this is fate finally getting it right."

He smiled. "Okay, I'll go with that," he leaned in and kissed her. "You should go see Brittany, she could probably use some good news," Jack said to Tommy.

Stephanie looked at him. "Just remember, she is going to look bad and feel worse. Try to listen to her and respect what she needs, but don't let her throw you out. She needs support and she is probably scared."

Tommy shook his head. "I know, thanks, and please call me if there is anything you guys need."

"You got it," Jack said as he and Stephanie were once again entwined together. Tommy chuckled as he left. He drove right to Brittany's hotel and he wasn't too worried when she didn't answer her phone. He knew the meds would have really kicked in and she was probably feeling terrible. He knocked on the door and when she opened it, he could see she must have had a rough night. She walked back to the couch to sit down, her face pale and beads of sweat on her forehead. She leaned back and closed her eyes.

"What have you eaten today?" he asked her.

She looked at him and smiled. "Nothing that seemed to like staying in my stomach."

He sat down next to her and took her hand. "Maybe you should go to the hospital," he touched her face, alarmed at the warmth.

She looked at him. "No, Tommy, this is all part and parcel of the meds. It will pass. If I can't keep things down in a few days, I'll go in for an IV," she closed her eyes. "I told you it wouldn't be pretty."

He ran his hand through her hair. "I just don't like to see you suffer."

"And that is why I told you to stay away. I can handle this, I will make it through," she said softly.

"I said I don't like to see you suffer, not that I can't be here. I want to be here, to help you and to take care of you. Have you taken anything for the nausea?" he asked, smoothing her hair from her face.

She touched his face. "Yes, but hold that thought," she ran to the bathroom.

He sighed and walked to the small kitchen area in the long stay hotel she was in. He grabbed some Gatorade and walked back over to the bathroom door, knocking softly.

"Are you okay?"

"I'm just going to lay here for a bit," she said softly and he pushed the door open. She was on the ground, her head in her hands.

"Red let me help you," he said.

She started to cry. "No, I don't want you to deal with this, please leave me alone."

He put the drink down and walked over to her. He gathered her in his arms and took her into the bedroom, placing her on the bed. She was weak and offered no objection to his help. He went and got a cool washcloth and the drink and came back. He moved her long hair away and put the cool washcloth on her neck. He let her stay still for a little while and then he went to get the thermometer. He checked her temperature and was disheartened at the high reading. "Brittany, can you look at me?"

She opened her blue eyes and stared up at him. "It's okay, Tommy. I will get through this. Just think of it as a hangover."

He smiled. "If this is like a hangover for you, I think I can handle my liquor a lot better than you," he said as she smiled, closing her eyes. He wished more than anything he could take this from her, but all he could do was sit there and be with her.

"How is Ron?" she asked through closed eyes.

"Came through surgery with flying colors," he said.

"Good, that's really good. I will try to go and see him tomorrow," she whispered.

He looked at her and smiled. "Let's just get through tonight," he put his arm around her and watched her sleep.

She woke up a while later and turned to look at him. "You're still here?" she asked.

He smiled. "Yes, why wouldn't I be here?"

She shrugged. "I don't know, but I'm glad you are," she snuggled up to him and fell asleep again.

Chapter Forty-One:

Jack sat by his father's bedside while Jenny took a break. Ron had been in and out of sleep since the surgery, but his vitals were steady. Jack noticed the yellow tint to his skin and saw that the latest bilirubin readings were still elevated. All to be expected, he knew, but still, he couldn't help but feel a twinge of worry. He wanted to see how the bile ducts were responding, but the report wasn't back yet.

"Hey, how are you doing?" Tommy asked him as he walked into the room. "How is he?"

Jack looked at him. "Stable, all seems to be good. His levels are still high, but that's to be expected," Jack ran his hand through his hair as Tommy sat down and handed him a cup of coffee. "Thanks," Jack took it and smiled.

"Has he been awake yet?" Tommy asked as he looked at his friend, noticing his tired appearance.

"In and out, but he really hasn't said much," Jack said as he looked at Ron.

"What's on your mind?" Tommy pushed him.

Jack looked at him. "What do you mean?"

Tommy smiled. "I have known you for a long time, man, and I know what you're thinking. You look at him lying there and you see your mom."

Jack didn't say anything, knowing his friend was right.

Tommy patted him on the back. "This story has a different ending. Ron came back into your life for a reason and he isn't going anywhere."

Jack smiled at him. "I hope you're right."

"I always am," Tommy said and Jack rolled his eyes.

"Come on, tell me one time I was wrong," Tommy chided him.

"Danielle, Emily, Stacey," Jack's eyes twinkled.

Tommy laughed. "Very funny."

"So who were all of those girls exactly?"

The men turned at the sound of Brittany's voice in the doorway. She was smiling at them.

Tommy smacked Jack who stood up and smiled. "I'm kidding. Hey, how are you feeling?" he walked over and hugged her.

"Much better, thanks. How is your dad?" Brittany smiled at Tommy as she walked over to him.

"He is holding his own. He should be out for most of the afternoon," Jack said.

"I'm so glad he was able to have the surgery," she smiled at them. "Where's Stephanie?"

"She had a meeting with a potential surgical candidate. She should be back here later this afternoon," he stretched his long frame as he walked over to the window. He turned and looked at them. "I can't tell you guys how much I appreciate you being here."

Brittany smiled and sat down, looking at Ron. "That's what family is for."

Jack looked at Tommy who seemed surprised by her words. The men grinned at each other as Jack walked over to Ron. "I couldn't agree more."

Ron began to stir and Jack looked at him. "Dad?" he asked tentatively. He was a bit alarmed at the yellow in Ron's eyes.

"Jack, hi," he said softly.

"You did great. Everything went really well," Jack said to him.

He nodded slowly. "Good. When can I get out of here?"

Jack smiled. "Probably not until you can stay awake through a whole conversation," he said as Ron drifted off to sleep again.

Tommy walked over and smiled at his friend. "I think he is going to be just fine," he patted Jack on the shoulder.

"Did you see the yellow? His eyes don't lie," Jack said.

"It is not uncommon for the Alkaline Phosphatase and Albumin levels to take a while before returning to normal after a hepatectomy. His bile duct may take longer to resume normal functioning, but it isn't anything to be concerned about unless it lasts. His kidney enzymes are normal and that is a good way to figure out how everything is functioning. His prognosis is really good, Jack," Brittany said and turned to see them looking at her funny.

She shrugged. "What? I did a fellowship with a hepatologist in London," she smiled as she stood up. "So listen to me, because I've seen the worst and this is not it. Ron is in good hands and I have a feeling he will be just fine."

Jack felt a lot better. "Thanks Brittany. I really appreciate that."

Tommy looked at her with more admiration. He just couldn't learn enough from her. He smiled. "Want to get something to eat in the cafeteria?"

She nodded. "I'm not sure what I can eat, but I'll try," she looked at Jack. "Do you want to join us?"

He shook his head. "No, I am going to stay until Jenny gets back, and then I'm meeting Stephanie. Thanks anyway."

"Okay, let us know if you need anything," Tommy said before they walked out.

******

"You know, you didn't have to come," Tommy said as they sat down in the cafeteria. She was looking very tired and he was concerned.

"I'm better; I think I'm over the worst," she took a bite of her jello. "Do you want to tell me how you are?" she looked at him and her eyes went right to his soul.

"I'm good, why?" he asked her.

She reached across the table and took his hand. "I know you haven't really told me about it, but I know how hard it must have been for you when you lost your parents. I just wondered if this was bringing up any memories."

He nodded. "A little, but my case was different. My mom was pronounced at the scene, and my dad, well, there was nothing that could be done. I mean, at first, there was a tiny bit of hope that he could recover from his injuries, but it rapidly changed. I think the worst was thinking, for a split second or two that I wouldn't lose both of them, you know. I wanted to give Julie some ray of hope. I mean I was older. I had gotten through high school with both parents. She was just a kid and she needed them," he wiped his face.

"Tommy, you needed them, too. Why don't you give yourself a break once in a while?" she smiled at him.

"I couldn't. I had to do what I could to make it better for her. I had to be strong and I had to show her that she wouldn't be alone. My parents always taught me that love was sacred and family was what we lived for. My dad and mom had such a great love and they were so in tune with each other. It never wavered, even when they fought. My mom worshipped my dad and he only had eyes for her. I don't mean to make their relationship out to be something it wasn't, I mean, they had their problems, but it was always important to work it out. They never lost sight of what brought them together in the first place, their mutual respect and trust for each other. I just wanted to make sure Julie got the same lessons I did, even it wasn't through them," he looked at her. "It's what my parents would have wanted."

She looked at him and played with an imaginary fleck of dust on the table. "If you are anything like your parents, I would think they would have wanted you to be happy, too," she smiled at him. "Tommy, Julie is an amazing woman and she is loved by an amazing man. She is starting a family and she is probably one of the most grounded people I have ever met. You did well, Tommy. I think your parents would be incredibly proud."

He looked at her, his eyes wet. "Do you think so?"

She nodded. "I know so."

****

Stephanie walked into the room and saw Jack sitting there with Jenny. She smiled at them as she made her way in. "Hey, how is everything?"

Ron opened his eyes and smiled. "Stephanie, hey."

She walked up to Ron and took his hand in hers. "Hi, I'm so glad to see you awake," she rubbed his hand.

"I think I am ready to go home." Ron said. "Maybe you can spring me out of here?"

Stephanie laughed and Jenny looked at her husband. "It doesn't matter how many people you ask, you are not going anywhere."

Ron sighed. "It was worth a try," he smiled and closed his eyes again.

Jack stood up and walked to Stephanie. "How was your consult?"

She hugged him. "Good. I think she will be a good candidate for surgery I just have to wait for some more results to be sure," she yawned.

"Will you let me take you home?" Jack asked her.

"We can stay if you want, I don't mind," Stephanie said.

"You two get going. I've got it from here. I promise I will call if we need anything," Jenny said and smiled.

"Okay, see you soon," Jack leaned in and kissed her cheek. He took Stephanie by the hand and they walked out.

"What should we pick up for dinner?" Jack asked as he opened the car door for her.

She sat down. "I don't know, I was thinking maybe Italian?" she said as she buckled her seatbelt.

"Sounds good to me. Do you want me to drop you off and then go get it?" he asked.

She looked at him and touched his arm. "No, we are both equally exhausted. I'll call it in while you drive."

He smiled at her. "Okay."

She looked at him with a twinkle in her eye. "Maybe we could just skip dinner and go for dessert? I was kind of in the mood for some peanuts and chocolate."

He cleared his throat. "Nice," he said as she burst out laughing.

******

Later that afternoon, Tommy was sitting in the main area of Britt's hotel room, watching some television when there was a knock at the door. He walked to open it and smiled when he saw Julie standing there. "Hey, what's going on?"

"I wanted to see how Brittany was doing. I didn't know you'd be here, although I should have figured," she smiled and he walked in and sat down with her.

"She is sleeping, finally. I hope she feels better when she gets up," he said.

Julie looked at him. "Are you okay?" she asked him.

He looked surprised. "Of course I am; why do you ask?"

She sighed. "It's just that, I worry about you. You have been through so much, Tommy, and you always put others before yourself. You had to take care of me after mom and dad died and you work with sick children, and now with Brittany, I just don't want you to go through any more loss."

He looked at his sister and knew she was scared for him. "I know, Jules, but you can't pick who you fall in love with. I am here for the long haul and believe me; I know it will be a long haul. HIV meds are very taxing to take and to adjust to, but when they work, they will enable Brittany to lead a long and healthy life. This is just a bump in the road. She is going to be okay."

"Tommy is right," Brittany said from the doorway of the bedroom. "I have been through this before and I know it will get better."

Tommy stood up and walked over to her. "You look better," he touched her face, happy at the coolness of her skin.

She smiled. "I feel better. Sleeping half the day helped a lot. Why don't you go out and get us some dinner so I can have some time to talk to Julie."

He looked at her and then at his sister. "Okay, I'll be back."

He walked by Julie and ruffled her hair and she smacked him. Brittany laughed as he left. She walked to the chair and sat down.

"I'm sorry, Brittany, I didn't mean to imply that you weren't worth staying with," Julie felt terrible.

Brittany smiled. "Please don't apologize. I know how hard this is to handle. You are Tommy's world and you worry about him and I would expect you to be concerned that he is with me. Having HIV is nothing to ignore and it is certainly nothing to take lightly, but I can promise you, I would never do anything to hurt your brother."

Julie shook her head. "No, you don't understand. I don't care about you having HIV. I mean, I care, but not in the way you think. My brother is so in love with you, Brittany, he is so happy. I miss that, seeing him so alive. I am grateful he found you and I am so amazed by how much more like the old Tommy he has become, like before we lost our parents. He has had to be everything for me for so long and I just want you to know how much I appreciate what you have given him."

Brittany was confused. "What do you mean? What have I given him?"

Julie smiled and came to sit down next to her. "You are as dense as my brother," she laughed and Brittany smirked. "You know, for doctors, I wouldn't think I would have to explain everything," she looked at Brittany. "You have made my brother open his heart to love. He was like an old man, living years ahead of himself because of circumstances out of his control. He took on his new role as parent and guardian without a second thought, but it broke my heart to see him give up on his own happiness. You made him live again. I can never thank you enough for that."

Brittany was touched by her words. "Thank you. I am honored that you have so much faith in me," she hugged her. Julie smiled and moved to get her phone, which was ringing.

"Hi Bill. I'm at the hotel with Brittany. Okay, I'll see you then. I love you too," she hung up the phone and looked apologetically at Brittany. "Sorry, I didn't mean to interrupt our moment."

Brittany laughed. "You didn't, moment was good," she leaned back into the couch, feeling a lot better. "So tell me how you and Bill met."

Julie grinned. "Oh my gosh, it was probably the most embarrassing moment of my life," she put her phone down and smiled. "I was a freshman at Michigan, studying nothing, because I didn't know what I wanted to do with my life. I had to contend with Tommy being this brilliant doctor, and I felt like nothing could compare, you know?"

Brittany nodded. "I can imagine that he was a bit concerned by your undecided major?"

Julie laughed, "That would be the understatement of the century. I swear he channeled our parents during that time. He was on my back constantly, and Jack didn't help, either. They were like this perfect tandem of intelligence and confidence, and I was so, well, not either one of those things," she laughed as she remembered. "Then I did the one thing Tommy forbade me to do."

"What was that?" Brittany was intrigued.

"I joined a sorority," Julie said and both girls laughed. "He was so against it, thought it would take away from my studies and I would never get into any programs and I would be corrupted by a fraternity boy," she smiled. "Mind you, both Jack and Tommy were in a fraternity together."

"The old double standard. I know it well," Brittany laughed.

Julie nodded. "Anyway, I wasn't really into the bar scene, but as a pledge, we had to perform these embarrassing acts for the sisters. I was sent to a fraternity bar night with my other pledges and we had the task of performing karaoke for the men. I was mortified, because I can't sing for the life of me, but it didn't matter. I got there and everyone was drinking, but I didn't, because I just don't drink, but that's a story for another time. Anyway, I acted drunk because it would have been obvious that I wasn't, and that would have gotten me in more trouble," she took a drink of her water and smiled at Brittany's mesmerized look. "I got to the microphone and thought I would pass out from humiliation and waited for the song choice, because the guys picked the songs for us. My song was "Billy don't be a hero" by Bo Donaldson and I just gave it my all, not knowing that the guys had set it up for me because of a certain fraternity member."

"Bill," Brittany smiled.

"Right. They all pushed him to the front of the stage when I was done and were teasing him relentlessly about his crush on me. I think I almost died of embarrassment and I ran out after I was done. I was standing outside the bar, feeling like an idiot when I felt someone's hand on my arm. I looked up and it was Bill." Julie smiled. "We have been together ever since," she picked up her eyebrows when she looked at Brittany. "But it hasn't been all smooth sailing, Tommy didn't like Bill at first and it was hard. It turns out that the fraternity brothers wanted me to sing that song also because Bill is a member of the Army, and he was about to be sent for training. Tommy was scared for me, but it didn't matter. I was and am so completely in love with Bill. I would follow him anywhere," she smiled. "He recently returned from a year tour in Iraq."

Brittany felt her heart swell at the story and in admiration for Bill. "What a beautiful story. Is Bill still active?"

Julie looked down at her hands. "He is, and I am praying he doesn't get called away. I love that Bill is a member of the military and I support him 100%, but with a baby on the way, I just need him here, with me," she looked at Brittany. "Does that make me selfish?"

Brittany smiled at her. "No, of course not. It is never selfish to want those you love to be with you and to stay safe," she realized the irony of her words.

Tommy arrived back and they all proceeded to enjoy a nice dinner. The women were quiet about what they talked about, and Tommy was dying to know. Julie left when Bill came to pick her up. They were going to pick out paint for the nursery. After she left, Tommy looked at Brittany. "So, what did she tell you?"

Brittany shrugged. "Just girl talk. You know a girl can't reveal her secrets."

He pouted. "Fine, but just so you know, I have secrets, too."

She stared at him and he relented. "Fine, I don't, but I could get some," he said and she smiled. Tommy stayed late into the evening until he was sure she was on the mend and then he left. They stood at the doorway before he walked out.

"Thank you for today," she said and touched his cheek.

"You can pay me back later," he said with a smile.

"Oh really? I look forward to that," she leaned in and he kissed her gently. She lingered on his lips for a moment before he left.

Chapter Forty-Two:

Stephanie knocked on Brittany's hotel room door a few days later and smiled when her friend opened it. She hugged her and Brittany smiled a big smile.

"Look at how cute that is!" she said, referring to Stephanie's maternity outfit.

"I just can't believe how big I am getting. It's only four and a half months, I think I will gain 50 pounds before this pregnancy is over," she walked into the room and sat down on the couch. Brittany followed her. "I was so glad when you called me to come over."

Brittany nodded. "I finally am over this last bout of flu symptoms from the meds and I missed seeing you. I wanted to make sure I was better before you came over. I don't want to pass on anything to you, in case it wasn't just the meds. With your own compromised immune system, I wanted to play it safe," Brittany said.

"But you're feeling better now? How is your viral load? Where is Tommy? How are things there?" Stephanie asked a bunch of questions at once.

Brittany laughed. "I am better and my viral load has continued to decrease, but it isn't at zero yet."

"And," Stephanie prodded.

"And Tommy is at work. Things are good," she blushed.

"Good? What does that mean? Britt, it has been almost a month since we got home from the Pocono's and from what Jack tells me; Tommy has been a fixture here. I want details," she scooted closer to Brittany.

The tall redhead laughed. "Tommy is amazing, Steph. I never thought I would ever meet someone like him. He is so gentle and strong and smart and my HIV truly doesn't faze him. He took care of me when I was sick and he is just the best thing that has ever happened to me."

Stephanie felt tears in her eyes. "I'm so happy for you guys. Tommy is such a great guy and I know how much he loves you. I just hope you continue to give him your heart."

Brittany stood up and walked to get some water. "I know what you mean, Steph, but there are still so many questions in my head," she sighed. "I finally get to go back to work tomorrow and there is a lot I need to deal with there. I also have to deal with the fact that this guy is still out there. And then there's my house," she ran her hand through her hair. "All of it has been in limbo while I have been here, recovering. Now that I am better, all of that has to be handled."

Stephanie nodded. "I know, but we are all here to help you. You don't need to face this alone. We are all with you, but none more so than Tommy."

Brittany smiled at her friend. "I love you, Stephanie. You are the best friend I could ever have and I am proud to have you in my corner."

Stephanie smiled back. "Just remember that when I'm begging for my epidural."

Brittany laughed and they went on talking about the pregnancy.

****

"So, how about we celebrate? You are officially back on rotation and able to see patients. I think a drink is in order," Tommy said as they sat at dinner the next evening.

Brittany smiled. "How about the non - alcoholic variety? I don't want to do anything to temp the stomach fates."

"Good point," he said as they ate.

After dinner, they went for a walk under the stars. Tommy had his arm around her and she had her head on his shoulder.

He stopped walking and looked at her. "Tell me something,"

She met his gaze. "What?"

"Tell me about your family," he said.

She looked at him, surprised. "What do you want to know?"

"You have mentioned your father a couple of times, but you haven't really said much about him. I just wondered if he was still a part of your life," Tommy brushed her hair behind her shoulder.

She crossed her arms around herself and was quiet for a minute. "My dad died when I was almost 12 years old. It was just us for most of my life, I never knew my mom; she left me with my dad when I was born. He was the best. He was so patient with me when he had no idea what to do with a little girl with frizzy red curls. He worked as a bartender and I went to work with him a lot," she smiled at Tommy. "I know it wasn't right for me to be there, but I stayed in the back and I listened to the musicians who came through," her face sparkled as she spoke of her dad.

"I was enthralled with the way they spoke through their instruments. My dad loved music and I begged him to show me how to play the guitar and the piano. I used to stay up late and listen to all kinds of music: jazz and rock, country and blues, it was the best," she was quiet for a minute.

"What happened to him? He must have died young," Tommy asked as they walked to a bench near the restaurant. They sat down and she continued.

"He was only 30. He suffered a brain aneurysm. He complained of a headache for a few days, but we didn't know any better, you know? He was under a lot of stress and I didn't know why, I was only 11. He collapsed at work and he was gone. They couldn't do anything," she smiled at Tommy. "He would have probably made it if he had just gone to the doctor when his headaches started."

Tommy shook his head. "You don't know that. There could have been a lot of underlying issues which contributed to the rupture," he touched her cheek.

She nodded. "I know that, but I still wish I could have done something," she looked at her hands. "After that, I was sent to live with my grandma. She was the only other family I knew. My dad was an only child and his mom was the only available person to take in an 11 year old. I am so grateful she did because otherwise I would have gone into the foster system. My grandma lived in London England, so I moved there with her and that's where I stayed until I signed my recording contract," she remembered it like it was yesterday. "I missed my dad so much, you know? I was all alone and in a strange place where the people spoke funny and drove on the wrong side of the road," Tommy smiled with her.

"But London was so magical. I was enthralled with the culture and the romance of the city. I started to read more and study music seriously. I took a chance at an open mic night at a bar I had no business being at and that's when I was discovered. My grandma was on board for a while, she got me to all of the proper lawyers and the contracts were looked over, but she wasn't really able to deal with the travel, so I was on my own a lot. She had a hard time with the death of her only son and she started to forget things." Brittany stood up and they began to walk again.

"I was back in the states when I was attacked, and when she found out, it kind of sent her over the edge. She was in a nursing home in London soon after, near where I went to school and shortly after I started classes, she passed away," she looked at Tommy and wiped her eyes. "She never knew I was HIV positive. I was in Paris when I got the positive result. When I came back, I just couldn't tell her."

Tommy put his arm around her. "I can't imagine having to deal with all of that alone. What about the people you trusted with your music? Wasn't there anyone who looked out for you?" he felt so sorry for all she went through. "I know how horrible it was for me going through such a loss, I don't know how I would have dealt with things without my friends."

She shrugged. "I spent a lot of time in the hospital after the attack and the people who had supported me were there at first, but the more it seemed like I wasn't going to be the same person I was, they stopped coming. I couldn't imagine singing ever again. It was a really dark time for me, because I didn't know what else I was good for. That's why I went to Paris. I needed to be with the only person I knew who would have my back."

"Stephanie?" Tommy asked.

Brittany nodded. "Yes. We had been really close growing up, but after I went to England, we didn't see each other for a while. When I got to Paris, she helped me so much. I don't know if I would be here if she didn't help me. I owe her so much."

"So do I," he said and hugged her as she shivered. "We should go."

"Yes," she said and they walked back to the car.

Tommy brought her back to his house and made some coffee when they got inside. He handed her a cup and sat down with her. "Are you okay?"

She smiled. "Yes, I'm good. It's just been a long time since I talked about all of this."

He sat close to her. "You are an amazing woman, Brittany," he said.

"You are pretty amazing yourself. I'm so glad I found you," she put her cup down and held his face in her hands. "You have made everything in my life better," her eyes were wet with unshed tears.

He leaned in and brushed her lips with his. She moved closer and intensified the kiss. He wrapped his arms around her and she felt her heart race. She looked at him and ran her fingers across his lips. She moved hungrily to his mouth and he enthusiastically returned her intensity. He positioned her back on the couch and she didn't stop him. He leaned into her and his hands ran down her neck to her shoulders. She pulled him down onto her and she relished the feel of his weight on top of her. She ran her hands down his arms and he stopped and looked at her, making sure she was okay.

"Don't stop," she pulled him to her and he went to reach his hand under her hair when her alarm went off.

Tommy sat back, looking at her. "Your meds?" he asked through his flushed face.

She nodded. "I'm sorry. I have to keep on a strict schedule while I'm adjusting them," she stood up and grabbed her purse. "Kind of a buzz kill, huh?" she pulled her meds out of her purse and walked to get some water.

Tommy followed her and wrapped his arms around her from behind after she swallowed the medicine. "There is nothing you could do that would make me not want you," he leaned in and kissed her neck.

She turned around in his arms and kissed him again. "I love that you say that and I believe you, but it's good that we were interrupted. Tommy, until my viral load is down, I need to be very careful. If I hurt you in any way, I would never be able to handle that," she ran her hands through his hair. "Would you settle for a little snuggling?"

"As long as you stay with me, I'm good," he said.

She hugged him. "I'm not going anywhere."

Chapter Forty-Three:

"I am so excited for tonight, Steph. I never thought I would be feeling like this, or would be so happy," Brittany said a week later as they ate lunch in the cafeteria.

"What's the occasion?" Stephanie asked her friend who seemed to be glowing.

"Well Tommy hasn't said, he just wants to take me out, but I have news of my own that I can't wait to tell him. I got the results from my latest blood work and my viral load is finally undetectable," she told her, unable to keep the excitement out of her voice.

Stephanie was so happy. "Oh Brit, that's wonderful news. I am so happy for you," she wiped her eyes. "Stupid hormones," she laughed as she wiped her eyes.

Brittany laughed. "You know, I wouldn't be here without you. You truly are my hero. You saved me from my sadness and because of you, I am happier than I ever thought I could be."

Stephanie hugged her smiled. "Your dad would be so very proud of you."

Brittany smiled. "I hope so."

******

"So what are we celebrating?" Brittany asked Tommy on the phone, as she got ready for their evening together.

Tommy smiled. "You'll see. I am allowed a few surprises. Just meet me at the restaurant at five."

"Why so early?" she played with a strand of her hair.

"The sooner we meet, the sooner I'll see you," he said and she smiled.

"Corny, but cute. I'll be there," she said.

"I love you," he said.

"I love you, too," she said and hung up. She turned to figure out what to wear.

Tommy smiled as he showered and got ready. He was still at the hospital because of a particularly long day of cases, and he wasn't sure he would have time to go home. He put on his black suit and the tie she liked and looked in the mirror. He was excited for this evening and what he planned. He turned to walk out when suddenly there was a bag over his face and a smell of chemicals before everything went black.

****

It was 5:30 and Brittany was waiting at the restaurant. She had called Tommy and it went right to voicemail. She texted him and figured he was probably called into an emergency surgery or consult. It was not uncommon for their profession; still, she was a bit anxious. She walked to the maitre d and asked again if there was a message for her. The gentleman nodded that he was sorry, but no, but he would be happy to seat her while she waited. She shook her head and smiled as her phone buzzed. She looked down to see it was from Tommy. Relieved, she opened to read the text. "Change of plans. Come to hospital, room 8090."

She thought that was weird, but he had said he wanted to surprise her, so she would go with it. She thanked the maitre d and left for her car.

****

Tommy opened his eyes and squinted at the light before him. He was tied to a chair; his wrists bound, his ankles as well. His head was pounding. He looked at the man standing in front of him, his back to Tommy. Finally, the man must have sensed Tommy staring because he turned around. "Good morning Dr.," he said. "Good thing I was able to text Barbie to tell her you changed venues. She is on her way," he put Tommy's cell phone on the table, out of reach.

"You son of a bitch, what did you do? If you touch her, I will kill you," Tommy said, struggling to get out of the chair, panic coursing through his veins.

"Sure you will. Looks like you're a little tied up at the moment. I will give you a show soon enough, when my girl gets here. She was only too happy to meet here instead of wherever it was you wanted her to go. It's kind of funny, actually, I wasn't sure how I was going to get her to come, but she kept texting you, worried about where you were," he said the last part with contempt. "So I texted her back and told her you wanted to meet here, for a surprise," he laughed. "She is sure going to be surprised."

"Look, what is it you want? I can give you whatever you need. She doesn't have to be involved. I am a doctor and I have access to money, drugs, whatever you want," Tommy was desperate.

"What do you think I want? What have I wanted from the day I first heard that voice? I had her, for just a short time, but she left me. I almost got her again, but she was feisty. She is just playing hard to get, and soon, I'll get her," he sneered. "I've been biding my time, you know, waiting for her to come to her senses, but then, all I saw while watching her was you. She looks at you the way she should look at me. You poisoned her and I need to fix that," he pointed a gun at Tommy. "I will make her watch while you die and then, she will finally be mine."

Tommy looked around for something, anything to help him. He tried to recognize where they were, but the room was bare except for some construction equipment. He figured it was part of the floor that was under construction. There weren't any cameras around here, but he knew there must be evidence in the locker room where he was taken. Was there a panic button anywhere? He knew she would be there any minute and he was frantic.

"You know, I don't know what she would see in you, with me, she had nothing to hide. I knew all of her, and I do mean all of her. I was able to give her an experience she will never forget," he sneered at Tommy.

Tommy knew he was trying to get a rise out of him, but it was all he could do to restrain himself. He kept calm and looked at him. "So how did you get me here? I mean, you don't look very strong. Is there someone helping you?"

The man smiled. "Wouldn't you like to know? You can insult me all you want, but the truth of the matter is; I will have her in the end."

"So you are just going to wait for her and then what? Shoot me and leave with her? Do you think she is going to go with that?" Tommy wanted to keep him talking.

"She won't have a choice. She belongs with me and she will see that," he said and smiled.

Tommy prayed she wouldn't come, but he knew it was inevitable. He needed a plan.

****

"Brittany, you look beautiful," Jack said as he saw her walk onto the floor. "What's the occasion?"

Brittany smiled. "I was supposed to meet Tommy for dinner, but he texted me and wanted me to meet him here, instead. I guess he got held up or something."

Jack shrugged. "I haven't seen him all day. I had back-to-back bypass surgeries, and I just found a second to call Steph. She said you guys had a nice visit this morning?"

Brittany smiled. "We did. She looks great. I can't wait to do your ultrasound later in the week."

He grinned. "I know. I can't tell you how happy we both are that you will be back at work tomorrow. Where are you meeting Tommy?"

She looked at him. "I have to check my phone again, but somewhere on the 8th floor."

He looked surprised. "I thought that floor was under construction," Jack said.

She nodded. "I did, too, but maybe there is an area he knows about? I don't know, but I guess I'll find out," she smiled at him as she walked to the elevator.

Chapter Forty-Four:

Brittany made her way down the dark hallway to the room number she had. She felt like something wasn't right, and she sent a text to Stephanie, telling her where she was going. She told her to check with Jack about the details because she didn't have Jack's number. She approached the door and opened it, walking in to see Tommy sitting in the chair, bound and gagged. She ran to him.

"Oh God, Tommy, what happened," she pulled the gag out of his mouth and he immediately spoke.

"Get out of here, now," he pleaded, but as he did the chemical smell permeated the room and she felt herself freeze. She turned around and saw him.

"Barbie, welcome home," the man said and she felt her knees go weak. She stood between him and Tommy.

"Please let her go," Tommy said, his chest tight with fear for her. "Just let her go."

Brittany turned back to Tommy. "I'm sorry, I'm so sorry," she moved to untie him, ignoring the bile rising in her throat.

The man grabbed her roughly and threw her back across the room, causing her to lose her footing and fall to the floor. She grabbed her arm, stunned for a moment.

"Get your fucking hands off her," Tommy said, feeling like he was about to lose his mind.

The man pulled her up and close to him, placing his mouth inches from her face. She strained away from him, struggling to stand when his hand crashed across her face.

"Stop it!" Tommy yelled.

"Did you think you could just walk in here and untie him and leave? I have waited too long for this, Barbie. I want you to watch him die. I want you to see the life go out of him and then there will be nothing holding you back. We can finally be together," he said, ignoring Tommy who struggled to get free.

She felt her fear grow and something more, her anger and hatred. She kept her eyes on Tommy, and he looked at her. "It's okay," he said softly.

The man tightened his grip on her arm and she winced, trying to hold it together. "Why are you so dressed up?" he asked, referring to her blue dress. He ran his hand over her chest, touching her breasts, and her tears began to fall.

"I will kill you, you son of a bitch," Tommy tried to get up, but couldn't.

He looked at Tommy. "Did I mess up something nice? I see you have a suit on, too bad I ruined your evening."

Brittany looked at him. "What do you want? Why don't you let him go?" she spoke with more authority than she felt.

He laughed. "If I don't kill him, you will never be free for me," he ran the gun across her face before pointing it at Tommy.

"No, no, please, I'll do whatever you want, please don't hurt him. I'll go with you, it's okay, I'll do anything you want," she said, her voice shaking.

"Brittany, no. It's going to be fine," Tommy said to her, willing her to look at him.

She did and her tears fell. "I can't lose you. Whatever he does to me, it won't be as bad as losing you," she whispered.

The man cleared his throat and looked at them. "Don't make me sick," he reached and grabbed her face with his hand, forcing her to look at him. "You shut up and watch."

"No, oh please, don't hurt him," Brittany cried and Tommy felt his heart break

The man aimed the gun at Tommy and fired. Brittany screamed and shoved him off of her. She ran to Tommy, who was hit in the thigh. He was bleeding fast and she grabbed her shawl and put pressure on the wound. She looked at him, beads of sweat on his face, his breath coming fast.

"Tommy, oh God, look at me, you're going to be okay," she cried as he struggled to look at her. She turned to look at the man. "Please let me get help. You need to untie him. The bullet hit an artery and he needs help now. I will leave with you, I will do whatever you want, just let me get him help," she screamed at him, struggling to stop the artery from pumping.

"I don't think so," he said and went to grab her. She found a strength she didn't know she had and shoved him hard. She heard a sickening sound as he fell back into the table saw which sat in the corner of the room, the blade protruding. He crumpled over the machine, impaled. She opened the door and screamed for help. She went back in the room and grabbed her cell phone and dialed 911. She put the phone down and let it ring. She ran to Tommy, who was passed out.

"Okay, okay, you're going to be fine. She saw he was wearing a tie and she quickly untied it and pulled it off. She tried to pick his leg up but it was tied down. She moved to his feet and tried to untie them, but the blood that was flowing from his leg made everything harder. She moved her hands back to his thigh and with effort, slipped the tie under his leg. She worked to make a tourniquet and saw the bleeding subside. She did her best to use her body to press on the wound.

She took his face in her hands and forced him to look at her. "Tommy, Thomas, you look at me right now. You will not leave me. You will not die, do you hear me?" she saw his eyes try to flutter open. "That's right, you can do it. Focus on me, I'm here, I love you and I'm here," she continued to apply pressure to his leg with her body while talking to him, her feet slid on the blood on the floor.

"Help us," she screamed and saw a site that brought her fear to the surface; the man began to move. She cried and held onto Tommy. "Oh God, please, help us," she screamed.

The police came toward the room and the man reached up, pointing his gun at Brittany and Tommy. "You bitch, you belong to me," he said to her. She turned and held onto Tommy, trying to shield him with her body. She held his head and prayed. There was a lot of commotion, police yelling orders and she could hear screaming. She just kept her eyes on Tommy, trying to keep him alive. Suddenly there was a shot and she closed her eyes, sobbing. She felt a pair of arms come to take her and she held onto Tommy. "No, please, no," she screamed.

"Brittany, it's me, it's Jack, let me help you," she turned and saw it was him and she moved, shaking uncontrollably. Jack looked at Tommy and yelled for help.

"He's been shot," she said softly.

Jack's heart broke for them. "I know and we're going to help him," Stephanie ran in along with other people and they cut Tommy loose, moving him to a gurney and calling out orders for blood and a surgical team to be assembled. Brittany followed behind them, walking past the dead body of the man who tormented her for so long. She had trouble keeping up with them, and she fell to the ground. Stephanie ran up next to her.

"Britt, hey, look at me," she touched her arm and looked at all of the blood on her. "Are you hurt?"

Brittany shook her head. "No, it's all from him. It's all Tommy's blood. I need to be with him, please," she went to get up but slid on the blood covering her feet.

"He is going into surgery. Let the doctors help him, we will wait outside the O.R," Stephanie said.

"No, I need to see him. He needs to know I'm here," she said, covering her face with her hands and seeing the blood all over. "Oh God, he lost too much blood. The bullet hit the femoral artery; he was losing so much blood," she began to crumple.

"Brittany, look at me," Stephanie said. "He is going to make it. You need to pull yourself together right now. He needs you strong and healthy," she took her friends hands. "Let's go get you cleaned up and we will wait for word."

Brittany didn't say anything; she just let Stephanie lead her to the elevator. She sat on a chair in the locker room while Stephanie wiped her face and her hands. She let her take off the dress she had on and put on scrubs.

She stood up and looked at her friend. "Is he going to die? He can't die," she said softly.

Stephanie smiled. "He won't. Let's go make sure of it," she took her friends hand and they walked to the O.R. Brittany waited outside in the hall while Stephanie went in to find out what she could.

Brittany stood frozen and looked at her hands, still stained with blood. She felt her heart breaking as she waited. She wrapped her arms around her waist and tried to blot out her thoughts. She looked as Stephanie came out.

"They repaired the artery. He lost a lot of blood, so they are giving him a transfusion. If you hadn't put the tourniquet on, he would have surely bled out. He had minor damage to the bone, but I think I know a good ortho who can help him with that if needed. He should be fine, sweetie," she said smiling as she smoothed her friends disheveled hair.

Brittany nodded, hearing her friend, but not processing everything just yet. "He's alive?" she asked.

Stephanie hugged her. "Yes, he is alive, Jack is helping them close."

"Okay, I need to see him," she said. "Is his heart okay?" she realized Jack was working on him.

"His heart is fine. You know Jack; no one touches his brother in the O.R. without him helping. Come on, I'll take you to his room, but he won't be there just yet," Steph said and took her friend's arm as they walked.

Chapter Forty-Five:

Jack sat in the locker room and put his head in his hands. Stephanie came in and he looked at her and wiped his face. She sat down next to him and hugged him. "You were amazing," she said to him.

"We almost lost him, Steph. I almost lost him," Jack said brokenly.

"Shh, I know, but you didn't. He is going to be okay and we can all move past this horrible nightmare," she said as she rubbed his back.

"If Brittany hadn't sent you that text and if she didn't put on the tourniquet, there would have been no chance," he continued. "They both would have been gone."

"Look at me," she turned his head to look at her. "He is going to be okay. You didn't lose him, okay?" she smoothed his cheek. "I love you so much and I am so proud of you," she hugged him again.

"I love you, too. I'm so glad you're here," he said and kissed her softly. "I need to go call Julie," he said.

"I'll go with you. We can call her together," she said and held his hand.

******

Brittany stood in the room and watched him sleep. His chest going up and down with each breath. The hospital gown half covered his torso, leaving his chest uncovered enough to allow the wires to lie unobstructed. His lower body was covered tightly with the sheet and blanket, there was a tube coming from his leg to allow for drainage from the incision. She walked over to the side of the bed that was clear and sat down, reaching for his hand and grasping it in her own. She leaned her head down on his shoulder and ran her other hand through his hair, feeling her tears fall, making his shoulder wet. She sighed and closed her eyes. "I'm so sorry. I'm so sorry," she repeated the phrase over and over before sitting up and looking at him, his eyes closed. She leaned in and kissed his cheek. "Tommy, you need to stay with me. I know the doctors said they repaired the artery and you should be fine, but I need to see your green eyes. Can you open them and look at me? Please?" she touched his face and put her hand on his chest. "Can you feel me here with you? I love you and I am not going anywhere. You're stuck with me," she looked up as Julie stood in the doorway. Brittany walked over and Julie hugged her, crying softly.

"Oh Brittany, I'm so sorry this happened. I'm so sorry that guy got to you both," she looked at Tommy. "He's going to be okay, right? I mean, Jack said he was going to be okay," she sobbed.

Brittany touched her face so she looked at her. "He will be okay. He is going to wake up and he will be fine," she smiled. "You need to take care of his little niece or nephew. You know Tommy would never forgive himself if something happened to you because you were worried about him."

Julie smiled. "I know, and I am. It's just that, he is my, well, everything," she said and wiped her tears. She walked to Tommy and leaned in and kissed his forehead. "I love you big brother," she said softly to him and stood back. Brittany swallowed her tears as she watched the scene. Julie turned to look at her. "Thank you," she said.

Brittany looked at her. "For what? If it weren't for me, none of this would have happened," she said, her tears escaping.

Julie hugged her. "You're so wrong. You made my brother wake up and live his life. You are the single most amazing thing to happen to our family and I am proud to have you in my life," she looked at her brother one more time and then at Brittany. "Take care of him," she said.

"I intend to," she said as Julie walked out and Brittany made her way back over to the bed. She sat down and let her fears come out for a moment. "Oh Tommy, I was so wrong for so long. I wasted so much time," she wiped her face. "Please don't leave me. Please come back to me," she said, taking her hand in his. She moved closer to him and leaned in close to his cheek. She sang to him softly and prayed he could hear her. She closed her eyes and put her arm gently across his chest, holding him as best she could.

****

Jack and Stephanie walked into the room and saw Brittany sitting with Tommy, who remained motionless. Jack walked over to her and touched her shoulder. She looked at him through her tear-stained face and sighed.

"Why don't you go take a break, I will sit with him for a bit," Jack looked at Stephanie who took Brittany by the hand.

"I don't think I should leave. He needs to know I'm here," she said sadly.

"He knows, sweetie, and I think you need to take your meds. Let me help you and Jack will talk to Tommy," Stephanie said softly.

Brittany looked at them, two of the three people she trusted in the world. She knew Jack wanted a minute, so she moved to Tommy and leaned in to gently kiss him on the forehead. She smoothed his hair and turned to walk out with Stephanie.

"I don't want to go far away," she said as the walked out of the room.

"Okay, let's sit here and relax a minute," she motioned to a bench in the hall close to the room. They sat down and Stephanie handed Brittany a bottle of water. "Do you have your meds with you?"

She shook her head. "No, but I have an extra set in my locker," she looked at Stephanie. "He should have woken up by now," fresh tears fell over her cheeks.

Stephanie hugged her. "He is going to wake up, I know it. You can't lose faith, Britt, He will come back to you and to all of us."

****

Jack sat down and looked at his best friend, the one who had been there for him through the worst moments in his life. He wiped his eyes and sighed. "What the hell is this? Of all the people I thought I would be sitting here watching, hooked up to tubes, hanging on by a thread, it was never you. I mean, come on, this wasn't the plan. Tommy, you are the closest thing to a brother I will ever have, and when I think of all of the things I have done in my life, I just don't see how I could have accomplished any of them without your support. But man, this isn't about me or what I need. You have a woman in your life that needs you. Brittany loves you so much and I know you worship her. You are different now, Tommy, alive and happy. You can't leave that. You need to wake up for her and for me," he reached down and touched his friends arm. "I'm begging you, please pull through this."

Stephanie walked up to her husband and wrapped her arms around his shoulders as he sat there. He touched her hands around his neck and turned to look at her through wet eyes. Brittany walked up and he stood to leave with Stephanie. He hugged Brittany and he and Stephanie walked out. Julie was in the hallway and they went to talk to her as Brittany sat back down with Tommy.

****

Tommy felt panic at his racing thoughts. He had to get her out of there; he had to save her. This guy was going to hurt her again and there was nothing he could do. He felt the ties around his hands and feet. He needed to get free. His heart was racing.

The machines were beeping as Brittany sat up with a start. She looked at the reading and saw his heart rate was too fast. She took his face in her hands. "Tommy, it's okay, wake up. Look at me, everything is okay," she spoke to him as the nurses ran in followed by Jack and Stephanie. Jack held them back. "Tommy, you need to look at me right now," she commanded him. His eyelids began to flutter and she touched his forehead. "That's right, baby, you're doing it, just a little more. Listen to my voice."

He opened his eyes and saw her blue eyes staring into his. She was smiling at him.

"That's it, everything is okay," she spoke soothingly to him, not moving her eyes off him. His pulse began to return to normal.

Jack motioned for the rest of the people to leave. He waited outside, letting her handle this moment. He smiled as Stephanie and Julie hugged him.

"Welcome back," she said as she stood over him, her hand never leaving his. "You are going to be okay," she said.

His eyes were wide as he remembered. "Red, he was going to take you," his face registered the panic he felt. "Did he hurt you?"

"Shh, he didn't, you saved me. He's gone, Tommy, and you are going to be okay," she leaned in and kissed him softly on the lips.

"I couldn't get free. He wanted me to watch him hurt you again. I did nothing," he said as a tear fell out of his eye, falling to the pillow. "He touched you again and I did nothing," he closed his eyes.

"Look at me," she said and he opened his eyes and focused on her. "I am right here. Nothing happened to me. But you, Tommy, I almost lost you," she said and wiped her eyes.

He focused on her and tried to smile. "It wasn't that close."

"Liar," she said and leaned in to kiss him again. She laid her head on his chest and this time he moved his hand to hold her to him.

"Were you singing to me?" he asked her softly.

"Yes. Could you hear it?" she asked him.

"It helped me open my eyes. I followed the music," he said softly. "So you see; your music did something wonderful," he closed his eyes, sleep taking over.

She looked at him and her heart felt like it would burst. "No, Tommy, you did something wonderful."

Chapter Forty-Six:

"Are you sure you are ready to go home?" Julie asked
Tommy as she helped him pack his stuff three days
later.

"Yes, for the last time, I am fine. I can't wait to get
home already. It's bad enough I work in this place, I
don't have to live here as well," he moved gently to the
side of the bed.

"Whatever. I just want you to take it easy. You can't
drive yet and you need to be able to change your
bandage covering at home. Are you going to be able to
do that?" she asked.

Brittany stood at the doorway. "I think I can help with
that," she smiled at them. "Your chariot awaits," she
said, pushing in a wheelchair.

"I can use the crutches; I don't want to sit in that," he
whined.

"You will do as I say," Brittany said with a stern look
that turned to laughter. "Come on; let me baby you a
little."

Julie smiled at them. "I'll get the door."

******
Brittany helped him get into the house and onto the
couch before she walked over and sat down next to
him.

"What can I get for you?"

"Come here," he motioned for her to get closer.

"I don't want to hurt you," she said unconvincingly.

"Not possible," he looked at her. "What's really going on?"

She looked at him; her eyes wet with unshed tears. "I'm sorry, Tommy. This is all my fault. I just want you to know how profoundly sorry I am."

He sighed. "You know how much I hate when you say that. Red, none of this is your fault. You saved my life in there."

"But you were in there because of me," she said emphatically. "How do I reconcile that?"

He smiled. "By living your life; by being happy and finally free of fear; by loving me and letting me love you, with no regrets."

She looked at him. "I don't know what I would have done if I'd have lost you."

He pulled her close to him. "You didn't and I am not going anywhere."

She reached up and touched his face. "I love you."

He held her to him. "I love you."

******

Jack and Stephanie came over that night and Jack stayed with Tommy while Stephanie took Brittany out for some supplies. Jack handed Tommy a bottle of water.

"Can't I have a beer?" Tommy asked.

"No, not while you're still on all of those pain meds," he said. "Besides, we need to talk."

Tommy rolled his eyes. "Now what? I told you, I am fine."

Jack sat down and smiled. "I need to ask you something."

Tommy looked at him, sensing it was serious. "Of course, what is it?"

"Stephanie and I want you and Brittany to be our child's Godparents," he said with a smile.

Tommy was quiet for a minute. "I don't know," he said and Jack stared at him. Tommy broke out in a huge smile. "Dude, of course I will. I would be honored. You are my family and I would be privileged to do anything for your little one," he stuck his hand out and Jack took it and reached in to hug him.

"Thanks man, you're the best," he said and they sat back and watched TV.

******

"So how is Tommy now that you got him home?" Stephanie asked Brittany as they loaded the car with things Tommy might need.

"He seems good, but I just hope he doesn't hide anything from me, you know, to protect me," she said.

"I don't think he will. Men are much less able to hide pain than we are," Stephanie said and they both laughed. "I think you will be able to sense what he needs."

"I hope so. I just want things to go smoothly for his recovery," she said.

Stephanie looked at her friend as they sat in the car, ready to leave. "Can I ask you something?"

Brittany turned to look at her. "Of course."

"Jack and I want you and Tommy to be Godparents to our child," she said, her eyes shining.

Brittany was speechless. "I am so honored, but Steph, with my HIV, I don't know if that's such a good idea."

Stephanie looked at her and smiled. "I know who you are, Brittany. I have seen you at the worst and at the best. I look at the qualities I want my son or daughter to have and you exhibit every one of them. You are strong and tenacious and talented and caring and honorable. I want my child to know strength of spirit and resiliency and I can't think of a better example than you and Tommy."

Brittany smiled at her friends' tribute. "Then I would be honored," she said.

******

"I am so glad to be home and that everyone is okay," Stephanie said as she and Jack walked into their house. She looked at her husband. "How did Tommy respond when you asked him to be a Godparent?"

Jack pulled her close to him. "He was honored. He is so excited for us and I think it is another way for him to fight and heal. I still can't believe how close I came to losing him."

Stephanie wrapped her arms around him and rubbed his back. "Tommy has gotten you through some tough things, hasn't he?"

He nodded. "When my mom died and my dad left, I was all alone. I had lost my support system and my family and really, my reasons for getting up in the morning. I never realized how much I had relied on the idea that my parents would always be there, and then suddenly, they were both gone. Tommy saw what was happening to me and he stepped in and made me straighten up. He made sure I went to school and had meals. His life was about to change worse than mine, but we didn't know that. He was just my friend, and there was nothing he wouldn't do for me."

"And then he lost his parents," Stephanie said. "How sad that must have been for all of you," she shook her head.

He walked over and sat down. "It was weird, you know? We were in our first year of college and things had finally seemed to be getting back to a new normal. We were at the bar when Tommy got the call," he remembered it like it was yesterday.

Stephanie sat down next to him. "What happened?"

Jack wiped his face. "They were vacationing in the Hamptons and were on their way back from an anniversary dinner. A drunk driver ran a red light and plowed into the passenger side of the car. Tommy's mom was killed instantly and his dad, well his dad seemed to hold on until he was able to see his son. Tommy had to tell Julie.

Stephanie felt her heart break at the thought of something so tragic. "I know how horrible it is to lose a parent, but I couldn't imagine having to tell a younger sibling about something so horrible. How old was Julie?"

"She was 12," Jack smiled. "Tommy used to hate when she tagged along everywhere with us, but after, well it was like he became her personal cheerleader. Anything she needed, he did whatever he could to make sure it happened. He sacrificed a lot and he suffered in silence. I don't mean in having to care for Julie, but in losing his parents. He never took time for himself, he always kept going, working hard at school, going home at night to help her with homework, he wanted to be her normal. He and I moved into his house together to raise her and Tommy was granted guardianship. He was always there, from that moment on. He promised his dad he would take care of her, and he never stopped," Jack stood up and turned to look at Stephanie. "I can't think of a better man to be a role model for our child."

She walked over to him, wiping her eyes at the tears the story brought up. "You forgot to mention something," she reached up and cupped his face in her hands.

He smiled at her touch. "What's that?"

"You; Tommy was able to make it because he wasn't alone. You helped him so much, Jack. He had you to lean on and he had you to help him. I think you underestimate the power you have over people," she leaned in and kissed his chest. "You are an amazing man, Jack, full of strength and passion. You walk into a room and it is instantly brighter. I was so very lost and your love saved me. You are my hero and the best person I know."

He wiped his eyes and looked at her. "You're the hero, Stephanie. You are my heart and soul," he leaned in and covered her mouth with his, his need pressing into her, overwhelmed by her love. She returned the intensity of the passion and he gathered her in his arms, his love, and his life.

Chapter Forty-Seven:

"I'm glad you're staying here," Tommy said as he moved to get up off the couch.

She walked with him to the bathroom in his room. "Me too. I'll be right outside, if you need help with anything, call me. When you're done in there, we can change the bandage," she said and he nodded. She closed the door to the bathroom to give him privacy and went to turn down his bed.

He opened the door a little while later, clearly tired from the exertion of moving around so much. She walked over to help him get to the bed. He sat down slowly, staying still for a minute. She took the crutches and put them against the wall, handing him some water and his pain pills. He took them and smiled. "Thanks," he said, handing her the cup. She sat down next to him.

"How are you doing?" she took his hand in hers, checking his pulse.

"I'm okay. I just need to change and go to sleep," he sighed. He motioned to the chair. "My shorts are over there. It will be easier to change the bandage if I wear those."

She went and grabbed the shorts and came back over to him. She handed them to him and he smiled. "Thanks," he said.

She turned around to give him some privacy. "I'll get the bandage materials ready."

"Okay," he nodded and leaned back to remove his pants. He struggled a bit with getting them off, but he managed to pull them down. He lay still for a minute, his shirt off, his pants down, his shorts on top of him, but not on him. She walked in and smiled.

"Can I help?" she asked him. "Strictly as doctor patient."

He looked at her. "I don't want to make you uncomfortable, although I am wearing boxers."

She walked over to him and smiled. "I'm a doctor, I can handle it."

"Once again, you are a gynecologist," he smiled.

She waved her hand. "Details. Besides, you helped me when I needed it," she grinned at him and moved over to take his shorts. She reached for them and he took her hand. "What is it?" she asked him, concerned.

"When I helped you, I didn't know you loved me," he said.

She smiled at him. "I think you did."

He smiled at her. "Thank you," he said softly, closing his eyes for a minute out of sheer exhaustion.

She took his pants and finished pulling them off his legs. She removed his socks and took his shorts and picked up his good leg. He helped move it into the leg hole. She went to his injured leg and gently lifted it, being careful not to move it too much. She slowly pulled the material over his legs, expertly maneuvering it over the bandage. He took the waistband and pulled them over his boxers. He sat up after he fixed them and she positioned him on the pillows before touching his face.

"You are doing great."

She went to the counter and grabbed her gloves. She cut away at the bandage covering his thigh and removed the part that needed changing. She worked and cleaned his skin around the wound and then re-bandaging his thigh. She felt her tears fall and he took her hand in his. "What is it?" he asked.

"Nothing," she said and took her gloves off. She put everything away and came back to the bed. "I just remember watching him shoot you, and I thought you were going to die. There was so much blood, and I couldn't get help," she wiped her eyes. "I felt so helpless."

He moved and touched her face. "It's okay, you saved my life. I am here because of you."

"You were shot because of me," she said softly, turning to look at him.

"I was shot because a lunatic was crazy," he said. "Red, you have to stop blaming yourself."

She nodded. "I know. I just love you."

He smiled. "Good, because I love you, too," he looked at her. "Are you going to sleep in that?"

She looked down at her clothes and smiled. "No, but I don't think I brought anything."

He grinned. "I love it when you wear my clothes."

"I suppose it's important to make the patient happy," she said with a smile as she walked over to his chair and pulled a t-shirt off the back. "I am going to go wash up. I'll be right back," she went into the bathroom and changed into his t-shirt. She loved to wear it as much as he loved her to. She washed her face and brushed her teeth before walking back to the bedroom and saw him waiting for her. She smiled. "Do you want me to stay in the guest room?"

He shook his head. "No, I want you to stay with me," he said softly.

She walked to the bed and crawled in, being careful to avoid his leg. She looked at him and traced a line down his face. "I love you," she said.

"I love you, too," he said and she laid her head on his chest and her arm across his torso. He put his other arm around her and they fell asleep.

Brittany woke up in the middle of the night and watched him sleeping. She smiled at how content he looked. She sat up carefully, not wanting to disturb him, and went into the family room. She stood at the window and looked out into the night, contemplating all that had happened. Hugging his shirt around her, she felt her tears begin and she didn't care. She made no effort to stop them or to hide. The weight of this whole ordeal just crashed onto her and she slid to the floor, holding her head in her hands. It was just too much. Whenever she closed her eyes she saw him getting shot and all of the blood, just so much blood. In the course of everything she had been through, it was always about her and how she had to adjust. Now, she had almost gotten him killed. She looked toward the bedroom and wondered if it would ever be okay. Could she ever let go of the fear and the memories? Could she ever let him get that close to her? She ran her hand through her hair and heard him.

"Red?" he called out.

She got up and walked to the doorway. "I'm here. Do you need something?" she asked softly.

He sat up carefully and turned the light on.

"What's going on?"

"Nothing, I was up and I didn't want to wake you. You need to sleep," she said.

"Come here," he said.

She wiped her eyes and walked closer. "Tommy, please, go back to bed, I just needed to clear my head."

He smiled and his unshaven face melted her heart. "I thought you were going to take care of me. I need you to come here," he pouted.

She smiled in spite of herself and walked over to the bed, sitting down facing him. He touched her face and she closed her eyes, letting fresh tears cascade down her cheeks. She wrapped her arms around his arm and laid her head on his shoulder. "Please talk to me," he said gently.

She shook her head. "I can't."

He moved closer to her. "Why not? I thought we were past this. I love you and you have nothing to hide from me. Please, baby, talk to me," he hated to see her so torn up.

She looked at him. "I love you and I want to be with you in every way, Tommy. I am just so messed up inside, you know? I look at you and my heart aches to touch you, but then," she looked away from him.

"But then what?" he asked her.

She shrugged. "I don't know."

"I think you do," he said. "Are you afraid I will hurt you?"

She shook her head. "No."

"Are you afraid you will hurt me?" he asked.

She looked at him. "Maybe," she said through her tears.

He sighed. "You and I are both doctors. We know what to do to be safe. Having HIV does not mean you can't have a sex life," he took her hand in his. "I think this goes deeper than that."

She looked at him. "What do you mean?"

"When you were raped, it was so much more than the physical attack. What that man did was condition you to expect pain and hurt from people. He left a wound that was so much worse than anything physical. He made you doubt your worth and your ability to ever be free of him. Brittany, you are such an amazing and sexy woman," he smiled at her. "You have made me happier than I have ever been in my life and my heart aches to be with you. You deserve to know what it means to be loved and touched in a way that makes you feel and know your worth," he looked at his leg. "If I wasn't incapacitated, I would love to show you," he smiled.

She was quiet for a minute. "I guess this was probably not the time to have this discussion," she smiled at him.

He shook his head. "No, I think it was the perfect time. We will be together, when you are ready, and when I can move," he grinned.

She moved closer to him and pulled his arm around her. She kissed his chest and moved up to kiss his mouth. She looked into his eyes and touched his cheek. "Okay," she said.

"Okay," he said and hugged her to him as she laid her head on his chest.

Chapter Forty-Eight:

The next week went by without incident. Tommy continued to improve and Brittany stayed close by. The day Tommy went in to have the bandage removed; Jack went with him.

"How do you feel, really?" Jack asked him as they made their way to the office.

Tommy smiled. "I feel good. I just need to be able to move around a little better. This is putting a crimp in my lifestyle."

Jack laughed. "Right, and what lifestyle might that be?"

Tommy looked at him. "Just walk with me and stop talking," he said and they both laughed.

Tommy went into the exam room and waited for the doctor while Jack continued to tease him.

****

Brittany walked into her house and closed the door behind her. She was glad to see the caution tape had been removed. Tommy was with Jack and she knew it was good for them to have some time together. She really needed to get her life back in order, and part of that would be getting her home back to normal. She put down the garbage bags she brought and walked into the foyer, looking around at the mess and sighing. She put her hair up into a ponytail and opened a garbage bag. She walked into the family room and began throwing away the broken pieces of debris on the floor. Most of it was replaceable picture frames and vases. She carefully removed the pictures from the broken glass and put them in a pile. She fingered the photo of her accepting her first Grammy. She smiled at the image showing her back then. She was so happy and truly honored to be recognized for her talents. She was also so naive. She had no concept of the dangers out there in the world and all that awaited her. Sometimes she wished she was that person again, so free and so open. She wondered where she would be if things had turned out differently.

She put the picture down and stood up. As much as she loved that life, she knew that she never would have met Tommy and that, by far, was the biggest blessing of her life. She continued to clean, trying to stay focused.

****

Tommy walked out of the office with no assistance and he was eager to get around on his own. Jack laughed at him. "Take it easy or you might wind up back in here."

"Not a chance," he said. "Want to grab a bite?"

"Sure, come on," Jack said and they headed to his car.

"So how is Stephanie doing? I haven't had a chance to see her lately. Is she feeling okay?" Tommy asked as Jack drove.

"She is, really. I try to stay focused on the whole idea that she will get through this okay, but," he said.

"But nothing. She is healthy and you both are going to have a beautiful healthy baby," Tommy said.

Jack smiled. "You sound like her."

Tommy laughed and they pulled into the diner. They made their way to a booth and sat down. Jack looked at Tommy. "I'm really glad you're okay," he said.

Tommy nodded. "You did a great job in the O.R."

Jack smiled. "How is Brittany? Is she dealing with everything okay?"

Tommy looked at him. "I think so, why?"

Jack shook his head. "No reason, I just can't help but remember the scene we walked into when we found you guys. It was heartbreaking."

Tommy looked at him. "What do you mean? What was the scene? Is there something I don't know?" he thought of Brittany's demeanor after and how upset she had been. Had he missed something?

Jack shook his head. "No, she just had to watch you sitting there, bleeding to death. When we walked in, she was like a barricade over you, trying to shield you and she wouldn't let go. I had to almost pick her up off of you. She was petrified and she was covered with your blood," Jack wiped his face. "I thought you were gone, man, so much blood."

Tommy felt sick to hear his description. "You guys saved me. I can't ever thank you enough."

Jack shook his head again. "No, man, she saved you. She had to sit in that room with you and that perv and she had enough of a mind to apply a tourniquet to your leg and lessen the bleeding. He had a gun on you both and he was going to shoot when the cops killed him. She just stood her ground and protected you at all costs. I owe her big time."

Tommy smiled. "We both do."

****

Brittany looked at her cell phone and smiled at Tommy's text.

"Where R U?"

"My house. Cleaning. How R U?"

"100% coming over."

"K ☺"

She smiled as she moved to her bedroom. She had made headway in the family room and wanted to see what she could salvage in her room. She put her dresser drawers back into their slots and began putting her clothes in bags. She knew she wouldn't be able to keep much of it, his smell was all over and she knew she couldn't wash it all away. She opened her jewelry box and saw that most of her things were still there. Thankful for the small surprise, she sat down and held the necklace her father had given to her. It was a locket and inside was a picture of him and the words "If music be the food of love, play on," she put in around her neck and held it in her hand. Wiping her tears away, she went about straightening the rest of her things. She was getting tired when she heard a knock at the front door. She walked and opened it. Tommy was standing there, unassisted. She threw her arms around him and he hugged her to him.

"You look wonderful," she said as he walked in. "Where's Jack?" she looked behind him.

"He left; I told him you would get me home," he said as he looked around and saw the progress she had made. "I wish you had let me help you."

"Don't worry, there's plenty more," she said and walked over to her couch. She sat down and wiped her forehead. She was sweaty and filthy.

He came over and sat down next to her. He wiped some dirt off her cheek. "Why don't you let me take you back to my place? I think you've done enough for today. We can come back tomorrow if you want."

She nodded. "Okay, I am a bit tired."

"Did you overdo it?" he was immediately concerned.

She laughed. "No, people who do work like lifting and cleaning get tired."

He smiled. "Just checking."

Chapter Forty-Nine:

Brittany drove Tommy up to his house and they walked inside. She put her bag of things down and turned to look at him. "Are you sure you feel okay? Just because you got your stitches out and can move around doesn't mean your body feels 100%."

He smiled at her. "I feel amazing. I just want to take a shower and wash all of this grime off."

"So do I," she smiled. "I wonder when the last time was that I dusted at my house," she fingered her hair.

He was going to say something, but stopped himself. She saw him pause. "What?"

He shook his head. "Nothing," he smiled.

"Are you sure?" she asked, walking over to him.

He nodded. "Yes."

"Okay, I will wait until you are done and then I will take my shower. Please let me know if you need help. I can put a chair in the shower if you want," she said.

He raised his eyebrows at her. "I don't think that will be necessary."

She laughed. "Fine, but I am waiting in your bedroom in case you need anything."

He looked at her again. "Okay," he said and went into the room.

She waited a minute and when she heard the shower running she went into his room and made sure she stayed in earshot in case he needed help. She pulled off her shoes and socks and checked out her foot. It was finally looking more like normal, although she knew she needed it set again. She looked in his mirror and smirked at herself. She looked filthy. Her hair was gross and her face had dirt smudges on it. She pulled her hair out of the ponytail and let it fall over her shoulders. She heard the bathroom door open and she turned around to see him standing there wearing a towel, his hair wet and dripping, and he was looking at her.

"What is it? Are you okay?" she asked him. His face looked like something was wrong. She walked over to him. "What's wrong?" she saw he had tears in his eyes.

"Did you protect me with your life?" he asked her. "Did you stand over me when he tried to shoot me again?" his chin quivered as he spoke.

She tried to look away, but she couldn't. "I would do anything for you," she said softly.

"I'm so sorry. I don't think I ever realized what," he began, but she stopped him.

"Enough. It's over and you're okay and I'm okay. I don't want to think about it anymore. I don't want to waste another minute," she said and pulled him to her in a passionate kiss. He wrapped his arms around her and she turned her head to allow deeper access of his tongue. He pulled away from her and saw her flushed face and her soft eyes. "Okay?" she asked him, wiping the water droplets from his cheek.

"Okay, I'm good. Go take your shower. I'll be right here," he said. She walked into the bathroom and closed the door, once again overwhelmed by her feelings. She turned on the water and walked in, letting the hot liquid flow over her. She washed her hair and her body and got out, wrapping a towel around her. She stepped out of the bathroom and saw he was still sitting in the same spot. He hadn't changed or moved.

"Tommy, what is it?" she walked over and sat down next to him.

He looked at her. "Nothing, I was just waiting for you. He looked at her, wearing only a towel. He saw her bruised arm and he touched her. "Is this from where he grabbed you?"

She nodded. "Yes, but it's nothing."

He shook his head. "I knew you were coming and I didn't know how to tell you to stay away. I just sat there and let him get to you, again," he emphasized the last word.

She shook her head. "No, Tommy. I wish you wouldn't say that. You were so brave. He was going to kill you. He almost did and I thank God you are okay," she put her arm around his shoulder.

He looked at her and smoothed her wet hair away from her face. "I thought he was going to get to you again, and I couldn't stop him," he blinked and a tear escaped.

She felt her eyes fill with unshed tears. "He didn't and we are both here and both okay. Let's get dressed and we can figure out how to spend the rest of our day," she looked at him. "Do you need help?"

He shook his head. "No, I'm okay."

She stood up and smiled. "Okay, be right back."

She walked into the guest room and closed the door. She put her head in her hands and for the millionth time, she tried to clear the images of him being shot out of her head. She put her clothes on and brushed her tangled wet hair. Walking out of the room, she saw he was still on the bed. She went quickly back to him. "Tommy, you're scaring me, what's going on?" she knelt in front of him and touched his leg. "You're getting cold."

He shrugged. "I don't know," he looked at her. "I'm sorry, I just keep thinking about the moment you came into the room. I just prayed for help, you know? I would have given anything to stop him from touching you again," he tried to stop, but his emotions just came out and he put his head in his hand. She sat down next to him and pulled him into her arms. She held him and let him get it out. She felt her tears fall with his as she tried to soothe him. He sat back after a minute and she held his face in her hands.

"I love you so much," she said brokenly. "You saved me, Tommy, in every way possible. Before, I wouldn't have been able to face tomorrow; but now, because of you, I look forward to it. It breaks my heart to hear you beat yourself up for even a second over this man. He took so much from my life; I can't bear to see him take your strength or your faith in yourself."

He pulled her to him and she pressed her mouth on his. He needed to feel her in his arms and she needed him to be okay. His kiss was searching, needy and desperate for reassurance. She met his passion and they kissed each other like they were the only people in the world. She stopped after a minute to catch her breath. He stood up and she looked at him, questioning him without speaking.

"I'm going to get dressed. I need to; will you wait in there for me?" he asked her, pointing to the family room.

"Of course," she walked out of the room, giving him his privacy. She walked to the guest room and looked in the mirror. She felt something different; she didn't feel nervous or anxious. She didn't feel fear or panic. She felt love and she felt hope. She turned and walked back into the family room and he was standing there. She smiled at him and wrapped her arms around herself. "Are you okay?"

He nodded. "I am. I don't know what happened, I just freaked out a little," he smiled.

She walked up to him. "You are amazing. You are so concerned for me and you don't even know how close you came to dying," she remembered the moment and shuddered. "He pointed the gun and he just pulled the trigger," she looked at him. "I tried to stop the bleeding, but I didn't know how, and you were fading away from me," she wiped her eyes. "You were trying to look at me, trying to help me and your eyes kept rolling back," she turned around and walked to the chair. She felt the need to sit.

"Hey, it's okay, I'm here, all good," he said and smiled. He sat down next to her and sighed. "I think we have had enough tears and sadness to last a lifetime. How about we make some new memories?"

She looked at him and smiled. "What did you have in mind?"

"The night we were going to meet, I had a surprise planned, but we obviously never got there. I had it all designed, romantic dinner, me looking handsome and debonair in my suit, sweeping you off your feet," he smiled and she giggled. "I wanted everything to be perfect for you. I wanted to give you a night that was fun and sexy and real. I wanted you to know how grateful I am that you gave me another chance after that awful introduction. I wanted to show you that you made the right choice."

She took his hands in hers and brought them to her lips. She looked at him. "You did all that, Tommy. You take care of me like I matter. You look at me like I am the only woman on earth. You are sexy and handsome and debonair and I have never been so completely in love with anyone. You know, I had my own surprise for you that night, and I can't believe I forgot about it until now."

He looked at her, surprised. "What?"

She smiled. "My viral load is undetectable. The new cocktail is working for now."

He picked her up in his arms and she wrapped her arms around him. He put her down and his eyes shone with tears when he looked at her. "I couldn't ask for any better news than that," he leaned in and kissed her.

"I agree," she hugged him and he held her for a moment.

"Why don't we have that dinner tomorrow night?" he asked her after a little while.

She smiled up at him. "I think that would be wonderful."

*****

Brittany went back to the hotel for the evening and Stephanie met here there. "Okay, spill, what's going on?" Stephanie asked her friend.

"Tommy and I are going out tomorrow and I want to look special. I was hoping you could show me how to do my hair like you used to when we were kids," she smiled at her.

Stephanie laughed. "I would love to. What are you going to wear?"

"I don't know; whatever I have here I guess," she frowned. "I really need to get all new clothes."

"There is a shop in the lobby, why don't we go down and see what we can find for you? I think tomorrow warrants a new gown," Stephanie beamed at her friend. "I foresee great things for you both."

Brittany felt her stomach lurch with nerves. She had been thinking about what might happen since she left Tommy. She looked at her friend who was so happy for her. She ran her hand through her hair.

"What's wrong?" Stephanie asked, aware of the sudden change in her demeanor. "Are you okay?"

She shook her head, "Yes, just nervous, I guess."

Stephanie sat down and took her friends' hands in her own. "Do you love Tommy?"

Brittany nodded. "With all my heart."

"Do you trust him?"

"Yes."

"Does he respect your feelings and your past?"

"Yes," she said softly.

"Then whatever happens, just remember that. Sometimes we get caught up in the idea of what we should do and how we should act, when really, we just need to be in the moment. Some things can't be planned and when they happen just out of spontaneity of being together, it is the most magical experience. Britt, I know you are scared of your memories and you live in the shadow of what happened, but maybe now it is time to truly move past it," she looked at her friend, the one who had been through such a traumatic ordeal, the one who stood before millions of people and showed her soul through her voice. The one who now sat there like a lost child, looking for guidance. "You are so much stronger than you give yourself credit. Tommy loves you, and I would bet that he hasn't pressured you to do anything you didn't want to do, am I right?"

Brittany shook her head. "No, of course not."

"Then it's up to you to jump. It's okay to let go and be with him, Brit., if that's what you want. I want you to know the kind of love you deserve and it can be so magical, so profound. I know you're scared, but giving yourself to someone, heart and soul is the most precious gift of all, and the most sacred," she smiled at her friend.

"But what if I hurt him?" Brittany said, vocalizing her deepest fear. "No protection is 100% effective."

Stephanie sighed and her heart ached for her friend. "You know that's not true. The medical research shows that with the proper precautions, it is perfectly safe. You are a doctor and so is Tommy. Sweetie, don't use your HIV as an excuse, if you want to be intimate with him, than do it, if not, then don't, but make it about your feelings, not your condition."

Brittany knew she was right. She hugged her friend. "How did you get so smart?"

"Good genes," Stephanie said and they laughed. "Now, how about a small shopping trip downstairs?"

"Okay," Brittany said and they went out.

******

"I can't tell you how glad I am that you're back at work. This place is boring without someone to mess with," Jack told Tommy as he stopped by his office the next morning. Tommy had come back to work to fill out charts and see patients. He had a few tough cases which needed his attention, and he hated to move people to different doctors when they were dealing with their children.

"I am sure you found someone else to annoy," Tommy joked with Jack. "How is Stephanie feeling? I haven't seen her lately."

Jack beamed. "She is amazing and beautiful and sexy and there are certain parts of pregnancy that we are finding very appealing."

Tommy raised his eyebrows as if he was grossed out. "Really? A simple 'she's good' would have sufficed."

Jack laughed. "There is no fun for me in that."

"As long as you're happy," Tommy smirked.

"So what's on tap today after work?" Jack asked. He knew from talking to Stephanie that Tommy had special plans set up.

"Just dinner. I am going by Brittany's house after I leave here to help her gather more things, and then we will go have dinner," he said.

Jack became serious for a minute. "How is she handling everything that happened?"

"What do you mean? I think everything is good," he said.

"I don't mean about you, but about what that ass did to her home. I know he's dead and gone, but he left some deep scars. Has she dealt with that? Have you talked to her about that?" Jack asked him sincerely.

Tommy ran a hand through his hair. "I don't know; she is just cleaning things up like it's just another step in the process of getting rid of this guy," he was quiet for a minute. "I guess in the midst of her recovery and then my getting shot, I haven't really noticed."

Jack nodded. "Okay, I just want to make sure you both are okay."

Tommy smiled. "I know and I think we are," he said, but Jacks words struck a chord.

Chapter Fifty:

Brittany carried the paint she bought into the house. She had been cleaning for a while and hadn't ventured into her music room, but knew she needed to face it. Carrying the paint into the room and putting it down, she looked at the mess that surrounded her and noticed for the first time how much destruction there was. He had focused on this room because it was the closest to her. He knew it would break her heart and it did.

She walked to the wall and looked at the crude spray painted words he had put in red. She fingered the letters and felt her anger begin to surface. She traced the pattern on the wall and tripped over something on the floor. She fell and looked down at a table leg that she had hit. She turned to see the mess of the sheet music that lay on the ground, some torn and some she found had paint on it. One she found had something else on it and her stomach churned as she realized he probably used her things to get off. She ran into the bathroom and scrubbed her hands clean, even though she hadn't really touched anything.

She went back into the room and as she looked at the wall, the images began to blur into his face. She saw him everywhere, smelled his chemical scent, saw Tommy getting shot, saw her life forever changed. She got up and opened the can of paint she brought and without thinking; she threw the paint onto the wall, the liquid splashing and dripping. She looked at the blue fluid as it covered the wall and peppered her skin. She felt her tears fall down as she took the can and threw it on the wall again. She continued to throw the pant and felt it splash on her face and her clothes, but she didn't care. She started to yell at him as she tried to cover his pollution.

******

Tommy pulled up to her house and was glad to see she was still there. He had been thinking a lot about what Jack had said and he thought it was probably a good idea to be with her while she cleaned. He knocked on the door but she didn't answer. He could hear something inside, so he listened and finally made out her yelling at someone. Fear coursed through his body as he pushed open the door and ran to her voice. He stood at the doorway and saw her, the blue paint splashed onto the walls. Her face and body had paint specks all over. She was covering over the mess he had made of the walls and yelling at him.

"Red, hey, Red," he said to her as he approached. She turned and saw him and kept throwing the paint on the wall.

"I am almost done," she said, a frantic look to her face. "I just need to cover it all up and then he will be gone," she tossed the paint onto the wall once more, splashing it over her and getting some on Tommy. He turned her to look at him.

"Brittany, stop."

She looked at him, her hands shaking in front of her. He took the can from her hands.

"But I need to cover it up," she said in a pathetically sad voice that broke his heart.

"No, you don't. He's gone and he can't hurt you anymore. Please let me take you out of here," he smoothed her hair, which had paint flecks in it.

"Maybe if I keep painting, things can go back to the way they were before. He never would have found me and gotten his smell all over me again and you wouldn't have been shot," she was struggling to keep her tears at bay, her resolve crumbling. She looked at him. "I just want the pain to stop," she said and sank to the floor.

Tommy sat down next to her. He pulled her into his arms and held her head to his chest. She kept her hands out in front of her, shaking with the emotion of the moment. He took a piece of ripped towel from the floor and wiped the paint off her arms, gently turning her face to look at him.

"You are going to be okay. The pain will stop and you will be able to move on," he said to her. "You just need to take time and deal with what happened."

She stood up and moved away from him. "I'm going to go back to the hotel."

He stood up and shook his head. "No, you're going to come to my house."

"Why? So you can 'fix' me? Aren't you tired of that, Tommy? Don't you want to be with someone who challenges you and inspires you and isn't," she stopped.

"Isn't what?" he asked her softly.

"Isn't damaged."

"Brittany, you aren't damaged. You are hurting and you're scared and you need to get out of the house that he vandalized. You can get through this and you deserve to be happy. Please just let me take you back to my house so you can clean up and we can make sense of this," he said with an air of desperation.

She looked at him and nodded. "I'm so sorry, Tommy. Every time I think I'm over it, I get so overwhelmed with fear. I don't know how to stop feeling this way."

"We are going to figure that out, but first, we need to clean you up," he said and led her to her car. She sat in the passenger seat and looked out the window as he drove back to his house. She let him take her inside and she walked to the bathroom and put her hands under the faucet, washing the paint off her hands and then walking out into the bedroom. She sat down on the bed and he walked over to her.

"Can I make a suggestion?" he asked her.

She looked at him and he smiled. "They make things called paint brushes."

She laughed despite her emotional state. "I suppose, in hindsight, I could have used a brush."

He shrugged his shoulders. "I'm just saying," he laughed with her and was pleased she seemed to be relaxing a bit.

She ran her hand through her hair and frowned at the paint she felt. "I think I need to take a bath. I need to just to wash everything away," she said and looked at him. "I'm sorry you had to see that, Tommy. I don't know what happened."

He came over and sat down next to her. He put his arm around her and sighed. "I know what happened, Red. You felt violated all over again. I shouldn't have let you go over there alone."

She smiled at him. "Let me?"

He grinned. "You know what I mean; I just wish I could take some of this pain away for you."

"You already have, so much," she looked at him and something changed within her. "Will you stay with me?"

He touched her face. "Of course, I'll wait right out here."

"No, will you sit with me, in the tub?" she asked hesitantly.

"Are you sure?" he asked her.

"I just want to feel safe and close to you. I just want to be with you, Tommy," she said softly. "I want to be with you, completely."

He smiled as he brushed her hair off her face. "Okay," he walked into the area with the tub and ran the water, filling it with some bubbles he had brought back from the resort.

She watched him and smiled. "What else did you take?"

"You'll see," he smiled and walked over to her. "We need to get your paint covered clothes off," he looked at her and saw her eyes were still wet with tears. "What is it?"

She shook her head. "Nothing, I am just so glad you're here."

He leaned in and kissed her. "Me too," he slowly reached to unbutton her sweater shirt, his fingers almost refusing to work the way he wanted. Her body heat was resonating from her skin and his heart beat faster as he moved the material away from her body, revealing a white tank top underneath. She was breathing heavily as he looked at her. She pulled him to her and her mouth searched for his. His toes tingled as the kiss intensified and she moved her hands to the hem of his shirt and then underneath the fabric, her fingers on his skin. Startled, he looked into her eyes. "Are you sure?"

She shook her head. "I want to feel your skin," she said as she picked his shirt up over his head and ran her hands over his muscular torso, relishing the feel of his warm skin beneath her fingers, moving her hands through the dark hair that covered his chest. She moved her fingers along his upper body, taking his hand in hers and bringing it to her lips.

"You have the most beautiful chest," she said softly as she leaned in and kissed his neck, her hands roaming over his nipples.

She was driving him wild and all of the months of waiting and hesitating to touch her were culminating in this moment. He stood there, frozen while she walked

SEE PROFILE

behind him and ran her hands over his back, leaning in
to kiss his shoulder blades as she ran her hands
around his waist from behind, resting her cheek on his
skin.

He clasped his hands over hers and turned to face her
before gently running his hand under her hair. He
looked into her eyes and he reached to the bottom of
her tank top and slowly pulled it off. His hands ran over
her shoulders, stroking her skin and making her melt
under his touch. In all the time he had cared for her,
seen her clad in her underwear, he had never allowed
himself to look, to feel for her. He couldn't, it wasn't
right, but now, standing here before him, he couldn't
take his eyes off of her. She was exquisite.

"You are so beautiful," he said. She looked down and
he picked her chin up and smiled. "Don't hide; I just
think you deserve to be told."

She met his gaze and let him leisurely move her bra
straps off her shoulders, her heart filled with excitement
and nervous tension. He slowly ran his fingers down
her arms as he moved closer and leaned in to her, his
lips meeting her neck. She moved her head to the side
and closed her eyes; feeling like her heart was about to
burst out of her chest. She leaned in to him and ran her
hands along his back as he reached behind her and
unclasped the soft material, which held the lingerie in
place. He looked at her as the fabric fell away and he
took her face in his hands. "Are you okay?" he asked
her.

She grasped his wrists with her hands. "So okay," she
said as she wrapped her arms around him, her chest
against his. He enveloped her in his strong arms and

held her, his hands on her lower back. She knew he was going slow with her and she adored his sensual side.

She felt her tears fall, but they were tears of release, of happiness and of love. She looked up at him and he lowered his mouth onto hers again, his tongue teasing her mouth and her mouth welcoming him. She stepped back and he kept his eyes on her as she moved her hands down his torso to the waistband of his jeans. She smiled at him as she slowly unbuttoned the material and pulled the zipper down. He pulled her to him again and nibbled her ear as she ran her hands under the top of his jeans and pulled them down slowly. He stepped out of the fabric and she looked at the beauty that was his body as she walked to him, reaching out to touch his hips. She traced a line across his navel and looked up into his eyes. "You are incredible, Tommy. I don't know what I did to deserve someone like you," she said to him, her eyes still brimming with tears.

He took her hand and walked to the tub. Turning to her, he ran his fingers down her abdomen to her pants and slowly pulled them down, running his hands down her legs and then back up to her thighs. She watched him move up her body and when he made his way back to her face she welcomed his mouth back to hers. She kissed him again as she reached down to remove the last piece of clothing he had on. She ran her hands down his legs as he had done for her and she stood back up, taking his hands in hers. They just stared at each other for a moment before he gently peeled her panties off and took her hand as they got into the tub and sat down, her back against his chest. He wrapped his arms around her and she leaned back and closed her eyes. He moved her hair from her neck and leaned in to her.

"I love you. You deserve the world," he kissed her neck and she turned her face to meet his mouth with hers. She held his arms around her and they just sat there, lost in the moment. He began to rub her arms, cleaning off the paint residue. He picked her arms up and ran his hands down the underside of her soft skin, loving how she moaned as he massaged her shoulders. He moved his hands over her breasts and she arched her back as he ran his fingers over her nipples.

She reached down and ran her hands over his thighs, feeling his muscles, being careful not to hurt his still tender injury. He put his hands over hers and hooked their fingers together. She felt the most amazing sense of calm and ease. She turned to face him and he studied her face, her features. He smiled as he touched her lips.

"Tommy, I," she took his face in her hands and pulled him to her so her legs straddled his, but they kept a distance. He nodded.

"I know; me too," he said through his own watery eyes and pulled her to him. He closed his eyes as she moved her hands over his body. She kissed his chest as her hands traveled down to his waist, brushing his groin. He opened his eyes and looked at her with a different expression. His green eyes were almost emerald with desire as he crashed his mouth onto hers. She kissed him back with equal passion and suddenly, everything was perfectly clear to her. This was real, this was true and this was love. She pulled away from him and he stopped.

"What is it? Did I hurt you?" he asked, concerned at her sudden stop.

She shook her head. "No, Tommy. I want you to make love to me," she said and he looked into her eyes.

"We don't have to do anything you don't want to do," he said; needing to be sure she really was ready for this.

"I love that you are so careful with me. I love that you want me to feel safe and you need to know that I do. I want to feel your body with mine. I want this," she said softly. "If that's what you want, too. If not, that's okay."

He smiled. "Like you even have to ask. Red, you already have all of me," he stood up and stepped out of the tub, his body glistening with the water and the bubbles. He reached out to her and she stood up. He helped her out of the tub and wrapped them in a towel together. He tenderly dried her off and picked her up gently in his arms, carrying her to the bed and placing her down on the soft plush sheets.

She lay back and reached for him, and he joined her on the posh material, carefully laying his body on hers. She ran her hands through his hair and kissed him deeply. He nibbled on her neck and made a trail with his tongue down the soft flesh of her chest and she arched her back to meet him. He used his tongue to tease each nipple and she could feel his erection against her leg.

He lavished her body with the attention it deserved and she adored the way he loved her. His tongue moved down to her navel and back up to her mouth.

"Can I touch you?" he murmured, looking deep into her eyes.

She nodded and he moved his hand to her center, rubbing the bundle of nerves and gently slipping a finger inside of her.

She moaned as the waves of pleasure took over her body and he moved his mouth to her breasts again while his fingers moved in and out.

The blue in her eyes looked almost translucent as she let him take her to the edge. She took his hand in hers and gently pushed him onto his back.

He watched her as she sat up and leaned into him, laying her body on his and moving down his chest, tracing a line with her mouth.

He was on fire for her and she was making him feel like he was in heaven. Her hands roamed over his body, exploring him in a way that left him feeling incredibly vulnerable. She moved over his torso, leaving a trail of wet kissed across his stomach.

"Can I touch you?" she asked softly, as he had done for her.

"Please do," he said breathlessly.

She smiled and ran her hand over his shaft, feeling emboldened by the moans coming from him at every stroke. She gently moved her body back over his until she faced him, her feelings mirrored in his eyes.

He sat up and pulled her to him before turning their position so she was lying on her back and he was over her. She ran her fingers over his lips and he met her again in a deep kiss. She wanted him, needed him to love her completely. She had never been more ready for anything in her life. She looked up at him and smiled. "Do you have what we need?"

He smiled. "Of course," he sat back and took the necessary precautions before moving back over her. She looked into his eyes as he slowly pushed into her, both of them overwhelmed by the feelings.

He moved until his hips met hers and he fit perfectly and intimately with her, in every way possible. Her eyes filled with tears at the power of the moment and the love she felt.

"Are you okay?" he asked her softly, seeing her tears. He stilled his movements and stroked her cheek.

"I'm amazing," she said and bent her leg to allow him more room. He smiled as he kissed her and began to move. He was slow and tender and affectionate with everything he did and she felt the most amazing sensations of love and trust. He linked his fingers with hers as they made love and gave themselves completely to each other.

A little while later, Tommy lay with Brittany on his chest. She looked up at him and he gently ran his hand through her hair. "What are you thinking?" he asked her softly.

She moved up closer to his face. "Thank you," she said simply.

"For what?" he brought her fingers to his lips.

"For giving me the most amazing experience of my life; for showing me that I can be beautiful and sexy; for being so patient with me; for being amazingly sexy and incredibly gentle," she ran her hand over his chest. "I just want to thank you," she kissed him.

He shook his head. "You are amazing," he said to her. "I don't know what I did to deserve your love."

She smiled. "I do have one request."

He raised his eyebrows. "What's that?"

She grinned. "I think I can get a lot better if I had a little more practice."

He laughed. "Oh really? Well I think I can manage that," he sat up and she giggled as he rolled her onto her back and pressed his mouth to hers again. Her arms wrapped around him and they both melted into their passion again.

Chapter Fifty-One:

"You seem different," Jack said to Tommy as they met the next morning before surgery.

Tommy couldn't stop grinning. "I don't know what you mean?" he said as he drank his coffee.

Jack laughed. "Whatever, man, I'm just glad you are back at work. You're sure you feel okay?"

"Better than I have felt in a long time," Tommy said and walked in front of his friend, leaving Jack shaking his head.

"Okay, so you aren't going to give me any more details? Jack asked him.

"Nope," Tommy said as his eyes twinkled.

******

Stephanie hummed to herself as she worked on filling in some of the charts she was working on. She was almost ready to go home and she was waiting for Jack to come by her office. She felt the baby kick and she put her hand on her stomach. "I know, baby, I promise we will eat soon," she spoke aloud and smiled. She walked to her desk and sat down, suddenly tired. She rubbed her eyes and sighed. "What should we have for dinner?" she talked to the baby and tried to just breathe. She felt a little spacey and she knew she just needed to relax a little. Maybe Jack was right and she should take time off, she thought to herself as she closed her eyes. She would do anything for her baby.

Jack made his way toward Stephanie's office when the nurse, Megan, who was always around Tommy stopped him. He couldn't believe he had ever suggested they date. She really was annoying. "Dr. Stephens, do you have a minute?"

Jack shook his head. "I'm sorry, I'm on my way to a meeting. Is it an emergency?"

She smiled. "Not really, I was just going to ask how Tommy, I mean Dr. Williams was doing. I haven't seen him much since he was hurt."

Jack glanced at her and tried to figure out her angle. "As far as I know he is doing great. Dr. Anthony is taking very good care of him," he focused on making sure she got the last part of the sentence.

"Oh, well if he needs a nurse, could you let him know I'm available?" she said.

Jack couldn't believe how bold she was and how inappropriate. "Megan, he is in a relationship. I think you should look elsewhere. Now excuse me," he said bluntly and turned to walk away, but not before he saw the anger in her eyes. "Weirdo," he muttered under his breath.

He walked to Stephanie's office and knocked. He didn't hear her so he opened the door and walked in, smiling when he saw she was asleep at her desk, her hands on her stomach. He walked over to her and leaned in to kiss her.

"I'm up," she said as she opened her eyes. She smiled when she saw it was him.

"Hi beautiful," he put his hand on her stomach. "Hi baby," he said to the small bump under her shirt.

She yawned and he laughed. "Are you ready to go?"

She nodded. "I just got really tired all of a sudden. I think I could use some juice or something."

He was alarmed and looked at her. "What's going on? What aren't you telling me? Steph, don't hide anything from me," he took her cheek in his hand.

She touched his hand. "Nothing, I am just tired and I felt a little spacey earlier, but I feel better now. I just need to remember to eat more often," she held his gaze so he would know she meant it.

He sighed and sat down. "I just worry about you. How about I take you home and we relax tonight?"

"That would be wonderful," she said and took his hand as she got up and they walked out.

"Hi Megan," Stephanie said as she saw the nurse standing in the hallway near her office. Jack stiffened at the sight of her and Stephanie picked up on it.

"Dr. Stephens," she said briskly as she eyed them and walked away.

Stephanie turned to look at her and then at Jack. "What was that about?"

"Let's just say she has the hots for Tommy and she doesn't seem to want to take no for an answer. I can't believe I ever told her about him and vise versa," he said.

She held his arm and smiled. "You wanted your friend to be happy and there is nothing wrong with that. Besides, if she wants a fight, I am fairly certain Brittany can hold her own."

Jack put his arm around her waist and felt much better. "I would agree," he said and they left.
*****
Brittany felt her stomach jump as she walked back into her office ready for work. It was her first real day back to seeing patients and she was having a little trouble forgetting all that had happened. So far, no one seemed to know who she was, or they were just being nice about keeping things quiet, but she still had it on her mind. She also had Tommy on her mind and the amazing day and night they had yesterday. She tucked a stray hair behind her ear as she walked to the nurse's station.

"Hi Dr. Anthony," Jade said as she walked up. "I am so glad you're back. This place has been crazy without you."

Brittany smiled. "It's good to be back. What's on tap for this morning?" she looked at the schedule, knowing she was only seeing patients for the morning, easing back in slowly. She didn't want to get run down.

"Here is the patient list. Do you need me to get anything for you?" Jade asked her.

Brittany smiled and shook her head. "No, thank you Jade. I'll be in my office if you need me," she turned to walk to some privacy, the thoughts of the previous day running through her head. She needed to figure everything out, from her house to the hotel to Tommy. What was she going to do next? She didn't think she could go back to living in her home, not after everything that happened. She also couldn't live in a hotel. She sighed and saw her office phone light up with a call. She smiled when she saw the extension.

"This is Dr. Anthony," she said softly.

"Hi, it's Dr. Williams," Tommy said with a smile.

"I know I was just trying to be professional," she smiled into the phone. "Where are you?"

"Waiting for my next appointment," he sounded a little down.

"What's wrong? You sound like something is bothering you," she played with her hair.

He sighed. "No, it's just a hard case. 12 year old girl with acute lymphocytic leukemia. I was called in to do the tumor removal and I was hoping to be able to give them all better news. Sometimes I wonder if I chose the right field," he said softly.

She smiled as she listened to him. "Of course you did. It takes a special person to deal with cancer and it takes an even more extraordinary person to deal with children with cancer. You knew what your calling was, Tommy, and this girl will be so much better off because of your care," she hoped he knew that was true. "Do you want to meet me for lunch after your appointment?"

"That would be great," he felt better already. "I am done after that, something about having to take it easy my first day back," he laughed. "I think Jack made sure I only had one case today."

"Remind me to thank him. You never slow down," she laughed. "Okay, I should be done before you, so I'll meet you at your office," she said.

"Sounds good. I love you," he said softly.

"I love you too," she added and hung up the phone.

The rest of the morning went by without incident and Brittany was relieved to be able to meet Tommy and then relax for the rest of the day. It had been a bit more taxing on her system to be there for so long, but she was holding up. She walked down towards his office when someone stepped in front of her.

"Will you please give me an interview? I have been waiting for you to come back," the man said as he stuck a camera in her face.

"Excuse me, I don't know what you're talking about," Brittany tried to walk past him.

"Hey, I know who you are and I'm not leaving without a scoop," he threatened her by blocking her way. "Are you here for a follow up? What's wrong with you? Is it serious?"

Brittany turned to look for help. She saw a nurse walking by and waved her over. "Will you please call security?" she asked the nurse calmly.

The nurse nodded and turned quickly to get help. Brittany faced the man. "You need to move and let me by."

"Tell me what happened? The beautiful redheaded sensation with the velvet voice. You were so popular, Barbie. When will you tell your story? The public won't stop until they know the truth. If you don't tell me, there are other ways of finding things out," he said in a sleazy manner, scooting closer to her.

Brittany felt like she was going to be sick. She looked down the hallway and saw Tommy step out of his office. She stepped to walk around the man, to go to Tommy, but the man grabbed her by the arm. She turned and smacked him as the security guards came up quickly. Tommy ran down the hall towards her.

"I guess there is more to the story," the man said with a smile as he snapped a photo of her. She stood shaking, rooted to the spot.

Tommy came up to her and stood between her and the man who was being held by security. He was livid, witnessing the exchange and seeing the fear which came back into her face. "What the hell is wrong with you? This is a place of business," he yelled at the man.

"Where there's smoke, there's fire, and I will get the first light," he said with a smirk. "I'll be in touch."

The guards moved him out to the elevator and Tommy turned around, but she was gone.

He ran down the hall towards the bathroom. He knocked on the door, but there was no answer. He walked in, not caring that it was the ladies room, but she wasn't inside. He ran his hand through his hair and turned to go to the roof.

She sat alone in the corner of the roof, hidden from view, letting the wind blow through her hair and trying to relax. She knew this was coming. She had escaped for so long, but now, the secret was out and it wouldn't die until she acknowledged who she was. She just wished there was some other way, any other way, to deal with this. She hugged her knees to her chest and put her head on her arms and just sat there.

Tommy stepped onto the roof and looked around. He didn't see her at first, but when he moved to the place he had seen her on one of their first meetings, he found her there, sitting on the ground. He walked over to her. "Red," he began.

She looked at him. "I'm sorry I missed lunch, I just needed a minute."

He sat down next to her. "What did that guy want?" he tucked a loose piece of hair behind her ear.

She looked at him and shrugged. "Me, my story. He knows who I am and he won't stop until everything is out," she laughed. "You know, it's kind of ironic. Here I am, back at work, the one thing that has remained untouched from my life before, and suddenly, it is the one place where I can't escape it. This is a public place and reporters can come here any time. It was kind of silly for me to think that they wouldn't find me, after it has been revealed that I am here and that I was at the hospital. It doesn't take a rocket scientist to search and find me here," she sighed and pulled her hair out of the ponytail she had it in. "They won't stop until they learn every sordid detail and then, there will be nothing left of me."

He sighed. "That's not true. You are so much more than a story," he looked at her and smiled. "Can we go back to my place? I don't want to stay on the cold roof."

She combed her hair with her fingers. "I need to finish packing my stuff at my house."

"I don't think you need to do that right now. I think you need a little Tommy medicine," he grinned.

She raised her eyebrows. "And what does that entail?"

"It's a very secret recipe which can only be revealed under the right circumstances. Are you interested?" he raised his eyebrows at her in a teasing manner.

"I might be persuaded," she rubbed her face and exhaled. "I'm tired, Tommy," she said softly.

"I know you are. Come on," he stood up and reached a hand out to her.

She stood up and wrapped her arms around her waist and shivered. "It is cold up here."

He looked at her with concern. "Let's go," he said, anxious to get her to safety and warmth.

She nodded and walked out with him.

Chapter Fifty-Two:

"So, did Brittany fill you in on her night with Tommy?" Jack asked Stephanie as they met in the locker room. He was waiting for the details he wasn't able to get.

She laughed. "He wouldn't say anything either, huh?"

Jack pouted. "He always tells me things. Girls ruin everything," he smiled.

"Oh really? And just what does that mean?" she touched his chest with her hand and moved her fingers down his torso before brushing his waist with her thumb.

"Oops, sorry, don't want to ruin anything," she said and turned to walk away.

"Oh no you don't," he wrapped his arms around her and she squealed.

"But you said girls ruin everything. Aren't I a girl?" she turned in his arms and pouted.

"No, you're all woman," he said and lowered his mouth onto hers. She wrapped her arms around his neck and deepened the kiss.

"Did you tell Tommy all about our nights in the Poconos?" she asked him. "Or about the chocolate?" her eyes twinkled.

"Of course not, that was just between us," he smiled and sucked on her earlobe.

"So, maybe whatever they did or didn't do is just between them," she closed her eyes, fighting the need to rip his clothes off and have him right there. What was this pregnancy doing to her?

"I will go with 'did'," he said and she smiled.

"Me too," she spoke as her hands trailed under his scrub top and over his torso. "We need to go home, now."

He shook his head. "Way ahead of you," he turned and she held onto his arm.

"Um, you kind of are," she motioned to his pants. He grinned and grabbed his coat, holding it in front of himself as he grabbed her hand and they ran out, laughing.

****

Tommy walked into the family room with the hot soup they had picked up on their way home. She took the mug he offered, holding it in her hands for warmth. He sat down next to her and smiled. "Part one, eat," he said.

She laughed. "I am, try not to worry so much. You are the one getting over a gunshot and losing half your blood volume."

He waved it off like it was nothing. "No biggie," he said and they both laughed. He looked at her with a serious expression. "Can I ask you something and have you hear me out?"

She put the mug down. "Of course."

"I want you to move in with me," he began and before she could say anything, he continued. "Hear me out, remember?"

She closed her mouth and nodded.

"Look, I love you and I know you love me. I know there are things that you still need to work out, but I hope none of those things have to do with your feelings about me. I want to help you to feel safe and I want to be there to hold you when you don't. I hate that you are staying in a hotel, with no connection to anything. You need to be in a home where you are loved and wanted. I want you to stay here," he exhaled and looked at her.

"Tommy, you will never be protected if I stay here. Things are going to start coming out and you will be tied to me and you will be dragged into the story. I wouldn't be surprised if your name is already out there. I think it might be best if I kept my distance for a while," she stood up and walked to the room where her bags sat. She picked them up and walked back into the room. "I love you and I don't need any time to work on that, but you simply don't understand what's coming."

He looked at her incredulously. "So you are just going to leave? It seems like that's your solution to all problems. It gets to be too much, so you bolt. What is it that you are so afraid of? The asshole that hurt you is dead, so you aren't running from him anymore. What is it? Is it me? Is it commitment? Is it love? Do you want to be alone?" he yelled at her, feeling his own fears come out in his words.

"You would think I would be used to it by now, people leaving, but to be honest, this is the worst. My parents were killed by a drunk driver, Jack's mom had cancer, they didn't choose to leave, but you, you are deliberately choosing to walk away and I don't know how to reconcile that. My only guess is that you don't want to be with me. I won't beg, Brittany, I won't chase you. If you go, than I don't want you to come back," he challenged her, praying she would stay.

Brittany nodded her understanding. "I see. If that's how you feel, I have no choice but to respect it," she turned and walked out the door, leaving him heartbroken and her own heart shattered.

****

"Hey Tommy, how are things going now that you're back at work?" Stephanie asked as she ran into him in the hallway. "I haven't seen you around lately."

Tommy smiled at her, but the truth was, he was specifically avoiding everyone. "I've just been swamped with a new case. I haven't really had time to do anything else," he hoped she would leave it at that.

Stephanie eyed him critically. "Okay, so how about you and Brittany come over to our house for dinner tonight? I think it's been too long since we all got together."

Okay, Tommy thought, obviously Brittany hadn't told her anything. He sighed. "I don't think so, Steph. Brittany and I broke up," he spoke like it was a bad dream.

She touched his arm and made him look at her. "What happened, Tommy? Are you okay?"

He shrugged. "I'm fine, probably for the best," he smiled at her. "Not every relationship can make it."

She shook her head. "I don't believe that, and neither do you. I know how hard you both fought your feelings for each other. Tommy, do you love her?"

He fought back the tears that threatened to escape. "Of course I do."

She smiled. "Then what's the problem? I know how deeply she loves you."

"It just isn't that simple. I'm sorry, Steph, but I have to go," he said and turned to walk away before he lost it.

Stephanie watched him leave and her heart broke for him. She had to help them, but first she needed to talk to Brittany.

Tommy made his way back to his office and closed the door. He picked up the stack of files on his desk and threw them across the room. He sat down on the couch and put his head in his hands, defeated. He had messed up and he had no clue how to fix it. He knew that she would never come back after he told her not to and she would never push herself on him after he told her to leave. He knew how fragile her trust was and he pushed her on it until she ran. The truth was he missed her. He missed seeing her and he missed holding her. He was lost and he needed the pain to go away. He heard a knock at his door and walked over to open it, hoping for split second it was her.

"Hi Megan, did I miss an appointment?" he asked, looking at his watch when he saw who it was.

She smiled. "No, I just wondered if you needed anything now that you're back at work and things seem to be calming down," she walked into his office. "I thought maybe we could have lunch sometime?"

Tommy tried to be tactful. "That's nice, Megan, but I'm not really interested. I am involved with someone right now."

"Oh, I thought you and Dr. Anthony broke up. I mean, I haven't seen her here recently and you seemed to be alone a lot," she said seductively, her proximity to him was inappropriate at best.

Tommy was more than a bit perturbed at the intrusion in his privacy. "You thought wrong, so thanks, but no thanks," he walked over and opened the door for her.

"Well, just so you know, the offer stands," she said as she walked out.

Tommy slammed the door and turned to his couch. This was a mess that he didn't know how to solve.
******

Everything felt different. It had been a week, but it felt like a year. The smell of the hospital seemed stale and the lights seemed dimmer. The people who walked the halls looked the same, but Brittany wondered if it would ever be that way for her. She tightened her ponytail as she made her way to the room to meet her next patient. She opened the door and saw Stephanie and Julie sitting there. She smiled despite her sadness.

"What's going on here?" she asked the women.

"Intervention." Julie said. "You and my brother need to fix this debacle and you need our help to do it."

Brittany sighed. "It isn't that easy. Tommy told me that we were over and I need to respect that. I owe him that much."

Stephanie shook her head. "You are so wrong. Sometimes you owe it to him to fight."

Brittany looked at her. "What do you mean?"

The girls exchanged glances. "My brother is a great guy. He has devoted his life to helping others and to being a great friend. He is, however, completely unsure of himself. When he challenged you to stay, he knew you wouldn't, he expected it. Everything good in his life has gone away and he is always left picking up the pieces. He wanted you to be the one to break the mold." Julie said softly.

"And instead I did what everyone else always does. I left," she said sadly.

"But you can fix it, Britt. He is so miserable and lonely and he loves you so much. I know he can be infuriating, but it's also what makes him so charming. Don't give up on him, please?" Julie said.

She exhaled. "I never have," she walked back to her office.

Chapter Fifty-Three:

Tommy was talking to his clients about their options for their eight year old daughters' treatment. They were handling everything really well and Tommy was optimistic about the prognosis. The only problem was the little girl was scared to death about having any treatment that meant she would lose her hair. She had beautiful red hair that looked a lot like Brittany's and the parents were at a loss as to how to help her accept the treatment. Tommy walked over to the little girl and smiled.

"You know, your hair will grow back after the treatment is finished," he said and she looked at him through small angry eyes.

"You don't understand because you're a boy," she crossed her arms and pouted. "I hate cancer and I hate this medicine."

Tommy nodded, "I know you do and I wish there was something else we could do for you, sweetie, but for now, this is our best option," he looked up and saw Brittany walking by, watching the scene. He smiled before remembering he shouldn't. He did, however, notice the little girl's eyes grow wide as she looked at her.

Tommy stood up and walked tentatively over to Brittany. "Hi, um I was wondering if you had a minute?"

She smiled a small smile. "Of course. What can I do?"

He filled her in on the little girls worries and she nodded. "Let me see what I can do," she walked over to the girl who was sitting with her parents. She knelt down next to her and smiled. "Hi, my name is Brittany, what's yours?"

The girl smiled at Brittany. "My name is Courtney. My hair looks like yours," she said as she touched Britt's hair.

Brittany smiled. "It sure does. I bet your pretty scared of what might happen if you take the medicine, aren't you?"

Courtney nodded. "My hair will go away," she sniffed and the parents looked like they might lose it. Brittany held out her hand to the little girl.

"Come here, I want to tell you a secret," she said and smiled at the parents who silently thanked her. She led the little girl over to a couch and helped her to sit down. "When I was your age, I hated my hair color," she said and the little girl's eyes grew wide.

"Why? You're so pretty." Courtney said.

Brittany smiled at her. "I was always getting teased. People called me tomato and carrot. I was so embarrassed by the color because it was so different from everyone else. But something wonderful happened to me that made everything change."

Courtney was hanging on her every word. "There was someone who I cared about a lot and he didn't pay attention to anyone and I thought he would never talk to me, but one day he did and it was all because of my hair. He called me 'Red' and it was this special connection just between the two of us. He was too shy to talk to anyone else and he was sad, but because of my hair, we became friends," she smiled.

"But what if I meet someone and he doesn't talk to me because my hair will be gone." Courtney began to cry.

"See that's just it. Whether or not your hair is there, you are a redhead and we have special abilities to find the good in people. We have red hair for a reason, to help people find happiness. You were born with red hair because you are a superhero and whether or not you wear your cape, or your hair in this instance, it is still who you are. You will just have to work a little harder to show people your heart while you wait for your hair to grow back. I also think I might know someone who will donate some hair so you can have a beautiful red wig," Brittany laughed when the girl realized what she said and threw her arms around her neck. Brittany hugged her back, wiping her own tears away. "Now why don't you go tell your mommy and daddy not to worry and that you will take the medicine and you will be okay? I will come and visit you when you are here."

Courtney shook her head and bounced back toward her parents who looked gratefully at Brittany. Tommy had watched the scene unfold and walked over to thank her.

"What did you tell her?" he asked her, fighting the need to hold her to him. Her face showed the sadness he felt in his heart.

"Let's just say that sometimes there is a benefit to having red hair. It took me a long time to realize that. Maybe Courtney can see it now," she looked at her hands and then back up at him. "How have you been?" she wondered if he would care if she kissed him.

Tommy wanted to tell her how miserable he was, how lost and alone he felt, but instead he shrugged. "Not bad, how about you?"

"Okay, I guess. I found an apartment to move into," she told him.

He met her gaze and felt his heart sink. She shouldn't be doing any of this on her own. He should be her partner and she should be able to rely on him to be there. "Oh, I guess that's good. You shouldn't have to stay in a hotel."

"Right," she sighed. "I wondered," she began and Megan interrupted them.

"Dr. Williams, I was looking for you in your office, but you weren't there. I was hoping we could grab that lunch we talked about," she touched his arm.

Brittany thought she would lose her lunch on the spot. Megan turned and looked at her. "Oh, excuse me Dr. Anthony, I didn't mean to interrupt."

"You didn't, enjoy your lunch," Brittany said as she turned and walked away as quickly as she could.

Tommy watched her leave, not sure what just happened. He turned and looked at Megan. "What was that about?"

"I just wondered if we could have lunch," she said, smiling.

Tommy glared at her. "I told you I wasn't interested, and I would appreciate it if you kept your distance. I am a professional and when I am at work I expect to remain professional. Excuse me."

******

Jack knocked on Tommy's door a few days later and waited. The man who stood on the other side of the door looked nothing like the happy vibrant man who was his brother. He looked like he hadn't shaved in a few days, or slept in that time. His clothes were filthy and the shades were down, even though it was the middle of the day. He was holding a beer in his hand and turned to walk back into the house.

"So I guess a simple 'how are you' is pointless?" Jack asked as he walked in. He moved to the shades and pulled them up, flooding the room with light.

"Dude, stop. I want it dark," Tommy said as he squinted.

Jack handed him the coffee he brought and took the beer from him. He sat down and looked at him. "You smell. Take a shower and get dressed."

Tommy looked at him. "No. I am not doing anything and I am not going anywhere."

Jack sighed. "What if I told you that she was just as miserable as you?"

Tommy shrugged. "You would be lying."

"Right, because I often lie to you," he sat down and looked at him. "Tommy, this is me, Jack. I am not going to let you fall apart."

Tommy ran his hand over his face. "Why don't you go home to your perfect life, Jack?" he spat the words out. "I am not you and I can't just make everything better by walking into a room. You don't get it. I can't do this."

Jack hadn't seen him like this before. He was worried and he knew Tommy was on a road that would lead to more sorrow. "Why don't you tell me what happened."

He looked at his friend. "I gave her an ultimatum and she left. I knew it was wrong, but I needed her to want to be here. I wanted her to stay. She doesn't trust me."

Jack shook his head. "That's not it and you know it."

"Whatever. It doesn't matter. I told her not to come back and she won't. If I have ever met anyone more stubborn than I am, it's her. And then she saw Megan," he stopped and ran his hand through his hair.

Jack raised his eyebrows. "What about Megan? What did you do?"

Tommy gave him a look. "I didn't *do* anything, but Megan keeps hanging around me and there was a moment when I thought Brittany was going to open herself up to me and Megan slithered in to the conversation. That was that, any door that was opened slammed shut. It's hopeless and it's over."

Jack shrugged. "I'm done listening to this. You have two choices. Sit here and wallow in your loneliness or clean yourself up and take control of your life. You decide," he got up and walked out, leaving his friend watching him and thinking about what he said.

****

"So, how did it go?" Stephanie asked as Jack walked into the house after leaving Tommy.

Jack sighed. "He is a mess and I'm worried about him. I don't remember him ever being so upset. He has always handled everything like it was just a bump in the road. I mean, he has survived horrible tragedies and he always finds a way out, but this is just," he sat down and ran his hand through his hair.

Stephanie came and sat on his lap. "This is just what?"

He shrugged. "This is his heart. He isn't the same guy. He seemed broken. I don't know how to help him."

Stephanie smiled at him. "You are amazing, Jack. You are so giving and loving, but unfortunately, you can't fix everything. If Tommy and Brittany are meant to be together, they will find their way back. We will be there to support them whatever happens," she ran her hand through his hair.

"I just want him to be as happy as we are," he said. "He deserves it."

Stephanie nodded. "So does she, but I think the next step has to come from one of them," she stood up and put her hand on her stomach.

"What?" he asked her.

She smiled at him and took his hand. She placed it on her belly and he felt the little flutter. His eyes grew wide as he looked at her. "Is that?"

She smiled as her eyes filled with tears. "That's our miracle," she wiped her tears.

"Why are you crying?" he leaned in and pulled her to him.

"Hormones," she smiled and he tilted her face up to look at him. He lowered his mouth onto hers and kissed her. She opened her mouth and let his tongue penetrate her lips. He probed her mouth and she played with the feel of his tongue against hers.

"What's wrong?" she asked him as she saw the tears.

He shook his head. "Nothing. Everything is just as it should be," he smiled. "Sometimes I just can't believe you are here."

She gently stroked his cheek before she took his hand in hers. "I am here because of you and your love."

Chapter Fifty-Four:

It had been over a week since Brittany walked out the door and things seemed to move a year in that time. Each day dragged on slower and slower and she hurt more with each day, not less. She went over the conversation they had the other day and then that nurse, Megan was there. Brittany didn't like the way she looked at Tommy, but honestly, it wasn't up to her. She wasn't surprised. Tommy was handsome and such a great guy, he deserved someone. Maybe it was better this way?

Sighing, she thought there was a slight connection when she had spoken to Courtney, but she knew it was nothing. She didn't want to see him walk away from her, so she left first.

She pulled up into her driveway and grabbed the boxes she brought. She had been going to the house daily and packing her things for storage. She had just left the apartment she was going to rent month by month. She was thinking of leaving, going back to London. She just didn't seem to care about anything anymore. She looked over and waved at Sadie, the elderly neighbor next door who always seemed to be snooping.

She packed up the rest of her music, the awards and the pictures that were salvageable. She sealed the boxes and moved through the debris with no emotion. The home she had made for herself now made her physically sick. She just wanted to take what she could and get out, never set foot inside these four walls again. She fought back the tears, which threatened to fall for Tommy. She shook her head. No, this was right, this was what was best. He just didn't understand and she never responded well to ultimatums. If he wanted it this way, she would respect his wishes. She just wanted to stop feeling so badly.

It hurt to breathe.

She worked and packed, finding herself hot and sweaty, but needing to finish. She hadn't been feeling great lately, but she knew the stress was probably to blame. It seemed like everything had an effect on her immune system. Moving to her bedroom, she decided against keeping any clothes, as most of them were destroyed or polluted. She threw everything out in garbage bags.

She walked into her closet and moved to the stepladder she had on the side. She reached up and pulled down the box she had kept hidden. She took it into the other room and placed it into the suitcase. She heard a knock at the front door and wiped the sweat off her brow. She sighed, not wanting to deal with anything right now. She just wanted to leave, make a clean break and once again, start over. She kept packing when the knocking persisted. She moved back to the music room and looked around, making sure she had removed everything. She saw the splashes of blue paint on the walls and felt flooded with the memories of Tommy holding her, taking her back home and finally, allowing her to feel the love he said she deserved.

He was wrong; she didn't deserve him. She heard a sound in the hall and she turned around, her heart pounding.

"Miss Brittany?" a voice called out.

She relaxed when she heard it was her elderly neighbor. "I'm in here, Sadie," Brittany said, wondering why she would just walk in.

"Sweetie, what happened in here? I saw all of the police here before and then the crime tape and now, this gentleman was worried about you and the door was partially opened. I hope you don't mind that I let him in," Sadie said.

Brittany looked, but didn't see anyone. "What gentleman?"

Sadie turned around, confused. "He was just here."

Brittany turned and walked into the other room and saw the reporter from the hospital standing in her family room, looking through her things. She was furious. "Get the hell out of my house," she said as he turned to look at her.

"I was invited in, for your protection," he said innocently, a sneer on his face.

"Sadie, call 911," Brittany said slowly, not moving her eyes off of him.

Sadie walked in and smiled. "No, Miss Brittany, it's okay, he is the man I told you about. He said he was your friend from the hospital."

Brittany felt her face was as hot as her hair was red. She kept her eyes on the reporter. "Sadie, please call 911. This is not my friend and he is not allowed in my home."

Sadie was obviously confused, but she recognized the seriousness in Brittany's voice.

"Should I go home and call?"

Brittany grabbed her phone from her pocket and handed it to her. "Please call."

The reporter looked at her and crossed his arms. "Why don't you just talk to me? What happened to you? Who did this to your house? Where were you all these years?"

Brittany felt her tears fall and she appealed to his sense of humanity. "This is my life you are messing with. This isn't sport and it isn't entertainment. You have no right to break into my home or stalk me at the hospital. It is my right to live my life as I see fit and you cannot bully me into talking or force me to give in to your demands. If I ever decide to tell anyone anything, you can be sure as hell it won't be to you or your paper," she felt a sudden surge of strength as she spoke to him.

He walked towards her, angry, and she backed away from him, tripping over the broken table that still lay there. She fell back and sat awkwardly onto her weak ankle. She screamed as she felt it snap and the pain shoot through her body. She saw a small piece of bone jutting out and her blood covering her foot. The reporter slunk back, not meaning for it to go this far. Sadie ran to her.

"No, Sadie, go away from me, it's okay. Did you call 911?" Brittany was trying to remain calm and cover for her fear and pain.

"Yes, I think I hear them," she said. "Let me put something over your foot," she walked closer to her and Brittany stuck her hand up.

"No, Sadie. You need to stay away from me," she looked at the frightened woman. "Remember, I'm a doctor, it's important that you let me take care of myself. I'm okay," she smiled at the alarmed woman.

The reporter eyed the scene, knowing there was more to it than that. "Why can't she help you?" he asked.

"Are you fucking kidding me? Get out of my house. Get out of my sight," she screamed as the police finally came in. She filled them in on the reporter and stated she wanted to press charges. The pain in her ankle was excruciating and she tried to stay alert. She looked up as the paramedics came in. She filled them in on her medical status and her heart sank when she realized the reporter was still in the room, within earshot. She lay back on the floor, finally giving in to the pain and passing out."

Chapter Fifty-Five:

Tommy put the finishing touches on his surprise for Brittany. He sat in his office and was getting ready to call her. He had thought a lot about what Jack had said, and he knew this was a once in a lifetime love. He had to fight and he needed her, plain and simple. He finally felt like he could get through to her and more importantly, he wanted her to know how committed to her he was. His phone rang and he saw it was Jack. He smiled as he answered. "I'm working on it."

"Where are you?" Jack asked him, his tone indicating all was not okay.

"What's wrong? What happened?" Tommy asked him, alarmed.

"Brittany is in the emergency room. There was an accident or something; I'm not sure. I don't know what happened exactly, something about a reporter accosting her in her house. Stephanie is in with her but she could probably use you, although she hasn't regained consciousness yet," Jack said.

Tommy was on his way to the floor.

"Regained consciousness? Oh God. Talk to me, Jack. What the hell happened?" he held his phone as he ran to the elevator.

"I'm not sure. She has an open compound fracture of the ankle, which was still weak from before. I don't know how it happened or anything more than she was at her house and a reporter got in and wouldn't leave. She was packing her things and he confronted her. I don't know how accurate that is, because it was based on the 80 year old neighbor's story who called 911."

Tommy was livid. How did he let this happen? How did they go from their wonderful evening together to this, in just days? He knew she would run if pushed, yet he pushed. He did exactly what she figured he would, and now, well he didn't know. He got off the elevator and ran down the hall to where they were. He saw Jack sitting there and ran to him. He sat down on a chair next to him, his leg throbbing from the exertion. "I need to see her."

"Stephanie is still in there. She will come out as soon as she can," Jack said. He looked at his friend. "What happened after we talked?"

Tommy exhaled sharply. "Nothing yet. I was working on trying to figure out the best plan of action," he stood up and felt sick. "I told her to leave and she did. I messed up the best thing that has ever happened to me because I wouldn't meet her halfway. It's always so cut and dry for me, you know? I am such a fucking idiot."

Jack smiled at him. "I highly doubt even a fraction of what you think happened, actually did. Why did you tell her to leave?"

He looked at his friend. "Because she was scared to let me in. She wants so badly to protect me and instead of understanding that, I told her that if she walked away from me, I wouldn't follow her. I told her we would be over."

Jack sighed. "Let me guess. She left?"

Tommy nodded. "She left."

"Haven't you learned anything from watching me all these years? Never give an ultimatum, it will always backfire," he said and smiled. "Good thing she loves you so much."

Tommy looked at him. "What do you mean?"

Jack laughed. "She walked away because you gave her no choice, but believe me, if you would have followed, she would have come back. You two are infuriating, man. Just admit your issues and let the crap go. You both need each other." They looked up as Stephanie walked out.

Tommy stood up, waiting for her. Jack looked at her, not liking the tired look on her face. "Tell me, please," Tommy said.

Stephanie sat down and they sat with her. Jack held her hand. "She has a Medial Malleolus Fracture which will require surgery to set. I would like the swelling to go down first, but because of the bone protrusion and her weakened immune system, I think we need to operate now. She is still unconscious, but she is being prepped for surgery. I still don't know what exactly happened."

"Do you think she can handle the procedure?" Tommy asked her.

"I do, but with her compromised immune system, the risk of infection and delayed healing is very real. She will have to be monitored closely after surgery," Stephanie said.

Tommy stood up. "Thanks, Steph. I'm going in to see her before they take her. We will worry about the rest later."

Stephanie sighed and Jack pulled her close. "Are you okay?" he asked her, smoothing her hair from her face.

She nodded. "I just feel so badly for her. She can't catch a break, you know? I just want her to be happy and feel safe and loved. I want her to feel like I feel with you."

He kissed her. "I think she will have that with Tommy, they just need to get there."

****

Tommy walked behind the curtain and swallowed the lump in his throat. He pulled up the little stool in the cramped room and sat down, taking her hand in his. He brought it to his lips and brushed her fingers with a kiss as he stroked her cheek. "Red, can you hear me? Can you wake up and look at me?" he asked, but she didn't move. He was watching the monitors and then he turned to look at her again. He felt his tears fall as he leaned in and kissed her softly. "Baby I'm so sorry. I let you down. I'm so sorry," she remained asleep as he spoke to her. "I'll be here waiting when you get out of surgery. I won't leave you again," he said as they wheeled her out.

Tommy and Jack waited in the O.R. lounge as Stephanie repaired the bone. Jack knew it would be a taxing procedure, but he also knew there was no one better to complete the operation. He looked at his friend who was sitting there, his mind a million miles away.

"Tommy, she's going to be fine," Jack said.

"I know," he stood up and crossed his arms. "I just want to know what happened. How did some reporter get into her house? Why was she even back there?"

Jack sighed. "She was packing up her things."

Tommy looked at him. "What do you mean? What aren't you telling me?"

Jack shook his head. "Nothing, Stephanie had been helping her to settle into an apartment nearby. She wanted to store all she could from the house and she signed a month to month lease. She wanted to cut all ties to that house. I know she was almost finished packing."

Tommy sank back down onto the chair. "I should have hired someone to go in and clean everything. How could I leave her alone to go through the mess that guy made of her life?" he was asking himself more than Jack.

"Stop beating yourself up. Both of you should have handled things differently, but now is your chance. You can both stop fighting and be together. It's not so hard when you realize what it is that's worth fighting for," he smiled as he saw Stephanie walk towards them.

"How did it go?" Tommy asked as he stood up.

"She did really well. There was so much damage to the tendons and ligaments around the fracture; I don't know how she managed to walk on it for so long since the attack. I was able to set the bone and it should heal nicely. She will need to be off of it for a few weeks, but we will deal with that when she wakes up," she sighed.

"What is it? Is there more?" Tommy asked her.

Stephanie looked at him. "I want to talk to you as a friend, not a doctor. I have seen so much in my time working at the clinic in Paris. I have dealt with people who have been abused and hurt and scarred from experiences. The one thing that needs to be there for someone to get back to any semblance of a normal life is the knowledge that there is hope. I worry a lot about Brittany and her ability to fight this, not because she is weak, but because she is tired of fighting. I have spent a considerable amount of time with her this past week, and she was just so sad. I don't want her to give up on life and even though this procedure was a success, there is more to her recovery than that. I don't mean to put this on you, and if you really don't want to be with her, then I will respect your feelings, but if you think there is a chance for you two, go for it. Stop fighting and be there for each other."

Tommy understood what she meant. "Thank you, Stephanie."

She sighed. "Go sit with her if you want and I will be in soon."

****

She slowly opened her blue eyes and wasn't sure if it was real. "Tommy?" she asked. "Is it really you?"

He felt his shoulders sag with her words. "Yes, Red, I'm here."

How could she think he wouldn't be?

"You don't have to be here," she said as her chin quivered and she closed her eyes again.

He put her hand to his cheek. "You're so wrong. As usual," he smiled as she looked at him again. "This is the only place I have ever wanted to be," he touched her cheek.

She looked at him and took his hand in hers. She felt such a sense of calm. "I miss you," she said brokenly. "But you should go."

He swallowed his tears. "I'm here and I'm not leaving," he held her hand to his lips and kissed her long fingers. He looked up as Stephanie and Jack walked in. Jack stood by the door and Tommy moved slightly to allow Stephanie to talk to Brittany. She smiled at her friend as she approached the bed.

"How do you feel?" she asked her.

"Tired," she closed her eyes.

Stephanie nodded. "Are you in any pain?"

"My back hurts, but I think it's more that I fell into the table. My foot is kind of numb," her eyes went wide as she remembered the incident. "Oh God," she said sadly, her blood pressure rising. Tommy looked at her, concern all over his face.

Jack and Stephanie picked up in her change in demeanor. "What is it? What's wrong?" Tommy asked her.

Jack approached the bed and stood with them. Stephanie looked from her to the men. "Sweetie, what is it?"

Brittany covered her face with her hands. "He knows."

Tommy was confused. "Who knows what?"

She looked at them with a mixture of despair and despondency. "The reporter who was hounding me was in the room when the paramedics came in to help me. He heard," she stopped and let her tears spill over her cheeks.

Stephanie knew at once what she meant. She looked at Jack and Tommy, who seemed confused. "The reporter knows about her medical status," she said softly.

Tommy felt a sense of anger in his gut that he wasn't sure could dissipate. He knew this was her deep seeded fear. He knew how much she agonized over this and how concerned she was with her personal privacy. He turned and walked out of the room. Jack turned and looked at him. He nodded to his wife and went after him.

"Tommy, hey, wait," Jack called to his friend. Tommy turned and looked at him, his eyes on fire.

"I need to find him and I will kill him if I have to," Tommy spewed.

Jack nodded. "I hear you, but this is not the way to go. You and Brittany need each other, the rest of it isn't important right now. She needs you to be with her through all of this," he grabbed his friend's arm. "Look at me; this isn't about you or what you need. This is about her."

"What am I supposed to do? How do I just let this go?" he asked him.

"I'm not asking you to let it go, I am asking you to stop and think. You need to figure this out with her and whatever actions come of it need to be as a united front," Jack said. "You need to go back there and be with her."

Tommy sighed. He nodded and turned to walk back to the room. They entered as Stephanie was administering some meds to the IV. Jack nodded at her and she smiled at Brittany before turning to leave with her husband.

Tommy walked to the bed and ran his hand through his hair before sitting down. She was sitting up more in the bed and she had pulled her covers all the way up to her neck, covering herself as she used to do. She looked at him and then looked at her hands. "Tommy, please go home. I'm fine."

He put his hands on top of hers and she felt her heart beat faster at his touch. She had been longing for him to touch her. "Look at me."

"I can't," her heart was crumbling.

He touched her chin and tilted it up to face him. "Tell me what you see."

She sighed. "Tommy, I can't do this."

"Tell me what you see," he repeated.

She blinked and her tears flowed down her cheeks. She looked into his eyes and reached up to touch his cheek. "I see what I lost."

He felt his own heart break. "Liar."

She closed her eyes and leaned back in the bed. "I walked away from you and I should have run into your arms. I ran and I should have stayed. I will never regret anything more than I regret leaving you. So you see, Tommy, I can't do this."

"I love you and if you would stop beating yourself up for a second, you might understand what I'm trying to say," he spoke through his breaking voice.

She looked at him and he took her hand in his. "You didn't lose me. I am here and it's not because I feel like I'm responsible, or because I think you are weak. It's not because of any obligation. Red, you are it for me. I want to be with you and I can't say it any other way," he pulled her to him and she hugged him, letting his arms envelop her and finally make her feel at home. After a few moments, she pulled back.

"How did everything get so messed up?" she asked softly.

He exhaled and shrugged. "I think we both got scared."

She looked at him. "Will you give me another chance?"

His heart melted at her words. "I wasn't sure you wanted one."

She looked at him with her eyes wide. "Why?"

"Because you left and didn't look back," he said simply.

"Because you told me not to," she said.

"Since when do you listen to me?" he asked her with a smile.

She smiled a small smile. "I'm sorry. I shouldn't have left. You were right and I always run when I get scared. But Tommy, I don't know how to trust myself to be happy and now, I am just so angry," she leaned back and exhaled, closing her eyes.

"How about we just get you better and then we can deal with everything else," Tommy said as he moved closer to her. He wanted to feel her again, touch her, and kiss her. He stroked her cheek and she turned to look at him, her eyes damp. He leaned in to her and gently brushed her lips with his. She reached up and put her hands on his cheeks. She pressed her lips to his and finally felt some of the heaviness lift off of her chest. She looked at him and pressed her forehead to his.

"I wish we could just go back to your place and start over," she said before leaning back in the bed, clearly exhausted. She shivered a little and he stood up and walked over to the side of her bed opposite her injured ankle. He gently sat down on the side of the bed and moved in next to her. She turned and moved closer to him, leaning her head onto his chest. He wrapped his arms around her, his body alive with electricity at her touch. She finally let herself relax, her tears falling as she tried to sleep, his presence the only medicine she needed.

"I'm here and I'm not leaving you, ever," he said softly as he smoothed her hair back. He watched her sleep and despite the horrors he knew they would face, he was happier than he had been in a long time.

Chapter Fifty-Six:

Jack walked in the hall outside the ladies room as he waited for Stephanie. He was relieved that Brittany seemed to be okay, but they had such a hard road ahead of them. He smiled when he saw Stephanie walk towards him, but he could see all was not okay. He moved quickly to her.

"Hey, what is it? What's wrong?"

She looked at him and wiped her eyes. "I'm sure it's nothing, but I am having some pain, like a contraction almost," she was scared and tried to hide it.

"Come here," he said and led her to a chair. He sat down with her and picked up his phone, calling the Dr. on call for Brittany. He hung up and looked at her. She was breathing slowly, trying to calm her nerves. "We are going to go and see that everything is okay. Let me get a wheelchair," he went to get up and she touched his arm. "It's going to be fine," he said and she nodded.

Jack wheeled her into the room where the doctor was coming and she was more relaxed. There had been no more pains, but both of them were wary. Stephanie looked at him. "I am sure it's just stress. I'm probably overreacting. I was standing for a long time during the surgery, so that's probably it."

He cupped her cheek in his hand. "There is no harm in checking everything out," he was nervous and knew that if anything happened to their baby, she would be destroyed. Who was he kidding; he would be destroyed as well. He helped her onto the exam table and held her hand.

"Let's talk about our next vacation," he said with a smile. "I think we need to go somewhere warm."

She laughed. "We just went on a vacation. Besides, I don't want to go too far away from our family."

He smoothed her hair behind her ears. "Okay, but I think we need some time to be together and shut everything else out. I just want to take care of you."

She looked at him and nodded. "We both need some time alone together."

They both looked up as the doctor came in.

****

Tommy was asleep in the chair when Brittany woke up an hour later. She felt better, although her leg was throbbing. She smiled as she looked at him. He must have felt her staring because he woke up and grinned at her.

"Hey," he said while yawning.

"Hi," she smiled and moved to get out of bed when he jumped up to stop her.

"What do you think you're doing? You can't get up," he said as he stood next to the bed.

"I am going to go home, Tommy. I need to use the bathroom and get dressed so I can leave," she said to him.

"Red, you need to stay here for a few days. You could develop an infection and you can't put any weight on your foot," he said emphatically.

She shook her head. "I know and I will be careful, but it isn't safe for me to stay here and I want to leave. I can take care of myself."

He shook his head. "You drive me crazy. How am I supposed to sit at my house and think about all of the things that could happen with you all alone? How am I supposed to keep you close without pushing you away?

She looked at him. "Does your offer for me to stay with you still stand?"

He wasn't sure he heard her correctly. "You want to stay at my house?"

She nodded. "If the offer still stands, I would."

He pretended to think for a minute and she laughed. "Of course it does. I want nothing more than to be with you all the time."

She felt a huge sense of relief. "Thank you."

He walked over to her and leaned in to kiss her. "Can you at least wait until we talk to Stephanie?"

She nodded. "Okay, but I need to leave before anyone finds me," she said.

He sighed. "Okay," he didn't know what to tell her. He couldn't guarantee that she wouldn't be stalked here.

He only hoped the reporter hadn't done anything to release what he knew.

******

Stephanie looked at Jack and let her tears fall down as she processed what the doctor had told them. Premature labor. She couldn't have this baby yet, it was too soon.

"Jack, what are we going to do? Oh God," she cried as another contraction ripped through her.

He looked at his wife and was heartbroken at her pain, but more importantly, he was so scared of what was happening. He took her hand and held it tightly. "We are going to have a healthy baby when it's time. Dr. Lacey is going to give you Magnesium Sulfate to stop the contractions and you are going to relax and stay calm. The medication will work," he smoothed her hair. "Baby you need to try to relax," he leaned in and kissed her forehead.

She nodded. "I know, but I'm scared. Jack, this baby is everything to us and we have waited so long. I can't bear the thought of something happening. I don't think I would make it."

He got into the bed with her and held her to him. "You need to stop talking and thinking like that. We just need to stay calm and try to let the medication work. Stephanie, you are the strongest person I know and the most stubborn. You can do whatever you put your mind to and this is just another battle we need to fight. Just try to breathe in and out, concentrate on that, and nothing else," he rubbed her back.

"Oh God, here is another one," she cried and he let his tears fall as he tried to help her.

"Listen to my voice and try to breath. You can do this, Stephanie, please look at me and concentrate on my voice," he got up and held her face in his hands, willing the contractions to stop, for all of their sake.

She looked at him and kept breathing, letting her body slowly relax. "I think we need to call Brittany," she whispered. "I know she is recovering, but she would know what to do. I need to know we are doing the right thing," she sobbed.

Jack nodded. "Okay, let me call the room," he picked up the phone and called Tommy and filled him in.

****
"Stephanie's in trouble, premature labor. She wants to see you," Tommy told Brittany after he hung up with Jack.

"Okay, let's go," she said simply. "Can you grab a wheelchair and I will put some scrubs on?"

He nodded and walked out, grabbing the chair. He came in and saw her sitting up, ready to go. He unhooked her IV bag and covered the area with gauze. He picked her up and placed her in the chair and they went to find the room. As soon as he wheeled her in, Stephanie began to cry again. Brittany looked at Tommy. "Can you help me into that chair next to the bed?"

He nodded and picked her up, placing her down in the chair. He looked at Jack and motioned for him to walk out into the hall with him. He let Brittany be with Stephanie and he looked at Jack. "Hey, talk to me, what happened?"

"She is having contractions, but it is too early. The chances of the baby surviving at this age are really low. She is a mess and I can't do anything to help calm her down," Jack stood there, looking into the room.

"What's going on in your head, man? How are you?" Tommy asked him.

Jack looked at him. "I am a horrible father. I don't deserve this baby or my wife."

Tommy was flabbergasted. "What the hell are you talking about? You are the best man I know, Jack. What on earth is wrong with you?"

He didn't meet his gaze. "I can't lose Stephanie. I just can't. She is so scared about losing this baby and all I can think about is how I can't lose her. What kind of a father does that make me?"

Tommy smiled at him. "One who is hopelessly in love with his wife? Jack, I don't blame you for being scared, but just because you are praying for your wife to be okay doesn't mean you don't want your baby to make it. Give yourself a break."

Jack looked at him. "If I have to choose, I don't think I can."

"You don't have to choose and you need to stop making this out to be more than it might be. Let's go back inside and see what Brittany thinks," Tommy said.

They walked back inside and saw the women talking. Brittany smiled at them. "I was just telling Stephanie here that it is kind of annoying when someone steals the spotlight from you. I was finally happy having everyone fawn all over me, and now she has to ruin everything."

Tommy grinned and walked over to her. Jack sat on the bed next to Stephanie. "Brittany seems to think we can stop the contractions," Stephanie said, visibly calmer.

Jack ran his hand through her hair. "I told you that," he smiled.

"I know, but you deal with the heart, not the uterus," she grinned and it was the first smile he had seen in a long time.

"No, I deal with you and you can do anything," he said, choked up.

Brittany sat back and smiled at all of them. "Dr. Lacey started you on the right dose of meds and as long as you relax, I don't see why we can't keep this baby inside its cocoon a bit longer. I think we simply need to keep your mind off of everything and see if you can sleep for a bit. I will stay and monitor things and if anything changes, we will act on it right away."

Tommy pulled up a chair and sat down. "Look at us," he said, the four of them all together. "We are one screwed up bunch of doctors," he said bluntly.

They all were quiet and then they all laughed out loud. "Nice, dumbass," Jack said.

He shrugged. "I'm just saying."

Stephanie looked at them and felt her heart swell. "You are all the best family I could ever ask for. Our baby will be so blessed," she wiped her tears away.

Jack held her in his arms and Tommy smiled at Brittany. She took Stephanie's hand and held it. "Do you remember what we used to do when we spent the night at each other's house when we were little?'

Jack looked at Tommy and the men looked at the women. "What?" they asked.

Brittany rolled her eyes and they all laughed. "You are both incorrigible. Get your minds out of the gutter."

Stephanie looked at her friend and smiled, her eyes shining with tears. "I didn't think you remembered."

Brittany leaned in and kissed her on the forehead. "Of course I remembered," she looked at Tommy and motioned for him to close the door. He did and came back and sat down. Brittany held her friends hand and looked at her. "Close your eyes."

Stephanie nodded and did just that. Brittany took a deep breath before she sang a beautiful lullaby. Jack felt tears come to his eyes at the beauty of her voice and he saw that Stephanie had fallen asleep and her contractions seemed to have stopped for the moment. He looked at Brittany, grateful for her help. He looked at Tommy who also was looking at Brittany. They truly were all blessed and they needed to remember that.

Brittany looked at the men. "Lets just sit and hope we have stopped things for now."

Tommy nodded and Jack smiled and Stephanie snored.

Chapter Fifty-Seven:

"I think it's time I took you home, you have been through too much," Tommy said to Brittany after they came back to her room. Stephanie was doing much better and seemed to be out of the woods.

"I would like that, but I'm okay, Tommy. I feel good, just tired," she smiled as she looked at him.

"Still, you are only a few hours out of surgery and you haven't been resting," he said sternly.

"All I did was sit with my friends. I put forth little to no exertion, so stop being so crabby. I am good and ready to take it easy and let you take care of me now," she grinned at him.

"Your wish is my command," he said as he turned to wheel her out.

****

"How are you feeling?" Jack asked Stephanie as she opened her eyes after sleeping for a while.

She smiled. "So much better. I think everything is back to normal. Can I go home now?"

He laughed. "Let's wait a little while and see what Dr. Lacey says," he played with her hair and stared at her.

"What is it?" she asked him, seeing his eyes wet with unshed tears.

"You really scared me last night. I felt so helpless and you know how I hate that," he said, masking his fear with a smile. "I can't lose you."

She touched his face and wiped his tears, "Everything is fine. You aren't going to lose me and we are going to bring our child into this world with love. I'm sorry you were so scared, but it's okay to feel that way. I was scared, too."

He leaned in and kissed her. "It isn't manly to be scared. I need to be the strong one."

She rolled her eyes. "Right, and wearing chocolate in places unmentionable is manly?"

He looked at her with a grin. "I think you thought it was very manly, I mean, you seemed to enjoy it immensely."

She raised her eyebrows. "It was okay," she kept a straight face for a minute and then burst out laughing. It was a sound that was music to his ears. He leaned in and kissed her again, this time deeper and needier. He pulled back and looked into her eyes. "You are my life, Stephanie. I love you more than I can ever explain."

She felt her own tears fill her eyes. "I love you, too. We are going to be okay, please try not to worry. This was a scare and now I will do whatever is necessary to keep our baby safe as long as possible. We will get through this, all of us."

"I will hold you to that," he said and they waited for the doctor.

****

"You know, you could put me down," Brittany smiled as he carried her into the house. "I have crutches and I am prepared to use them."

Tommy placed her gently on the couch, so her legs were out in front of her on the pillows. He stood up and smiled. "Nope, not taking any chances," he walked to close the door and put her things down. He came back over to her. "What can I get you?"

"Nothing, I'm good," she smiled.

He nodded and sat down on the chair opposite her. "Do you want to tell me what happened?"

Her happy expression disappeared and she sighed. "Does it matter?"

"Yes, it does. I don't want you handling everything yourself. I want to be your partner in this, all of this," he said sincerely.

She glanced at him and smiled. "I thought you were seeing Megan."

His eyebrows shot up. "What? Why would you think that? How could you think that?"

She shrugged. "She is after you. She is always hanging around and she kept insinuating that she was 'helping' you through some things. She touched your arm in front of me."

Tommy smiled. "And that bothered you?"

She looked at him. "No," she said and grinned. "Yes, a lot," she sighed. "But I didn't blame her, because you deserve the attention. Tommy, you are worth all of it."

He moved closer to her. "Megan makes me sick. She is clingy and needy and there is not a subtle bone in her body. Besides, she has no chance."

"Why is that?" Brittany asked him, aware of his proximity to her.

He picked up her hand and placed it on his chest. "Because this is what you do to me," he said, feeling his heart beat faster. "No one makes me feel the way you do. I love you, completely. I was wrong for giving you an ultimatum and I am profoundly sorry about that, but even if you never came back, I couldn't look at another woman. You are the one for me."

She felt her eyes grow wet with unshed tears. "You are simply amazing," she pulled him to her and pressed her mouth against his. After the kiss he pulled away and smiled at her.

She leaned back against the couch and closed her eyes.

"We should get you into bed. You need to rest," he said.

She nodded. "Okay."

He stood up and looked at her. "Do you want to stay in the guest room?"

"I want to stay where you are," she said.

He nodded. "Good choice," he gathered her in his arms and she didn't object. He walked into his bedroom and placed her onto the covers.

"Can you give me the bag I brought so I can change?" she asked.

He walked over and got it, handing it to her. "What else do you need?"

"I need to take my meds, so I just need some water," she said and he went to get her some water from the bathroom. She pulled her shirt over her head and flinched at the pain in her back. Tommy walked out and saw her.

"Oh Red, what the hell happened?" he walked over to her, checking out the bruise on her back. It covered a good quarter of her lower back.

She pulled the blanket up, covering herself and he immediately moved away. "I'm sorry, I didn't mean."

She shook her head. "No, I'm sorry. I don't care if you see me, Tommy. I guess it's just a habit," she moved the blanket and ran her hand through her hair. "When I fell, I hit some of the broken table pieces. It's nothing," she said and went to put her pajama top on, having trouble pulling it across her back.

He held the fabric for her to put her arms through and he walked in front of her. "It is most certainly something. Why do you continue to lesson your pain for me?"

She shrugged and tried to button her top, but her fingers were clumsy. "I don't know, I think it just gets tiresome. I don't want you to look at me and see a big bruise."

He smiled. "When I look at you the last thing that comes to mind is a big bruise," he reached and tilted her head to meet his gaze. "I just wish I could do more to help ease your pain."

She moved and motioned for him to sit on the bed next to her. "I think there are a few things you could do to help."

He raised an eyebrow. "Really? Like what?"

"You could kiss the pain away," she said with her eyes looking at his lips.

He grinned. "Where does it hurt?"

She looked at him. "All over."

He smiled at her and then his face took on a serious gaze. "I really missed you," he said as he smoothed her hair away from her face.

She touched his chest and nodded. "I love you so much. I don't think I have had a full night's sleep since I walked out that door."

"I think all of that will be better now. Everything is going to work out, I believe it," he said and she smiled as she leaned back onto the bed and closed her eyes. He moved to finish buttoning her shirt and pulled the covers over her. She fell asleep almost instantly.

Tommy watched her sleep and couldn't remember a time where he felt so content and happy. He changed into his pajama bottoms and moved back to the bed. He got in gently next to her, being careful to not disturb her. He turned and looked at her, her beautiful red hair framing her face and falling around her shoulders. He reached out and ran his hand over her forehead, moving the stray hairs out of the way. She moved in her sleep and put her arm over his chest, leaning her head on his torso. He settled in and held her to him, both content and home.

Chapter Fifty-Eight:

Brittany woke up a few hours later and saw him watching her. He smiled as she looked at him. "What is it?"

"Nothing, I just missed your face," he said as he traced her jaw line with his finger.

She looked at him and moved to sit up a little. She struggled to move her leg. "Ugh, this needs to come off."

"Not for a while. Do you want something for pain?"

"No, I'm okay," she glanced at him and took his hand in hers. She linked her fingers through his and looked at him. "I've been thinking about something."

He tried not to let her touch drive him crazy. "What?"

"I think maybe I should tell the press who I am and what happened to me," she said softly.

He never broke her gaze. "Do you think that will help you to move on?"

She closed her eyes and sighed before sitting up. "Tommy, I have spent so many years running and hiding. You were right, I have never dealt with the extent of damage my attack had on me. I healed from the physical trauma, but to be honest, the fact that I am HIV positive has always been that thing I couldn't bear people finding out."

He cupped her face in his hand. "Why?"

She shrugged and looked at him, her gaze piercing. "I guess that I thought I could hide the extent of how deeply he violated me. I felt so dirty, Tommy, and every time I took a pill and felt so badly after it was like he was always there, hurting me again. If everyone knew about it, the looks and the comments would feel like an assault again," she moved the covers and tried to get up, but her leg hurt her. She picked up her knee with her hand and moved to the edge of the bed with her legs hanging over. "People can be very cruel and judgmental. I just don't want to go through it all again, and in public. But I don't think I can stop the news from coming out, so maybe I can do it on my own terms," she ran a hand through her long hair.

Tommy moved behind her and wrapped his arms around her waist. He leaned his head on her shoulder and kissed her neck. "I think you are the strongest person I know and if you want to do this, then I am behind you all the way. I just want to make sure you are ready and if you don't want to, then we should see about having this reporter arrested. You shouldn't be forced into revealing anything you don't want revealed."

She turned and looked at him. "I wish it were that easy, but I'm afraid it's out there now, and if not this guy, then someone else. I need to take control of my life and this is the only way I know how to do that."

"Okay, then what do we need to do?" he asked her, not really feeling comfortable about her going through this, but knowing it was her decision.

"I have people I can call. There is a reporter who I was close to before and I am sure she will be happy to tell my story. She works for Rolling Stone and she is ethical and responsible. I'll call her tomorrow," she grabbed the crutches from the side of the bed and stood up slowly. "Are you sure you're okay with this? It won't be the same after everyone knows who I am."

Tommy walked over to her and brushed her hair over her shoulders. He exhaled and looked into her eyes. "It will be the same because I know who you are and I love you. It doesn't matter what the world thinks, I only care about what you think and what you feel. I just don't want to get left behind."

She touched his chest with her hand. "Not a chance. You can't get rid of me that easily."

"Promise?" he asked as he leaned in to kiss her.

"Promise," she said as their lips met. She ran her hands down his torso and he felt his heart pound as his blood pumped faster.

"I missed the feel of your skin," she said as she glanced at him through her semi closed eyes. She ached to touch him and her longing for his hands on her was reaching a breaking point,

"You just had surgery, Red, this isn't the best idea," he said into her ear as he kissed her cheek.

"But I need you to touch me. I miss your hands and your face," she leaned into him and moved her hands to his waist. She almost lost her footing and he grabbed her in his arms.

She yelped and he picked her up in his arms. "See, too soon," he put her back down on the bed.

"I still miss this," she said as she ran her hand over his chest. "I mean you."

He laughed and she blushed.

"I'm not going anywhere," he smiled as he leaned in and kissed her some more.

They were interrupted by the doorbell and they looked at each other. Tommy shrugged and carried her to the couch before walking to the door. He looked out, but didn't see anything. He opened the door and there was a large box on the ground and a note. He didn't know what was going on, but he figured he should take it in.

******

"How are you doing?" Jack asked Stephanie as he tucked her into their bed at home.

"Happy to be home and happy to have the baby still where it should be," she smiled.

"So can you handle staying home for the rest of the pregnancy?" he asked her as he sat on the side of the bed.

"I'll do whatever it takes, but you do know that bed rest doesn't imply never getting out of bed. I will take it easy, but I can move," she smiled at him and gave him a look that he knew too well.

"I know, but for just a few days won't you let me take care of you?" he said and leaned in to kiss her. His lips lingered on hers and she moved to kiss him again.

"Why don't you come here with me?" she said softly.

"I don't think that's really what taking it easy means," he said, his eyes twinkling.

"We don't have to do anything, at least I don't," she said and emphasized the last part.

He laughed. "Oh really?" he moved to the other side of the bed and sat down. He put his hand on her belly and looked at her.

She could see his mood was a bit hesitant. "What is it? Talk to me," she ran her hand through his hair.

He shrugged, choked up and silent.

"Jack, please. Tell me what you are thinking about," she put her hand on his.

He looked at her and angrily wiped his eyes. "I'm just not sure I'm cut out for this."

"For what?" she asked him, her heart broke at his sadness.

"Being a dad. I mean, I haven't had the best model and I just faced my first test and I think I would have failed if I had to go through with a choice," he looked at her. "I don't want to lose you, and I don't want to lose our baby, but," he stopped and sat up, his legs over the side of the bed, his back to her.

She moved to him and wrapped her arms around him from behind. She rested her head on his back and he clasped her hands in his own. "Baby, it's okay to have doubts and to be scared. I wouldn't want you to be any other way. This is a scary adventure and we are going to be facing a lot of tests, but if we stay true to each other and always face things head on, we will be okay. I love that you are vulnerable and squishy. You are the manliest man I know, but your heart is pure little boy," she smiled as he turned and looked at her.

"What I'm trying to say is that it doesn't show weakness or make you any less of a man to tell me your scared or that you have doubts about anything we are facing. I have doubts, too, but none of them have to do with they type of man I married or the type of father you will be," she leaned and kissed him. "You are my hero, Jack. You are our child's hero and you don't need to do anything other than be who you are to earn that title."

He pulled her to him and pressed his mouth to hers, thanking her for the sentiment through his gentle kiss. He moved away and pulled off his top, getting into the bed with her. She moved to his chest and laid her head on his shoulder, holding him and reassuring him that everything was okay.

****

Tommy stared at the box on their doorstep and looked around again for someone, anyone who might have left it. He saw nothing.

"What is it?" Brittany asked him from the couch.

"A box and a note," he said. He picked up the note and turned to look at her.

"What does it say? Who is it from?" she asked him. She got up and grabbed her crutches and made her way closer to him.

He opened the note and read it out loud.

"Dear Dr. Tommy

You are a good doctor to babies and this one needs help. It was born a runt and my friend said it was going to be put to sleep, which I didn't understand because I was sick and you fixed me, so I was hoping you could fix him, too. My mom said not to give it to you, but I knew you would understand and the lady doctor told me I had super powers and I think my power is to help this little one find you. I think you can help him like you helped me.

From

Courtney"

Brittany looked at him and he looked at the box. "Open it," she said with a smile.

Tommy opened the box and a tiny little puppy looked up at him. Brittany squealed and he looked at her. "Oh, no way."

She nudged him. "It's so cute," she said.

"I am not having a dog. I refuse," he said and crossed his arms.

"Arf, arf, arf," the dog jumped and cried. Brittany gently leaned down until she was sitting on the floor and could reach the box. She picked up the little puppy and it immediately began licking her face. She smiled and laughed and looked up at Tommy.

"I'm not keeping it," he said. He closed the door and sat down next to her. The puppy jumped over to him and curled up on his lap.

Brittany smiled. "I think he is keeping you," she moved closer to him and kissed Tommy's cheek.

"I don't want a dog," he said. "My schedule won't allow it," he began to scratch the dog's head as he spoke.

She leaned on his arm. "Okay, so we will try to get it a home, but for now, he needs things."

He looked at her. "What do you mean, things?"

"Food, toys, a bed, a collar, a leash, you know, baby things," she said.

He rolled his eyes. "You can't be serious."

She looked at him and raised her eyebrows. "Courtney trusted you with his care and you need to take the challenge. Are you scared of a little ball of fuzz?"

He looked at her as the little ball of fuzz peed on the floor. He sighed and she tried to stifle a giggle. "Great, this is just great."

An hour later Tommy was still grumbling to himself as he drove home with $200 worth of 'things'. He walked into the house and saw her asleep on the couch with the puppy sleeping on her chest. He had to admit it was a beautiful sight. The dog was cute and Brittany was so happy. He walked closer and put the bags down and the puppy woke up and yawned. Brittany opened her eyes as well. "Hey, did you find everything?"

He snorted. "If by 'everything' you mean the next mortgage payment on the house, then yes."

She held the puppy to her like a baby. "Thank you," she said.

He sighed. "Whatever," he said and smiled at her. He leaned in to kiss her and instead got a puppy tongue. "Seriously?" he wiped his face.

She tried to hold it, but she burst out laughing. He looked at her and started laughing as well. "Oh, I see how it is," he said. "Two against one?" he leaned in and tickled her and then he looked into her eyes before pressing his mouth on hers. She pulled him to her and intensified the kiss.

"You should rest, it's been a long day," he said and smiled at her. "I'll watch the dog," he added reluctantly.

Tommy watched her as she slept shortly after he got her back into the bed. He was so glad she was here and that she wanted to stay. He hated that she was going through so much pain, both physically and emotionally, but he knew that as long as they were together, they would make it. He settled in to work on some paperwork, keeping an eye on the puppy sleeping in the fancy new bed he had purchased. He rolled his eyes and kept working.

"Are you fucking kidding me? Get out of my house. Get out of my sight," she screamed as the police finally came in. She filled them in on the reporter and stated she wanted to press charges. The pain in her ankle was excruciating and she tried to stay alert. She looked up as the paramedics came in. She filled them in on her medical status and her heart sank when she realized the reporter was still in the room, within earshot. She lay back on the floor, finally giving in to the pain and passing out."

"No!" she screamed and sat up. Tommy nearly jumped out of his skin before running to the bed.

"Hey, it's okay. Look at me, please. You're safe, Brittany, baby, look at me," he held her face in his hands and wiped her tears.

She took a deep breath and turned away from him, trying to calm herself. She felt sick.

Tommy grabbed her some water and knelt in front of her on the side of the bed. "Here, drink this," he took her hand and handed her the cup.

She picked it up but her hand was still shaking. She shook her head. "No, it's okay, I just need a minute."

He took the cup and put it down. "What happened?"

She looked at him, his eyes shining with love. "Just a bad dream."

He raised his eyebrows. "Just a bad dream?" he smiled. "Care to elaborate?"

She looked at him. "I keep seeing the reporter in my house and I know he heard everything and I'm just so mad. I feel like I should have handled everything differently."

He cupped her cheek in his hand. "We are going to handle things together from now on. I should have been there. I should never have made you choose. I did everything wrong."

She took his hand in both her hands. "No, Tommy. You did everything right. I just love you so much," she let fresh tears fall.

"What is it? Don't cry?" he said.

"Will you just hold me for a little while?" she asked him.

"It would be my honor," he said and got into the bed behind her. She moved gently between his legs, her shoulder against his chest. He wrapped his arms around her and she hugged his arms to her. She turned slightly and put her cheek on his chest.

"I'm so sorry I hurt you," she said, needing him to believe her.

"Shh, Red, stop this. We were apart and now we're together. Everything is going to be okay," he held her to him. "Please just let me love you."

She reached up and pulled his face to hers. He lowered his mouth onto hers and kissed her deeply.

She returned the passion and his hands moved to the front of her shirt. She took his hand in hers and placed it on her chest. He kissed her again and moved his hand under her shirt, running his fingers along her skin. She moved to his shirt and ran her hands under the fabric. He looked at her.

"This is silly," he took his shirt off and she grinned.

"Much better," she said and pulled her shirt off as well, melting into his chest with his strong arms around her. She breathed in his scent and kissed his torso. She felt so safe and so content. It almost seemed as if all of the problems they had to face weren't so bad.

Tommy ran his fingers up and down her arm, moving to her stomach and back to her fingers. He thought his heart might burst at the love he felt for her. He moved her hair to the side and kissed her neck and she moaned at his touch.

"Are you okay?" he asked her.

"I am so happy. I love you so much," she said as she moved slightly to move to the side of him. She needed to stretch out her leg. He helped her to get comfortable and he propped himself on his elbow as he looked down at her.

"As soon as that cast is off, we have a lot of time to make up for," he said.

She reached up and cupped his cheek in her hand. "I will hold you to that," she closed her eyes, exhausted.

He smiled as he moved and covered them with a blanket. He held her and they both heard the distinct sound of whining. Brittany opened her eyes wide. "I forgot about the baby."

He sighed. "The baby?"

"Bring him here," she said.

"He is not sleeping on the bed. There is no way I am bringing that thing on the bed with us," he said and looked at her.

She stared at him and he sighed. "Fine, but just this once," he got up and picked up the little puppy who promptly curled up between them and fell asleep. Brittany smiled at him before falling asleep herself and Tommy held his little family to him as he too fell asleep.

Chapter Fifty-Nine:

Tommy woke up and saw she wasn't in bed next to him. He got up and walked to the other room to see what was happening and realized she was on the phone, so he sat down and waited for her. She hung up after a few more minutes and turned to look at him, holding the puppy in her arms. "Well, it's all set," she put him down and he scampered to Tommy.

"What is?" he asked as she moved to him with her crutches. He stared at the creature on the floor as it looked at him.

"That was Danielle, the contact from the paper I was telling you about. She was thrilled to hear from me," Brittany sat down on his lap, smiling at the squirming pup.

He played with her hair. "When was the last time you spoke to her?"

"Before I was attacked," she sighed. "Tommy, I did so many things wrong back then. I just felt like Barbara Rose died in that moment and I let her. I cut all ties with that life and I never thought I would want to go back."

He put his arm around her waist. "Do you? Do you want to go back?"

She smiled at him. "No, I really don't. I love my life and I love being a doctor. I think I just missed the music so much, you know. It was such a part of who I was and who my dad raised me to be and when I stopped singing, I just left all of the influences in my life, the

things that made me who I am, I just abandoned them,"
she touched his face and ran her fingers over his lips.
"I want to bring some parts of that back."

He took her hand in his and kissed her fingers. "I think I
would like to help you with that, if you'll let me."

"You don't have a choice," she grinned. "You're a part
of me now and I love that most of all," she leaned in
and kissed him. He smiled but then he saw a bit of the
light go out of her eyes.

"What is it?"

"I guess I'm just afraid of what will happen next. I know
that after I give this interview, things will change. I
might lose my job," she sighed.

"Why would you think that?"

"Before, I couldn't go anywhere without someone
watching me. There were cameras in my face all the
time and I had hardly any privacy," she stood up and
hobbled a little to the window. "But it was okay, you
know? I loved singing and when I was giving a concert
for so many people, I was free. Everything was so
clear," she smiled at the memory. "And then he took
me," she wrapped her arms around her waist.

Tommy stood up and walked over to her. "Do you want
to talk about what happened? Can you tell me what
you went through?"

She turned and looked at him. "What do you want to
know?"

"I want to know everything. I don't want you to carry any of this around by yourself. I know I can't take away what you went through, but I don't want you to hide it from me," he wrapped his arms around her from behind.

She loved the feel of him holding her, but she wasn't sure she could do what he asked. She didn't know where to start.

****

"What are you doing up?" Jack asked Stephanie as she walked into the kitchen.

"I am going crazy sitting on the bed. Jack, I can't just sit and do nothing. I need action," she said as she sat down on the couch.

He grinned at her. "I thought you might say that, so I spoke to Dr. Lacey and she said since you haven't had any contractions for two days, you can come off bed rest, but you still need to stop working and take it easy."

"Oh thank God. I want sex," she said and walked over to him.

He laughed. "That's what you want? I thought you would want to go for a walk or a drive, but you want sex?"

She shrugged. "We all have our vices, mine happens to be you. Like I have said before, I am perfectly capable of taking care of myself," she turned to walk away.

"Not so fast," he said as he wrapped his arms around her. He pulled her to him and she giggled. "You know we need to wait a little longer for anything extracurricular. The last thing you need is to make your body contract."

She pouted. "Fine, but I never thought I would be the one begging for sex from you."

He leaned in and kissed her. "You never have to beg, but you have to be able to handle me and all of my magnificence."

She smiled and ran her hand over his groin. "Oh really?"

He shuddered at her touch. "Don't start something you can't finish, Stephens."

She leaned in and kissed him, plunging her tongue into his mouth. "I'm not the one who seems to be rising to the occasion," she broke the kiss and turned to walk away. He felt empty as soon as she broke the connection.

"Where are you going?" he whined.

"To satisfy another craving," she looked at him as she pulled a chocolate bar out of the cabinet. She opened it and used her tongue to trace a line up and down the bar before wrapping her mouth around it.

Jack thought his eyes would bug out of his head. "Okay, now you're just being mean."

"I'm going back to bed; maybe you can join me and bring your magnificence with you?" she turned and walked away, leaving him unable to move for a moment.

****

Tommy walked back into the house dragging the puppy behind him. Brittany laughed at him. "What? It doesn't know how to walk on a leash."

"Of course he doesn't, you have to teach him," she scooped him up in her arms. "Did the baby go potty outside like a good boy?" she spoke to him in a little baby voice.

Tommy washed his hands and walked back over to her. "How hard is it to walk on a leash? He already knows how to walk, it isn't brain surgery."

She looked at him and then back at the puppy. "Tommy is a big meanie. Don't listen to him. He is just jealous because I am choosing to cuddle with you instead of him."

Tommy crossed his arms across his chest. "You know, I made potty today, too. Why don't I get a reward?"

She laughed. "Let me see what I can do," she put the dog down and moved closer to him. She put her hand on his thigh and leaned in and kissed him. He pulled her to him and wrapped his arms around her. Suddenly there was a growling sound and Tommy felt something pull his pant leg.

"What the?" he looked down and the puppy was tugging on his pants, trying to pull him. Brittany looked down and smiled.

"He wants to play with you," she said.

Tommy looked at the dog. "He is kind of cute, but he needs a name."

Brittany nodded. "I know, but I can't decide on one. What do you think?"

He sat down on the floor and the pup jumped into his lap, falling over Tommy's calf. Brittany joined him on the floor and he pulled her into his lap. They looked at the dog that ran across the floor and tried to pick up a toy. "He looks like a Tramp."

Brittany looked at him. "He is not a tramp, he is a mini schnauzer through and through."

"He looks like Tramp from Lady and the Tramp. Julie made me watch that all the time growing up. He said and leaned his head on her shoulder. "He is like me."

Brittany looked at the puppy. "Tramp, come here," she said and the puppy bounded towards them.

Tommy smiled. "It's like us. You're my lady and."

"You're my Tramp?" she asked and smiled. "You're no Tramp, Tommy. You're my superman," she moved around and pushed him gently onto his back on the floor. She moved to lay on him and ran her hand under his shirt. She leaned in and kissed him passionately.

He ran his hands up under her shirt and she yelped in pain.

"What is it? Did I hurt you?" he asked as she recoiled and sat up quickly.

"Tramp jumped on my cast," she said as she moved her foot over.

Tommy lay back and sighed. "Of course he did," he looked at her and groaned as Tramp came and jumped onto his face.

Brittany smiled despite her throbbing leg. "I think we have created a monster."

Chapter Sixty:

"I don't understand why we had to do this together. I have other things to do today, like talking about what we need to do to be ready for tomorrow," Tommy complained as he drove the car and Brittany sat holding Tramp in the passenger seat.

"He needs his first check up. I can't take him myself yet and if you went alone you would probably give him away," she said as she scratched the puppy's ear while he yawned.

He looked at her and smiled. "You are too attached. What if the vet says he has some weird disease or something?"

She glanced at him. "We are both doctors and we don't deal with 'weird' diseases. He is our responsibility and we will take care of him. Courtney gave him to you for a reason. Besides, you are a pediatric surgeon, you should have a soft spot for babies."

Tommy sighed, but laughed. "Correction; pediatrician, not veterinarian. I handle humans, not mutts," he glanced at her again. "And she only gave him to us because you told her she had powers and apparently rescuing mutts and giving them to nice unassuming doctors is one of them."

She squeezed his arm. "Don't be nervous, I am sure his checkup will be fine."

He raised his eyebrows at her and then shook his head. "Whatever you say, but I don't care one way or the other."

****

"What do you mean he has a heart murmur? What are we going to do to fix it? Is it going to impact his quality of life?" Tommy was agitated and he was holding Tramp while questioning the doctor.

Brittany smiled. "He is a new dad, please excuse him," she touched Tommy's arm. "Why don't we let Dr. Burton tell us what we need to know?"

He smiled. "Sorry, I guess I got a little worked up."

Dr. Burton grinned. "It's okay, I have three kids myself."

Tommy began to object but Brittany stopped him. "Is this something he may grow out of?"

The doctor shook his head. "Yes, being that Tramp is a runt, it is entirely possible he will grow out of the murmur and the hernia can be reduced when he is neutered."

Tommy almost fainted. "Hernia? Neutered?"

Brittany and the doctor laughed. "Maybe you want to wait outside?"

Tommy sat down. "I'm fine."

The doctor smiled. "Okay, then let's give him his shot and we will be all set."

"Shot?" Tommy asked and Brittany glared at him. "Sorry, shutting up now," he sat down and they all laughed.

******

"He is not being neutered," Tommy said as he drove them home.

Brittany smiled at him. "I think we can discuss that later. Poor little Tramp is wiped out from his adventure," she stroked the dog's chin as they drove. "And Tommy is wiped out from being so worried," she smiled at him as they pulled into the driveway. Tommy walked Tramp while Brittany used her crutch to walk back in the house.

Tommy put Tramp down when they got inside and he walked to his bed by the window and went to sleep. "Poor little guy, he is exhausted," Brittany said.

Tommy peered at him, his little body jumping every so often. "Is that normal? Do you think he is having some sort of reaction?"

She crossed her arms in front of her body and didn't think could be any cuter. "Tommy, come here. He has the hiccups."

Tommy walked over to her and smiled. "I just don't want you to worry," he said sheepishly. She smoothed his hair behind his ear. "Hey, maybe while he is asleep we can have some fun?"

"What kind of fun?" she asked him, smiling as he picked her up in his arms. She laughed as he sat down on the couch with her on his lap. "I could have made it to the couch."

"It was more fun this way," he said as he ran his hand under her hair and pulled her to him for a kiss. She put her hands on his cheeks and savored his kiss, letting his tongue dance with hers. He moved his hands to her torso and she melted into him when the doorbell rang.

"Ugh," Tommy said. "What now?"

She got a surprised look on her face and stood up. "I forgot that I invited everyone for dinner."

"Everyone? Why? We didn't cook," he said.

"No, Bill and Julie are bringing the pizza and Stephanie said something about Jack bringing the chocolate. I wanted to tell them what I'm doing tomorrow with the reporter," she walked with her crutches to the door.

Tommy smiled. "I think that's a great idea," he said as she opened the door and the four friends came in.

"Tommy, come take the pizza, we need to see the baby." Julie said. She and Stephanie walked in and went towards Brittany. "Where is he?" Stephanie asked.

The women made their way over to Tramp who bounded to see them and Tommy shook his head as Jack and Bill eyed him.

"Of all of us with kids on the way, you had to go and have one first?" Jack said and patted him on the back. He looked at Stephanie holding Tramp and smiled. "He looks just like you."

"Shut up," Tommy said and put the pizza on the table. The men walked over to where the women were with Tramp and Julie looked at her brother.

"So did you have any trouble at the vet today?" she asked him.

He walked over to Brittany and shrugged. "No, I was just trying to calm Brittany down. She was concerned about a few things."

Brittany patted his chest and smiled. "Tommy is wonderful when I have concerns. He doesn't let anything rattle him," she eyed him and he smiled a silent thank you.

Stephanie held Tramp as he fell asleep in her arms. "He is so cute, Jack. Don't you just want one?"

Jack shook his head. "No."

Tommy smiled. "I am sure there are others who need homes, should I call?" he said, grinning at his friend.

"No, we have a very human baby who will be here soon enough. I don't think we have time for anything else," Jack said, glaring at Tommy.

He shrugged. "I'm just asking."

Stephanie smiled at them. "Jack is right, but I will be here often since I can't do much else for a while," she walked over and sat down on the couch."

Brittany sat next to her. "Are you doing okay? No more contractions?"

Stephanie smiled. "No, all is calm, but I am not taking any chances. I will be home for the rest of the pregnancy."

Jack walked over and sat down. "We will find enough things to occupy your time."

Bill walked over to Julie and put his arm around her. "So tell us what's going on with you two? We are all dying to know why you needed to talk to us."

"Yes, you sounded so cryptic on the phone." Julie smiled, hoping it was good news for them. She rubbed her own large belly and exhaled.

Brittany took a deep breath.

"Actually, I just wanted to let all of you know something that will be happening tomorrow," she looked at Tommy who put his hand on her leg and smiled reassuringly at her. She nodded and looked at the expectant faces of the group. "You all have been the closest thing to family I have known in a long time. You have supported me and made me feel welcome when you really had no reason to, I mean, except for Stephanie, I was a stranger to all of you," she stood up and walked with her crutch to the chair in the middle of the room.

"I have a past that I have kept hidden for a long time, partly out of anger and partly out of shame, but I think mostly out of fear," she looked at each of them. "I don't know how much you know about what happened to me, but about 12 years ago, when I was known as Barbara Rose, the singer, I was attacked and held by the same guy who shot Tommy. He took a lot from me at that moment and left me with scars that were so much deeper than the physical assault. I let the person I was die in that moment and I never looked back," she ran her hand through her hair and saw the tears in the eyes of her friends.

"Until recently, I thought I had everything under control. I had a great practice in London and I was managing my disease, and everything seemed to finally be settling into place. Then I got the opportunity to move here and be with the only family who had been with me through everything," she smiled at Stephanie. "I figured it was time to stop running, and to stop being so alone."

Tommy felt a sense of pride and love for her while he watched her do what he knew was so hard. He also knew tomorrow was going to be 100 times harder and more revealing. He held Tramp on his lap as he continued to listen with everyone else.

"They never caught the guy who attacked me, and apparently he had been looking for me all this time. He found me here and you know what happened next. The thing is, when he found me, so did a reporter, and one who won't stop until he gets the whole story. He was the one in my house when I hurt my ankle."

Bill spoke up. "How is that possible? There should be protection out there for you and laws to protect your privacy? How could this guy get so close to you? I'm a detective and I can help you."

Julie nodded and Brittany smiled. "The paparazzi are a unique group of people. I am a story and that is their lifeblood. The thing is, I had been dreading this happening for so long, it is such an issue with me and I have so many deep-rooted fears about people knowing the extent of what happened. But now, I think I can handle it," she looked at Tommy. "Now I'm not alone."

Stephanie felt her tears fall as she watched her friend. She was so happy for her and for Tommy and she knew this was right. She looked at Brittany. "So what happens next?"

Brittany sighed. "I tell my story on my terms. That's the crux of why I wanted you all here. Tomorrow I am meeting with a reporter who I know and trust and we are filming an on air interview. She is going to break the real story, and after that, whatever happens, happens. I just wanted you to know and not be blindsided by anything," she exhaled. "I guess that's all."

There was a bit of silence when Jack walked over to her. "I think I can speak for all of us when I say that we are honored to know you and be your family," he hugged her.

Stephanie walked over to her. "You know how much I love you and no matter what; I'll be there through it all," she hugged her.

Julie wiped her eyes and walked over to Brittany. "You are simply amazing. I thought you were brave for putting up with my brother, but now, I am in awe. Thank you for letting us into your world," she hugged her.

Bill joined his wife. "I know that being in the military is hard and it takes a lot of courage, but in all of my years of service, you are probably one of the bravest and strongest people I have ever met," he hugged her.

Brittany wiped her eyes and was overwhelmed by the love and support she felt. She knew it was going to be hard to live through the next day, and she knew that later tonight, she would have to tell Tommy everything, all of the details of her attack, and she knew she needed to do that, but right now, this was perfection and she was simply going to enjoy it.

Tommy walked over to all of them and grinned. "How about we eat?"

Everyone smiled and Brittany was grateful for the attention moving from her. She stood up and grabbed her crutches. "So Jack, What kind of dessert are we having? Stephanie said you were bringing the chocolate and peanuts?"

Jack turned about every shade of red and turned to glare at his wife who was the picture of innocence.

"I think it's too soon to bring that out, maybe later tonight," Stephanie smiled and everyone began talking about other things. Jack shook his head.

"You are in so much trouble later," he whispered to her.

"Promise?" she smiled and walked to the table.

Chapter Sixty-One:

"So, tell me what's on your mind?" Tommy asked Brittany as they sat in the family room after everyone left. She was sitting with her back against his chest and he was running his hand through her hair. Tramp was chewing on a toy on the floor.

"I am grateful for our circle of friends and family. I am grateful for you," she said softly.

"But," he pushed, knowing there was more.

"But I am scared to death about tomorrow," she sighed.

He wrapped his arms around her and held her to him. "What are you afraid will happen?"

She held his arms around her and closed her eyes. "I don't know."

He smiled. "Liar."

She laughed. "I can't help it."

"Liar."

Another laugh.

She turned around and looked at him, smiling. "Tommy, what if there is someone else out there who tries to get to me? All these years, I have kept myself separated from my past for a lot of reasons, and although so many of them are not important anymore, one big one remains."

He nodded and cupped her cheek on his hand. "I know, but you can't live in fear. There are people out there who may try to exploit what happened or may try to appeal to you on a level that is unsuitable at best. The only thing I can tell you is to live your life the way you feel most comfortable. You can share as much of your story as you want or as little. It is not up to you to placate the minds and questions of the world, only to give yourself peace and freedom from nosy reporters and the misinformed public," he stroked her cheek. "I think you might be surprised by the response. I think more people love you than you ever realized."

She looked down at her hands and then back up at him. "I only care about one of those people," she leaned in and brushed his lips with hers before crashing her mouth on him, kissing him passionately.

"Yip, Yip, Arf," a little voice broke their connection. They both turned to see Tramp standing there next to a little yellow puddle, looking so proud of himself. Tommy groaned and Brittany laughed.

****

"Did he go?" Brittany asked as Tommy came back inside with Tramp. She had cleaned his little accident and was getting his dinner ready.

"Yes, he did everything. I asked him why he couldn't just always do that outside, but he didn't answer me," he put the little pooch down and smiled as he ran toward Brittany and his food. She pet his head as he began to eat.

"Boys are a mysterious bunch. Just when you think you have them figured out, they go and surprise you," she said as she smiled at him.

Tommy walked over to her and wrapped his arms around her. "You think so?"

"Mmhmm," she said as she laid her head on his chest.

"What do you want to do now?" he asked her, not wanting to release her from his arms.

"I would love to take a bath, but with this cast, that isn't an option. I guess I can take a shower and try the cast cover we have," she looked at her leg. "I know they will take care of my hair and makeup tomorrow, but I would like to clean up tonight," she said.

He grinned at her.

"What?" she asked as she smiled at him.

"I could give you a sponge bath," he said, his eyes sparkling.

She looked at him and smiled. "Will you be gentle?"

"Only if you want me to be," he leaned in and kissed her.

A few minutes later she was sitting on the bed and he was getting a few things ready. Tramp was sprawled out on the floor next to his little dog bed and she smiled at his full belly. He was just so cute. She tried to calm her butterflies as she thought about everything. She had only been intimate with Tommy once and so much had happened since then, she was feeling nervous all over again. She loved him and wanted to be with him more than anything, she just doubted herself and her ability to give him what he needed. She heard him approach and she turned and smiled.

"So, are you ready for some doctoring?" he asked her.

She nodded. "I am."

He spread out a towel and put some things down on it. He walked over to her and helped her stand up. He still couldn't believe how beautiful she was. It didn't matter how many times he looked at her; she mesmerized him. She noticed him staring and touched his face. "What's wrong?"

He blushed. "Sorry, sometimes I wonder why you're here with me. You could do so much better," he stepped back.

She was surprised by his words. "I don't like when you say that. You are all I will ever want and all I will ever need. You're it for me," she kissed him. "You know, I was just wondering if you would be better off with someone else, someone who can give you everything you need. Sometimes I wonder if that's me."

He smiled at her. "Aren't we a pair? Red, you are everything I want, everything I need and everything I could ever imagine in a partner. I don't want you to ever doubt that," he ran his hand under her hair.

She stepped back and smiled at him, her fears calmed by his touch. She looked into his eyes and pulled her shirt off. She reached behind her and unclasped her bra, removing the material and standing in front of him.

Tommy swallowed the lump in his throat and motioned for her to lie on the bed. She did and he moved to take the washcloth he had and squeezed out the excess water. He sat down next to her on the bed and slowly began to wash her, running the fabric over her neck and her torso, being careful to avoid her breasts. He wanted to save that. He took a bottle of lotion from the basket and squeezed a generous amount into his hands. He rubbed his hands together and moved them to her shoulders, massaging her and moving them down her arms and back up, rubbing her skin. She put her hands on his and stopped him.

"What is it?" he looked at her, not wanting her to see how badly he wanted her.

"I think this was a bad idea," she said, her breath coming faster.

"Did I hurt you?" he asked her, feeling his anxiety brewing.

She sat up and looked at him. "I need more. I need you," she pulled him down onto her and he pressed his mouth onto hers. He felt his heart pounding as he plunged his tongue into her mouth, tasting her and feeling her hunger for him in her aggressive kiss. He leaned back and she ran her hands under his shirt before he pulled it off entirely. She leaned up and wrapped her arms around his neck and pulled him into her. He let his hands roam down her body and he unzipped her pants. She lay back on the bed as he pulled her pants off, being careful around her cast. He ran his hands up her legs and she moaned under his touch. He looked at her and her sapphire eyes were full of desire. She reached for him and he linked his hand in hers and lay down on her, moving enough to avoid her cast. She ran her hands up and down his back as he moved down her chest. He relished the sensations her body was giving him and the pleasure he was able to give her. She moved him onto his back and ran her fingers over his face, tracing his mouth and smiling when he sucked on her finger. She ran her fingers down his torso and to the trail of hair which led to his groin. She leaned in and kissed him passionately while she ran her hand under his waistband.

He moved his hips at her touch and she smiled into his mouth. She backed away and used both hands to pull his sweats off, revealing his arousal still hidden under his briefs. She ran her hand over the bulge and he thought he might lose consciousness. She leaned down and kissed his torso, running her tongue over his nipples and letting her hair cover his neck. He held her hair back from her face, wanting to see her and watch her mouth work his body. She smiled at him and scooted down closer to his waist.

Tommy felt like he was in a dream. He never thought he could feel so much love and desire for another person. He knew that she was vital to him and he knew he loved her, but he had never felt the depth of connection he was feeling until now. It was as if she was his breath, his heart and his soul. He didn't know how that happened, or when it happened, but somehow, it did. He watched as she moved his briefs off, allowing his erection to spring forth. He felt such a need for her to be closer to him. He reached out and touched her, feeling she was too far away. She turned to him and moved back up to his face. He wrapped her in his arms and turned her into her back. He slowly moved down her torso and gently moved her panties off of her, staring at her beautiful body. She felt tears come to her eyes and he smiled at her. "God how I've missed you. You take my breath away."

She shook her head. "I just love you so much," she said. "I've missed you so much," she stroked his cheek.

He reached over and took the necessary precautions before moving between her legs. He looked into her eyes and saw himself there. He leaned in and kissed her softly, gently entering her as he did. She bent her good leg and allowed him more room. Her hands ran up and down his back as he moved in and out of her. She allowed herself to give in to her feelings, moving with him and becoming one with the moment. He leaned in to her as he felt her body shudder and he buried his head in her neck. She let herself go and Tommy could feel her contracting around him and it caused him to let go with her. He felt every ounce of strength he had go into her and he didn't know if he was able to move.

Brittany pulled the covers over them, holding him to her. He moved to the side and she wrapped him in her arms. She ran her hand through his hair. "I love you," she said softly.

He snuggled to her, looking into her eyes. "I love you more."

"Not possible," she said and he leaned in to kiss her again.

Chapter Sixty-Two:

Brittany and Tommy arrived at the studio and she immediately felt a rush of memories flood her mind. The odor of the lights and the cameras thrust her back into a time in her life, which was both amazing and heartbreaking. Tommy turned to see she was standing there, rooted in place. He walked back to her and cupped her face in his hands. "Hey, what's going on?"

She looked at him. "Just having a little trouble," she wiped her eyes.

He smiled at her. "You know we don't have to do this."

She nodded. "I know, but I kind of do. It's time I stopped hiding, but this is just really hard. I don't know what might happen."

He pulled her to him into a hug. "All you need to know is that I am here with you and nothing will change how much I love you and how amazing our future will be. This is just a step in that direction," he ran his hand under her hair and looked into her eyes. "You are safe and you are stronger than you give yourself credit."

She shook her head. "No, Tommy, you are my strength and you keep me grounded. I just love you so much."

He wiped her tears away and kissed her. "I love you, too," he hugged her again and felt her cling to him like he was her life preserver.

******

Jack and Stephanie arrived at the studio and met
Tommy who looked nervous and anxious. "Hey, how is
Brittany doing?" Stephanie asked.

He ran his hand through his hair. She is in makeup and
wardrobe. She is scared to death but hiding it well. I
am so glad you guys are here."

Jack smiled. "Of course we are here. This is a huge
step and we want to be a part of it with you guys. We
will be your studio audience."

Tommy nodded. "Good, that's good," he looked up as
Brittany walked towards them. His heart stopped when
he looked at her. She had her hair blown straight,
which made it longer than he had ever seen it. Her
makeup was subtle and glamorous, looking like she
wasn't really made up, but Tommy knew different. She
was wearing a blue pantsuit, which mostly hid her cast.
She looked like a movie star.

"Hi," she smiled at all of them.

"Excuse me, can you sign this for my daughter?" a
stagehand came up and held out a picture of Brittany in
front of her. She blushed and nodded, scribbling her
signature on the sheet.

She shrugged at her friends after the man walked
away. "Sorry, I guess I should get used to that again. I
am honored that you guys came"

Jack smiled. "We wouldn't miss it. How are you?"

She took a deep breath. "Aside from the fact that my
hands won't stop shaking and I feel like I might throw

up at any second, I'm fabulous," she laughed, only half joking.

Tommy still hadn't said anything and she sensed his apprehension. "It's okay, it's still me, just a lot of stuff."

He felt an overwhelming need to protect her, to get her out of there, but he knew she needed to do this. He just felt helpless. "I know; I just want everything to be okay."

Jack and Stephanie took their seats out of view of the camera and Tommy stood with her, just staying close for as long as he could. Suddenly they heard a voice.

"Barbara! I can't believe it's really you," a short woman with gray hair and a very expensive black suit walked up to them and Brittany turned around and smiled.

"Danielle, hi," Brittany hugged the woman. She looked at Tommy and smiled. "This is Tommy who I told you about."

"So nice to meet you," she shook Tommy's hand. "I just can't believe it. Do you know how amazing this is? People are just going to flip when they see you. You are absolutely stunning and your hair is simply gorgeous," Danielle touched Brittany's locks.

"Danielle, I can't tell you how much I appreciate you doing this for me. I am afraid the story is going to come out, and I would just rather people hear my story on my terms," Brittany said.

"Honey, you are going to get me ratings unlike anything I have ever seen," she smiled. "Are you ready to start?"

Brittany took a deep breath. "I think so."

Tommy squeezed her hand. "I'll be right there," he pointed to the chair next to Jack and Stephanie. He turned to walk away and she pulled him to her for another hug. She felt like a lost child again, alone in a scary world. "You can do this," he whispered in her ear. "And when you're done, we will have another sponge bath to remove this makeup," he grinned at her and she smiled while blushing. She nodded at him and walked to the oversized chair and sat down, Danielle sitting on an equally oversized chair across from her. The makeup woman came and touched up both of their faces and the boom mike was lowered. Brittany attached her own mike to her lapel and tried to calm her pounding heart.

Tommy watched her, marveling at how she was able to transform herself into someone so completely different and still, he saw his Red in her face. He silently wished her luck.

The show began and there was a montage of Brittany as Barbara Rose. There was concert footage and charity work along with many glamorous signings and award shows. It ended abruptly and the camera panned on Danielle.

"Good evening everyone. This is Newsline 10 and I'm your host Danielle Flatts. This evening we bring you a remarkable story of survival and recovery. It is the never before told story of a young girl who had the whole world at her fingertips, but in one horrific moment, lost it all. We all remember her as Barbara Rose, beautiful, talented and giving. We also remember how she vanished, never to be seen again.

Tonight, her story is told and the voice that was known around the world for its pure quality and emotion will return again."

Tommy watched Brittany and saw her smile for the camera, but he could see her fear behind her eyes. He looked at Jack and Stephanie and they smiled at him, but he could see their concern as well.

"So Barbara, can you tell us where you have been all this time?" Danielle asked her.

Brittany smiled. "Actually, I go by Brittany now. I have been living my life for the past 12 years. I am happy now and I have been enjoying all that this life has to offer," she took a deep breath. "I went through something 12 years ago that facilitated my move out of the spotlight and out of singing. It is only recently that I have begun to embrace some of the things that meant the most to me back then."

Danielle nodded. "Right, so what exactly happened the night you disappeared? Can you share with your fans what you went through?"

Brittany exhaled and Tommy didn't like how pale she looked. He kept his eyes on her, trying to give her his strength.

"After one of my concerts, I was in my trailer, winding down like I did after every show. It had been a particularly long show because the audience was really into it and I think I came back for three encores," she smiled as she thought about the show. "I was really tired and I was waiting for something, I don't remember what exactly, maybe food to be delivered?" she paused and shook her head. "Whatever it was, I remember hearing a noise outside the trailer and I opened the door to look outside but didn't see anything. To make a long story short, I walked out to look and suddenly found myself being chased. I ran for a long time before finally finding shelter, but it wasn't enough, he found me and grabbed me," she stopped and looked at her hands.

Stephanie felt her tears fall down her cheeks as she watched her friend relive such a horrible moment in her life. She could still picture Brittany showing up at the clinic, battered and bruised. She could still see the terror in her eyes when she heard her diagnosis. She put her head on Jack's shoulder and he put his arm around her.

Tommy kept his eyes on her. He concentrated on his breathing and just looked at her. He fought every urge he had to run up there and take her away, but he knew he couldn't save her from this. Damn that reporter.

Danielle smiled at her guest. "Can you tell us what happened next?"

Brittany took a sip of water and Tommy could see her hands shake. "I was held for about 24 hours before I was able to escape."

"What happened while you were held?" Danielle asked her.

Tommy saw Brittany shudder. He went to stand up but Jack held him back. He sat down and ran his hand through his hair.

"I was assaulted numerous times. I got away and got help," she looked at Danielle. "Can we take a break?"

Danielle nodded and signaled for them to cut. Brittany pulled the mic off and got up quickly, walking on her cast to the safety of the bathroom. She went in and made her way to a stall and emptied the contents of her stomach. She sat down on the carpeted floor after she cleaned herself up and sobbed into her hands.

Tommy ran after her and Danielle stopped him. "Maybe she needs a moment alone," she said and he looked at her.

"Maybe she needs me," he said. "I think enough people have left her alone when she needed them the most. This isn't just a story, this is her life," he walked to the bathroom and went in.

His heart broke as he saw her, sitting on the floor, her head in her hands, the long red locks flowing around her, covering her fingers. He flashed back to the time he found her on the roof after Jack was shot and she was so vulnerable and so alone. He knew how she felt because he had felt the same way. They had been through so much since that moment, and he never wanted either one of them to go back to that sad and lonely place. He made his way over to her and sat down, reaching over and moving her hair behind her shoulder. She looked up at him; her blue eyes brimming with unshed tears. She shrugged and didn't speak. He pulled her into his arms and held her. She wrapped her arms around him and held on tightly as he rocked her. "I'm so sorry, baby," he repeated over and over.

After a few minutes, she pulled away from him. "I feel so ridiculous reacting this way, like it's happening all over again. Tommy, it's been 12 years, how can I still be so messed up?"

He wiped the tears off her face and smiled. "You are not messed up. You were violated in the worst, most invasive way possible and I don't think you have ever allowed yourself to deal with that. You have moved on and made a life, but deep down, you still see yourself as that girl, alone and afraid," he smoothed her hair back some more. "But baby, that's not who you are. You have buckets of strength and you have the courage to do this," he ran his hand through his hair and smiled at her. "I remember the first time I realized just how strong you were," he said.

"When was that?" she looked into his emerald eyes.

"When we were in that cave and I was afraid you weren't going to make it. You had a collapsed lung and were minutes from losing consciousness and possibly your life, but you gave me the courage and strength to help you. Do you remember what you told me in that moment?" he took her hand in his.

"No, I don't remember much of that time," she said softly.

"You told me it was okay, and whatever happened, it wasn't my fault. You tried to protect me from blaming myself if you didn't make it," he kissed her hand. "You were in incredible pain and your only concern was for me. I have never forgotten that."

She smiled at him. "I love you and I don't know how you found me or why you decided to take a chance, but I am so grateful you did," she looked down. "I do remember some things about the cave."

"Oh really? What things?" he asked her softly.

"I remember feeling safe despite the fear and I remember feeling like maybe there was a reason I survived," she spoke with emotion.

He felt his own tears wet his eyes. "Ditto," he said as he softly kissed her.

Chapter Sixty-Three:

A few minutes later, Brittany was back in the chair and the makeup artist was fixing her face. Tommy was sitting back with Jack and Stephanie and they all were anxious to get this over with. Danielle smiled at Brittany. "Are you ready to continue?"

Brittany shook her head. "Yes, thanks."

"So, Brittany, can you tell us what happened after you got away? What have you been doing all these years?" Danielle prodded her.

Brittany looked at Tommy who smiled encouragingly at her. She looked at the camera.

"There is something else I need to say. About a month after my attack I tested positive for HIV." They all heard the audible gasp of the room. Danielle didn't know this piece of news and she was visibly shaken. Brittany continued.

"The only reason I am sharing this bit of information is so that people will hear the truth. I have been living with HIV for 12 years and am healthy and happy. Many people struggle with the stigma of this disease and it needs to stop. I was petrified of revealing this and that is the ultimate reason I kept myself hidden for so long, but now I know that was wrong."

Danielle looked at her. "What made you change your mind?"

Brittany smiled for the first time in the interview. "I found someone who showed me my worth."

Tommy felt his heart swell. He didn't think he could be any prouder of her.

"Well, I want to thank you for being so candid, Brittany. What is next for you?" Danielle asked, wiping her own tears.

"Living my life with the man I love and the friends who support me. I have been so incredibly blessed my whole life, and I never want to forget that. Whatever happens, I want it to be on my terms, and not anyone else's," she said with strength. "It is time I take control of my future."

Danielle nodded. "So can we expect a tour anytime soon?" she smiled.

Brittany shook her head. "No, that part of my life is over. I am happy with my career and with my life. Music is a part of me and I will always have that, but it is time to move forward."

Danielle looked at her. "What career is that?"

"I would like to keep that private. I just want people to understand that I am so thankful for the support and kindness of my fans and I will never forget how much they meant to me," she smiled.

"I can't thank you enough for telling your story. Will you sing for us one last time?" Danielle asked her.

"I would love to," Brittany said. She had written a song for this moment and wanted it to be a surprise to Tommy. She stood up and walked to the piano they had brought out into the studio. She sat down at the bench and moved her good foot to the pedals. She adjusted the microphone and began to play.

Tommy stared at her and Jack leaned over to him. "Did you know about this?"

He shook his head. "No, she didn't tell me she was going to sing."

Jack smiled and hugged Stephanie to him. They all watched Brittany.

She moved her hands over the keys and softly pressed her fingers down to create a soft, beautiful sound. She closed her eyes and let the music flow through her body. She opened her eyes and began to sing.

Life can take you places you never wished to be
Situations happen and fear becomes your only trusted
friend
Sometimes the darkest moments can break your spirit
down
And sometimes there is someone who makes you
breathe again

Love is the reason, not simply the result
Trust can be given and faith can be found
Pain can abate and truth can be revealed
But when you're stuck in the moment it feels like
there's no end

It's in those instances you see your worth
It doesn't matter what you thought or what you believed
to be true
Letting go of the fear is the hardest part

But when you do, the most extraordinary things are possible

There was a small piano interlude where Brittany played the most beautiful bridge. She closed her eyes and a few tears escaped. Tommy was mesmerized by the melody and Jack and Stephanie were both affected.

I was alone and I was content
I walked through my life with me as my only friend
I played it safe because I was scared
I looked up one day and love was there

The time for waiting is over
The time for living is now
The hope for tomorrow is near
And love is the answer

Love is the answer to the questions we don't ask
Hope is the freedom to take a chance
You are my reasons and you are my truth
I will love you forever, my heart, and my life

Love is the answer to the questions we don't ask
Hope is the freedom to take a chance
You are my reasons and you are my truth
I will love you forever, my heart, and my life

The music stopped and Brittany put her hands down. Danielle walked over to the piano and smiled. She wiped her own tears away and thanked Brittany again. The cameras turned off and the interview was over.

"Thank you Danielle, I really appreciate this," Brittany said.

"You are an inspiration and I thank you for allowing me to tell your story. It will air tonight," she said.

Brittany nodded and stood up, but her legs were shaking. Danielle reached out to help her.

"Are you okay?"

Brittany smiled. "Yes, I just think the nerves are taking over a bit," she sat back down.

Tommy made his way over to her and thanked Danielle who walked away. He looked at Brittany. "Need a hand?"

She took a deep breath. "I think I could use both hands," she smiled and he took both of his hands and cupped her face. He leaned in and kissed her.

"Let's go," he said and she stood up. He put his arm around her waist and they walked out of the studio.

****

"I can't believe everything that has happened in the last few months," Stephanie said as she and Jack walked into their house. "So much can change in such a short amount of time," she sat down on the couch.

Jack joined her and pulled her feet up onto his lap. He pulled her shoes off and began to massage her feet. "I know what you mean. I think about the past and I remember when I met you and how lonely I was, but how stubborn we both were," he smiled.

"We wasted so much time, Jack. We need to always appreciate each other," she moved to lie down on the couch next to him, resting her head on his lap. He smoothed her hair away from her face. She took his hand and placed it on her stomach.

"I love you so much, Steph. I don't need anyone to remind me how lucky I am. All I have to do is look at you and our growing baby and my heart feels so full," he said.

She looked up at him. "You know, it won't be long before the baby will be here. Are you scared?"

He exhaled. "Terrified," she looked at him and he smiled. "Well I am."

She sat up. "What are you scared about?"

He shrugged. "I don't know how to be a dad. My only form of reference walked out of my life. I know he has been trying lately, but I harbor so much anger and resentment, I just don't want to do that to our child."

She touched his face and smoothed his cheek. "You are going to be the most amazing father, Jack. Do you know how I know that?"

He felt tears prick his eyes. "How?"

She shrugged. "Because of how you love me. You take care of me and you respect me and you put the needs of everyone else above your own. You are intelligent and witty and you also have a heart that is the best and most genuine I have ever known. You are funny and romantic and my best friend. All of those qualities are what a child needs to feel love and respected."

He wiped at his eyes. "You left something out."

She snuggled up to him, "What's that?"

"I am incredibly handsome," he grinned.

"No, I didn't forget that, it's just that some things are only for the mommy and not for the baby," she ran her hands under his shirt and he lowered his mouth onto hers.

Chapter Sixty-Four:

Tommy and Brittany walked into the house and Tramp ran up to them from his spot in the kitchen. Tommy scooped him up quickly and took him outside. Brittany walked to the couch and sat down, pulling her hair up into a ponytail. She had so many thoughts and feelings running through her mind. She leaned back onto the couch and closed her eyes. A few minutes later she felt wet paws on her and a tongue licking her face. She opened her eyes and held Tramp while he jumped all over her. She couldn't help but smile.

"So, I think it's time for you to eat something and relax," Tommy said as he sat down.

Tramp bounded over to him and he picked the puppy up and put him on the floor.

She looked at Tommy and started to say something, but stopped.

"What is it?"

"You just haven't said anything since we left the studio."

He sighed. "I know."

"Why? Is there something I said that bothered you?" she had felt there was something on his mind, but he wasn't letting on.

Tommy looked at her. "You didn't say anything that bothered me, but I need to know what you went through, all of it. I feel like it is this huge barrier between us at times and I don't know how to get through it because I don't know what it is. When I listened to you tell what happened, I realized that I don't know enough about your past and about what made you the strong woman you are today. I don't mean to make you uncomfortable or angry, but if we are going to move forward, I think it would be best if you told me what you couldn't tell earlier."

Brittany nodded. "You're right, Tommy, but I guess I hoped to spare you that information."

"I love you and I don't want you to hide anything from me. I don't even know the date you were attacked."

"April 25th. I was taken on the 25th and got away on the 26th. I pretty much told everything about how he got to me earlier, but when I woke up, I was tied to a chair in some cabin-like area. He was taking pictures of me and he developed them in the cabin. There were photos hung up all over," she stood up and wrapped her hands around the pillow she picked up with her. "There were pictures of me singing and walking down the street in locations all over. It was like he wanted me to know how long he had been following me. He had been to my house and at my bedroom window. There were also pictures of me sleeping in my bed," she wiped her face with the back of her hand. "He had also taken pictures of me tied up in the chair."

Tommy listened, taken aback at the date, but kept it quiet for now, remaining silent. He needed to hear this. He needed her to get it out. The rest could come later.

"I was kind of out of it, from the chloroform and the beating. I tried to fight, but I really didn't know what was going on, until," she stopped for a minute.

Tommy walked over to her. "Until what?"

She turned around and looked at him. "Until he ripped my shirt off and put his hands all over me. I remember hoping that I would just die, you know?" she walked back toward the couch and looked away from him. "He apparently couldn't do what he needed to do with me in the chair so he threw me on the floor and pulled my clothes completely off. He held me down and pressed his body on me, pinning my arms under my body and then he raped me and then he stopped and then he raped me again. I lost consciousness after the 3rd time."

Tommy wiped his face as he listened to her and he felt sick to his stomach. He didn't know how someone could do something like this to another human being. He couldn't imagine the fear she must have felt and the pain she had to endure.

She turned around and looked at him. "When I came to, I was naked and in pain, but I was alone. He had taken pictures of me naked and at different stages of the attack. I grabbed the remnants of my clothes and put them on and ran out of the cabin and to the street. I flagged a car down before I passed out again. When I woke up, I was in the hospital, three days later," she shrugged and sighed. "That's the gist of it. Do you want to know anything else?"

Tommy looked at his hands. "Brittany, what year was this?"

She was surprised at his question. "1999, why?"

He started to cry and covered his face. Tramp scratched his leg, concerned at this change in his human. Brittany moved to him. "Tommy, what is it? What's wrong?" she knew it was something more than the story. She put her hand on his thigh.

Tommy looked at her through his wet emerald eyes. "April 25, 1999 was the day my parents were killed."

Brittany sat there, stunned, not sure she heard him correctly. "No, it couldn't be the same day, it just couldn't," her tears fell down her cheeks as she spoke aloud, but to herself.

Tommy felt the anxiety he hadn't felt for so long coming back all around him. He stood up and walked into the bathroom, closing the door behind him. He needed a minute to figure out what the hell was happening to him. He turned the water on and splashed his face, trying to wash away the intensity of the feelings he was having. He looked in the mirror, the droplets of water hanging off his chin. How could this be true? How could they share such a profoundly horrible experience on the same day? What did it mean? He sat down on the closed toilet seat and took some deep breaths, collecting his thoughts.

Brittany watched him walk away and gave him a minute before she walked to the bathroom. She knocked on the door and waited. "Tommy, can you come out?" she waited for a little bit and then walked to the couch and sat back down.

There was silence and then the door opened. He stood there with his hands in his pockets, his face showing the fatigue of the day. He sighed. "Sorry, I just needed a minute."

She walked back over to him and touched his face. "I'm so sorry."

He was confused. "Why would you be sorry?" he held her hand in his own.

She pulled him to her and hugged him, laying her head on his shoulder. He was surprised, but wrapped his arms around her as well. They stood there in the bathroom doorway for a minute, their arms around each other. Brittany stepped back and cupped his face in her hands. She traced a line down his cheek and leaned in and kissed him softly. "I'm sorry you had to lose your parents in such a horrible way and I'm sorry that I'm bringing it all up again for you," she touched his cheek. "I'm going to change. Take all the time you need to be alone, but when you want company, I'll be waiting," she turned and walked into the guest bedroom. She sat down on the bed and pulled her leg with the cast up onto the mattress. It was throbbing and needed to be elevated. She started to pull off her suit and change into something more comfortable, but after she removed her jacket, she leaned back on the bed and exhaled. She pulled her ponytail out and lay back on the pillow, closing her eyes for a minute.

Tommy walked into the room and smiled when he saw her. She was lying on the bed and Tramp was curled up in the crook of her leg. He walked over to the other side of the bed and sat down. She opened her eyes and looked at him. "Hi, I was just resting my eyes," she smiled.

He grinned at her. "Do you always snore when you rest your eyes?"

She playfully smacked his arm. "That was Tramp."

Tommy raised his eyebrows. "Right, blame the dog." They both laughed.

There was an uncomfortable silence and then Brittany moved her leg a little. "Quite a day, huh?"

He nodded. "You could say that," he looked at her leg. "Do you want something for pain?" he was concerned at the look on her face when she moved.

"No, I just want this cast off. It weighs a ton and my leg is throbbing," she said.

He smiled. "Tomorrow we go back and your wish should be granted. Hopefully the cast can come off."

She closed her eyes. "That will be amazing."

He looked at her, laying there, her eyes closed and her face beautiful. He reached down and traced a line across her mouth. She opened her blue eyes and smiled at him. "Do you want to talk about it?"

He shook his head. "Not really."

She sighed. "I can understand if it is too much to deal with. I also understand if you look at me and see what happened, and not the woman you fell in love with," she sat up and took the blanket off the side of the bed and covered herself up. "I think maybe you should take some alone time. I can go out for a while, or just go for a ride. I think maybe you need some time to sort through everything. I am just going to change," she stood up and walked into the bathroom. He watched her leave and ran his hand through his hair in frustration.

He looked at Tramp who appeared to be smirking at him. "What do you know, all you do is look cute and lick yourself," he said and Tramp cocked his head as if he understood him. Tommy sighed. "I think I have royally screwed everything up."

Brittany sighed as she sat on the closed toilet seat. She remembered when Tommy had helped her right after he saved her life. He had taken such good care of her, treated her with respect and tenderness. She had never felt the fear she did when she had been near others. She always had a hard time in business meetings and classes where people would stand too close to her. She never went anywhere and she never really did anything social because she carried around such a horrible stigma, at least in her own mind.

With Tommy, it had been different from day one. Granted, he was an ass when they met and she didn't like him very much, but it was quickly apparent that under his tough exterior, there was a heart of gold. Brittany saw herself in him, a kindred spirit, or so she thought. She sighed and wiped the tears she felt dampen her cheeks. This was his pain, too, and she needed to respect that. He was allowed to take some time to process everything.

Brittany opened the door of the bathroom and didn't see him. She walked out and changed her clothes, pulling on Tommy's shirt that she loved to wear. She grabbed a pair of yoga pants and put them on, frowning at how loose they seemed. She needed to be sure to eat more and take better care of herself. She walked into the other room and saw him sitting on the couch, waiting for her. She walked to get her coat.

"You know, if you leave, Tramp won't know why," Tommy said.

Brittany smiled. "I'm not leaving forever, I just think you need some time away from me. Everything has been so heavy, and tonight I think it just became too much," she ached to talk to him and to help him deal with everything. She just didn't know what was the right thing to do.

Tommy couldn't bear her leaving. Everything that had happened since they came back from the shoot was wrong. He wanted today to be so different, so much better for her. He wanted to have a wonderful evening and take away all of the sadness the interview brought up. He had failed and failed horribly. "I don't know what to say, I just have so much going through my head," he looked down.

She walked over to him and leaned in and kissed his forehead. "It's okay, take some time. I'll leave you alone for a bit," she touched his hand and turned and walked out, leaving him watching her, knowing he should stop her, but sitting there, doing nothing.

Chapter Sixty-Five:

Brittany sat in the bar at a restaurant near the house. She wasn't sure where to go, and her car ended up there. She was wearing a baseball cap and her hair was in a ponytail through the back of the hat. She was nursing a drink and watching the news playing on the bar television. She sighed as she looked at her phone, which was silent. She finished her drink and asked for another, drinking it faster.

"Hey, you might want to slow down a little," a voice said from next to her at the bar.

Brittany looked over at the man sitting there. She turned back to her drink. "I've got it covered, thanks."

"I'm just saying, a girl like you might get into trouble, drinking alone like this," he said with a sneer.

Brittany turned and laughed. "Really? A girl like me? What the hell do you know about me?"

The man moved closer to her. "I would like to know more, if you'll let me."

She suddenly became aware of the potentially dangerous situation around her. She shifted in her seat. "I'm waiting for someone, so if you don't mind, I would just like to sit here in peace until they come."

He shrugged. "I'll wait, for now," he sat back down at his seat.

Brittany sighed. She was relieved after a minute when the man left. She finished her drink and ordered another. She knew she was drunk, but she didn't care. She would call a cab later. Right now, she didn't want to think about anything, or feel anything. She played with the straw in her glass when a sound made her heart jump in her throat. She looked up as the big screen television in the bar suddenly had on the beginning of her interview. She looked around and saw most of the people at the bar were watching. She looked at the screen and then back at her drink. She finished it and motioned for the bartender to come over. "Can't you change it to something else?"

"Are you kidding? Everyone has been waiting for this show to come on." The bartender wiped the counter and smiled at her. "You should watch, you kind of look like her."

Brittany pulled the cap further over her face. She sighed and nodded, picking up her cell phone and making a call. She watched while she waited, feeling the effects of the alcohol and the interview taking over. She stood up and walked out of the bar, needing some air and doing her best to remain upright with her cast and her level of intoxication.

****

Jack and Stephanie finished their dinner and Jack smiled at his wife. He reached over the table and played with her fingers. She looked up at him.

"What are you thinking?" she asked him softly as she wiped her mouth.

"We have to discuss names," he said.

She grinned, "I know, do you have any ideas?"

He shrugged, "Maybe, how about you?"

She nodded, "Kind of."

He stood up and pulled her up with him and walked over to the loveseat. He sat down and pulled her onto his lap. She moved slightly. "I'm going to smush you."

"Not a chance," he held her to him. "Do you think we are having a boy or a girl?"

Stephanie touched her stomach and leaned back against Jack. "Sometimes I feel like it's a boy, but then, I wonder if I really have any idea what that feels like. I just want everything to go okay and I want you to be happy," she ran her hand down his thigh.

"Baby, I am the happiest person in the world," he wrapped his arms around her. "I will be happy with a boy or a girl, it doesn't matter. I am kind of excited that we don't know."

She nodded. "I know, I thought about asking but then I figured it would be one last surprise, you know?"

He leaned in and nibbled on her neck. "I think we will have many more surprises."

She felt her resolve crumble as he moved his lips over her shoulder blades. She turned and found his lips with hers and plunged her tongue into his mouth. They began to move toward the bedroom when Jack's phone went off. He groaned and looked at it.

"It's the hospital," he said. She backed off of him and let him take it. He hung up and sighed. "I need to go in for an emergency," he looked at her, so beautiful and so eager for him. "I'm sorry."

She smiled. "I'll be waiting when you come back."

He leaned in and kissed her again, lingering before grabbing his keys and walking out.

Stephanie watched him leave and smiled at how blessed they were.

******

Tommy had enough time alone. She had been gone for a couple hours and he was through thinking. The longer she was gone the more he thought about how much he had screwed up. He knew she didn't think that way, but this day should have been all about her and he made it about him. He just wished he could go back a few hours and do everything differently. He ran his hand through his hair when he heard a car drive by. He looked outside and saw it wasn't her. He sat back down and pet Tramp while he turned on the television. He flipped through the channels and stopped when he saw the show starting about her. He sat there, mesmerized by her on TV. He watched her, talking, telling her story, and exposing her soul to virtual strangers and millions of others who were watching. He saw every expression as if it was a road map to her heart. She was so strong on the outside, but Tommy knew what was really happening. He shook his head. She should be here with him, and he should be taking her mind off of everything that had happened. He looked down as his cell phone buzzed.

"Hey Stephanie, what's going on?" Tommy said into the phone.

"Brittany called me to pick her up, but Jack took the car to go in for an emergency. She told me not to call you, but I can't get there right now," Stephanie said and sighed.

Tommy was worried. "What happened? Where is she?"

Stephanie relayed where Brittany was and Tommy smiled.

"Drunk?"

Stephanie laughed. "I think very much so. She never drinks like that, Tommy, so I think today just got to her. I would ask why she went off on her own, but I guess I'll leave that to another day."

Tommy blushed. "It's a long story. Thanks for calling me, Stephanie, I'll get her."

He hung up and grabbed his keys, heading towards the bar. He pulled up to the parking lot and walked in, looking for her. He saw the people there watching the interview on television and he felt his heart drop at the realization that she was probably trying to hide from everyone. He walked to the counter and asked the bartender if he had seen her.

"She left about 15 minutes ago, walked outside while she waited for her ride." The bartender wiped the bar and smiled at Tommy. "Is she your girlfriend? You're a lucky man."

Tommy nodded, concerned. "She walked out by herself? Why didn't she wait inside?"

He shrugged. "She didn't seem to like the show on tv. She asked me to change it, but the whole bar was mesmerized. She walked out after that."

Tommy turned and saw the big screen with Brittany's face on it. He turned and walked out, looking for her and hoping she would be okay with him being there.

He looked around the parking lot and didn't see her. He shivered, feeling the cold go through him. What was she doing outside for so long? He was beginning to get nervous when he didn't see her anywhere. He saw her car and he walked over to it, relieved when he saw her sitting in the passenger seat. He walked over to the car and stood in front of it, waiting for her to see him. She opened the door and stepped out.

"You're not Stephanie," she said softly, and then started laughing.

He grinned at her. "Are you drunk?"

She shrugged, "Maybe a teeny bit," she held her fingers up and made a small pinching motion. She turned to walk and almost fell over. Tommy grabbed her and she dissolved into giggles.

"You're so sexy, Tommy. You're my sexy hero and I'm your pathetic loser," she said with an air of sadness and he knew it wasn't all the alcohol talking.

Tommy helped her to his car. "Time to go home," he said, helping her into the passenger seat and then drove them home. She had her head rested on the window the whole drive. "If you need to get sick, please tell me and I'll pull over."

"Pshaw, I can handle my dink, my drink," she said.

He laughed. "Sure you can," he pulled up to the house and got out. He went to help her and she got out on her own and stumbled to the door. "Let me help you."

She put her hand up. "No, I can do it. You need time alone and I didn't ashk you to help me," she said and opened the door. She walked in and Tramp ran up to her and she smiled at him before tripping over the puppy and sprawling to the floor, Tramp running for safety to the kitchen. "Oof, ouch," she said as she landed hard on the floor.

Tommy walked over to her. "Are you okay?" he reached to her.

"My bruises have bruises. I'm just going to stay right here for the night," she put her head down and lay on the floor.

Tommy sat down next to her and smiled. "What happened at the bar?"

She looked at him. "I ordered drinks and I drank them, that's what happened."

She sat up and sighed. "Look Tommy, I'm fine. I just need to shleep."

He nodded. "Right."

"So just take my eyeballs out and I'll be fine," she said.

He stood up and helped her up. She wobbled and he gathered her in his arms. "Come on, time for bed."

"Ooh, fun," she said and leaned her head against his shoulder and sighed.

He loved the feel of her on his skin. He put her down on the bed and smiled. "I am going to take Tramp out. Can you just sit here until I come back?"

She nodded. "I'm good."

He shook his head and laughed as he took the pooch outside for a bathroom break. He praised Tramp for doing his business and then walked back inside to find Brittany asleep on the covers in her clothes. He smiled at her and walked over to the bed. He gently undressed her and put her nightshirt on. He placed her under the covers and she never stirred. He lay next to her and smoothed her hair around her face. He felt such a burst of love for her and he just wanted her to know that. Today was so hard for her and then to find out their common tragic date was just so painful. He made her handle it on her own and he wouldn't make that mistake again. He held her to him as he fell asleep.

Chapter Sixty-Six:

Tommy and Jack met for breakfast the next morning. Brittany was still asleep and Tommy figured it would be best if she stayed that way as long as possible. Stephanie had been nesting all morning and Jack was happy for the distraction. They had picked up Brittany's car first and dropped it back off at the house.

"So, how did it go after you got home?" Jack took a drink of his coffee. Was she better after you came home and the interview was over?"

Tommy held his cup in his hand. "Before or after she went to the bar and got plastered?"

Jack smiled. "I see, so talking wasn't on your mind?"

Tommy sighed. "She told me more about the attack after we got back."

"Why?" Jack asked.

"I needed to know more, you know? I thought it would be better for her to lessen the load she carries," he said.

"And, was it too much for you?" Jack asked his buddy, knowing that wasn't the case.

"Of course not. Dude, her attack was on April 25 of 99," Tommy said softly.

Jack was quiet for a minute and then he knew exactly what was so profound. "Oh God, man, the same day?"

Tommy nodded. "Karma, huh?"

Jack shook his head. "Nope, destiny," he smiled. "Maybe both of you suffered such a horrific experience on the same day only to come full circle and make your blessing mean more."

Tommy smiled. "Tell Stephanie I said thank you."

"For what?"

"For making you human," Tommy said and Jack smacked his arm.

"Come on, let's go," the men began to walk up to the counter when Tommy's eye caught an image that almost stopped his heart. Jack saw it too, at the same time.

There was a tabloid magazine fresh on the stands with a picture of Brittany huddled on the floor of her house with the headline:

Teen Idol ravaged by AIDS weeks to live

"Oh God," Jack and Tommy said and looked at each other.

It took Jack a while to calm Tommy down enough to let him drive home. Both men were livid at the irresponsibility of the reporter and the paper for printing such erroneous lies. Tommy knew this was exactly what she was afraid would happen. Going on the TV show wouldn't matter because people would see this everywhere and draw the wrong conclusions. He drove home, hating the morning news he was going to have to give her. He walked into the house and went into the bedroom, surprised to see her gone. He picked up Tramp who was yipping and barking and trying to lick his face and walked into the kitchen. He saw her note on the counter.

"Went to cast appointment be back after. Thanks for taking care of me last night and for getting my car. Love you."

He put the note down and sighed. What were the chances no one would say anything to her? He looked at Tramp and nodded. He needed to go to the hospital.

****
Brittany walked onto the ortho floor and tried to keep the pain in her head from showing through her face. She had not had that much to drink in a long time and she was a bit angry with herself. She felt badly that Tommy had to get her and she figured the least she could do was go to her appointment and come home finally free of the cast and they could talk, because she needed him to hear a few things. She smiled at a few patients who walked down the hall and noticed they were staring at her in a strange way. She looked at her clothes, making sure she remembered to put them on, and then shrugged. She made her way to the desk to check in.

****
Jack walked into his house after breakfast with Tommy and looked for Stephanie. He was worried about her stress level, but she needed to know what they saw. He saw her in the nursery, sitting on the rocking chair they had purchased. The room was empty except for that because they were waiting until the baby was born

to finish decorating. It was a bit of a superstition. She had her eyes closed and her hands on her stomach. Jack felt his heart melt at the sight of his precious cargo and his love. He stood in the doorway and watched her and she opened her eyes, sensing his gaze.

"How long have you been standing there?" she asked him with a big smile.

"Not long," he walked into the room. "How are you feeling this morning?"

"Fine, happy, fat," she said.

"You are not fat. I love your body," he said and put his hand on her belly while he knelt down next to her.

"You have to say that, it's your job," she smiled at him.

"No it isn't, it's a perk. I love telling you how beautiful you are and I love loving you," he leaned in and kissed her.

She touched his face with her hand. "How was breakfast? Did you find out what happened with Tommy and Brittany last night?"

Jack sighed and Stephanie looked at him, concerned. "What is it? What happened?"

"Stephanie, do you remember the date Brittany was attacked?" he asked her.

She nodded. "Of course, April 25, 1999. I remember because it was right after I arrived in Paris. I was so upset I was far away from her," Stephanie looked at him with a puzzled expression. "Why?"

Jack sat down on the floor next to the chair and Stephanie moved to face him. "Tommy's parents were killed the same day."

Stephanie's face showed the horror she felt. "Oh my God, the same day? How could it be the same day?" she was asking a rhetorical question, but it seemed too surreal.

He shrugged. "Brittany finally told Tommy the specifics about her attack and when she told him the date, he freaked out. He didn't know how to handle it, and so he shut down a bit."

"And Brittany walked out," Stephanie added.

He nodded. "They so need us to help them."

She grinned. "We are so mature," she moved closer to him and kissed him. "So she went out and got drunk?"

He shook his head. "It appears that way. Tommy picked her up and she fell asleep so they didn't talk. He went with me this morning to give her some time to sleep. But Stephanie, something else happened."

She smoothed his hair down. "What is it?"

"When Tommy and I were walking back from the restaurant, we saw the front page of the tabloids. There was something really bad," he wiped his face.

Her face took on a look he knew all too well. "Did they say she had AIDS?"

"How did you know?" he asked her, confused.

"Jack, Brittany has been living with the fear of this disease for years and it is unfortunately what people who still live in ignorance and fear think. She has come across people who find out she is HIV positive and automatically figure she has AIDS. As far as we have come as a society in dealing with the AIDS crisis, we still have so far to go," she wiped her tears away. "This is Brittany's worst fear and it breaks my heart that she will have to face this kind of prejudice; especially after she has just revealed so much of herself."

Jack felt his heart break for their friends. He pulled her into his arms and held her. "I'm sorry, Stephanie. I wish I could punch each and every ignorant person."

She laughed. "Punch? Really?"

He shrugged. "It's the least I could do."

"But then your beautiful hands would be bruised and I like those hands to be used for a much more tender purpose," she said.

He smiled. "Such as?"

She wrapped her arms around his neck. "Making me something to eat?"

He laughed and pressed his mouth to hers.

Chapter Sixty-Seven:

Brittany smiled as she looked at her naked leg. The cast was off and she was waiting for the x-rays. The doctor seemed pleased with how everything looked and the surgery seemed to be a success. She wanted to take a shower and relax with Tommy. He headache seemed to be dissipating and she was feeling so much better about everything. She looked up as the doctor came in.

"Everything looks great, Brittany. I want you to go to physical therapy to increase your strength and balance, but I don't see any reason to recast at this time, but you need to wear the walking boot for at least a couple weeks. I want to see you back in four weeks," the doctor said.

"Great, thanks so much," she said and stood up. The doctor went to walk out and turned to her.

"I'm so sorry to hear about what you went through. I hope you have a strong support system in your life," he said and then walked out.

She sat there for a minute. What the hell was going on? She got up and grabbed her coat and purse and walked out into the hall. She continued down the aisle and more stares were evident. She began to feel uneasy and she realized suddenly what had happened. The show aired last night. She couldn't believe she had forgotten that.

She remembered seeing it at the bar and everyone watching. She hugged her coat around her body and walked towards the door, keeping her head down and pulling her hair up into a bun. She wished she had a hat. There was a time she wouldn't have gone anywhere without a hat, or the ability to disguise herself. She had hated that and she didn't want to go back. She walked by the pharmacy on her way to the parking garage and saw a sight that crushed her. She walked in and grabbed the tabloid, her hands shaking. She turned to the story and saw the picture of her huddled on the floor of her house, her leg broken and her face ashen. She felt sick when she read the headline and she looked for a chair to sit down. She dropped the magazine and ran out of the store, finding a bench and sitting down, quickly. She felt her walls go up and her world get considerably smaller. She looked around and knew she needed to get out of there. She made her way up to her office.

Brittany got off of the elevator on the floor of her office and was immediately surrounded by cameras. She stood there, taking a minute to figure out what she should do. She looked up at the faces of the people standing there and smiled before moving through them and the security guard who held them back. She thanked the guard for holding the media near the elevator and she made her way to her office, not saying a word to anyone. She walked into her office and closed the door, walking to the couch and collapsing, finally letting her emotions out.

Tommy made his way to the ortho floor, hoping to catch her before she ran into any trouble. He quickly realized that wasn't going to be possible. There were media personnel all around the main floor of the hospital and he knew why. He also knew she must have seen them. He called her cell phone to see where she was, but it went to voice mail. He texted her instead and looked down as his phone vibrated and he saw she was in her office. He got off the elevator and saw the swarm of reporters at the lobby area. He walked through the mob and made his way down the hall toward her office. He felt his phone again and looked down at the number. He picked it up.

"Hey," Tommy said to Jack.

"Did you talk to her yet? Did she see?"

"The hospital is crawling with reporters. I don't know if she saw the tabloid, but she sure as hell knows it's out. I'm on my way to her office now," he said.

"Stephanie and I are coming in. We want to be there with you guys," Jack said.

Tommy nodded. "Okay, that would be nice."

Tommy knocked on the door to her office and waited a minute. She opened the door and he walked in to find her packing her things into a box. "Red, what are you doing?"

She kept working. "Packing my stuff."

"I can see that, but why?" he asked her.

She kept working and he walked over and took her hands in his. "Stop for a minute and talk to me."

She looked at him, her long hair still in a bun. "Tommy, do you know why I didn't want anyone to know about my HIV before?"

He sat down on the couch. "Because you're a private person and it isn't anyone's business?"

She shook her head. "Maybe that's a part of it, but really, it's more than that. If people didn't know about my HIV, then they wouldn't be watching me, waiting for," she stopped for a minute.

"Waiting for what?" he pushed her.

"Waiting for me to show signs of AIDS," she walked over to the couch and sat down next to him. "If people didn't know about it, then I could live my life without always waiting for something bad to happen. When the public hears HIV, they don't know what that means. It isn't always a means to an end. Now, if I sneeze or cough, people run the other way. If I get a paper cut, it's such a big deal to everyone else. I know one thing has nothing to do with the other and if I get sick, then I get sick, but it was just easier to be somewhat normal. Now that's gone forever."

He sighed. "I am so sorry about this, Red. You don't deserve any of this."

She put her hand on his knee. "Did you see the tabloid this morning?"

His heart broke a little more. "Yes. I think you should sue."

She shrugged. "It doesn't matter. The damage is done. People will believe I have AIDS and there is nothing I can do to change that. That's why it is best for me to leave the practice here."

"But why? I don't understand that. You are the same doctor you were yesterday. It shouldn't matter what other people think," he touched her cheek.

"I wish it were that simple," she stood up. "This isn't just about me. This is a hospital and people come here to get help. They don't need to deal with the added pressure of my celebrity. It isn't the nurse's job to dodge reporters or answer questions about me. It isn't the orderly's job to protect my secrets. It isn't my colleagues jobs to look over their shoulder because someone is watching them, looking for information on me," she wrapped her arms around her waist. "It was stupid of me to think I could live like this forever."

He wished he had something to say to make it better, but he knew she was right about the attention she would attract. He just wasn't ready to help her give in. "Red, can we just go home and get some distance from this and talk a little? We didn't get to talk last night because I acted like a selfish child and you felt the need to leave. I wanted to talk this morning but we didn't get the chance. Can we please talk now?"

She turned and looked at him. "Tommy, you weren't selfish last night. We are dealing with some really unchartered territory here and you have every right to be profoundly affected by learning the date of my attack. I just can't believe it was the same day you lost your parents," she sat down next to him and took his hand in her own. "I am so sorry you had to go through those emotions again yesterday."

He brought her hand up to his mouth and kissed her fingers. "I need to tell you some things, but I want to do it at home. Will you please let me take you home?"

She nodded. "Okay, but I need you to leave without me. I don't want anyone connecting your job to my craziness."

"Are you sure that's it, or do you not want to be seen with me?" he knew it wasn't true, but he hated that she still excluded him in her pain.

She looked at him with an incredulous glare. "How can you even ask me that? How can you even think that? Tommy, you are the only thing in my life that is real and true," she shook her head and grabbed her purse.

He stood up. "I'm sorry, I know that, it's just that you always keep me at a distance, Red, you never let me all the way in."

She turned to him, her eyes blazing. "How much farther do you want to go? Do you want to get so close that the only way they know to get to me is to hurt you? Do you want them to upset your practice so the only good you can do in medicine is from behind a desk? Do you want them to go after Julie or Bill or Jack or Stephanie? It isn't that simple, Tommy, you just can't see it like I can. It's easy for you to get mad at how I react, or blame me for being scared, but you just don't want to see the truth. You don't give me an inch," she turned and ran out, going the back way down the stairs and out into the corridor behind the hospital.

"Fuck," Tommy said as he ran his hand through his hair. He opened the door and saw Jack and Stephanie heading toward the office. He looked at his friends and hoped maybe they could help him get through to her.

Chapter Sixty-Eight:

"So maybe you just need to give her some time and she'll come home," Jack said as he and Tommy waited for Stephanie to join them in the hospital cafeteria. They had all stopped there after exhausting a search for Brittany.

"No, you don't understand, man. She's right. I have impossible standards and I don't give an inch. I never stop to look at things from her point of view and to be honest, I don't know if I can. I have no connection to a life in the spotlight, where random strangers want to know everything about me. I would hate that and yet I push her on every aspect of her privacy," he sighed.

Stephanie walked up to the table and sat down. "Any ideas?"

Jack shook his head. "No, but I suggested that Tommy just go home and wait. I think she will come home after she takes some time to think."

"It's possible she will just come home, but I'm not sure," Stephanie sighed. "Tommy, you need to stop blaming yourself for any of this. Brittany has a lifetime of issues that she is fighting through and you are the best most important part of her future."

Jack smiled at his wife. "What can we do for you?"

Tommy shook his head. "You guys are the best, but I think whatever happens is what's meant to be. You should go home and relax. I'll call you if I need anything."

Stephanie felt sad for them, but knew he was right, they needed to work things out on their own. "Tommy, just remember one thing."

He looked at her. "What's that?"

"She may say it's the celebrity aspect that scares her the most, but it isn't. Brittany can't make her HIV go away. She lives with a fear in her gut that you are going to have to watch her succumb to this disease and the more everyone talks about it and puts it out there, the more in her face that possibility becomes. The press is relentless and they will pick at every piece of her. I am not saying you shouldn't push her on her issues, just understand that below all of it is the fear this disease puts you through. Famous or not, life and death issues are paralyzing. I just think she needs to know that you can handle that," she took Jack's hand. "Not everyone can."

Jack knew she was talking about them and his heart swelled at what she said. He knew how hard living with Multiple Sclerosis was for Stephanie and he was honored she allowed him to share her journey with him.

Tommy nodded, thinking about what she said. He watched them leave and ran his hand through his hair. He wasn't sure what to do. He got up and made his way to his car. He drove home and saw her car was in the driveway. He felt a sense of relief that she was there, but he was afraid she had built her walls so high he wouldn't be able to get in. He walked through the door and saw her sitting on the couch with Tramp. She looked at him as he came in and she put Tramp down who ran to him.

Tommy picked up the pooch and scratched his ears before putting him down and Tramp ran back to Brittany. Tommy walked over and stood opposite her. "You got your cast off."

She smiled. "Yes, it's weak but the bone healed well. I need to start therapy next week."

He nodded. "Good."

"Tommy,"

"Red," the both began and they both laughed.

"Go ahead, please," he said to her.

She played with her hair as she stood up and walked to face him. She felt her eyes fill with tears as she looked at him. "I'm sorry, Tommy. I really am. I don't know what to do that's right. I am so scared of doing the wrong thing," her tears fell down as she spoke to him, his heart breaking at her anguish. "You are the most amazing thing that has ever happened to me and I don't want to ruin that, but just because you want me to be okay with everything and you say the right things, doesn't make it okay. I am so afraid of this, Tommy, and you don't see why. You refuse to look."

He didn't flinch at her words, but challenged her. "Tell me what I don't see."

She looked down. "You only see what you want to see. Tommy, what does our life look like? Do you see yourself as a father? I do, but not with me. I can't give you children. I can't be the woman who you deserve and in truth, I could be your downfall. I just don't know why you want to go through this with me. You could do so much better."

He was angry. He was angry that this was how she saw herself and he was angry with himself for not recognizing it sooner. "Brittany, the man who attacked you is dead, why do you allow him to live?"

She was stunned at his words and the pain she felt was real. She looked at him, unable to say anything.

"Let's be honest. You believed him when he told you that no one would want you. You allow his voice to be the one you hear when you think about love. You look in the mirror and you see his mark on you. You think that because of your HIV you are forever doomed to live a life of solitude. I think that's a load of shit and if I have to tell you every day of my life that I think you're worth it, then I will. I will work every minute to undo the damage that jackass did to your sense of worth and your ability to love yourself. But Red, you have to meet me half way. You have to want to try. I can't be the only one who wants this relationship. If you don't want to be with me, then I'll respect that, but let it be because you don't love me, not because you're scared," he stood there, waiting for her to make a move.

She looked at him and felt all of the air go out of her lungs. She felt faint and she sat down on the floor. He was at her side in an instant and took her face in his hands. "Hey, what is it?" he asked her, berating himself for always pushing her so damn much.

She took a few deep breaths and took his hand in hers. "I just didn't feel well all of a sudden, it's okay, it will pass," she said softly and Tramp ran over to them. She looked up at him. "I just need a minute," she closed her eyes and let her tears escape, concentrating on her breathing and trying to stay centered. She needed to answer him; she needed to be who he deserved.

"Here," Tommy said as he handed her some water. He held her wrist in his hand and checked her pulse. "Your pulse is really slow. What did you eat today?"

She took her hand away from him and looked into his eyes. "Stop, Tommy, please."

He sighed. "I'm sorry. I don't know what to do."

She didn't feel well, but she tried to ignore it. "Listen to me for a minute, please."

He sat down and nodded.

"You're right about a lot of things, but not everything. I don't think of myself as worthless or a loser. I know what my value is and when I think of love, I don't think of my attack, I think of you and how it feels when you hold me and when you love me," she closed her eyes for a minute.

"But then I see the other side of me, the illness, the meds and the constant precautions you have to take to be with me. It isn't fair to you that you can never make love to me without protection, or we can never be spontaneous. My whole life has been about waiting for this disease to push forth and I know it will. We can ignore it, or act like it isn't a real possibility, but it is. My viral load has fluctuated constantly and my meds haven't always worked. The press is onto me now and they will push and push me until they get to you and then," she stopped and wiped her face.

He looked at her. "And then what?"

She shook her head. "Nothing, I'm tired, Tommy, I'm so tired of dealing with HIV. I hate it so much," she began to cry as she spoke with a hatred he hadn't heard before. "I hate that it took everything from me and I hate that it's taking you away from me and I hate that this monster infected me. I just want it to go away, you know? Is that too much to ask? I just want one moment of my life with you to be free of fear and I want us to not have to think about this anymore. I just want to feel good and be healthy," she stood up and walked into the bathroom, closing the door behind her.

Tommy felt like a piece of garbage. He really had no idea of the fight she had with herself on a daily basis. He accepted her HIV as a part of who she was, but he never considered how she had accepted it, or how she dealt with it. He looked at the bathroom door and walked over to it. He was going to knock, but she opened it, looking white as a ghost. "Red, what is it? Please, talk to me," he was scared for her.

She shook her head. "I just need to rest. I'll be fine," she moved to the bed and sat down quickly. She looked at him. "Please let me be alone, Tommy. Please don't make me go through this with you here."

"Go through what? Baby what is it you're going through?" he sat down next to her and pulled her into his arms. He held her as she cried and he smoothed her hair back behind her. He didn't know what was happening, but he felt his own heart breaking at her sorrow. He held her tightly, trying to make her feel safe, trying to push away her fear. He felt her sit back after a minute and held her face in his hands, wiping her tears with his thumbs. "Can you look at me and talk to me, please?"

"I had to change my meds again this morning after the doctor and after drinking too much last night, I am having trouble getting my body adjusted. I don't mean to scare you and I'm sorry. I really just need to sleep. Please, I just need a minute to sit still."

He nodded and stood up and went into the other room. He called Jack and Stephanie to come over. He paced through the house while he waited for them and thought he was going to go out of his mind with worry. Why did she have to adjust her meds again? He didn't know what was happening, but he needed his family to help him. He stood at the door to the bedroom and watched her sleeping. He heard the door and went to open it. Stephanie looked at him and nodded, heading towards the bedroom. Jack went into the family room with Tommy.

Stephanie walked into the bedroom and felt her tears come to her eyes. She had been there, feeling so badly and not being able to explain to anyone why. This disease made everything worse and Brittany was fighting the demons of the virus and her heart. Stephanie walked over to her, taking her friends hand in her own. Brittany opened her sapphire eyes and focused on Stephanie. She gave her a small smile and nodded her approval for the company and Stephanie sat down on the bed next to her. Brittany looked at her. "I feel selfish about it, but I'm glad you're here."

Stephanie smoothed her friend's hair down. "I'm glad, too. Did you take the Retrovir? The side effects can be hard after you drink a lot of alcohol and if you don't eat, you know that. You should have your blood count checked; you are probably anemic. Are you sure you don't want to go to the hospital?"

"No, I've been through this before, it will pass. I just need to get through it, but I messed everything up, Stephanie. I think I might have lost Tommy and I don't think I can survive that," she cried and Stephanie smiled softly.

"I don't think that's possible, sweetie. Tommy loves you so much, but you have to let him in. It isn't fair to keep him on the outside of your HIV. He can't help you if you don't tell him what's going on," she continued to rub Brittany's back while her friend lay on her side. "I used to think that if I let Jack see my struggle with MS, he would somehow think less of me or not be able to handle the daily struggles."

"How come you let him in?"

"I had to. I couldn't live without him," Stephanie smiled. "Love is bigger than your disease, Brit. Love is about both of you being 100% open with each other about everything. If he is the man you and I both think he is, he will rise to the challenge. He might even surprise you. You have been fighting this disease alone for so long, don't you think it would be nice to have someone to fight with you?"

She sighed. "Yes, but I feel like it's unfair. Tommy is amazing and has so much to offer the world, what can I offer him?" she hated feeling so powerless. "I just don't want him to be my caretaker. I don't feel like my health will ever be in control."

Stephanie nodded, "I understand that, but you need to look at it in a different way. Tommy sees you as his partner. He wants you to be with him through the struggles and the triumphs. But Brittany, I think you forget that for Tommy, long term is not a guarantee."

Brittany looked at her. "What do you mean?"

Stephanie smiled. "He lost his whole life in a split second. His parents were taken from him in an instant and he had to live with all of the regrets and the loss he felt. When he sees your illness, he doesn't see what might happen in the future, he is living in the now because he knows that nothing is guaranteed. You have to understand that you are a part of him and by shutting him out, in order to protect him, you are hurting him," she stood up and sighed. "I get it. I really and truly do, but you need to hear this. Get out of your own way and let yourself be loved. You will find it will make you a better person in every way," she hugged her friend and walked out.

Chapter Sixty-Nine:

Brittany got up and went into the bathroom. She looked at herself in the mirror and splashed some water on her face. She heard what Stephanie said and she knew her friend was right. She was wise beyond her years and she spoke from a place of love and of respect. Brittany knew it would take all of her courage to give Tommy all of her fear, but she felt, for the first time, like she truly wanted to.

Tommy walked Jack and Stephanie out and went back into the bedroom. He saw her sitting up in bed and he smiled at her. He went to walk and stepped on something that screeched. "Shit," he said and saw Tramp look up at him with a guilty apologetic face. "Are you okay?" he picked up the little pooch who proceeded to lick him all over. Tommy put him on the bed and watched him walk. "Did I break him?"

Brittany laughed at him and shook her head. "I think he'll live," she smiled as the little dog frolicked onto Tommy's pillow and chewed on his shirt. "He seems no worse for wear."

Tommy sighed and sat down. "What did Stephanie have to say?" he kept an eye on Tramp.

She looked at him. "Girl talk," she sat up and took his hand in hers. "I owe you an explanation."

He braced himself for whatever she might say.

"You are right. I don't let you in all the way. I make assumptions about what you can handle and I discount my worth in your eyes. I let my past dictate my future and I don't want to do that anymore. But Tommy, you need to understand that sometimes, I might need help letting you in. The things I have to deal with at times can be ugly and scary and it's okay if you don't want to deal with it. I struggle with my health every day. The meds I take are hard to manage and I hate how they make me feel, but I need them to live a healthy life. I wake up and I'm tied to a schedule. I go to sleep the same way. It's frustrating and irritating and sometimes I get so mad that I take it out in ways I shouldn't. I need to work on that. But there is one thing that is really important for you to know," she touched his cheek.

"You said that if I didn't want to be with you let it be because I didn't love you, not because I'm scared," she smiled and leaned in to him. "I want to be with you and I love you more than I could have ever thought I was capable of loving anyone. You have me, all of me, and I am so profoundly grateful for that," she leaned in and brushed her lips on his. He wrapped her in his arms and moved on the bed only to hear another squeal.

"Dammit," he swore and they both laughed as Tramp jumped on them.

"I need to ask you something before we go any further," he said seriously.

"Okay," she looked at him, not knowing what was coming.

"What is it?" Brittany asked him as they sat on the bed. She looked into his green eyes and tried to figure out what was on his mind.

Tommy stood up off the bed and walked to the window before turning around and looking at her. "You said something earlier that struck something with me and I need to know why you feel that way."

She stood up and walked over to him. "Okay, what is it?"

"Do you want to have children?" he asked gently.

She sighed and looked down. "It doesn't really matter what I want, Tommy. There are some things that are out of my control."

"You didn't answer my question. Do you want to have children?" he asked her, taking her cheek in his hand and tilting her face up to look at him.

She met his gaze and felt her eyes fill with tears. "I can't want children, Tommy."

He wasn't sure he heard her right. "What do you mean? How is that an answer?"

She moved his hand from her face and turned to walk back to the bed. She sat down and sighed. "You are so amazing, Tommy. You are funny and smart and handsome and amazing. You deserve a family with a ton of kids," she wiped her tears away as she spoke. She smiled at him. "You should coach little league and go to daddy daughter dances and chaperone parties and heal their wounds and make memories to last a lifetime. It's just not in the cards for me."

He walked over to her and held her hands in his. "You still didn't answer my question. It's a simple yes or no."

"It's anything but simple."

"Not true. You are looking at it from your head and I am asking you to show me what you feel in your heart. It's not that difficult."

"Why do you do this to me, Tommy? Why do you push and push until I am so exposed that I can't hide even if I wanted to?" she wiped her face.

He knelt in front of her and put his hands on her thighs. "Because you have been hiding for so long. You don't need to hide and you don't need to be scared that what you say will make me want you any less. I heard you before and you said that you see me as a father, but not with you. I want to know why you feel that way. Brittany, you have so much love in you to give to others. You hold yourself back out of a self-imposed punishment and it needs to stop. You deserve to be happy."

"When you say it like that, I almost believe it," she said softly.

He smiled. "It's the truth."

She nodded. "I hear you, but I think I just need to figure out where to go from here. I can't help but feel selfish about wanting things I know I shouldn't."

He shook his head. "Do you think Stephanie and Jack are selfish?"

Her eyes opened wide. "Oh God no, they are going to be the absolute best parents. I have no doubt in my mind about that. But Tommy, I am not Stephanie. I am not healthy enough and I am not stable enough to care for myself, let alone another human being. Maybe one day I will be, but I don't see it right now. And the chance of passing my HIV to a baby is real."

"So I will take that as a yes, you want children," he smiled at her. "All things being equal, if you felt healthy enough, you see yourself with kids?"

She looked at him. "Yes, but"

Her stopped her. "No buts, therapy is over for today."

She smiled at him. "Why does it have to be over? I think I need some more intense therapy."

He raised his eyebrows. "What did you have in mind?"

I haven't been able to take a real shower in a long time because of my cast, and now that it's off, I would love to stand under the water for a while," she stared at him. "Would you care to join me?"

He grinned. "In a strictly therapeutic manner?"

She shrugged. "If that's what you want, but I was hoping we could be a little less professional."

He couldn't stand it any longer. He leaned into her and pulled her to him, his mouth finding hers and her lips meeting his. He got up and pulled her up to meet him and walked into the bathroom, turning the shower on and turning to face her. He gently unbuttoned her shirt and moved the fabric off her shoulders before pulling his shirt off. He pulled her into his arms and she wrapped her arms around him, relishing the security of his body. She rested her head on his chest and closed her eyes, feeling a sense of comfort that only he could ever bring to her. She looked up into his face and pulled his mouth onto hers. They kissed each other and he ran his hands under the fabric of her bra and removed the material. She reached down and unbuttoned his pants, reaching her hands under the waistband of his briefs and pushing them down a little. He pushed his hips into her and she ran her hand over his lower back.

Brittany removed the rest of her clothes and stepped into the shower. She turned and looked at him as the water cascaded over her. She watched as he pulled off the rest of his clothes and stepped into the shower with her. The water flowed over her face and her hair and Tommy stood behind her, massaging her shoulders and lathering her hair with shampoo. She leaned back into him and he wrapped his arms around her, his hands running over her body, gliding with hers. She turned in his arms and raised her hands to his shoulders and up to his face, pulling him to her, feeling his erection pressing against her waist. He stepped back and looked at her, smiling at her and moving slowly to make sure all of the shampoo was rinsed off of her. She moved and ran her hands up and down his body, lathering and rinsing him completely. She turned and shut the water off.

Tommy grabbed a towel and wrapped it around her. He rubbed her arms to warm her and he looked into her face. "Are you okay? Do you need me to stop?"

She nodded. "I'm good, I just need to sit down for a minute," she smiled. "But I'm not about to stop our therapy."

He smiled and wrapped a towel around his waist.
"Come on," he said and stepped out of the shower,
picking her up in his arms. He carried her into the
bedroom and placed her down on the bed. She
shivered and he pulled the towel more over her body.
He moved and stepped over a sleeping Tramp before
grabbing some lotion he had in the basket from the
Poconos. He came back to the bed and she smiled at
him, needing him with her.

"How about a warming massage?" he looked at the
bottle in his hand. "It's supposed to warm as you
massage it in."

She raised her eyebrows. "Let's try it?"

He opened the towel she wore and squeezed some of
the lotion onto his hands. He rubbed them together and
then placed them on her chest, massaging up to her
shoulders and down her breasts. They both felt the
warmth of the liquid and Brittany closed her eyes.

"Are you okay?" he asked her, concerned for her.

She pulled him onto her. "I need you Tommy," she felt
her eyes grow wet with unshed tears. "I just need you."

He leaned in and pressed his weight on her, letting the
lotion react between both of their bodies. She ran her
hands up and down his back as he moved his mouth
over her lips. He sat back and grabbed his protection,
putting it on and turning to look at her. She reached up
and pulled him to her, wrapping her arms and for the
first time, linking her legs with his as he entered her.
He buried his head in her neck and she ran her hands

up through his hair as he began to thrust in and out of her, slowly at first and then faster. He put his hand under her lower back to help support her as they moved together. She gently pushed him over onto his back and straddled his waist as he placed his hands on her hips. She moved her body back and forth and placed her hands on his chest for support. She leaned down onto him and lowered her mouth on his. He wrapped her in his arms as they both rode the wave to orgasm. She stayed on him for a moment after they were finished and she felt her heart slow to normal. She moved off of him and lay there, exhausted.

Tommy cleaned up and joined her on the bed. She immediately curled up into his side and he put his arm around her. He ran his hand through her wet hair as she rested her head on his chest. "I love you," he said.

"I love you too, so much," she added. "I still can't believe you're really here with me."

He looked at her. "I know what you mean. But I think, right now, we need to start believing in our love and our future."

She smiled. "Okay, I think you're right."

"I always am," he said.

She rolled her eyes and went to respond when his phone rang. He sighed and looked at the number. He dialed the hospital and spoke to the nurse. He hung up and sat up.

"What is it?" she asked him.

"It's Courtney. She was brought in with a spiking temperature and her blood work shows elevated white cells," he ran his hand through his hair as he got up.

"Do you think the cancer is back?" she asked him, knowing it probably was.

"Probably, but I'll know more when I get there," he looked at her. "Are you okay staying here alone?"

She smiled. "Of course. Call me when you know something."

He nodded and kissed her before leaving.

Chapter Seventy:

Brittany was asleep when her phone rang an hour later. She blinked and answered, not recognizing the number.

"Brittany? It's Julie, is my brother around? He didn't answer his phone," she said, obviously upset.

"He was called into an emergency, sweetie. What's wrong?" she asked, concerned at her tone.

"I just need some help. Bill and I had a fight and I left, but my car broke down and it's raining out and I don't know what to do," she was sobbing.

"It's okay, I'll come get you. Tell me where you are," Brittany was already getting dressed.

"There's more." Julie said, her voice breaking. "My water just broke."

****

Brittany was writing a note to Tommy when she heard the doorbell. She went to answer it and saw Stephanie standing there. "Hey, what's going on?"

Stephanie shook off the rain from her umbrella. "When did it start to storm so badly?" she asked. "Jack got called in for an emergency and he said that Tommy was called in, too, so I figured I would hang out with you and see how things went after we left."

Brittany smiled. "Well, you can stay here, but I have to go and get to Julie, she is in trouble and I was on my way to get her."

Stephanie was concerned. "What happened?" she looked at Brittany. "You can let me come with you or after you leave I will follow you."

The women smiled at each other. They went to the car and Brittany shivered at the cold air and driving rain and took a minute to catch her breath. She had trouble breathing when the air was thick since her lung injury. She put her medical bag in the back seat and got into the car while Stephanie got into the passenger seat.

"She and Bill had a fight and she left. She said her car broke down and her water broke. She was really upset and wanted Tommy, but he is in an emergency so I will get her."

"Why didn't she call 911? Do you know where she is?" Stephanie asked as she called Jack's cell phone to leave him a message about where she was.

"She didn't seem to need an ambulance. She just wanted a ride so I am hoping she is waiting in her car for me. I didn't know we were supposed to get this big of a storm," Brittany turned her windshield wipers on higher. "She told me roughly where she is, so I am hoping we can find her. I called her back, but her phone went to voice mail."

"She must be so scared. I wonder what the fight was about? Bill seems like a great guy," Stephanie said, worried for Julie.

"I agree and I am hoping it was just end of pregnancy stress and nothing serious," she looked around. "I should have let you drive, you're much more familiar with this area than I am."

Stephanie looked at the streets. "We are close to where she should be, just over that bridge and there is the wooded area she should be near."

Brittany nodded and turned over the bridge. They drove down the deserted street and looked for Julie. They found her car on the side of the road and both women let out a sigh of relief. They drove up closer and Brittany pulled over. She looked at Stephanie. "Stay here while I go get her."

Stephanie nodded. "Okay."

Brittany looked at her. "I'm serious. You are almost eight months pregnant and your health is my main concern."

Stephanie nodded. "I know. I won't move."

The women exchanged glances and Brittany was sufficiently sure her friend wouldn't leave. She got out of the car and was almost immediately drenched by the rain. She went to Julie's car and looked inside, but she didn't see her. Shit, she thought, where would she have gone? She walked to the other side of the car and yelled for her, listening as best she could. She saw her out of the corner of her eye, sitting under a tree nearby. Brittany ran to her.

"Hey, sweetie? Come on, let's get you in my car," Brittany said as she touched Julie's face. The woman was soaking wet and shivering.

"I am afraid to move. The pain is really bad. I locked my keys in the car with my phone and so I was just waiting." Julie said through her tears and chattering teeth.

Brittany helped her to stand up and supported a lot of her weight while she helped her to the car. She opened the back door and Julie sat down and stretched her legs across the seat. Stephanie turned to help her. "Hey Julie; here, take this," she handed her a towel to dry off.

Brittany ran to the front of the car and got in, ignoring the coldness and the soaking clothes she was wearing. "Okay, we need to get you to the hospital," she began to drive. "Can you tell us what happened?" she asked, hoping to keep her mind off of what was happening and to help her relax a little.

Julie wiped herself off as best she could and closed her eyes. "Bill is going to leave," she cried.

Stephanie looked at Julie as Brittany continued to drive. "What do you mean?"

"Bill was called to report for duty." Julie said sadly. "He is going to leave and I don't know when he will come back. He was gone to Iraq a whole year last time."

Brittany felt terrible for her. "Okay, but right now you need him with you and we need to deliver a healthy baby for you both. When does he need to leave?"

"In three days. I can't do this alone. I need him," she cried. "Oh God," she yelled as another contraction came.

"Just try to breathe, you're going to be fine," Brittany tried to drive down the road, but the rain was coming down in buckets. She looked at Stephanie who nodded.

"I think we should pull over and wait for the weather to clear up. There is a campground on 4th and I know there are cabins there. I bet we can find a place to take shelter while we wait," Stephanie said.

She pointed Brittany in the direction she should go and they were almost there when there was a crack of lightning and a tree fell right in front of the car. Brittany swerved and avoided the damage, but the road was totally blocked. She turned to her passengers and smiled. "Sit tight and let me see how close we are to the cabin."

Stephanie held Julie's hand and nodded. Brittany got out and gasped as the wind and rain hit her face. She ran down the street and saw the cabin close by. She went back to the car and sat down, struggling for a minute to catch her breath.

"Okay, I think I can drive closer. We are going to be fine, just hang in there," she backed up and drove onto the grass and over the rocks to get them closer. She tried to go slowly so Julie wouldn't be jostled around more than necessary, but she needed to get there. They got close to the cabin and she turned the car off. She turned one more time to them. "Let me get the door open before you come in."

She ran to the cabin and was relieved to find the door open. She went in and saw there was a fire place and a bed. She went back to the car and grabbed the bag she brought and took it back inside before going out one more time to get Julie out of the car. She and Stephanie helped her walk into the cabin and sit down on the bed. Stephanie started a fire and lit some candles. Brittany helped Julie take off her wet clothes and she covered her with the blanket she brought before grabbing her gloves and checking the progress.

Julie was panting and in a lot of pain. "Please, I can't lose my baby," she cried.

"I am the best there is, sweetie, no one is going to lose anything here tonight," Brittany said with confidence. "I do, however, think we are almost ready to deliver a baby," she smiled at her. "You are almost fully dilated."

Stephanie sat by Julie's head and smoothed her hair from her face. "Just think of the stories you will be able to tell about the night of the birth."

Julie cried. "I was so horrible to Bill. He loves me so much and he is so excited for this baby. I am honored that he serves this country and I made him feel so badly. I am such a horrible person."

Stephanie smiled as she rubbed Julie's arm. "I highly doubt that. Bill knows you are scared and that you love him. I am sure he is going out of his mind with worry and as soon as this storm dies down, you will be together with your baby. You can't worry about anything else right now. You are not alone and you will never be. You have Tommy and Brittany and Jack and me. We are all family and we will see to it that you are okay."

Julie looked at her. "I wish my mom was here," she said softly.

Stephanie wiped her tears away. "I know, honey, but I think she is, we just can't see her. She is holding your hand with me."

Brittany came back to them after getting some materials ready. She was frozen to the bone and her chest hurt, but needed to keep it together. She could feel the effects of her meds still bothering her, but she simply couldn't be concerned. She handed Stephanie a bottle of water to drink and she gave Julie some ice chips to chew. "I know it's not much, but I was only able to grab a few things. I didn't know we would be stranded, but this will do," she put her hair up into a ponytail and grabbed more gloves. "Okay, let's see where we are."

Chapter Seventy-One:

Jack and Tommy walked into the locker room after a crazy night of emergencies and procedures. This storm had come out of nowhere and after he saw Courtney, he was pulled into the ER. Tommy was exhausted and just wanted to go home and crash.

Jack looked at his friend. "How are things with Brittany? Stephanie was concerned about her."

Tommy ran his hand through his hair. "She is better now. We talked and things seem a bit clearer. I just hate the way these meds mess with her, it isn't fair."

Jack nodded. "I know, but we need to be grateful for the meds and the hope they give us," he knew what Tommy meant, but he was eternally grateful for Stephanie being healthy.

There was a commotion at the door and Jack and Tommy looked up to see Bill coming in to the locker room. Tommy stood up, immediately concerned. "Bill, what is it? What's wrong?"

"Julie is missing and so are Brittany and Stephanie," he said and Jack and Tommy both looked at each other.

"What do you mean, missing?" Tommy asked him as Jack called Stephanie on his cell phone.

"No answer," Jack said and felt his heart beat faster. "What happened?"

Bill sat down and exhaled. "I was called back to active duty and Julie freaked out. I knew she would and I don't want to leave her like this, but I have a duty to my country and I need to serve," he spoke like it broke his heart to leave. "Anyway, she got really mad and asked me to give her some space, so I did, but when I came back, she was gone and the roads around our house are terrible. I went to your house to see if she was there and Stephanie's car was in the driveway but no one was home. None of them are answering their cell phones and the roads near our house are blocked off because of falling trees," he looked at the two terror stricken men's faces.

"There's more. Julie has been having contractions all day and I'm afraid she may have gone into labor."

Jack realized there was a message on his phone and he listened to it before hanging up and checking the time. "Stephanie left a message that she was going with Brittany to pick Julie up because Julie was in labor. She said she would see us here soon. That was over an hour ago," he grabbed his coat.

"What are you doing?" Tommy asked.

"If they are out there, they need us. I'm going to find my wife," Jack said.

Tommy nodded. "We'll all go. Come on."

******
"Okay, so tell us some stories about Tommy and Jack when you were growing up," Stephanie said to Julie as Brittany listened to the baby's heartbeat. They both had been trying to keep Julie calm while she progressed through labor, but all three of them knew they needed to get her to a hospital.

"They were they best, but so annoying to always have around." Julie said in a soft voice. "It was like having the most overprotective parents ever. When Tommy wouldn't let me do something, Jack would back him up and it was impossible to get away with anything. No matter what I did, they were on to me."

Stephanie smiled. "I can imagine how hard that must have been."

"And all of my friends were in love with one or the other of them. It was ridiculous," she said and smiled, but then screamed. "Oh God, I have to push," she cried.

Brittany nodded. "Okay, you need to bear down and push when I tell you to. Try to hold the push for 10 seconds," she looked at Stephanie. "You ready?"

Stephanie nodded. "You can do this Julie. You can do it."

"I want Bill to be here. I need him," she cried.

"I know, sweetie, but you need to be a mom first. Your baby needs you to do what you can to help," Brittany said.

"Okay, Oh God," she screamed.

"Now, deep breath and push," Brittany said and Julie pushed while Stephanie helped hold her up. "There you go, you're doing it, keep pushing Julie almost there," Brittany said as she tried to move her hand around the baby's head, afraid the cord was around the baby's neck. "You need to push again."

"No, can't, too tired." Julie said and closed her eyes. Stephanie looked at Brittany who shook her head.

"Julie, look at me right now," she demanded.

Julie opened her eyes. "I need Bill."

Stephanie took the other woman's face in her hands and spoke to her. "You don't need anyone but your strength and your power which is massive. You have survived so much in your young life Julie; you can do this. I need you to do this and Brittany needs you to do this, but most of all, your little baby needs you to be strong. Now I know you can do this. Let's push this baby out right now."

Julie looked at her through her tears. "It hurts so much."

"I know, but it will be over soon and the pain will turn into a miracle," Brittany said and held Julie's legs back while she tried to help her with the next contraction. "Here we go, push," she pressed on Julie's stomach while she pushed and the head finally came out. She grabbed her suction bulb and suctioned out the baby's nose and mouth and kept the cord from restricting the baby's breathing. She looked up at Stephanie and Julie and smiled. "One more push," she nodded. "Now, push," she heard Julie scream as Brittany delivered the baby.

Julie and Stephanie waited and heard nothing.

"What is it? What's wrong?" Julie cried.

Brittany was working on the infant, rubbing it down and removing the umbilical cord, which was indeed around the baby's neck. Stephanie saw but Brittany shook her head almost imperceptibly, telling Stephanie to keep this from Julie. "Brittany is working, don't worry," Stephanie said.

Brittany was working feverishly on the baby and all she could think of was Tommy. She couldn't let anything happen to his family. She tried one more tactic when suddenly the wail of the infant pierced the air.

Julie cried and Stephanie joined her. Brittany held up the baby and smiled. "Here is your son," she placed the boy on Julie's chest and covered them with a blanket. Julie held her son and the women all laughed and cried. Brittany saw Julie looking pale, so she motioned to Stephanie to take the baby. "Julie, talk to me, tell me what you feel."

"I'm just really tired. I don't feel well," she closed her eyes and Brittany looked down to help with the rest of the birthing process and was alarmed by the amount of blood loss.

"Stephanie, we need to get her out of here. She is losing too much blood," Brittany said as she began to do what she could to help.

Stephanie held the baby to her and looked at Brittany and Julie. They needed help fast.

****

"Where the fuck are they?" Tommy asked as the men drove toward Bill's house.

"We're going to find them, Tommy, don't worry," Jack said.

Bill was on the phone with his contacts from the military, hoping for some kind of assistance. He hung up and shook his head. "They are swamped but will let me know if they find anything."

"This is ridiculous. We have to find them," Jack said. He had tried to remain calm, but the more they drove in the horrible weather, the more fearful he became. Stephanie was a month from delivering and she had already experienced early labor. He didn't want to think about what might happen if she went into full labor out here.

Tommy knew they needed to find them. He thought about his sister, scared and hurting. He knew how much she wanted this baby and if anything happened to either of them, he didn't know what he would do. And then Brittany, God, she had been through so much and now this, he knew she would do anything she could to ensure both Julie and Stephanie's safety, but at what cost? He felt the enormity of the situation come over him and he stopped the car.

"What is it?" Bill asked him.

"We need a plan. This is pointless, just driving in this horrible storm with no way to know where they are. We can't just waste time," Tommy yelled.

The three men looked at each other, all lost in thought over their loves.

******

"Okay, so I think we are okay for the moment," Brittany said. She had stopped the bleeding she could see and there didn't appear to be anything more serious going on. Julie was likely out of it because of sheer exhaustion, but the fact that she had been out in the rain for a while before they got to her could mean she was dealing with some other complications. Luckily for all of them, Julie was by far the healthiest. Brittany looked at Stephanie who cradled the infant in her arms and lovingly protected him. She smiled at the scene and knew how amazing of a mother her friend would be. She walked over to her. "Are you okay?"

Stephanie looked up at her friend with tears in her eyes. "He is so perfect and beautiful. He needs his mom."

Brittany smoothed Stephanie's hair with her hand and smiled. "Julie will be fine. We just need to get her out of here and to the hospital. I think I am going to try and go to the car and see if I can get my Onstar to work. I forgot about that and although our cells aren't working, they should be able to trace the satellite from the car. I will try and call Tommy from the car as well. You need to stay right here and protect the baby and sit with Julie. I wrapped her up enough that she should be stable barring any other complications, but it's important you don't go near the door. The baby needs to stay warm and dry."

Stephanie didn't want her to go. "Brittany, you need to stay here. It is still coming down in sheets out there and you are not in good health. Please stay here."

Brittany sighed. "Stephanie, this is Tommy's family. His sister and his nephew are everything to him. I have to make sure they are safe," she wiped her face. "I need to do this."

Stephanie nodded and watched her walk out. "You're so wrong, you are Tommy's family," she said and wiped her tears away.

Brittany ignored the driving rain and the cold and ran to the car. She slipped a few times but got up and made it to the car. She got in and closed the door, pushing the blue button on the rearview mirror. She breathed a sigh of relief when it rang and she was able to hear a voice on the other end. She wiped her tears as she relayed all she could about where they were and the conditions they were in. The person on the other end said they would call the paramedics, but the weather was a problem for them to get through. They would make sure it was a top priority. Brittany asked if they could call Tommy and patch him through to the phone. She waited and shivered while the phone rang.

"Hello?" Tommy's deep voice rang through her car.

"Tommy? It's me. I am so glad you can hear me," Brittany cried.

"Red, where are you guys? Is everyone okay? We have been worried sick," Tommy motioned to the men that she was on the phone.

"We are stranded in a cabin at the campgrounds on 4th. Julie and Stephanie and the baby are safe inside and I came to the car to call you." She coughed and tried to catch her breath.

Tommy felt his heart race at her words. "What do you mean the baby?"

Brittany smiled. "Julie had her baby. Is Bill there? Put him on the phone."

Tommy handed Bill the phone. "Brittany? Tell me what happened."

Brittany smiled. "You have a gorgeous son, Bill. He is beautiful and healthy."

"I have a boy? I have a son?" he said and felt the biggest smile come across his face. Tommy and Jack patted him on the back. "How is Julie? Is she okay?"

"She is hanging in there, but she needs you. She had a rough time of things, but she was a trooper. You have an amazing wife," Brittany said. "She wanted you to know she was sorry about yelling at you. All she wanted was for you to be here with her for the birth. She loves you so much."

Bill tried to keep his emotions in check. "Tell her I love her more. We are going to get to you guys, please try not to worry. I will get people there, I promise."

"We know that. And Bill, Congratulations," Brittany said.

"Thanks. For saving them both." Bill said and handed the phone back to Tommy.

Jack grabbed the phone. "Brittany? It's Jack. How is Stephanie?"

"She is fine, Jack. I tried to convince her not to come with me, but she is rather stubborn. I was afraid she would follow me on her own," she smiled.

"You're right. She would have. But she is okay?" he repeated.

"She is fine. She has been caring for the baby and sitting with Julie. No labor pains or problems at all. She is fine," Brittany said and coughed.

"Are you okay? That doesn't sound good," Jack was concerned and Tommy grabbed the phone.

"What is it? What aren't you telling me?" Tommy asked her.

"Nothing, baby, I am fine. Just get here, okay?" she said and coughed, trying to hold it in. Jack motioned for him to switch places so he could drive while Tommy talked.

"You need to go back inside and keep warm until we can get there. Do you hear me?" he yelled into the phone.

"Tommy, I think I figured something out," she said, smiling to herself.

"What's that," he asked, tears filling his eyes as he heard her voice becoming weaker.

"I think this was my purpose. I think I was supposed to help your family and I did it, Tommy. Despite everything, I did it," she said and coughed again.

His heart broke at her small voice. "Yes, you did it, but that's not all you need to do, Red," he punched the car and Jack touched his arm.

"Let's just get there. She'll be okay," he said to him. "Let's just get there."

"Britt, can you get back into the cabin?" he asked her.

"I'll try," she said. "I love you."

"If you don't think you can, then stay there. I don't want you stuck in the rain," he said. "We will be there soon."

"Okay. Don't worry," she said.

"I love you, too," he said and looked as the call ended. He looked out the window, his heart torn in a million pieces.

Chapter Seventy-Two:

Brittany got out of the car and fell back with the wind. She stood up and made her way back to the cabin. She opened the door and stepped in, seeing Stephanie and Julie still safe and sound. Stephanie stood up to come to her but Brittany held up her hand. "No, stay there. I have a cough and I don't want to get near any of you anymore unless I have to."

Julie opened her eyes and looked at them. "Hey, what happened?" she asked. "How is my baby?"

Stephanie turned and handed her the bundle and smiled as Julie kissed him. She touched his face and Stephanie turned to look at Brittany.
"I talked to the men and they are on the way. The paramedics are also on their way. You just need to hang on a little while longer," she coughed into her arm.

"Brittany, come by the fire and get warm," Stephanie said, knowing her friend was in trouble.

"No, I need to go to the car and grab my meds. I have some things that will help me with my breathing, but I left them there. I just wanted to make sure you were all okay," she moved so Julie could see her. "Sweetie, Bill loves you and wanted you to know how much. He can't wait to see you," she smiled and turned to Stephanie. "And Jack was so worried about you, too. You both have precious cargo and need to stay safe. No matter what, you stay safe."

Stephanie wiped her tears away. "Please don't go out there again."

Brittany coughed hard and held her chest. "I have to get my breathing treatment. I'll be back," she looked at them one more time and walked out.

******

Jack drove as quickly as he could through the driving rain and tried to get Tommy to talk to him. Bill was on the phone with his military base, trying to get them to help, but Jack could see something was very wrong with Tommy's demeanor.

"She was saying goodbye to me," Tommy said as he looked out the window. His expression was reminiscent of when Jack drove Tommy to tell Julie that they had lost their parents. Jack couldn't let him go back there again.

"What do you mean? She didn't sound that bad to me. She is probably tired, dealing with two pregnant women and a delivery in the middle of all of this weather. I am sure she was just exhausted," Jack tried to sound convincing, but even he knew that Brittany had sounded like she wasn't getting enough air.

"She said goodbye because she thinks her work here is over. She saved my family and she said that was her purpose. She has had problems with her lungs since the collapsed lung repair. With stress, she might have another collapse and there is no one to help her," he slammed his hand on the dashboard.

"You need to calm down and hold it together. We all need you, man, but none more so than Brittany," Jack said.

Tommy didn't say anything; he just kept looking out the window.

****

Stephanie held the infant while Julie slept. She was beyond worried about Brittany, but she would do as she asked, and stay put. She knew it was the right thing to do, but she would never forgive herself if something happened to Brittany. Stephanie sighed. She should have been back by now. She smiled as Julie looked at her. "How are you feeling?" she asked the new mother.

"Tired and sore, but better than before." Julie looked around. "Where is Brittany?"

"She went to the car to get some meds for her breathing. I think she is having some trouble with her lungs," Stephanie said. "She should be right back," she didn't want Julie to get upset.

"Okay, but I wish she would have stayed here," she said and took the baby from Stephanie for a moment. She looked at her. "He is so beautiful, isn't he?"

Stephanie smoothed Julie's hair and smiled at them. "He is absolutely beautiful. Bill is going to be beside himself when he meets his son. You are both so lucky."

Julie nodded. "Soon this will be you. Are you ready?"

Stephanie laughed. "I plan on being in a hospital with lots of drugs, and then I'll be ready." Both women laughed when they heard a commotion outside. Stephanie stood up as the door opened and a man in uniform came in.

"Hi, I'm Lieutenant Draper. We got a call from Corporal Kastan that his wife and her friends were stuck here. Is that you?"

"I'm Julie Kastan, Bill is my husband. This is Dr. Stephanie Stephens. We are very happy to see you," Julie said softly.

"We have a medical ambulance ready for you, the paramedics are pulling up as we speak," the officer said.

Stephanie felt tears of relief fall down her face. "Our friend is out there. She went to the car but she should have been back by now. She may be in distress."

"We will find her," the man radioed to someone to look for Brittany.

There was more commotion and Jack and Bill ran in. Jack grabbed Stephanie and hugged her before inspecting her for any injuries. "I'm fine, really. I have been sitting here the whole time," she touched his face as he kissed her and put his hand on her stomach. "I'm okay, babe."

Bill walked to the bed and looked at Julie and the bundle she held. He knelt down next to the bed and touched her face. "Hi."

Julie let her tears fall down her face. "Hi. Do you want to hold your son?" she touched Bill's cheek. "He's perfect."

The soldier nodded, at a loss for words. He took his son from Julie and held him, staring at the perfect tiny face, which was sleeping peacefully. He looked at his son and then back at his wife.

"Thank you," he said to her.

She smiled at him. "I love you."

He sat down next to her and held her to him with their baby. "I love you both."

Tommy walked into the cabin and took in the scene before him. He saw his sister and her husband and he saw Jack and his wife, but he didn't see her. His heart was gone and he didn't know what to do. He forgot how to breathe for a minute and turned white. Jack went to him. "Hey, look at me."

"Where is she?" he asked in a voice that was unlike his usual one.

Jack turned to look at Stephanie. "She went to get her meds a while ago. I told the Lieutenant and they are looking for her. She should have been back by now," Stephanie let her tears fall. "I'm so sorry Tommy; I shouldn't have let her go."

Tommy nodded, unable to do anything else. He ran outside to help look. Jack went to follow but Stephanie called to him. "No, please stay with me, Jack. I'm scared and I can't sit here alone anymore. Please stay with me," she cried.

He took her face in his hands. "It's okay, you're okay and we are all going to be okay. Shh," he pulled her to him and held her. "Stephanie, I just need to make sure they get to her. I need to be sure he makes it," he said, his eyes filling with tears.

She nodded and closed her eyes, her tears spilling over. "I know; you're right. Go and help him," Jack kissed her and turned to run after Tommy.

Jack saw him standing there, talking to the Soldiers and then he saw Tommy collapse, the soldier trying to help him.

Oh God, Jack thought to himself as he ran to him.

Chapter Seventy-Three:

Stephanie took the baby while Bill helped the paramedics get Julie secured on the gurney. She was worried about Brittany, but was trying to stay strong for everyone. She looked up as Jack walked in, his face ashen. She almost collapsed, but she held the baby and sat down on the chair. She couldn't bear it. He came over to her and knelt in front of her.

"Please don't say it, Jack. I can't," she began to cry.

He touched her leg and shook his head. "They can't find her. They looked everywhere, but there is a lake near the car and they are afraid she may have fallen in," he wiped his eyes.

"Oh God. Where is Tommy? He needs to be with us," she sobbed and Jack took the baby from her.

"He is in the ambulance. He collapsed when they told him and they are making him sit there while I came in to talk to you. I wanted you to know what happened, but I need to go back out to him," he wiped her tears away. "We aren't giving up yet."

She took the baby back and nodded. "Okay. Please tell him we love him."

He kissed her and nodded at Bill who heard what he said. They all agreed silently not to tell Julie yet. Bill took his son and Stephanie put her head in her hands.

Jack made his way to the ambulance and was pleased to see the rain had let up. He stepped into the back where Tommy was sitting, the paramedic by his side.

Jack looked at the medic and motioned for him to give them privacy. When the man left Jack moved and sat across from Tommy.

"Hey, look at me. Don't do this, Tommy."

Tommy didn't move. He didn't speak and he didn't respond to Jack. He simply sat there.

"You're freaking me out. You need to snap put of this and think logically. Brittany might have gone somewhere to get warm and she might have passed out. There is no reason to think she fell in that lake. You need to pull yourself together and think," he yelled at him.

"The Army couldn't find her, what the hell makes you think I can?" Tommy looked at him.

"Because you love her and it's what you need to do," he sighed when Tommy looked at him. "Look, I don't know where she is, if she is okay or not, but there is something I do know. You have always been the strongest person I know, man. You have survived so much and I know that it isn't meant to end with a tragedy like this. You can't give up. You can't shut down and you can't quit on us. Julie needs you and Brittany would want you to be there for everyone."

Tommy stood up and looked at Jack. "I need you to let me deal with this my way. Go be with your wife and tell Julie I love her. I need some time, please respect that. I'll meet you at the hospital later," he walked out of the ambulance and into the wooded area.

Jack shook his head. "No, Tommy, I can't do that," he stood up and watched as they loaded Julie and the baby into the ambulance. Bill went with them and they left. Stephanie came out next and Jack walked to meet her. He went with her into another ambulance and they sat down.

"How is he?" she asked him.

"I am giving him a little time alone, but after you and Julie are settled, I will go back to him. He needs to come to terms with this, whatever it is," he said. "I don't know what to do to help him, but I need to be with you right now," he kissed her hand.

"It's okay, Jack. If you want to go with him, I'll be okay," she said.

He shook his head. "No, I'll give him some time. He needs that," he held her in his arms as he signaled to the paramedic to take them.

Tommy watched both ambulances leave and stood there, looking at the vast landscape in front of him. He didn't know what to do. He sat down on the wet ground and looked up at the clearing sky, the stars beginning to show brightly. He spoke into the air.

"Mom and Dad, it's Tommy. I know I haven't spoken to you in a long time, ever, actually, since you died, I guess because I didn't know how to explain what was going on in my head. I have spent a lot of years angry with you. I realize that isn't productive or even rational, but I felt like you left me with so much pain and way too much responsibility. But I did everything you wanted me to do and I have to believe you would be proud of me."

"The thing is, I need your help. I haven't asked for anything or felt pity for my situation, but I am in trouble. I need Brittany. I need her to be okay and to be in my arms. I don't want to be greedy, but I feel like maybe you owe me. I need something extraordinary to happen to me and I need it to be now. Please, I'm begging you," he put his head in his hands and sobbed.

After a few minutes he stood up and collected himself. He didn't know what he expected; it wasn't like his parents were just going to talk to him and suddenly Brittany would walk in, but he was at a loss as to what to do.

****

"Excuse me, I am in the middle of a meeting," the doctor said. She stood up and looked at the family sitting there. "I'm sorry, I will be right back," she walked to Tommy and led him out to the hall. "What is your problem? Are you an idiot? Can't you see I am in the middle of something?" she hissed at him.

"I'm sorry, but why do you need an entire conference room to talk to a pregnant woman and a guy? You could accomplish the same thing in your office, you know, the things each of us have here?" he said in a sarcastic tone.

"Who the hell are you? It is none of your business why I am in here and you are completely out of line. I have half a mind to call the chief of staff and report you for harassment," she yelled at him.

******

It had seemed like a lifetime ago when he had first spoken to her. He had barged into her life and she stood up to him and didn't take any of his crap. He challenged her at every turn and she demanded complete honesty and sincerity in everything they did. He loved her completely and he just knew that without her, he would be destroyed. He remembered another poignant moment.

Brittany sat in silence and wiped the tears, which had fallen down her cheeks. She stood up from her desk and walked over to him. She knelt in front of him and took his hands in hers. "You have nothing to be sorry about. You are right to feel the way you do and I am sorry I gave you the wrong impression about how you need to react. In case you haven't noticed, I am not the best at expressing my feelings. I think it has been a long few days for you and I think you are on overload," she stood up and he felt her break their connection. "Look, I am not the one to get involved with. You have so much to offer, Tommy, you need to leave me and go live your life. I am not your problem to fix and I don't need to be rescued. I am happy with my life," she lied.

Tommy stood up and nodded. "Okay. I get it," he turned and walked to the door. "But I don't think you're happy, and neither am I," he said and left the office, leaving her alone again.

How wrong they both were. He turned to head back to his car, dejected and alone.

******

Julie sat in her hospital bed with Bill and their baby. She looked at her husband and wiped her tears away.

"Where is my brother?" she asked softly. "I am not dumb. I know something is wrong. Please, just tell me where he is and where is Brittany?"

Bill sighed. "Jules, we need to focus on what we can do right now, and that is be the best parents to our boy. I don't want you to get upset about anything. I need you to be healthy and strong for our son, especially if I have to leave soon," he took her hand in his. "Tommy will be here later."

She looked at him and let her tears fall. "What happened? Please, Billy, tell me the truth."

He could never handle it when she called him that. He looked at her and smoothed her hair behind her ears. "Brittany is missing. Tommy stayed behind to help look for her. He will be here later."

She listened to him and let it register. "Is he all alone? Did anyone stay with him?" she asked in an alarmed voice.

"He wanted to be alone for a bit. I will go back and get him soon," Jack said from the doorway. He and Stephanie walked into the room. "Jules, you know your brother, and if he needs some time alone, it's best to give him that."

She closed her eyes, knowing he was right. There was no one closer to either Tommy or Julie than Jack and she knew he would never do anything to put either of them in danger. "This is all my fault. How will he ever forgive me?" she sobbed.

Stephanie walked over to the bed and touched her hand. "This is not your fault, sweetie. It is just a terrible accident."

Julie shook her head. "If I didn't call Brittany, she would never have come to get me and she would be fine. I took everything from Tommy, his freedom, his fun, his happiness and now I took his love," she sobbed and Bill held her. Jack took the baby in his arms.

Bill's phone rang and he looked at it. Julie motioned for him to take it and Stephanie sat with her. He walked into the other part of the room and answered, hoping it would be information they could hold on to. Jack handed Julie her son and he and Stephanie sat with her.

"Jules, I have known you your whole life. I know how much Tommy loves you and he would be absolutely destroyed if he knew you were feeling one ounce of guilt over any of this," Jack looked at the baby. "Look at your son and know that whatever happens, he needs you and you need to be there for him, all the way. Tommy helped to bring you through one of the toughest things anyone could ever go through, and we will do the same for him, if we need to."

Stephanie wiped her own tears away as she listened to Jack speak. Her heart was breaking for all of them, but she was most worried about Brittany. She didn't know what happened to her. They all looked up as Bill came back over.

Julie could tell by his expression that it was bad. "Don't sugar coat it. Tell us what they said."

"That was my Sergeant. They got permission to drag the lake tomorrow morning," he ran his hand over his face.

"Oh God, oh my God," Stephanie said, her face white.

"Hey, you need to calm down, baby. I can't deal with you getting sick. Please, try to breathe and stay calm," Jack put his hand on her forehead and made her look at him.

"She can't be gone. I can't take it, Jack. She has lived through so much pain in her life and she finally found such a profound love with Tommy. It isn't fair. She can't be gone," Stephanie sobbed and Jack held her to him.

Julie looked at her husband and Jack. "You both need to go to Tommy. I don't care what he said or what he does. He needs his family and he needs to feel support. Please go to him."

Stephanie nodded. "She's right. I'll stay here with Julie and the baby. Go and get him, please," she wiped her face with her sleeve.

Bill nodded and Jack agreed. "Okay, we'll be back."

They walked out, leaving the women to pray for a miracle.

****

Tommy had been wandering back towards his car for a while, hoping against hope that something might happen. He knew it wasn't to be, but he still tried. He looked up as he saw Jack's car pull up. He turned away, sighing. He just wanted to be alone.

"Tommy, you need to come to the hospital," Jack said as they walked to him.

Bill walked up with Jack. "Your sister needs to see you. She is really worried," he hoped that might make a difference.

Tommy looked at them. "Julie has you, Bill. She will be fine. I am waiting for the police to come back. They need to keep looking."

Jack looked at him. "Did the Soldiers talk to you?"

Tommy stared at him. "What are you talking about?"

Bill walked over. "They are going to drag the lake in the morning."

Tommy looked at him and then at Jack. He turned around and ran to the bushes, emptying the contents of his stomach. Jack gave him a minute and walked up to him. "Tommy, please."

"Get away from me, Jack. I mean it, leave me alone," Tommy said in a voice that was full of anguish. "You can't fix this for me."

Jack stood there, unmoving. "So what, you can sit out here and die? You're just going to let this be the end for you? You can't do that, man, I won't let you."

Tommy walked up to him, challenging him. "Why not? Do you honestly think you can stop me?" he shoved Jack.

"Will it make you feel better to hit me? Go ahead, but it won't bring her back. Do you want to blame someone? Blame me, but it won't bring her back," he stood up to his brother, his friend, and challenged him.

Tommy turned around and walked away, but Jack grabbed him. "Where are you going?"

"To find her. Last time everyone gave up and I was able to find her. If I didn't look for her, she would have died. She is waiting for me and she knows I will find her. I can't let her down," he said.

Jack sighed. "Then I will go with you."

"Me too." Bill said.

Tommy looked at them and shook his head. "I can't live without her. I have to find her."

"Okay, man, it's going to be okay," Jack said.

Tommy broke down and put his head in his hands. Jack grabbed him and held him while he sobbed.

Chapter Seventy-Four:

She looked at him, anger flashing in her eyes. "All of my lingerie is gone. That fucker took my underwear. Who does that? When it is enough?" she screamed.

Tommy felt sick. He walked over to her. "Come on, we need to leave. There is no reason for you to go through this," he tried to take her hand but she was on a roll.

"What will it take for him to stop?" What can I do so he will leave me alone? Should I make myself look ugly to him?" she walked over and grabbed a scissors from the desk. She took a handful of her hair and went to cut it off. Tommy jumped and grabbed her hand.

"Stop it," he said. "That's enough."

She looked at him and burst into tears. "I have to do something, Tommy. I just let him win every time. He will never stop until I'm dead. I can't do this anymore. This was my home, my sanctuary," she looked at him. "I painted each room, you know. I decorated and I felt safe here. I was the real me when I was here. Nothing touched me from before. Nothing got inside and now, it's all corrupted. I feel like I will never be free."

He shook his head. "I am going to say something that is very cliché right now, but I think it's true," he took a deep breath. "When my parents died, I was afraid to put anything away. I kept their things exactly as they were for the longest time because I felt like if I packed their things or removed their toothbrushes and personal items, then I was losing them from my life. I was erasing them from what they had built and I was dishonoring them. I didn't want to make it like they had never existed, but I also couldn't come home and look at their things and know they were never going to use anything again. I look at this house as something similar. You can't look at this place without seeing all of the sadness, but that is something that can be fixed. This home is what it is because you made it that way. It is because of you that it was a safe place. It isn't this house; it's what you made of it. You can do that again. If it isn't here, it will be in a new house, but it will be just as safe and just as 'you'. We can fix this. You can win, Red. I learned that and I will help you learn that, too."

She looked around the room and then at him. "I think I have a lot to learn from you," she took his hand. "Thank you."

Tommy shook his head to clear the memory. He looked over at Jack who was talking with Bill. It had been a few minutes since his meltdown and Tommy had pulled himself together. He walked over to them and Bill nodded to him. "Hey, I just got a call from some of my Army buddies who are going to meet us on the south side of the park. If there is anything we missed, they will help us. They're the best in the business."

Jack smiled and Tommy nodded. "Thanks," he said sincerely.

About a half hour later, the men were all split up and searching the grounds one more time. Bill's friends were thorough to the point of exhaustion and Tommy was grateful. It was becoming apparent, however, that they were not finding anything. Jack was afraid that Tommy was going to collapse any minute from sheer emotional and physical exhaustion, but he also knew that he would stay with him as long as it took him to accept the truth, whatever that may be. He walked up to Tommy when they all heard yelling coming from across the park. The men took off running and soon found what happened.

There was a Soldier standing over a large tree, which had fallen on the ground. Tommy and Jack ran up to him with Bill close behind. The Soldier was tending to something and Tommy jumped over the tree and felt his heart in his throat. There, on the ground, pinned under a massive tree branch was Brittany. She looked dead and for a minute, Tommy thought he was as well. He fell to the ground next to her and touched her face, checking for a pulse. He couldn't feel anything and he yelled for Jack to help him. The two men tried to feel for a heartbeat and finally Jack thought he felt a faint pulse. Tommy looked at her and couldn't see the rest of her body because the tree covered her. He looked at Jack and the Soldier. "What are we going to do? We have to get her out of here," he cried.

Jake, the soldier, nodded and was on the phone with someone, coordinating some form of help. Tommy smoothed her wet hair away from her face and leaned in close to her. "Red, I'm here, just hold on, please," he spoke to her, not knowing if she could hear him. He looked at Jack who was on his cell phone with Stephanie telling her what was happening. Tommy reached down and tried to feel for her hand. He grasped her fingers and moved her arm up to his chest. He sat down facing her and held her free arm to him. He didn't know what the damage was to her body. He couldn't tell if her bones were crushed beneath the weight of the tree or if her lungs were working. He looked at the paramedics who ran up to the scene and he yelled for them to give him the materials to start an IV.

Jack watched the scene and knew it was probably a lost cause, but who was he or anyone else to say that. If there was a will, there was a way and he had to help them. He handed Tommy some gloves and he put some on as well. He saw Tommy's hands were shaking so he put his hand on his shoulder. "Let me, just talk to her," Jack said and Tommy nodded. He stepped back and moved to the other side of her face. Jack worked fast and got the IV placed securely in her arm. He hooked a bag up and moved to assess the rest of her injuries. He was able to move some of the branches and could see the tree did not impede her legs. It appeared the trunk was lying right on her torso. He wondered how long she had been lying there, suffering. He looked at her and Tommy and saw himself and Stephanie. He shook his head and tried to shake the image out of it.

Tommy just sat there, touching her face and talking to her. He turned to Jack. "We have to get the fucking tree off of her. What are they waiting for?"

"You know they can't just move it without running the risk of doing much more damage to her. There is no way to tell the extent of damage she has to her body and if the tree is pressing on anything and we release that pressure, she could bleed out quickly," Jack said.

He knew that, but Tommy also knew she didn't have the time to wait. He looked up as the soldiers with the tree cutting equipment came over. One of them knelt down next to Tommy. "We are going to cut the tree next to her body on each side and hopefully that will enable us to lift the main section off of her with the least amount of stress to her body. You should move aside while we cut."

Tommy shook his head. "I'm not going anywhere."

The Soldier nodded. "I hear you. If she were my girl, I wouldn't do anything differently. I have always loved her music," he smiled at Tommy.

Tommy looked back. "I have always loved her."

The men went to work cutting the tree slowly and surely. Tommy covered her face with his body as the tree was shredded. Finally, the work was done and Jack monitored her vitals while they moved the last chunk of tree off of her. The paramedics covered her quickly with a blanket and loaded her onto the stretcher. Tommy looked at Jack and he shooed him in with her. "We will meet you there."

Tommy sat with her in the ambulance, not knowing at all how injured she was. They didn't want to move anything until she was in the E.R. where they could adequately address her needs. He just held her hand and put his hand against her cheek while they rode to the hospital.

****

Jack found Stephanie waiting for him when he arrived with Bill. Julie was waiting for Bill so he went to her and Stephanie jumped into Jack's arms, as much as she could jump being so pregnant. She touched his face and smoothed his shirt, inspecting him for any damage. "You are not to leave my side again," she said through her tears.

He leaned in and kissed her softly. "No problem there," he said and buried his head in her neck. She held him and felt her relief flood over her. After a minute they sat down and she took his hand.

"Do you think she has a chance?" she asked him.

Jack looked at her, unable to lie to that face. "I don't know. Stephanie, it's bad."

She nodded. "Okay, then we will help her in any way we can. Do they know what happened?"

He shook his head. "No, I would guess she collapsed and the wind brought the tree down on her. With any luck, she didn't know what was happening. I can't imagine what it would have been like if she was lying there, knowing what was happening, and being unable to move or call for help," he put his head in his hands.

"Shh, it's okay. She is here now and Tommy is with her. Whatever happened, it doesn't matter. We just need to hope it is something she can get through," she held him to her and prayed for their friends.

Chapter Seventy-Five:

Tommy stood in the room while the doctors worked on her. She was intubated and on a ventilator while they cut her clothes off and assessed the damage. He looked at each and every person in the room, making sure she was safe from any gawkers. He waited by her while they worked, knowing how much she hated when strangers looked at her body. He needed to protect her any way he could. He watched all of the universal precaution marks on the room and he fought the urge to rip everything down. He hated that her HIV was always the first thing people had to consider. He knew they were doing everything they needed to do, but it broke his heart. One of the doctors called for help when they went to remove her shirt because it was covered with blood and he needed assistance.

"I'll do it," Tommy said, walking over to help.

"Dr. Williams, I don't think you should be here," the doctor said.

"I'll do it," he said and ignored the statement. He pulled the fabric off of her body, feeling his tears fall as he saw the bruising on her torso and the deep gash across her chest. Her abdomen was distended and he motioned for them to call the surgeon. He knew she had internal bleeding and needed surgery now.

"We are waiting for the results of the x-rays and we will take her. Please let us work," the doctor said. "We will do everything we can."

Tommy nodded and stepped back. He continued to watch the scene in front of him as if he were in a fog.

He couldn't think clearly, he couldn't comprehend the image before him. It was just a few hours before that he was making love to her and talking about their future and the possibilities that lay before them. How did this happen? How could this happen?

They finished prepping her for surgery and the doctors walked out to get ready. She was lying there, covered and waiting to be taken in and Tommy walked over to her. He leaned in and kissed her on the forehead. He smoothed her still damp hair and traced a line down her cheek. "I love you and you are not allowed to give up on me. I mean it, Red, you are not allowed to leave. I have more left for you to do here. You have a life to live with me and you can't bail on that. I don't know what to say to make you want to fight. I am just going to be selfish and ask you to do it for me. I can't live without you. I can't breathe when you're not near me. I have lost so much in my life and I have survived because I was making my way to you. You showed me that I could want more and now that I do, you need to be there with me. I love you, completely. Please fight for us," he leaned in and kissed her cheek, letting his tears fall on her face. He took her face in his strong hands and held her. "This is not the end, baby. I am with you all the way," he moved while they wheeled her out. He sat down on the chair and closed his eyes.

"Tommy, hey, what's happening?" Jack walked into the room with Stephanie. They saw the mess all around and knew she had been taken to surgery.

"What's the extent of her injuries?" Stephanie asked.

He shrugged. "I don't know. Her torso was crushed under the weight of the tree. Her abdomen was distended, so there is bleeding somewhere. I don't know if her lungs are working or if her chest can be repaired. I don't know what they can do. I don't know how she will survive."

Stephanie walked over to him. "How did you survive when your parents died, Tommy?"

He looked at her. "What do you mean? I had to, for Julie."

"But how did you do it? Did you just turn around and say 'oh well' and live your life?" she pressed.

He shook his head. "Of course not."

"Right; it was hard and painful and at times agonizing, but you did it because that's what you had to do. Brittany is no different. Her scars might be more physical, but they are just as moveable as yours were. She can do this, don't underestimate her," Stephanie said softly.

"I won't, but how much can one person go through before they simply stop fighting?" he asked.

Jack walked over to them. "You'd be surprised. How about if we go see Julie while we wait? She needs to see you for herself."

Tommy looked at him, like he forgot she was even there. He nodded. "Okay, but I don't want to go far. Let me tell them where I will be."

****

Bill came out of the room when he saw Jack approaching. He stood with Jack and Stephanie while Tommy went in to see his sister. He nodded to Bill as he walked past him. Julie was sitting in the bed holding the baby when she looked up and saw Tommy. She began to cry as he came to the bed.

"Oh Tommy, I'm so sorry. This is all my fault," she cried.

Tommy hated it when she cried. "Jules, stop crying, you know I hate that," he sat down next to her. "Can you introduce me to my nephew?" he smiled at her.

She wiped her face. "Tommy, this is David. Just like daddy," she handed the baby to him and he let his own tears fall.

"Mom and dad would be so proud of you, Jules. Look what you did?" he held the little boy in his arms, his dad's namesake, and felt a sense of peace. The little boy grasped his finger in his tiny fist and Tommy almost lost it. He looked at his sister who was watching her son. "I am so proud of you. You are going to be the best mom. I wish they could be here to see him."

She nodded. "Me too," she whispered. "But Tommy, I need to know that you're going to be okay. I can't stand it if you're sad or hurting," she began to cry.

He looked at David and then at her and smiled. "Jules, do you remember the nights after mom and dad died and you had trouble sleeping?"

She nodded. "I was afraid to sleep because I was afraid when I woke up you would be gone, too."

Tommy put his hand on her leg. "And do you remember what I told you?"

She blinked and her tears fell down her cheeks. "You told me that no matter what, you would always take care of me. You said that even if I wasn't with you, I could always call you, and you would come."

"And have I ever let you down?" he smiled.

She shook her head. "Not ever," she said softly. "But Tommy, I'm not a little girl anymore. I just don't want you to think that I don't need you anymore. I don't think I would make it if anything happened to you. You're my family and I love you."

He handed David back to her and leaned in and kissed her forehead. "Nothing is going to happen to me, baby girl," he used to call her that and she hated it, but now, it was endearing.

"How is she, really?" Julie asked.

He wiped his eyes. "Not good, but we are going to do everything we can to help her. She is in surgery."

Julie touched his hand. "She saved my life and little David. He wasn't breathing and she saved him and she saved me when I lost consciousness. I owe her everything, Tommy."

He nodded, unable to speak for a moment. "We both do."

Chapter Seventy-Six:

Tommy walked back into the hall and saw Jack and Stephanie there. Bill walked back into the room with Julie. "I'm going to go back and wait by the O.R."

Stephanie nodded. "You should eat something."

"Tramp!" Tommy yelled. "Oh no, he has been alone all this time. He needs to eat and go out. He doesn't like to be without Brittany."

Jack looked at Stephanie. "We can go and let him out. We'll spend some time with him and then come back."

Tommy gave them his house key. "Thank you," he told them where his food was and what he needed. He turned back to the O.R. after they left. He sat down and waited for word.

Jack and Stephanie walked into Tommy's house and closed the door, turning the lights on behind them. Stephanie called out to Tramp who was nowhere to be seen. Jack walked to the family room and looked for him, but saw nothing. Stephanie walked to the bedroom and smiled. Jack walked up behind her and she leaned her head on him. Tramp was curled up in a ball on Brittany's pillow, snoring deeply. Jack put his arm around Stephanie as they watched for a minute until Tramp finally must have sensed someone was there because he sat up and yipped.

Stephanie walked into the room and smiled. "Hi Tramp," she said as the little dog stretched and went to walk to her but fell off the bed. "Oh," Stephanie grinned as the little dog shook it off and bounded to Stephanie.

He began to tinkle in his excitement. "Jack, take him out, quick before he makes a puddle."

He scooped the little dog up and put his leash on before walking outside. Stephanie grabbed some paper towels and wiped up the small mess. She finished cleaning up and walked into the kitchen, pulling Tramps food out and preparing his meal. She filled his bowl and turned to put it down when she saw the note on the table, which Brittany had left for Tommy. Stephanie touched the paper and felt her tears fall as she realized how quickly everything had changed for all of them. Tonight should have been so happy. The birth of a child was such a blessing and now, Brittany and Tommy were fighting for just one more moment together. Jack walked in and Tramp ran to Stephanie before moving to his bowl of food.

"What's wrong?" he asked her as he saw her fresh tears. He walked over to her and touched her face.

"It's just not fair, Jack. Tommy and Brittany deserve so much more than this. It's just so sad," she shrugged and he pulled her to him.

"Let's go sit down in the other room," he said and led her to the couch. She sat down and he sat next to her. "Look, this is terrible, there is no way around it, but we can't change what happened, we can only take what we are given and do the best we can with it. I truly believe this will work out like it should, you need to think that way, too."

Tramp ran into the room and Jack picked him up. The little dog licked him all over and Stephanie couldn't help but smile. He was such a little cutie. He walked over to Stephanie and curled up next to her, not quite able to get onto her lap. She ran a hand over him as he rolled onto his back, wanting his belly scratched. "It's hard to be positive when everything is so bad. It just breaks my heart to watch the people I love go through so much."

He nodded. "I know, but all we can do is be there for them and help them by doing whatever we can to make things easier."

She was quiet for a minute. "You were there when they found Brittany, how bad was it? I need to know the details."

He sighed. "Why? What is the point of going over that? You can't do anything to change what happened, baby, and the more you focus on the bad parts, the harder it is to see the good."

She smiled. "I appreciate what you mean, Jack, but I have always been someone who looks at things with an analytical eye. I like to know what I am up against and then I can figure out what I have to do to get through the problems. I know that there is more to it than that, but I need to know the details so I can approach this the right way," she wiped her eyes. "I need to try and fix it, please?"

His heart broke for her and for the helpless feelings they all had. "Her torso was crushed under the tree. Her arms and legs appeared to be free, so it is likely contained in her chest and abdomen. We couldn't see anything specific because they didn't remove any part of her clothes out in the field. We wrapped her up and took her, so I don't know the details. She had a pulse, but it was weak. Tommy was afraid her lung had collapsed again, but I don't know if that was true or not. She was taken into surgery because of internal bleeding, but other than that, none of us knows until they look at everything," he sighed.

Stephanie nodded. "Thank you. I think we should go back to the hospital and wait with Tommy."

He looked at her. "Maybe you should stay here? I don't want you to have any problems, Stephanie. You are eight months pregnant and your health is also a concern. This has been an intensely stressful evening and I worry about you."

She put her hand on her stomach. "I know, and I am okay, really. I will not do anything to risk our child or my health. I just want to be with my family and help them the best I can. I promise you, I will take it easy."

He nodded, "Okay."

****

Tommy was going out of his mind with worry. It had been a long time since they had taken her into surgery and he hadn't heard anything. He knew that it might mean nothing, but it might mean everything. He made his way to the O.R. to find out for himself what was happening. He went into the prep area and put on his surgical scrubs. He decided to scrub in and see what he could do. He was washing his hands when a few nurses came out. Tommy looked at them as he scrubbed. "What's happening?"

One of the nurses looked at him. "Dr. Williams, I didn't know you were scrubbing in."

"I am and I would like to know what is happening," he finished scrubbing his hands and turned to look at them.

The two nurses looked at each other and Tommy shook his head. "Never mind, I'll found out myself," he pushed into the O.R. and one of the nurses helped him with his gloves. He walked behind the surgeons and stood there, looking at her vitals. "What's going on?"

"Dr. Williams, you need to leave," the surgeon said.

"I am not going anywhere. Tell me what is going on?" he said.

The alarms began going off and the doctors all worked furiously. "We need to close her up and wait to finish. She isn't going to tolerate any more right now."

Tommy felt his heartbeat increase. He watched them work on her, and then the dreaded flat line. He moved closer and watched them work. "Dammit, come on," he yelled.

"Dr. Williams, get the hell out of my way or I will have you thrown out. This is the third time we've lost her and I will be damned if you get in my way," the doctor yelled and continued to work on her. "Paddles," he yelled. The nurse charged them and handed them to him. "Clear," they shocked her heart and Tommy felt like he was going to faint.

He turned and left the O.R. and pulled off his gear before running into the bathroom. He got sick again and sat there, trying to catch his breath. He felt his tears fall and he held his head in his hands, trying to hold it together. He stood up and walked out, afraid to hear what happened.

Jack walked into the locker room and saw him. "Hey, I was looking for you. I heard what happened in the O.R. Are you okay?"

Tommy sat down and exhaled. "No, I'm not. Is she dead? Just tell me, please, I need to know."

Jack shook his head. "No, she is alive and being moved into a room," he sat down next to him as his friend covered his face again. "Look, I know you're scared, but you can do this."

Tommy looked at him. "Did they tell you what they had to do in there?" he was ashamed to have left before he even knew what had happened to her.

Jack sighed. "They removed her spleen and part of her liver. They repaired her lung, which was damaged again and she has numerous cracked ribs. They repaired the internal bleeding, but she will need some work on her heart, the left ventricle was damaged, but we will need to wait until she is more stable."

Tommy looked at him. "You'll do that?"

Jack nodded. "Of course."

Tommy nodded, happy to hear that. He looked at him. "What is it you aren't telling me?"

"There may be a problem with her larynx. There was damage and until she regains consciousness, there is no way to know the extent of the damage," he said. "It isn't clear if her voice will be affected, but it's likely."

Tommy stood up. "She won't sing again," he turned to look at Jack. "It's too much. I just need to go be with her."

Jack nodded. "Come on."

Chapter Seventy-Seven:

Tommy walked into the room when she was finally
settled. She was wrapped tightly in bandages and her
neck was also wrapped. She had a sheet loosely over
her and her arms were about the only thing
unobstructed. He moved to the side of the bed and sat
down, finally alone with her and finally breaking down.
He cried as he held her hand in his. He had to be
strong for everyone, but here, with her, he could let his
guard down and be the person who was inside, scared
to death that everything he ever hoped for was about to
be taken away. He didn't hold back, he simple cried
like his heart was breaking, which it was.

He looked at Brittany and kept his hand on her
shoulder. He wanted her to feel that he was there. He
wanted her to know she wasn't alone. He needed her
to wake up and he hoped it would be soon. He kissed
her hand, which he held in his other hand and put it
against his cheek.

*He walked to the closet door and pulled out her guitar,
fully restored to its previous form. He brought it to the
bed and placed it down in front of her. "I just wanted
something to be able to be fixed," he sat down facing
her, the guitar between them.*

*She looked at the guitar and ran her hands over the
beautiful wood. She grasped it and picked it up, looking
at it from all sides. She put it down and looked at him,
tears in her eyes. "I don't know what to say."*

*He smiled and raised his eyebrows. "Is that good or
bad?" he wasn't sure.*

He remembered the moment she opened up to him about her music and then when she sang to him, the beauty of her voice was amazing, but more importantly, it was a piece of her that she had lost, which he had helped her to get back. If it were gone now, forever, it would just be the ultimate act of cruelty, and validation in her mind that nothing good ever lasts. He smoothed her hair away from her face and she moved slightly at his touch. He leaned in closer to her.

"Hey, Red, can you open your eyes and look at me? You're safe and I'm here," he spoke to her and rubbed her cheek. She began to flicker her eyes and he smiled. "That's right, try a little harder and you're almost there. Come back to me and let me see those blue eyes."

Brittany opened her eyes and focused on Tommy. He was looking at her, holding her hand. She could see that, she could see him, but something felt wrong. She felt heavy, like there was something on her. She remembered the tree and she began to panic for a minute. Her eyes opened wide and her tears fell.

"Hey, you're okay, look at me," he could see she was scared of something. He touched her face and held her chin, looking into her eyes. "It's me, Tommy, you are safe," he spoke firmly and she seemed to hear him. She began to calm down a little, an effect he always had on her, since their first meeting. He wiped his own face as he looked at her. "I love you, so much," he couldn't stop his tears from falling.

She tried to move, but her arms felt like lead. She looked at him and tried to speak, but she just squeaked.

He smiled. "Don't talk, you are still recovering and are on a lot of meds. Let me talk for you," he smiled as he took her hand and held it to his cheek. "I love you, Tommy, and I will not leave you," he looked at her and she closed her eyes and nodded a tiny nod. She squeezed his hand softly. "Good, and how about this. I will spend my life worshiping Tommy and reminding him that he is the most handsome and sexy man I have ever met," he smiled as she rolled her eyes at him. "Too much?" he asked. She smiled a little and closed her eyes, asleep again. He leaned closer to her face. "I will spend the rest of my life worshiping you, my love. You're going to be okay," he lay his head down next to hers and kept his hand on her.

She would not feel alone again.

****

Jack walked into the room and smiled at Tommy and Brittany. His friend was out, exhausted and snoring a little. Brittany was still asleep, her hand in Tommy's. Jack touched his friend on his shoulder and Tommy sat up.

"Hey, it's just me," Jack said and sat down.

Tommy ran his hand through his hair and sighed. He looked at Brittany and then back at Jack.

"You look like shit. Why don't you go home and eat something and take a nap?" Jack said to him.

Tommy nodded. "I don't want her to be alone. I'm fine."

Jack crossed his arms. "I have been instructed by the ladies to get you to go home and if you think I am going to head back to Julie's room and face my wife and your sister and tell them I failed, you are crazy. I will stay here with Brittany until you come back. Your dog needs you, too. He pished in the house. I thought you would have raised him better," Jack grinned at him.

Tommy looked at Brittany again. "She woke up for a minute."

Jack looked at her. "That's great. Was she able to communicate with you?"

He shook his head. "She squeaked when she tried to talk. I told her it was because of the trauma and the meds. She freaked out a little, but I think it was just the gravity of everything. She didn't say anything, just listened to me. I think she was able to follow what I said, but she was out of it in about a minute."

"You know that's a good sign," he walked over to the machines next to the bed and looked at the readings. "She appears to be stable, Tommy, please, for all of us, but especially her, go home for a few hours. With the meds she is on, it is unlikely she will wake up again, and if she does, I'll be here and Stephanie will be here. She will be okay with that."

Tommy stood up and leaned in and kissed her softly. He walked over to Jack and hugged him. "Thank you. You'll call me?"

"If she blinks, I'll call you," he hugged his friend and Tommy walked out. Jack sat down next to the bed and looked at Brittany. He prayed she would pull through, for all of their sakes.

****

Tommy walked into his house and Tramp came bounding up to him, yipping in his excitement. Tommy sat down on the floor and the pup jumped onto him, licking him all over. Tommy let his tears fall and smiled at the pup. He sighed as he got up and grabbed the leash, taking Tramp out for a minute. After he got back inside, he walked into the bedroom and sat down on the bed. He lay down and held her pillow to him and cried until he felt something against his face. He opened his eyes and saw a small ball resting against his face and Tramps wet nose pushing it against him. Tommy smiled and threw the ball and Tramp bounded after it. After doing that a few times, both boys fell asleep, exhaustion of a different kind taking over each of them.

******

Jack and Stephanie sat with Brittany and Jack had his hand on Stephanie's stomach. She had her feet up on the recliner chair in the room and was eating a sandwich. He smiled at her.

"What? I have to eat."

"I didn't say anything, I'm just glad you are okay. I am glad you're eating and I'm glad you're with me," he said.

She fed him a piece of the sandwich and he took a drink of his water before giving it to her. She finished and looked at Brittany, who hadn't made a move since Tommy left.

"I wish she would wake up."

Jack looked at Brittany as well. "I think she is waiting for Tommy. They both needed their sleep."

"What did they say about her voice?" Stephanie asked.

He shrugged, "It's unclear until she wakes up. It is also dependent upon her lung damage. She needs both to sustain any singing," he sighed. "None of it's relevant if she doesn't recover."

Stephanie shook her head. "I know."

They both looked up as Tommy walked back into the room, looking somewhat refreshed. Stephanie smiled at him and he walked over to hug her.

"How are you feeling?" he asked her.

"I'm good, stop worrying about me," she smiled and stood up with Jack.

Tommy looked at Brittany and Jack walked over to him. "No change, but no worse. She hasn't opened her eyes again. Are you sure you are ready to be back?"

Tommy smiled. "I'm good. Take your wife home and have a good nights sleep."

"You'll call if you need anything?" Stephanie asked.

"Of course," he said and watched them leave. He sat down next to the bed and leaned in to kiss her. He sat back down and saw her open her eyes and look at him. "Hi beautiful," he smiled at her.

She reached her hand up to his face and touched his cheek. He leaned in closer to her and held her hand in his own. "I love you," he said softly.

She closed her eyes and swallowed before she looked at him. "I love you," she whispered, her voice barely audible.

"Jack and Stephanie just left, they were here while I went home for a little bit," he said as he looked at her.

"Tramp," she whispered.

"He is all set, don't worry," Tommy smoothed her hair around her face.

"Julie and baby?" she whispered.

"Beautiful and amazing. His name is David and he is perfect," Tommy said.

She let a tear fall. "Like your dad."

He nodded and wiped his own eyes. "Just like my dad," he moved closer to the bed as she looked like she was trying to say something more. "What is it?"

She took a deep breath and winced at the pain. "You're my life and I will not leave you. Don't ever doubt that," she smiled and he leaned in to kiss her softly. She touched his face and let her tears fall. He sat back and looked at her. "Okay?" she whispered.

"Okay," he said, amazed at how those simple words made him feel like a weight was lifted off his shoulders.

Chapter Seventy-Eight:

Brittany woke up a while later and looked around, taking a minute to remember where she was. She was in the hospital, but why? She tried to move, but all she could do was pick up her arms. She lay there as memories came flooding back to her. She delivered Julie's baby and she remembered there was a lot of blood, but she was able to stop it.

Was Julie okay?

Yes, Tommy had said so, right? Was that real? She remembered being worried about Stephanie and Julie and knew their only hope was for help to come to the cabin. She couldn't allow Stephanie to go into labor, there were too many complications that might arise and she wouldn't be able to help her. She remembered having trouble breathing while there, but needing to call for help.

More images flashed in front of her. There was the car and the Onstar, which worked perfectly. Brittany had moved to the trunk to get her meds and she remembered falling down after a particularly rough coughing bought. She tried to get up but the water made the ground slippery. She fell down the hill and hit a tree and was happy to finally stop moving. She sat against the tree and was trying to gather her strength when there was a loud clap of thunder and she saw the tree next to the one she was leaning against begin to sway. She remembered watching the tree crack and she tried to move, but she simply had no energy. She could see the tree falling and she was suddenly crushed under it. She could feel the pain and the fear.

She didn't want this to be the end. She couldn't let it be the end.

"Tommy?" she called out in a squeak. She moved, forgetting about being in the hospital bed, and her body reminded her by screaming out in pain. She touched her face and felt the bandage on her neck. Something was wrong with her voice. Something was terribly wrong. "Oh please, Tommy?"

He heard her as he came out of the bathroom and ran to the bed. "Hey, I'm here, you're okay," he took her hand and she looked into his eyes.

"I wasn't sure you were here," she said in a hoarse voice.

"Where else would I be? You're stuck with me," he smiled at her, but saw she was agitated. "Tell me what's wrong."

"I was so scared, Tommy. Not like before, with him, but because I thought I would never see you again," she cried as she spoke. "I would never do that to you, if I could help it, I would never leave you."

Tommy moved closer to her and tried to comfort her. "Shh, Red, it's okay, I didn't think you left me. You don't have anything to be sorry for. Please don't cry," he felt so helpless that she was so distraught and he hated it when she cried.

"Tommy, what's wrong with my voice?" she asked softly.

He looked at her. "Hopefully nothing. It will just take time to heal," he couldn't lie, but he couldn't tell her everything.

"I want to see my chart," she said.

"I don't think you should."

She looked at him. "Don't do that to me, Tommy. Don't treat me like I'm weak. I may be hurt and I may need time to heal, but I have always been in charge of my own health and I need to know what I'm facing," she met his gaze with wet eyes. "I know something is wrong."

He put his head in his hand and sighed. "Red, can you listen to me for a minute?" he looked at her and touched her face. "I don't think you're weak. I want you to be in charge of your medical care and I would never keep anything from you, but, you died three times in the O.R," he choked up when he said that and she squeezed his hand. "You are not alone in this and you need to trust me to be with you all the way, but I can't do something that will bring you more pain and I can't watch you hurt unnecessarily. I just need you to get stronger before we look at anything else because if you get worse, none of it will matter," he let his tears fall and didn't even try to stop them. "I don't care if you hate me, I just need you in this world."

She heard him and she understood. "I'm scared, Tommy. I hate this, being in a hospital and being dependant on other people. I am afraid to look at my body and see what happened and I am afraid of being helpless. But do you know what my biggest fear is?"

"What?" he asked softly.

"Not having you hold me again. Not feeling your skin touching mine. Not feeling your lips against me. It would be the cruelest thing ever to have brought you into my life and then all of a sudden it was all gone," she wiped her face with her hand.

He smiled. "That's why we need to make sure that doesn't happen. We will have many years together and a lot of naked time," she blushed a little and smiled.

"Am I scarred? Is my body damaged? I remember being stuck under the tree and I could feel the weight crushing me. Am I ugly?" she was serious and needed his honesty.

"Do you remember what happened when I first told you that I loved you?"

She nodded. "You didn't want me to leave the resort."

He smiled. "And do you remember what you did?"

She let more tears fall as she remembered. "I looked into your eyes."

"And what did you see?" he prodded.

"I said that there was no sadness or pity, no regret or remorse. I just saw the man I found myself in love with," she wiped her tears.

"And what do you see now?" he wiped her tears away.

"My hero," she said.

"Ditto," he said and leaned in to kiss her softly. For now, this would be enough.

Chapter Seventy-Nine:

Stephanie came in to see Brittany a few days later and was happy to see her sitting more upright in her bed. She still had her middle wrapped tightly, but her neck was uncovered, revealing a dark bruise. Brittany smiled when she saw her friend.

"Hi," she said in a very hoarse voice. She reached her hand for Stephanie to come sit down.

"I'm so glad to see you awake. Jack made me wait and rest for two days before he would let me out of the house," she sat down and smiled. "I would have argued harder, but I knew Tommy was taking good care of you."

"I'm glad you rested. How do you feel? Any contractions?" she asked her.

Stephanie laughed at how concerned Brittany was for her when she was in the worst shape. "I'm fine. How are you feeling? You know, you really gave us a scare."

The tall redhead nodded. "I know. For a while there, I thought I wasn't going to make it."

"Where is Tommy?" Stephanie looked around the room for his things.

"Home with Tramp, poor doggie. He is so confused," she coughed and doubled over in severe pain. Stephanie held a pillow for her to hug against her chest.

"Sweetie, you shouldn't talk so much. You have numerous cracked ribs," she sat on the bed and helped Brittany until she could breathe normally. "Are you okay?"

Brittany began to cry. "No, I'm pissed off," she wiped her face and laughed a small laugh. "It wasn't supposed to be like this," she whispered.

Stephanie smoothed her friends' hair away from her face. "I hear you. But you know the saying, man plans and God laughs."

Brittany nodded. "I just hate being in the hospital. Every time the door opens I am afraid of who might come in."

Stephanie sighed. "I know, but we were all careful about not putting you here under your real name. The doctors know, of course, but if anyone tries to find you, they will have a hard time."

Brittany squeezed Stephanie's hand. "Thank you."

Stephanie stood up and smiled. "We would do anything for you, sweetie."

Brittany wiped her tears again, grateful for her family.

About an hour later, Brittany was feeling sorry for herself for the millionth time that day when she saw Tommy walk into the room. He had his coat on and he was carrying a bag, but he seemed to be walking funny.

"Hey," she whispered. "Are you okay?" she was concerned something was wrong with him.

He closed the door to her room and looked around before opening his coat to reveal Tramp hidden inside.

Brittany's whole face lit up with joy when she saw the pup and Tramp began to whine with excitement when he saw Brittany. Tommy smiled and walked over to the bed, sitting down and putting Tramp on the blanket next to her. He immediately jumped onto her and Tommy caught him before he hurt her. She reached out and picked him up, letting him lick her face, but avoiding her middle section. She let her tears fall and soon Tramp settled down next to her on the bed and rolled onto his back, assuming his traditional pose for a belly scratch. She looked at Tommy.

"Thank you. How did you know I needed both my boys?"

He sat on the edge of the bed and leaned in to kiss her. She held his face close to her so the kiss lasted longer. He saw her throat was uncovered and he tried not to stare at the terrible bruising. She still didn't press him on the damage she sustained, but he knew it was coming. He pulled a treat out of the bag for Tramp and the pup began to munch on his dessert. Tommy pulled out a small bowl and poured some bottled water in it for him as well. Brittany smiled at the care he took of their little boy.

"We are in so much trouble if anyone sees him here," she said.

"Then we will have to be sure no one sees him," he said, looking at her with a grin. His expression became more serious as he touched her face. "How are you feeling?"

"Fine."

"Liar," he smirked. "Tell me what's on your mind."

"I wish I was home with you and Tramp. I hate being here. But I also need to figure out why my voice is so scratchy. I wonder if the intubation tube bothered me more than usual. I need it to get better soon because I was thinking about something," she whispered.

He felt like a jerk, not telling her the truth. "What's that?"

"When you were called away and Julie went into labor, you had to work on Courtney, right?" she asked softly.

Tommy nodded.

"Is her cancer back?" Brittany asked sadly.

Tommy nodded. "Yes."

She shook her head. "I thought so."

He looked at her. "Why?"

"I thought she might like to learn how to play the guitar. I know I said I was done with singing for the public, and I am, but maybe I can use my voice to help people, lift their spirits, do something for charity," she looked at him. "I need a purpose, Tommy. Maybe this is it?" she seemed to have a renewed sense of hope at her realization.

He didn't know what to say to her. "You have a purpose, you're a great doctor. You saved my sister and her son. What is wrong with having that?"

"Nothing, but I honestly don't think I will be able to continue my practice. There is just too much out there and I don't think it's going to be realistic to go about my life like it was before," she sighed and coughed again, doubling over in pain. Tommy gave her the pillow and held her to him, trying to help her sit in a position, which would help. Tramp scratched his arm and nudged him with his nose, concerned at the commotion. She sat back and tried to breathe calmly, her hands shaking.

"When was the last dose of pain meds?" he asked her as he pet Tramp, reassuring the pup all was well. Tramp continued to stare at Brittany, not convinced.

"I'm okay. The sooner I am off such high meds, the sooner I can leave," she said and touched the pup who promptly flopped onto his back again for a scritch.

Tommy smiled at him but sighed. "You need to be here for a while, Red. Do you understand how precarious your health is?"

She exhaled. "I know, but I'm scared, Tommy," she scratched Tramp's ears.

"Of what?" he was grateful for her talking to him, and not shutting down, like in the past.

"That I might not leave," she let her tears fall. "I don't want to spend my time in the hospital, as a patient. I don't want to feel like this is where I belong. I mean, look around you, the reminders are all over. I can't escape it when the room announces it at every turn. I know it's necessary and I know it's to protect everyone, but it just gets to me, you know? Outside of the hospital, I am not a hazard label."

His heart broke a little more every time she said things like that. "You are going to get better. Your viral load will move lower and you will heal. You won't be here forever."

She nodded. "I hear you, but I'm just not okay with that. I feel like every time I am here, it is for longer and longer and I am not ready for that."

"But this isn't immune related, baby. You were injured by a tree; it's not from anything else," he took her hand in his.

"But don't you see, Tommy, it's always immune related. That's what happens when you're HIV positive. It always comes down to that. I can't just get a scratch or an infection without the fear that it will be the one that turns into something more," she ran her hand through her hair and winced at the pain in her chest. "I'm sorry; I don't mean to keep focusing on it. It's fine; I'm just having a pity party."

He looked at her hand in his own and shrugged. "You don't have to be sorry. I don't focus on your HIV because I can't. I don't want to even consider the possibility that you might leave me, but I also know that I'm a coward. I can look the other way, but you never can. I can see the numbers improving and you can feel the disease growing. I am the one who should apologize. You can always talk to me about your fears and how you're feeling. But I need you to always fight, for yourself and for our future," he implored her. "And just so you know, I am the king of the pity party. Can I bring the beer?"

She smiled as she held Tramp to her. "I would prefer champagne."

He laughed. "Whatever you want."

Chapter Eighty:

Jack came home after work with Stephanie's favorite carry-out. She was sitting on the couch with her hands on her stomach and her eyes closed. She was breathing evenly and he thought she was asleep. He put the food down and she opened her eyes and smiled at him. "Did I wake you?"

"I smelled the food. I'm starving," she moved to the package and he pouted. "What?"

"All you want me for is my food," he said.

She turned to look at him with a breadstick in her hand. "Oh, no, I'm sorry," she walked over to him and pulled him to her for a kiss. "Hi honey, how was your day?" she smiled at him.

He laughed. "Eat your breadstick."

She grinned and took a big bite. "Oh my gosh, this is so good."

"You used to say that about me," he said.

"I can't eat you right now," she said with a straight face.

He moved closer to her and reached over her to take his own breadstick. "If you really wanted to, you could find a way to handle my breadstick."

She laughed. "Really? Is that the best you've got?"

He shrugged. "It's been a long day. Did you see Brittany?"

She nodded. "I did. She seems better, but I know she isn't out of the woods, and she doesn't know about her voice yet."

Jack sighed. "I know. Tommy is really struggling with how to tell her and what to tell her. She also needs more surgery and I don't think she knows that, either."

She stood up and walked over to get some water. "I think she knows more than we all think. Brittany has an amazing threshold for pain and for emotional baggage. I just hope she lets us all help her," she walked back and sat down.

Jack spooned some of the pasta into a plate and grabbed two forks. He sat down next to her and smiled. "I think we should share."

She looked at him incredulously and he laughed. "I'm kidding. Here," he gave her the plate and grabbed his own. They ate and talked about his day, it was perfectly normal and they both relished that. After they finished and he was loading the dishwasher, she walked up behind him and tried to wrap her arms around him, but her stomach got in the way. She sighed and he turned around, smiling at her. "I love you, my sexy wife."

She rolled her eyes. "I'm a whale."

"No, you're my amazingly beautiful better half," he leaned in and kissed her, lingering on her lips for a minute. She held his face in her hands and relished the feel of him so close to her.

She backed away for a minute and he noticed her expression change. "What is it?"

She looked at him. "I think my water just broke."

****

Stephanie was settled into the bed at the hospital and was breathing and waiting for Jack to finish the paperwork. She had been very calm and retrospective since her water broke. It was like she was coming full circle and for once in her life, she knew her purpose in this world. She was meant to be Jack's partner and they were meant to be parents. She remembered their journey and how far they had come and now, it was just as it should be.

"Okay, they are prepping the O.R. and we should be able to meet our baby soon," Jack said as he came into the room. The baby was still turned the wrong way and since Stephanie had her own health issues, they decided on a c-section. He sat down and took her hand in his. "How are you doing?"

She smiled. "I'm fine. I was just remembering something," she breathed in and out evenly as she felt another contraction beginning.

"What's that?" he asked her.

"Oh God, shit," she yelled as the pain ripped through her body.

"Just try to breathe, it will be over soon," he said.

She glared at him. "Really? It will be over soon?"

He knew there was no right way to respond to this, so he simply smiled at her.

"You're lucky you're cute," she said as the pain subsided. She looked at him. "I wish Brittany were here."

Jack sighed. He felt terrible that she was missing this. If there was one person who was instrumental in both of them getting to this place, it was Brittany. She worked so hard on their behalf. He looked at her and took her hand in his. "I know. I wish she were here, too."

"Ask and you shall receive," Tommy said as he wheeled a smiling Brittany into the room. Stephanie burst into tears and Brittany shook her head.

"You didn't think I would let you go through this without me, did you?" she whispered.

Jack walked over to Tommy and hugged him, giving the women a little privacy. "Thanks, I know it wasn't easy to get her up."

"Are you kidding me? Once she heard you were here, she would have walked here without me if I didn't take her," he smiled at her. He knew how much pain she must be in, but it didn't show for a moment on her face. This was all about Stephanie and Jack.

"I'm scared," Stephanie said to Brittany. "I just want my baby to be healthy."

Brittany reached over and smoothed Stephanie's hair away from her sweaty forehead. "There is no reason to believe you won't have a perfectly healthy baby. You have done everything right and now you are about to bring a baby into this world," she motioned for Jack to come over. He did and Tommy stood behind her. "You both need to listen to something."

Stephanie smiled but then cried as another contraction took over. Brittany was the only one not fazed by the screams. Tommy looked at Jack and both men were white. Brittany helped Stephanie breathe and then looked at the men.

"Come on, you are both doctors," she said hoarsely, rolling her eyes.

"My patients don't scream," Tommy said.

Stephanie was panting. "It's okay, it stopped," she held Jack's hand and her breathing calmed.

The nurse came in and smiled at them. "They are just about ready to take you in, Dr. Stephens."

"Thanks," Stephanie said as the nurse walked out. She looked at Jack and Tommy and Brittany.

"Okay, so listen. Everything in there is going to move very fast. I know you are both doctors, but it's different when it's you. Take the time to be in the moment. Bringing a child into this world is such a magical experience, and you both are going to be the best at it. Don't worry about anything. The commotion and the craziness in the O.R. doesn't matter. Just like when this child was conceived, it is just about you two and your family. Take it in, enjoy it, and treasure it. You are both so very blessed," she said and wiped her tears.

The nurses came in to take Stephanie and Brittany had Tommy wheel her back. Stephanie squeezed Brittany's hand as she was wheeled out, and Jack kissed Brittany's forehead, both of them at a loss for words.

"We will be waiting right here," Tommy said.

Jack hugged him again and went to get ready.

"Are you okay?" Tommy asked Brittany.

She nodded. "I'd like to wait here, in case I am needed," she said and Tommy sat down next to her, holding her hand in his own while they waited.

Chapter Eighty-One:

Jack looked at Stephanie and he didn't know how it happened. He didn't think it was possible, but he felt a love that was more intense, more powerful, deeper and stronger than anything he had ever felt. She had just given him the most precious gift in the world, and he was simply overwhelmed. She looked at him, her own tears mirroring his. The nurse walked over and looked at Stephanie. "Would you like to hold your baby?"

Stephanie nodded and took the bundle in her arms while they continued to sew her up. Jack sat down next to them. Stephanie looked at him. "Look what we did?"

He was at a loss for words. "Thank you for this miracle, Stephanie," he leaned in and kissed her.

Stephanie looked at the baby. "You are safe and loved and we couldn't wait to meet you," she let her tears fall as Jack held his family.

Tommy and Brittany looked up as Jack came out of the O.R., grinning like a little kid. He walked up to them. "It's a girl!"

Tommy yelled and picked him up in a bear hug. Brittany smiled a huge smile and breathed a sigh of relief. "How is Stephanie?"

"She is amazing and beautiful and went through the C-Section like it was nothing. The baby is 6 lbs, 2 oz and 19 inches long."

"That's great for being a month early. Very well developed. Congratulations, Jack. Please give

Stephanie a hug for me," Brittany said. Tommy looked at her, knowing she needed to get back to her room.

Jack knelt in front of the wheelchair and took her hands in his. "We owe you so much. I can't wait for you to meet her," he kissed her on the cheek and hugged Tommy one more time before running back to his girls.

Tommy looked at Brittany. "That child is going to be the most spoiled little girl."

Brittany nodded. "Can you take me back now? I am not feeling really great," she put her hand to her face and wiped her eyes.

He touched her forehead, alarmed at the heat. "Okay, let's go," he wheeled her out of the room.

******
Jack walked into the room and smiled at the sight before him. Stephanie was sitting up in bed with their daughter and she was examining the little baby. He walked up to the bed. "What are you doing?"

"Checking her, making sure she has 10 fingers and 10 toes. She has 15 hairs on the top of her head and if you watch her closely, I think she has a dimple. Come here," Stephanie smiled at her husband.

Jack sat on the bed as Stephanie moved over a little to make room. He leaned his head next to Stephanie's and they looked at their daughter. He was choked up, as he had been numerous times in the past few hours. He still couldn't believe she was real.

Stephanie looked at him. "Why don't you take her for a bit?"

He swallowed and gently took her in his arms. He sat back and looked at his sleeping baby. "She looks like a doll," he whispered.

Stephanie leaned her head on his shoulder. "She is the best of both of us."

The baby yawned and both parents marveled at her.

"Was that her first yawn?" Jack asked. "Should we write it down?"

Stephanie laughed and held her stomach. "No and no. She has yawned about a million times. Apparently being born really wipes you out."

Jack noticed Stephanie's discomfort. "Do you need any pain meds?"

She shook her head. "Nope, I'm good, just sore," she touched the baby's hand and ran her finger over her cheek. "I am so glad she is healthy. Of all the things I prayed for the most, her being healthy was at the top."

Jack nodded. "I knew she would be. She is already my little champ. Just like her mom."

Stephanie looked at him. "So, don't you think she needs a name? Baby girl Stephens just doesn't do her justice."

He nodded. "I agree. Are you set on what we talked about?"

She smiled. "I am, but I think we should ask her."

He smiled. "I agree," he looked at his baby girl. "Sabrina Amanda Stephens. Is that a name worthy of such a beautiful girl?"

Stephanie smiled. "What do you think, little Bee? Is that okay with you?"

"Bee?" Jack smiled. "Cute. I think it's perfect," he looked at little Sabrina and his heart swelled. "I hope you know how excited we are to meet you. Your mommy and I have been so anxious for you to arrive. Apparently you were, too, because you got here a little early. But we're ready and we are so excited. I can't wait to show you off."

Stephanie wiped her tears away. "What do you think she'll be like?"

He looked at his wife. "I hope she is more like you than me."

Stephanie shook her head. "No way, she is going to be daddy's little girl. Besides, you are the most perfect person I know, so she should be just like you."

Jack sighed. "I don't think she should date until she's 30." Bee cried when he said that and they both laughed. "Okay, 29."

"It doesn't matter, she will marry David. I already have it planned. They will grow up together and fight all the time, but soon learn that they would be incomplete without each other," she smiled at them.

"David is never coming over," he said. "I forbid it."

Stephanie smiled. "Good luck with that," she yawned.

"You should get some sleep because they are releasing you tomorrow," he said.

"I'm so glad. I can't wait to bring her home," she said.

Jack nodded. "I can't wait to have all my girls at home where they belong."

Jack stood up and put Sabrina in the little bassinette near the bed. He got back into the bed with Stephanie and held her while they both watched their baby sleep. They were beyond thrilled and they looked up as Tommy walked into the room.

"Hey, come in and meet Sabrina Amanda," Stephanie said.

Tommy grinned. "That's beautiful. I know Amanda comes from Jack's mom, but what is the significance of Sabrina?" he walked over and looked at the baby.

"Sabrina is a name I have always loved, ever since I watched Audrey Hepburn in the movie. It means Princess and that's what she is," Stephanie smiled. "But the character also had a strong love of family and a respect for all around her. Those are some of the qualities I hope she embodies."

Tommy nodded. "It's a beautiful name."

Jack looked at him. "So, what's going on? How's Brittany?"

Tommy wiped his eyes and looked at them. "That's kind of what I wanted to talk to you both about."

Jack looked at Tommy's expression and motioned for him to come and sit down. "Tell us what's happening."

"I know this isn't the right time, but I don't trust anyone else," Tommy sighed.

Stephanie took Jack's hand in her own. "What is it?"

"I need Jack to operate on Brittany," he said.

Jack nodded. "Tell me what happened?"

"Her heart was damaged by the tree, there is an aortic rupture that they just found on the echo. When they initially went in, they knew there was more damage that would need to be repaired, but they didn't realize the extent. It isn't her lungs, but her heart and she needs the best cardiac surgeon, and that's you," he wiped his face. "I know it's a lot to ask."

Jack looked at Stephanie and they both looked at Tommy. "Will you stop?" Jack asked. "It's not too much to ask. Is there an O.R. booked?"

Tommy shook his head. "No, they were trying to assemble a team and were calling Kingsley in. I told Brittany I wanted you, but she didn't want to bother you. She's not going to be happy with me that I came to you, but I don't care. This is her life."

"Kingsley is good, but I'm the best. Tell them to prep the O.R. and I'll be there to look over the tests and scrub in," Jack said.

Tommy smiled gratefully. "Thank you."

"Once again, just stop. You both are family," Stephanie said. "Bee and I will be fine while you are both gone. We need to talk about some things alone, you know, mommy/daughter talk."

Jack leaned in and kissed her and then kissed a sleeping Bee in the bassinette. He and Tommy walked out. Tommy was quiet as they walked and he had his arms crossed in front of him. "I don't know how this was missed. Her lungs are not the problem. They took out her spleen and repaired the bleed but didn't inspect everything else? How did I not see what was happening?"

Jack looked at him. "Aortic rupture is often missed when a patient presents with multiple injuries. It would explain her chest pain, shortness of breath and throat problems. It is just easy to overlook. I will go in and fix it and she should feel much better."

Tommy nodded and looked at him. "I'm going to go in with her while you get ready."

"Okay, but I forbid you to come into the O.R," he looked at Tommy. "I mean it, I can't do my job if you're there."

"Okay, just please save her," he said.

"It's what I do," he smiled as Tommy rolled his eyes, secretly grateful for his friends' arrogance.

Chapter Eighty-Two:

Tommy walked into Brittany's room and stopped at the doorway while he watched her. She was huddled on her side, propped all around with pillows to make her more comfortable. She was facing away from the door, so she didn't notice him. He could see her struggling to be comfortable. He wiped his face and headed to the side of the bed she was facing. He smiled at her. "Hey baby," he said as he kissed her forehead before sitting down.

"Hi," she whispered. "I missed you."

"Sorry, I had something I had to take care of. How are you feeling?"

"Okay," she spoke with small breaths, as taking deep breaths hurt too much.

"Why do you always try to protect me? You can tell me the truth. Besides, I can see it all over your face," he smoothed her hair behind her ears.

"It's no big deal. I'm actually glad because I should feel much better after they repair this. I should be able to get up and around much easier," she looked at him and a tear slipped down her face. He brushed it away.

"I hope so."

"Is someone with Tramp? Maybe you should go home instead of sitting here. I'll be fine and I will most likely be out of it for a while after the surgery."

"Bill and Julie took him to their house for a few days. He will fit right in with David," Tommy sighed. "I need to tell you something."

She looked at him and smiled. "Jack is doing the surgery."

He looked surprised. "How did you know?"

"Tommy, I knew you wouldn't let anyone else touch my heart, at least except you," she closed her eyes.

"I love you," he said.

"I love you, too. Don't worry," she said.

He took her hand in his own and kissed it, knowing that was easier said than done.

****

Stephanie sat with Bee in her arms and smiled at her baby girl who had latched hungrily onto the tiny bottle. "Hi Sabrina Mandy. Do you recognize my voice? It's mommy, the one who has been talking to you for the past eight months. I am so honored to meet you," she held the girl's tiny hand in her own. "Your daddy will be back soon, but he had to go and help Auntie Brittany and Uncle Tommy. Daddy is strong like that. He is very good at fixing things that seem beyond repair. He fixed me and because of him, we made you and that is by far the best thing we could ever do," she took the bottle away and put Bee against her shoulder and rubbed her back, waiting for a burp. She heard the little release of air and smiled. "That's my big girl," she picked her knees up and put Sabrina against her legs, looking at her and watching her fight to keep her eyes open.

Stephanie felt such an enormous sense of love and protection for this little life that was equal parts her and Jack. It really was hard to wrap her mind around all of this. So much had happened to get to this point and there was simply nothing more important than making Sabrina happy.

She looked up at a knock at the door and smiled as Tommy stood there. "Want some company?" he asked.

She looked at Sabrina. "Actually, I think someone would like to meet her Godfather now that she is awake."

Tommy walked over to the bed and Stephanie handed him Sabrina. He held the little girl in his arms and sat down next to the bed. He felt tears fill his eyes at the precious cargo he held. "Stephanie, she is just beautiful."

She beamed at Tommy. "I think she has Jack's nose and sometimes, I think I see a dimple, but I'm not sure. It's still early."

"You and Jack are going to be the best parents. You know, when Jack and I were in high school, he was so sure that he would remain a bachelor. His mom used to fight with him all the time about how much the right woman would change his life. He heard it from her and of course from my parents as well," he smiled as Bee grasped his finger.

Stephanie had never heard him talk about his parents. "What about you? Did you see yourself as a married man?"

He shrugged, "I don't remember thinking much about it as a kid. I mean, I loved how in love my parents were and the example they set was quite something. But after they died, my life took such a different turn. It was just making sure Julie was okay and continuing with school. Nothing else mattered," he put Bee against his shoulder and she fell asleep.

"And now?" she pressed him, smiling at the picture of Sabrina being so immediately comfortable with Tommy. He seemed to have that effect with everyone.

He rubbed the tiny baby's back and looked at Stephanie. "I just need Brittany to be okay. I don't know what happens next."

"I think you do, but you don't have to talk about it with me," she smiled.

He rolled his eyes at her. "Jack warned me you do things like this."

She laughed. "What things. I don't know what you mean."

He grinned. "You just have a way of getting to the heart of the issue. You're right. I know what I want, but I don't know if it's possible. I don't know if the future I see is one that Brittany wants, or will be able to have."

Stephanie smiled as he handed the sleeping infant back to her. "I think it is. And Jack should have also told you that I am always right."

Tommy laughed. "You have been so good for him. I have never in my life seen Jack so happy and so relaxed. You both are an inspiration to me," he looked at his watch. "I'm going to head back to the O.R. I hope they are done soon."

Stephanie looked at him. "Tommy, you deserve to be just as happy. You both do. Thank you for coming by and spending some time with us."

He leaned in and kissed her cheek. "I would do anything for Jack's girls. Always know that."

"We do. Give Brittany a hug for us," she smiled and wiped a tear away.

"I will," he turned and walked out.

****

Jack walked into the room later that evening and smiled at Stephanie and Sabrina. They were both sleeping and he walked over to his daughter and leaned in and kissed her softly. Stephanie sat up and smiled at the scene. "Hey, how did it go?"

He walked over and kissed her. "It went great. I fixed the valve and was able to stabilize some of the cartilage around her broken ribs, which should make her feel much better. I am hopeful she is done with the surgeries and with the intense pain, and she can begin to heal. I left Tommy with her, but I told him to go home and rest because she will be out of it for a while."

Stephanie smiled. "He isn't going to leave."

Jack grinned. "I know, which is why I ordered a bed to be brought in next to her for him. He is exhausted and needs to sleep."

"So do you. You just performed a long surgery after having a baby. Why don't you go home and get some sleep?"

"Technically, you had the baby, I just sat there, so I really can't take credit for that, and wherever you are, is where I want to be," he yawned.

"Okay, then come here in bed with me and get some sleep," she scooted over in the bed and smiled at him. He took off his shoes and socks and got into the bed with her. He wrapped his arms around her and she held his hands next to her heart. "You are my champion, Jack. I am honored to be your wife," she said, but he simply snored.

Chapter Eighty-Three:

Tommy sat up in the roll away bed they had brought in the room for him. He watched her sleeping and was happy to see a little color back in her cheeks. Jack had said that there was a lot of damage which should have been repaired earlier, but because of the condition she was in, it was probably best that they let her get stronger. It just killed Tommy to know that she was in so much pain for days and they could have fixed that. She never complained, and she never felt sorry for herself, but he knew this had been an emotionally painful time. Stephanie having her baby had been something that Brittany had been waiting for and to not have been able to help was heartbreaking for her. He knew that. He also knew that it was because she had risked her life to help his sister that she was in this mess. He ran his hand through his hair and sighed.

"Tommy?" she said in a soft voice.

He moved to her and took her hand in his. "Hey, Red, I'm here."

She opened her eyes and he saw the familiar ocean blue pierce him. She smiled. "I missed you."

He grinned. "You know, it's good for a couple to have some time apart. It makes our reunion that much better."

She nodded a tiny bit while still smiling. "How did everything go in the O.R.?"

He smoothed her hair away. "Fabulously. You know I will never admit it to him, but Jack is the best there is.

He fixed the rupture and he was also able to repair the torn cartilage from the broken ribs. That was why there was more pain than usual for cracked ribs. You should feel much better now, although the ribs and now your sternum have to heal."

She closed her eyes for a minute. "How are Stephanie and the baby? Did they name her? Is everyone okay?"

"Everyone is perfect. Sabrina Amanda Stephens is perfect as is her mom," he said.

"Sabrina Amanda? That's different, I like it," she said quietly. "My voice feels stronger than before."

He nodded. "That's because of the rupture. It was infringing on your throat and vocal chords. We thought your larynx might have been damaged before, but it turns out it was all from your heart. Jack figured it all out."

"You didn't tell me you thought my larynx was damaged," she said, eyeing him.

"You're right, because we weren't sure what was wrong," he lied a little.

She squeezed his hand. "That's not why you didn't tell me," she looked at him. "Tommy, I am a much stronger person now than when you met me and that's because of your love and faith in me. I can take anything that comes as long as we face it together. As long as you want to be with me."

He hated that he once again had underestimated her. "I guess I am still learning how to be the man you deserve."

She reached up and touched his stubble covered cheek. "Baby you're so much more," she pulled him gently to her for a kiss. "I love you."

He looked at her and kissed her again. "I love you too," he said, glad she closed her eyes so she didn't see his tears.

******

Brittany was sitting up in her bed a few days later. She was feeling so much better and she couldn't wait to go home. She missed Tramp. She smiled as she thought about it. Okay, she missed Tommy and Tramp. She laughed a little at herself and held her chest. Although it was a million times better than before, her chest still was extremely painful. She knew Tommy would be back soon to see her and she wanted to clean up a little for him. She had been up a few times to use the bathroom, but always with assistance from the nurses and she wanted to look at herself, something they didn't let her do. She felt her hair, which was gross, and she figured she could try one of those dry shampoos until she could take a shower. She was glad they had stopped her IV earlier, and although the port was still in her arm, she could move without impediment. She stood up and got her bearings before holding the rail as she walked slowly to the bathroom. She felt so much stronger and she closed the door behind her and turned on the light. She turned and looked at herself in the mirror for the first time since she had been brought in.

****

Tommy carried pictures of Sabrina and David with him as he made his way to see Brittany. He was excited to tell her she could go home later that day and that Jack and Stephanie were home and ready for visitors. He got to her room and saw her bed was empty. He realized she was in the bathroom so he put his stuff down and went to check her chart. He heard a noise and went to the door of the bathroom. "Brittany? Are you okay? Do you need any help?"

He waited for an answer, but only heard sniffles. "Can I come in? What's wrong?" His heart was beating fast as he waited.

"No, Tommy, you can't see me," she said in a pathetically sad voice.

Relieved she had spoken to him, but not sure what she was talking about, he continued. "What do you mean? I think we've seen each other before."

"No, Tommy, not like this, I'm repulsive," she cried.

"Let me in, Red," he pleaded.

"No."

"I'll come in if I have to, these doors don't lock."

There was silence for a minute and finally she spoke.

"Fine, come in."

He opened the door and saw her sitting on the floor of the shower, a towel covering her. She looked at him. "See, I'm fine, now you can go home."

He closed the door and looked at her. He could tell she had been crying. "Um, I don't think I would consider you sitting on the shower floor to be fine," he walked closer and sat on the closed toilet seat. "Care to share?"

She looked down. "Tommy, I'm hideous."

He still didn't follow. "Red, I don't understand what you mean?"

She looked up at him. "My body looks like Frankenstein. I am revolting."

He finally got it and he shook his head. "No, you're not revolting."

She shrugged. "I think he's finally right."

"Who?"

She looked at him. "Never mind. Can you leave me alone so I can get dressed?"

"Nope."

"What do you mean, nope?"

"You aren't going back to that place of isolation. Besides, you can't get dressed by yourself. You are a week removed from open-heart surgery," he stepped into the shower and held out his hand to her.

"Tommy, I don't want you to look at me," she said sincerely.

"I got that, and I am trying not to be insulted that you think so little of me."

She shook her head. "Every feeling I have isn't a reflection of you. This isn't about insulting you, it's about."

"What?" he asked softly. "What is it about?"

"Being attractive to you. Tommy, you look at me like I am the most beautiful thing you have ever seen. I don't want that to change when you see me. I am not trying to be insulting, it's just when I saw my body, it repulsed me and I am scared that he was right," she repeated the same phrase again.

He reached down to her and wrapped his arms around her as gently as he could. He pulled her up slowly with him so she was standing and then he helped her sit on the closed seat. He knelt in front of her and she continued to hug the towel to her body. He took her face in his hands. "Who was right? Baby, tell me what's going through your head?"

She struggled with the words at first, but she finally looked at him, her tears spilling down her face. "The man who attacked me told me that no one would ever be able to love me. He gave me this disease as a reminder of how alone I would always be. He told me that no one would ever be able to look at me and not see my HIV, but you changed that. You looked at me with nothing but love and I don't want that to change. I don't want him to be right," she wiped her face. "I'm sorry, there is nothing you have ever done that would make me think you would react with anything other than love, but suddenly, he is back in my head and I'm scared. I don't want you to leave."

He took her hand and helped her to stand up. "Come here," he said and turned her to face the mirror with him behind her. He reached around her and gently took her hands, allowing the towel covering her to fall away. He held her gaze in the mirror as her tears fell down. She moved to cover herself up. He took her hands in his and brought them to his lips. "Do you know what I see?"

She shook her head. "No," she said through her tears.

"I see the woman I love more than life itself," he moved her hand to the scar on her chest and held his hand over it. "I see a reminder of how you saved my sister's life and delivered my nephew despite horrible circumstances. The fact that you see it as something that would make me want to leave is just proof that as far as you have come, we still have work to do undoing what that shithead did to you," he held her hands at her side and looked at her face in the mirror. "I love you, scars, HIV, stubbornness, arrogance, beauty and intelligence, I love all of you," he turned her gently so she was facing him and put his hands on her shoulders. "I love you, completely, and that's not going to change."

She looked into his eyes and had no words. She tried to hug him, but she couldn't lift her arms without pain so she simply leaned gently into him and put her head on his shoulder. He wrapped his arms around her and held her to him. She felt like she had won the lottery. "Can we go home?" she asked him.

"I think so," he said.

"Can I put some clothes on?"

"Not on my account."

"I'm cold."

"Liar."

She stepped back and looked at him. "I'll tell you what, when we are home, we can both be naked. Until then, this is too one sided."

He pretended to think it over. "Okay, I suppose I can go along with that," he grinned and reached over to grab a new gown. He helped her put it on and tied it in the back. Before helping her back to the bed where she sat down. He sat down next to her.

"Can I clear something up really quick?" he asked.

She looked at him and could tell from his expression he was trying not to laugh. "What is it?"

"Frankenstein was the doctor, not the monster, so technically," he said and smiled.

"Nice," she said and put her head on his shoulder.

He laughed and held her to him.

Please follow the Family by Choice series as the series continues with Book 2, *Love Endures*, now available. For more information and sneak previews, please stop by www.nadlersnovels.com or follow Robin on Twitter: @buka163090 or
facebook: www.facebook.com/nadlersnovels

59404649R00377

Made in the USA
Charleston, SC
03 August 2016